ACTS OF KINDNESS, ACTS OF CONTRITION

The Red Edition

~ a love story ~

by

Sylvia Ross

ii

Dedicated to my husband Robert E. Ross
And my sisters,
Nancy Fanucchi and Theresa Cord

Acts of Kindness, Acts of Contrition
The Red Edition

Special Note: Though the character, Jeanne French, was an actual person and is portrayed in a manner consistent with public record and the author's memory, this book is a work of fiction. All other characters and events are merely literary invention.

Other books by the author are:
LION SINGER, 2005
BLUE JAY GIRL, 2010
ACORNS AND ABALONE, 2011

Her work is included in the following anthologies:
THE DIRT IS RED HERE, Margaret Dubin, Ed.
SPRING SALMON, HURRY TO ME, 2008,
        Margaret Dubin & Kim Hogeland, Eds.
SEAWEED, SALMON, AND MANZANITA CIDER,
        2008, Margaret Dubin & Sara-Larus Tolley, Eds.
THE ILLUMINATED LANDSCAPE, A Sierra Nevada
        Anthology, 2010, Gary Noy & Rick Heide, Eds.
LEAVES FROM THE VALLEY OAK, 2010,
        Mary Benton & Gloria Getman, Eds.

**Acts of Kindness, Acts of Contrition was a finalist for the James D. Houston Award

Table of Contents

Chapter   Page

Acts of Kindness, Acts of Contrition

Chapter 1: Venice Boulevard

I'm a godless old woman. When I was very young I prayed for the gift of faith. I thought it was something others had that I didn't. As I grew older, I realized faith was something others needed and I didn't. The earth, sky, moon, the stars and planets, this whole known universe was, and still is, more than enough for simple kinds of people like me.

It's late in the afternoon. All our work is done, and my dear old man is resting in the house. Hummingbirds are feeding on coral aloes. The dry country flowers blaze on spikey stems. A rich plain stretches out below this west-facing patio. From beside the cactus garden, as the shadows grow longer, it is clear enough today to see California's Coast Range rising on the other side of the great San Joaquin Valley. I sit here, and like counting knitting stitches, or rosary beads, I count my sins. Only mine. Counting the sins of others would add unnecessary weight to my own penitential list. My sin list has changed over the years since I was a child. I no longer differentiate so carefully between what is venial and what is mortal. The quality of sin itself has changed somewhat in my lifetime.

This afternoon, examining my conscience, I ask myself if I ravaged the earth's resources by wasting a paper towel. No. I carefully conserved. Did I treat others fairly and with kindness? Yes. I try to do that every day. Did I indulge in any petty vanity, and so doing overlook someone else's need for attention? No. Maybe yesterday, but not today. I promise to make amends for yesterday.

This resolution made, my mind opens to the memory of someone I knew a long ago time, during the time of parties and frivolity following the Second World War. Her name was Jeannie.

She was kind to my friends and me when we were children. She wasn't young, but seemed to be. Our parents liked her too. She was always looking for ways to help people. The neighborhood where we lived gave her nothing in return for her kindnesses but attention and affection.

I want to tell you about the way my life played out after her death and to tell you about some of the other children who knew her and knew me. Jeannie French was the person who first compromised my certainties between sin and virtue, yet her benign presence has been with me for most of my life.

To tell you what I want to tell you, I have to start in the beginning and try to recall whom I was then. I can't tell you the month or season when this story began. I lived in a place where seasons changed little. I was too young to read a calendar. I could only read a few words: STOP, GO, Lazlo's Liquors, The Diner, Culver Market, and of those few words I could only read two out of context. I know only by inference that the time was late in 1939 or early in 1940.

There was much I didn't know, but I could see my hands and feet and knew who I was. I was Lynn Horvath. My mother was Marianne Horvath. I knew I lived on Venice Boulevard in Culver City. I lived in a big brick building in an apartment. If I got lost, I was supposed to tell people who I was and where I lived, but I never got lost.

My father was Lazlo Horvath. He worked downstairs in his store. It was next to the shoe shop and in front of the dressmaker. The door to the dressmaker was on the side street. Daddy's and Mr. Conti's shops' doors were on the Boulevard. In the daytime Mama stayed in the apartment, but I went outside. I liked to wander through the alley or play in the cactus garden someone planted in the lot between the high brick wall of our building and the low stucco wall of the diner.

At first, I thumped down the steep wooden stairs of our building on my bottom. As I grew older and steadier I'd hold onto the wooden balusters and jump with both my shoes down from step to step. At the bottom, there was a big door to the boulevard. That door was too heavy, but if I turned and ran down the hallway's first floor tunnel, the door at the end of the hall was usually unlatched. If not, I hit its wooden staves hard until the door popped open. Sometimes I got a splinter, but I always got out. Pushing behind trashcans, climbing in and out of discarded crates, I never cared if I tore my pinafore or my shoestrings were dragging.

In the cactus garden between the diner and our building, pebbles and twisted stickery leaves littered the ground. There were spiders, moths and little bugs that would tickle when they crawled up my hand. My mother didn't like it when I took them upstairs to our apartment. The cactus garden had a cat. He had fluffy long hair. Mama didn't like him either.

Downstairs, Mr. Conti had a dog. He and the dog smelled like the shoe repair shop. Daddy smelled like soap and shaving lotion. The dressmaker didn't like me. But the diner ladies did. I learned to sort out the people who lived in our building by voice, size, smell and the way they moved. Mr. Tyler's feet stomped. Mrs. Harrigan lumbered up the stairs. Miss Butler tripped along. Mrs. Harrigan sighed often and smelled like flowers. Miss Butler smelled like cigarettes. My mother smelled like me.

Usually, the tenants and people in the houses on the streets behind our building left me alone. Once, a woman in one of the houses was nice to me. She smiled and talked to me, but then her claw hand held me by my wrist. She led me back to our apartment and scolded my mother. After that I was careful to avoid people who were friendly. When I came home, Mama would get up, wash my face and hands, and fix something for me to eat if I came home hungry. She didn't talk very much, but she liked it when I talked to her. She didn't like me jumping about punching pillows and wiggling. When I was in the apartment, I tried to keep all the parts of my body still. One day, in a gruff and mocking voice, I told her that the dressmaker said,

"Git yurself home, little girly!" Another day, "Mr. Conti's dog let me pet him." And on another, she laughed when I told her that a lady on the sidewalk was mad and told a man, "I'm not going with you. Just go by yourself. I'll never go there again!"

But then I told Mama something that man said back to the woman. She put her hand across my mouth and frowned. I learned that there were some words that weren't to come out of my mouth, even if other people said them.

My mother was charmed when I mimed the tenants, shopkeepers, and people on the sidewalk. She didn't notice that although I knew my colors, I neither mentioned the color of anyone's eyes or hair, nor described details of their clothing. My mother had been an only child and none of her friends had children. Overlooking the clues that might have qualified her judgment, Mama determined that I was precocious merely because I talked to her. I'd imitate the sounds of traffic and sing out birdsongs in high-pitched trills to make her laugh. I told her what the cat in the cactus garden said, using the words of his language, *aaaaaaaaaaq, rrmmwraao or wwaaak.* I chattered on until her sweet voice said, "Now Lynn baby, all that energy tires Mama out." Then, she went in the bedroom to lie down. She put a scarf over her eyes, and wouldn't look at me.

Though my memory began more with episodes than sequences, I knew there were few rules. I wasn't to go inside anyone's house or apartment, and I was not to go near the curbing in front of the shops because I might tumble into the street. Mama warned me the boulevard's cars and trucks would "run over my head." I believed her. A clanging bell on the Red Car that went back and forth on the boulevard's median and the signal arms on the corner pole ratcheting either STOP or GO, added their noise to grinding gears, squealing brakes, and the e-yah, e-yah of car and truck horns. I understood danger through its noise. Hearing the lilting drift of my mother's light voice against the roaring chaos of the boulevard, I absorbed all the meaning in her words. I didn't want my head run over. I wasn't supposed to bother people, which suited me. People who smiled at me seemed much like the woman who had once taken my hand. I avoided them.

There were no other children where I lived. Sometimes I saw them going into the diner with their families. They were funny and had big eyes. Now and then they smiled at me. I didn't talk to them. I hid in the cactus garden and peeked out. I wasn't supposed to bother Daddy, but sometimes I'd sneak into his store. The sparkling windows and the rows and rows of shiny bottles reflected light from the boulevard. It glittered in the store. Daylight from the big south windows glancing on all the cylindrical glass and spearing down the gleaming floors created a brilliant palace. It was bright enough in the store to tantalize my faulty and resistant vision. It smelled of fragrant tobacco as my grandfather did, and also smelled sweet, strong and good like the contents of the bottles. Mostly when I snuck in, Daddy lowered his eyebrows and shooed me back out.

~~~<<=>>~~~

Chapter 2: Beth Horvath

Only one bad memory stays with me from that time. It was almost dark when Daddy found me in the cactus garden. My mother had been calling me, but I didn't want to go in. I'd piled a collection of stones on the ground in front of me and refused to leave them. Daddy left the store and came to get me. He yanked me up and dragged me, fighting him, down the gravel path toward our building. Then he dragged me along the sidewalk to the door. I was still fighting and screaming. One of my legs was skinned to bleeding by the gravel and concrete, and my other leg was scraped. I was twisting to loosen his grasp and hitting at him with my free hand. Daddy threw me up over his shoulder, and I bit him as hard as I could. He put me back down and shook me and shook me. When he stopped, I kept screaming, "No! No!" I kicked and hit at him.

Daddy pulled me up the stairs by my arms. He threw me down hard on Mama's rug. Dirt was ground into the scrapes on my legs, and my back and ribs hurt from thumping the stair treads. I sobbed into the scratchy wool of the carpet, smelling its animal smell, and I felt that my life was over. He slammed the door and went down the stairs to the store.

When I stopped sobbing, Mama put me in the bathtub, cleansed my legs and put a stinging antiseptic on them. She washed my hair, rinsed it with a rubber spray attached to the faucet, and said if I stayed out late again. She had put a latch high up on our apartment door so I couldn't get out. I was careful after that. I never wanted to be trapped indoors, and I wanted to make her happy. I loved my pretty, quiet mother passionately. I knew even early on that while my mother was the center of my life, I was not the center of hers. And after that day, I knew enough to be frightened.

There were lots of good things. Mama and I went to see my grandfather. We left in her car in the early morning when it was still dark. We didn't get to the ranch until almost lunchtime because Mama said it took five hours to get from Culver City to Madera. Sometimes I stayed at Grandpa's. He had a cow and chickens, and a pump in the kitchen at the sink and one out in the yard. I had my own bed in a room that used to be my mother's. She always came and took me back home.

One day, Mama took me to a movie. It was called *Gone with the Wind*. We had to go downtown because Mama said the movie would never come to Culver City. The theater was dark and the screen bright. I liked it until a horse got scared and was trying to run away from fire. I tried to climb into Mama's lap, but she sat me back down and said, "If you close your eyes everything bad will disappear." I closed my eyes. The bad things didn't disappear. I still heard the horse's screaming and the crackling of the fire. But I didn't cry. Mama didn't like crying.

Mama's cousin Verna met us afterward in a restaurant that had trees and waterfalls indoors. When we finished eating, Verna smoked a cigarette. Then we walked to a building that had bright balconies and metal stair rails. Light came down from a big window in the ceiling. We went out by a different door and found a streetcar. It went to Pasadena. I went home with Verna on it. Aunt CeCe liked me, but Verna didn't.

"That child is too scared to ask for a drink of water when she's thirsty," Verna complained to Aunt CeCe.

In a few days, Mama and Daddy picked me up in his big car. They were laughing. I was happy to see my mother.

My mother must have loved me, because after that she gave me a baby to be my very own. The baby was so small she was the right size for my arms. Baby Beth peed in her diapers. Mama explained how she held the fingers of her left hand tightly together and put them between the diaper and Beth's stomach, and the pins in her right hand would never stick the baby. If her hand slipped, the pin would stick the fingers of Mama's left hand instead. I helped by putting my fingers in between the diaper and Beth's little pink stomach while Mama was diapering her. Mother never let the pins stick me. She was proud that I was three years old and willing to endure a pin's stab to protect my sister.

Mama said, "It's my job to clean the house and cook. It's Daddy's job to make money for us. And, it's your job, Lynn, to take care of your sister. You must keep always protect her and keep her from harm."

Daddy and I loved the baby. Daddy loved her so much he never stopped looking at her and singing to her. Once when he was singing his Magyar songs, I came to Beth's basket. He was happy. He said, "Look adet pretie bebi. Baidt is Leen's sistair."

Daddy couldn't speak English right, but Mama and I could. I tucked my head down so he couldn't see me smiling.

Uncle Sandy and Rozsika had a record player. It went around and played Magyar music instead of the news. Uncle Sandy was Daddy's brother. He and Rozsika danced with me when I stayed in their house while my mother was in the hospital getting Beth. After Mama and my new sister were home, Uncle Sandy and Rozsika brought us *palacsinta* sprinkled with powdered sugar. I showed them that I knew how to support my baby's head with my arm.

Rozsika smiled at me she said, "You zo lucky hev litlee bebi."

I nodded. I knew I was lucky. And I knew Rozsika practiced and practiced to say so many words in a row in English.

My sister learned to sit up, then to stand in her crib. Grunting fiercely, she'd frown and shake the crib's railings until it moved back and forth and banged into the wall. Beth made such a racket that Mama lifted her down to play with me.

Before my sister could walk, Daddy opened a new store in a hilly neighborhood closer to the beach. Uncle Sandy came to manage Lazlo's Liquor's downstairs. Uncle Sandy stood me on a wine barrel so I'd be tall and taught me the coins in the cash register. He let me put them in the right place when customers paid. If there weren't any customers, I taught him how to say more words in English.

Daddy bought a house high on a hill in Palms, nearer the ocean. His new Lazlo's Liquors was down the hill and around the corner. Mama said that she could smell the clean Pacific from our hilltop. The garage was big enough for both cars.

Families lived in our new neighborhood. They weren't like apartment people. They were like us. They had children.

~~~<<=>>~~~

Chapter 3: The View from Breeze Terrace

By January 1947, I was in fifth grade. My tenth birthday was approaching. We'd lived in Breeze Terrace for six years. Beth was seven. My sister was so smart St. Blaise School skipped her up from second to third grade. Her eyes blue, her eyelashes dark, and her cheeks and lips were pink. She wasn't freckled or squinty like I was. Her hair was blond and wavy. Mine was straight. Mama thought her mouth was too wide, but people commented that Beth was beautiful. Mama said it was because she inherited Daddy's deep-set eyes and curving cheekbones along with Mama's fair coloring. I wished I had.

Our brother Stevie was five. He and Beth had asthma, but he was sicker than she was. Stevie had eczema on his face, arms, and legs too. Stevie had Daddy's dark eyes, but he didn't look like Daddy otherwise. He was thin and spindly and Daddy was tall and strong. Stevie was old enough for public school, but Catholic schools didn't have kindergarten. He had to wait until he was six to start. When I started first grade I was only five but Sister Mary Anselm took me "on condition". Sister never took boys "on condition."

Mrs. McCauley, my best friend Delores's mother, drove the nuns if they had to go places like to the doctor. Nuns couldn't drive. Mrs. McCauley told Mama they said my sister was the first child to skip a grade at St. Blaise in five years. Mama reminded us that being smart in school didn't mean much. Being smart in school didn't mean we were smart in the world.

"Daddy has lived in the United States twenty years and still has trouble with English," she said. "Your father obviously isn't good at school subjects, but he certainly knows how to make money. My father, your grandfather, had a college degree, and he was a perfectly useless man. He didn't make enough money to buy tobacco for his pipe. Don't you girls be vain because of what you know. It's what people *do*, not what they know, that shows intelligence."

I didn't like Mama saying mean things about my grandfather. But Beth was vain, and so was I. On the state tests twice a year, only three kids in my class ranked higher than I did. They were boys. Next year, when she was in fourth, Beth would probably beat even the smartest boys. She liked winning. Grandpa died when I was barely six. Beth and Stevie didn't remember him at all. Before he died, he bought me a radio so I could hear *Let's Pretend* and *The Little Brown Church of the Air*. The radio was still on my night table. Things lasted better than people.

Beth and Stevie didn't have to do much work. They had asthma. In the Bible story of Mary and Martha, I was Martha. Mother bragged that I was competent. Beth got to be Mary. Stevie was sick a lot. If he were coughing, I knew to prop pillows up behind him, and to pat his back to bring up phlegm blocking his airways. I'd wash his face and hands with cool water to make him feel better, and kept the bubbler's water jar filled. I put eucalyptus oil drops in it if my brother were wheezing. Beth was never as sick as Stevie. She never had to stay in the hospital to get oxygen. My mother was happy I could do things to help.

My father was never happy with me. I thought he resented me being so healthy when my sister and brother were sick. I didn't like being healthy because it meant I had to do everything, but Mama's friend Jeannie was a nurse. When I complained, Jeannie told me that God put vital people like us on earth to take care of the sick and injured and do what they couldn't. I should be very proud of all I could do.

Stevie had friends up and down the block. Asthma wasn't catching so no one was afraid of him. Public health nurses didn't put quarantine tags on people's doors for asthma like they did other sicknesses. When our brother wasn't sick, he played outside like we did. Mama wouldn't let any of our friends come inside.

Elsa was our cleaning woman. Elsa looked for reasons to criticize; so I avoided her and didn't offer to help her. But, when she wasn't there, I did all the work she would have done. Mama did the hard things like cooking and ironing our father's white shirts. Elsa's job was to scrub the kitchen and bathrooms, sweep, mop, and vacuum, do dishes and laundry, and iron the ordinary things like our school uniforms and Mama's everyday dresses. Elsa didn't like children, even helpful ones. Mama said Elsa was a housekeeper.

At school, Laura Baronovich said, "A housekeeper works all week and gets Sunday and part of Wednesday off. Cleaning women usually only come once a week."

Her father was a cinematographer. They lived in Cheviot Hills where the streets curved and houses had bay windows. In Laura's opinion, Mama was wrong. Elsa was only a cleaning woman who came more often than usual. She worked for us four days a week, because our mother had been crippled by an accident. Mama could walk with a cane now. But she'd rather limp than look old. Our mother was as every bit as vain as Beth and I.

Daddy worked six days a week. There wasn't enough time for him to do all the yard work. Mr. Hasekura, our gardener, was kind. He never rolled his eyes at Mama if she asked him to do something the way Elsa did. He took time to show Stevie how all the tools worked. Mama hired Mr. Hasekura so that he and his family could re-establish themselves after the war. Mama said they were innocent Americans and lost their property. That could have happened to us too, because Daddy was Hungarian.

During the war the FBI watched our house and our stores. A blue car was parked in front of the Herrick house sometimes. Ronnie and Michael Herrick used to watch the FBI watch us. The FBI thought that the Nazis might try to intimidate Hungarian Americans into being spies. That was silly.

Daddy said Europe was full of "...boorocradts and bortergardts. Amerrica vas free and hadt golten streedts." He loved America. Hungary was just where he was from.

The Second World War started just after we moved to Breeze Terrace. Our father had been in the First World War, but on the wrong side. When the Second World War ended, we kids had a parade around the neighborhood. Ronnie and Michael Herrick took turns carrying a flag, and Diane Taylor twirled her baton.

Adrian put hibiscus in her hair and tooted a penny whistle. Beverly, Adrian's little sister, and my little sister, Beth, were only five. They wore tutus from their dance class. Other kids dressed up too and carried little flags. I wore a cowboy hat Grandpa had given me. It was too small by then, but I wore it anyway.

That evening, Mama told us that America only won the *first* part of the war. We didn't have a parade when we won the second part. It wasn't the same. At school Sister Mary Philomena told us that America didn't torture or kill civilians like Germany and Japan did. And then, the summer after I was in third grade, we did do all those things to Japanese women and children. Mama said I didn't understand the situation. We had to kill civilians to save democracy.

My sister and I had a double set of friends, at school and home, because we didn't go to public school like most of the kids in the neighborhood. My best friend at St. Blaise School was Delores McCauley. Her mom had a baby that died. Then her mom cried until Mary, Mother of Sorrows gave her another baby. Mrs. McCauley named the new baby Delores in thanksgiving. *Dolors* meant sorrow in Latin. We'd known each other's worst secrets since first grade. Mine was that I had trouble at home and the police could take me away from my mother if they found out. Her worst secret was that her middle name was the ugliest name in the whole world because it had *sin* in it. Delores said people only said it right in Ireland. My school friends never got to know my home friends. They lived on the other side of Culver City and my home friends lived in our neighborhood in Palms. Public schools were in districts and Catholic schools were in parishes. They didn't match. Kids in our neighborhood had a short bus ride to public. It was long to St. Blaise.

At home my best friend was Adrian Claussen. I liked her better than anyone except for my sister and brother, but there were some things it wasn't safe to tell Adrian even if I knew she'd never tell. Adrian and Beverly's mother was our mother's best friend. Her name was Louise Claussen. If Mrs. Claussen accidentally heard us talking, she'd naturally tell my mother. Jeannie French and Helen Porter were Mama's other best friends.

Daddy's friends were Hungarians and none of them lived near us. We saw them at St. Stephens's at Magyar festivals or in Palm Springs or Lake Arrowhead on Sundays. We liked them and their wives. They were older people like Daddy. Their kids were grown.

Our street was the highest hill in Breeze Terrace. From our living room window we could look fifteen miles across Los Angeles and see the tower of city hall. From our kitchen window, we could see a glimpse of ocean looking the other direction. On our side of the street, behind the back yard fences, was open land. There was a wide path and then sand cliffs. It was okay if we played there, as long as we didn't bother the farmers working below us. Adrian and I found tiny seashells when we dug into the cliff fissures. We thought of dinosaurs or Noah and a sea covering the world. Adrian wasn't a Catholic, but Mormons studied the Bible too. She knew about the ark. Sister Mary Immaculata said it was okay to believe in both the science of paleontology and the Word of God, because the definition of time was different when the Bible was written. I needn't worry about which came first, Noah or dinosaurs.

Some of the men in the neighborhood, Mr. Harris, Mr. Rader and Mr. Taylor, worked at Douglas Aircraft. They wore neckties like Daddy and Mr. Claussen even though it was a factory because they worked in offices. Other men worked at Hughes or North American or at MGM or Twentieth Century Fox. Dr. Bryant taught at UCLA. Dr. James was a medical doctor in Santa Monica. Mrs. Morgan was a teacher. She was the only mother who had a job. Adrian's aunt Charlene worked, but she was a widow, not a mother.

Daddy's dream was to move to Brentwood. It was higher than Breeze Terrace. We looked at lots for sale there. Mama thought our hills were high enough. Daddy talked to the real estate salesman. Mama smiled and acted nice, but she wouldn't get out of the car to look at the lots with their little strings and flags. Afterward, we had a picnic of sandwiches, potato chips and orange soda under the trees along Sunset Boulevard above the polo grounds. The polo players and ponies were practicing down below us.

"Brentwood has only half our view," Mama told Daddy. "It backs right up into the mountains, Laz. It's too closed in. We have a three hundred and sixty degree view from Breeze Terrace."

Beth and I knew what three hundred and sixty degrees meant. We explained it to Stevie by drawing circles, half-circles, and quarter-circles in the dirt with twigs. Then we ran to the edge of the trees and looked down at the polo field. Stevie clung to the fence, watching. He wanted to ride a polo pony. Beth frowned. Her face tightened up. A sentence from the library book in my desk at school, *"Mrs. Harwell's face showed grave suspicion,"* suited Beth. She was often suspicious of things Stevie and I admired: cats, dogs, birds, bugs, streetcars, road tar, the cliffs, junk piles, and now polo ponies. We ran to strip some leaves from the trees. The smell of eucalyptus oil in the bubbler was good for asthma. The smell of the leaves might be good for my sister and brother.

Daddy thought buying a lot in Brentwood was a good investment, and it was going to be a prestigious place. Mama won. Beth and I were glad because we didn't have to leave our friends or our school. Our little brother liked Brentwood; but it was only because of the polo ponies. He didn't want to leave his friends either.

~~~<<=>>~~~

Chapter 4: Evading the Gestapo

Stevie, crashing his tiny cars and trucks or running the noisy Lionel on its tracks, was all that Mama could handle. The Claussen house was so crowded we'd get stepped on in their house. Adrian and Beverly's grandmother lived with them. She had her own room, but the girls shared a bedroom with their aunt Charlene. Besides that, what in our house was the dining room, in their house was a bedroom for visiting relatives. Everyone seemed to want to come and live in California, and most of them stayed with the Claussens until they got settled. Between our mother's need for peace and quiet and the Claussen family's need for the opposite, we girls spent a lot of time outdoors.

One afternoon, two weeks before my tenth birthday, my sister and I went to find Adrian and Beverly, but they had gone to one of their grown-up cousin's house. Adrian was helping with the cousin's children; her sister went along to go somewhere. With nothing else to do, Beth and I walked down to our father's store. My sister could coax Daddy to give us treats, a soda or something from the candy counter.

On racks out in front of Lazlo's Liquors, every newspaper told of a gruesome murder. I began reading while my sister went inside. A moment or two later Beth came out with a Hershey bar for each of us, and one to take home for our brother. Beth glanced at the headlines, and she began to read too. We nibbled at our candy as we examined the grainy photos of the murdered woman. The headlines called the victim The Black Dahlia. She looked like a movie star. I folded what was left of my candy into its wrapper and put it in my sweater pocket and tried to slip a copy of the Herald

Express from the rack. The metal bar jammed. I struggled to get the newspaper out without tearing it.

Daddy came to the store's doorway. He frowned and pointed at the bank of newspaper racks. "Thees news is nodt goodt for girls," he said, as he waved us off. "Go home. Play vid kidz. Go somverr elz."

I didn't move quickly enough, and he came to yank my fingers away from the rack's bar. A burr on the metal bar cut the soft part of my hand below my thumb. Before I could put my hand to my mouth so my spit would clean the wound, Beth grabbed me and pulled me away. We turned for home. My little sister looked back to smile at Daddy and blow a kiss. I didn't. I was angry.

"It's not fair," I grumbled. "Why send us to school if he won't let us read. Daddy is like the Gestapo. He's censoring us about the papers. Next, he'll turn Nazi and take our radio."

Beth slyly said, "But Lynnie, he gives us candy."

We nibbled slowly to make the chocolate last as we climbed the hill. Beth wondered if the victim in the paper was someone famous. I was thrilled by the word murder. It was a true-life drama like a radio mystery, like The Whistler, or The Shadow, but real.

In the evening, Mama needed to lie on the sofa and ease her swollen leg and foot by propping it on a pillow. I did the dishes and cleaned the kitchen. In the dining room, Beth and Stevie helped Daddy count the day's receipts from the stores. Afterwards, Stevie played in the living room or listened to the radio with our parents. Beth came in to dry the dishes and keep me company. Then we finished our homework. Our parents listened to Gabriel Heater and Walter Winchell and read the paper. Mama had Stevie bring the paper into the kitchen to us when she finished. We read it after we finished homework. We didn't read all of it. Just the parts we liked.

This night, Mama came into the kitchen. Instead of giving us the paper, she only gave us the comics. She had a look on her face that meant we weren't to complain. We were used to the whole paper. Beth liked to look at the fashion ads. I liked to see how many different foreign countries would be named.

The second section had neat-o stuff like obituaries and vital statistics: how old people were when they died, how many got married, how many baby girls were born and how many baby boys. My sister looked at me. We knew Daddy told our mother what happened. They weren't going to let us read about The Black Dahlia. This time Beth was angry. She brought her pale eyebrows down almost over her eyes and pulled the corners of her mouth down. I raised an eyebrow at Mama but didn't say anything.

"You girls settle down." Mama said, and she limped back to the living room.

After she went through the swinging kitchen door, Beth said, "That's not fair."

"That's what I told you. It's censorship. It is just like Nazis. We're being Gestapo'd."

"Mama can't do this to us. I'll tell Daddy on her."

"He was the one who started it."

As the evening closed on our bedtime, my intrepid little sister tiptoed down the hall, through the kitchen, into the service porch and dug the newspaper out of the paper drive box. Beth tucked the first section of the paper under her robe and tiptoed back to our room. I closed the door softly and draped my robe along the crack at its base. Our parents never opened our door until they went to bed. We perched up on Beth's bed and read every word about the murder. The Black Dahlia captivated us, and we wanted the police to capture her killer and put him in the electric chair.

Our sneaky and defiant actions brought their own punishments. My sister had nightmares that week. I tried to convince myself that because I didn't have nightmares, I was braver than Beth. But while her terrors came at night and ended with the week, mine came in the daytime and never went away. Dreams seemed to work things out faster than thoughts. I began to be frightened of all men even our neighbors. I imagined any man might pounce on my almost ten-year-old body and kill me. *Brutal butchery* and *savage slaying,* phrases in the newspaper became realities to me, not mere abstractions from Dick Tracy or from the sinister adventure serials at the Palms Theater. I'd read of murders before, but The Black Dahlia was real to me. The range of men's capabilities expanded far beyond what I already knew.

My obsession with the crime should have worn itself out. Adrian and Beverly weren't interested in it. At school my friends weren't interested. Delores was, but her interest only lasted a day or two. My fears grew as days passed. I made my sister cross the street if a man was coming down the sidewalk on our side. My heart raced if a man sat near us on the bus. He might be a murderer. I pretended I was normal. If Beth saw I was scared, she'd get upset and then she'd get sick.

A week later we took the January mid-year state exams that kept all private and parochial schools accredited, and my sister and I did well and were happy when our scores in each area were sent home.

Soon, my birthday arrived with its special dinner and coconut cake. Among my presents was a Madame Alexander ballerina doll. Beth was squinty with envy. She shouldn't have been, because on her birthday she'd received a gorgeous doll from Madame Alexander that was equally beautiful. Madame Alexander dolls weren't to play with. Mama kept them in their boxes. My real presents were Levis and a flannel shirt I'd wanted and a red wool sweater Aunt CeCe had knitted. I loved my birthday. It fit between Christmas and Valentine's Day. I finally was ten. My friends already were.

~~~<<=>>~~~

Chapter 5: The Soft Whirr of the Projector

Everyone found our father attractive and paid attention to him. Mama said it was because of his good looks and accent. Men liked him, and women hung around Lazlo's Liquors taking a long time to decide what kind of cigarettes to buy. Some neighbor women would drop in on Sundays when they knew he was home. If they'd been coming to see our mother, they would have come when Daddy was at work. His voice was like a cat's purr. Once Jeannie told Mama that our father's voice was sexier than Charles Boyer's.

Mama laughed and said, "That's because Hungarians are sexier than Frenchmen."

Then Mrs. Porter said, "So, you know about Frenchmen, Marianne?"

Adrian's mother said, "She wasn't born married, you know."

Mama and the women all laughed.

Beth and I didn't know about Frenchmen, but we knew about Hungarians. They kissed women's hands. Whenever Daddy did that we'd start laughing, but the women seemed to like it and got silly. Mama wasn't jealous. She told her friends she didn't worry, because she always knew where he was. That was true. He was always at work, or else he was with us. Besides, my father liked my mother better than anyone else but maybe Beth and Stevie. My father didn't even like the American women he flirted with. We heard him tell Mama that American women ran around like "cheekens vidt headtz cut ov."

Our father liked things in this order: Mama and Beth, Stevie, America, the merchandise in our stores, our garden, his Hungarian friends and their wives, and last, the neighbors and customers who came into the stores. His mother lived in Hungary. I didn't know where to put her on the list. *Nagymama Erzsébet* wouldn't come when Daddy brought Uncle Sandy and Rozsika to America just before the war. She was too old now.

Uncle Sandy died last winter. I just turned nine. Beth was six and Stevie was four. On the way to his funeral, I wanted to go with Rozsika. Rozsika only had Mrs. Toth with her and seemed lonely for us. Daddy looked angry, and Mama made me get into the second limousine with our family. Daddy leaned back in the corner of the seat. He had his arm around Beth and was crying into a handkerchief with a brown plaid edging. Stevie was sitting on Mama's lap looking out the window. He was still only four then and understood that he shouldn't look happy when no one else was, but he loved the limousine. Stevie and I sat across from Mama. It felt odd riding backwards and knowing that we were following our uncle's coffin to the cemetery. I didn't cry, though. Mama didn't cry over things. I didn't either.

"Everyone who loves me dies, I whispered to myself.

Mama heard me. "I'm not dead, and I love you. Shush."

"First Grandpa and now Uncle Sandy. It's not fair," I said, keeping my voice low.

"Nothing is fair. Don't whine." She bent forward and whispered. "Stop thinking about yourself so much. Your father lost his only brother."

"Well, I lost my only uncle," was in my mouth, but I didn't say it.

At the grave, Father Király from St. Juliana's sprinkled holy water on the casket. Father Kennedy from St. Blaise was there too. Stevie got restless, and I took my brother down the hill away from the crowd around Uncle Sandy's grave, so he could run around. The dead people wouldn't mind a little boy running around. Beth didn't come with us. She stayed holding on to Daddy's hand.

Daddy's friends were all there. The Hungarian men we

knew worked in the studios. That's why they came to Los Angeles. Mr. Szepp was a cameraman. Mr. Voros designed backdrops. Daddy came here, back in the 20's, in service for a Hungarian film director named Korda. The director went back to Europe, but Daddy stayed here and became a citizen. He bragged that America was the only place in the *verruldt* where a servant could become a rich man with servants of his own. He must have thought Elsa, Mr. Hasekura, and the clerks were his servants. He paid them. Maybe they were.

When the prayers were done, I saw Mama talking to Rozsika. Stevie and I ran back up the hill. Rozsika bent down and kissed me. She picked Stevie up and hugged and kissed him over and over. She had tears because her husband died, but she was happy to see us. Beth held her hand and I cuddled up next to her. Mama pulled us away. Daddy was over by the limos waiting for us. He stared at Rozsika, and she turned her back. They didn't like each other. She was a widow now.

There was going to be a big funeral party somewhere, but kids weren't invited. The limo was going to drop us off, and Mrs. Voros would watch us. She was bringing strudel for us. We'd have our own funeral party. In the limo before we got home, Stevie fell asleep against me. I tried not to fidget so he could sleep. His head was heavy and turned my arm numb, but I didn't mind.

After our uncle died, Daddy had to close the Washington Boulevard store until he hired Auggie Friedman. Clerks helped out in both stores, but Daddy didn't trust them enough to let them manage. Auggie wasn't handsome or friendly with the customers like Uncle Sandy had been. Daddy thought he'd be bad for business, but Mama said that didn't matter at all. "In liquor, the merchandise sells itself," she said. "A clerk doesn't have to be handsome; he has to be dry and honest. That old bachelor is both."

She made Daddy laugh, and he began trying to kiss her neck. She pushed him away. She always pushed him away, but we knew she liked it.

On Sundays if Mother's leg hurt, Daddy planted flowers and pruned the trees. If her leg didn't hurt, he took us places.

Besides Palm Springs, our father took us to rodeos, carnivals, the Ice Capades, pony rides and to the beach. He liked Will Rogers State Beach best. Zuma was the prettiest beach, but Mama couldn't climb down the path. The only place we didn't go was to public swimming pools because our parents were afraid we'd catch polio. Whenever we had special events, our father made movies of us. All Beth's birthday parties were in the little round 16-millimeter film cans. Uncle Sandy came back to life again and played with us in the movies. The projector could run backward. We went up the slide instead of coming down. Planes landed tail first at Douglas. We laughed ourselves silly.

There was always a party somewhere in Breeze Terrace. We kids had birthday parties. The grown-ups had cocktail parties, barbeques, and parties for any old reason. Our family was invited to all of them because of Daddy. He rented theater movies for his and Mama's parties. We watched Charlie Chase, Laurel and Hardy or Abbott and Costello while the grownups drank high balls and talked. Later, our friends went home to their babysitters and we went to bed. The movies would change to John Wayne and Maureen O'Hara, Humphrey Bogart and Lauren Bacall, or Errol Flynn and Betty Davis. If Beth and I cracked our door open, we could hear the soft whirr of the projector, and under the actors' voices we could hear the adults clinking their glasses and laughing. We'd fall asleep listening.

Beth had only been two when Mama tripped and fell from the high stairs on our back porch. Mama was still in the hospital when our brother was born three months later. Our mother and Stevie came home in a wheelchair. Nurses came in shifts. Mama blamed the accident for giving Stevie asthma, but Beth had asthma too, so that wasn't reasonable. Neither my sister nor I contradicted our mother, but we knew she was wrong about asthma.

While our mother was in the hospital, Beth and I stayed with Uncle Sandy and Rozsika. Rozsika took good care of us until we could go home. Nurses were there for our mother. After the nurses left, a housekeeper named Beryl lived with us, but she didn't stay. When she quit, another one came.

After she quit, someone else came, then someone else. Finally Elsa came and she stayed.

On Elsa's days off, I could lift the baby, help Beth in and out of the bathtub, make beds, empty the hampers, and clean the bathrooms and the kitchen. I wasn't tall enough to hang my brother's diapers on the line. Eventually I grew tall enough. The garbage pail had to be hosed out and relined with newspapers after the truck had emptied it. I had to do that twice a week. Usually it had maggots in it and there was slimy liquid at the bottom. It smelled horrible. Daddy said the garbage pail wasn't Mr. Hasekura's job. Elsa said it wasn't hers. There was no one but me for that kind of work.

If my mother hadn't been crippled, things would be better for all of us. I was resentful. I knew resentment showed ingratitude for a good home, but I wished my father didn't hate me, and that my sister and brother weren't sick so much, and that Elsa would have to clean the garbage can. Sister Mary Immaculata said that we could ask God for anything, but what was the sense in praying for an accident not to have happened? I never heard of God making time run backward like movie film.

~~~<<=>>~~~

Chapter 6: Stunning Women and Rich Husbands

Last summer, Daddy sold Mama's green Plymouth and bought a new car for her. Mama's old car was a coupe. Daddy's car was a sedan. The new Studebaker didn't have a clutch so it was easier for her to drive. She could go to the grocery store and the beauty parlor to get her hair and nails done like the other mothers. Ruthie from Breeze Terrace Beauty didn't have to come to our house anymore.

Mrs. Porter, Mrs. Claussen, Mrs. Bryant, Mrs. Morgan and Jeannie French were Mama's best friends. Mrs. Bryant couldn't come visit much. She had babies to care for. She didn't have cleaning woman to help her even once a week. Dr. Bryant was a professor at U.C.L.A and didn't get paid very much. What Mama said about intelligence being sort of useless was probably true.

Mrs. Morgan couldn't come visit because she taught English at Venice High. Her little boys were Stevie's friends. Mama said nursery school made the Morgan boys wilder. Maybe it did. Mrs. Morgan was the only mother I ever met who worked.

Of Mama's friends, I'd known Mrs. Claussen the longest. She'd taken Beth and me to parties, dancing class, and music lessons with her daughters since we were little. Mrs. Claussen came from a theatrical family. One of her nieces was married to Errol Flynn, a movie star. Another was married to a music director, and another to an animator who got credits. Adrian and Beverly were the youngest cousins in the whole family because their mother had been their grandmother's last baby.

Mrs. Porter was loud and said rude things that made people laugh. Beth and I liked her. The Porters didn't have any kids. Jeannie French was our favorite of Mama's best friends. She let kids call her and her husband by their first names. Mama disapproved, but Jeannie told us to do it anyway. Our mother thought Mrs. Claussen was the prettiest of her friends. As Mama put her make-up on one morning, she said, "Louise Claussen doesn't even need mascara. She comes from a family of stunning women. That's how they could get such rich husbands. The Claussen girls will be stunning someday too."

Mr. Claussen wasn't really rich, but I knew what she meant. The Claussen girls were my sister's and my best friends, and it made us jealous of them. Beth made a face. While she helped herself to some of Mama's rouge, my sister corrected our mother. "Jeannie French is the prettiest of your friends, Mama."

Mama shook her head.

My sister was confusing personality with looks. She was wrong. Jeannie was the nicest, but I didn't think she was the prettiest. Mrs. Morgan was the prettiest. She had light brown hair twisted up in a bun and hardly wore any make-up.

When I said Mrs. Morgan was the prettiest, Mama corrected me. "Lynn Horvath, you can't mean what you're saying. Vivian Morgan is about the most pathetically washed out woman I ever met."

Time slid into winter and it was a rainy winter. Last year, for Valentine's Day we received hand-painted valentines from Daddy's cousins in Budapest. It was exciting because it was the first mail we had received from Hungary since the war.

Every other month we sent heavy boxes of sugar, coffee and cigarettes to his cousins as well as to *Nagymama* in Hungary. The valentines from this year were in the secretary in the living room with the other important things. Daddy was Magyar, but Mama was only plain American. Magyars celebrated Valentine's Day with presents and treats more than Americans did. We'd get more presents than we did for birthdays and way more than the valentines our friends got from their parents. We'd go out to dinner at a fancy restaurant on La Cienega. Maybe we'd go to one with candles and a trolley of desserts to choose from.

This year, Mama might get a new coat. She found a curly Persian lamb she liked in a Beverly Hills shop when she took Stevie to the doctor. We knew Daddy would buy it for her. Our mother had dimples and smiled a lot. Maybe Mama was the prettiest. Last year Beth and I got dresses of real silk that had flowers on a yellow background. Beth's still fit her. Stevie was as tall as she was. She didn't grow very fast but she wasn't the shortest in her class so Mama didn't worry.

~~~<<=>>~~~

Chapter 7: Kérem Szepen

Drizzly rain came down on Monday, and we had to wear our raincoats though it would probably be clear when school was out. It was the best week of the whole year. There would be no school on Wednesday the 12th for President Lincoln's birthday, and we would have a Valentine's party at school on Friday the 14th. Delores and Pat O'Hara's mothers were arranging it for my class. But as we and I jumped off the bus Monday afternoon to get home, Donny and Melvin were waiting for us. That was unusual. Although public school got out earlier than our school did, kids on our block never came to meet us.

The boys' eyes were big and their faces pale. Melvin, who was older than I, was hunched over his handlebars, one leg down for balance. Donny had dumped his bike down on someone's lawn and was sitting beside it. The brothers told us that Jeannie, Jeannie French, our friend, had been found murdered.

"It's just like The Black Dahlia," Melvin said. "Jeannie's body was found way across Sepulveda this morning. By Douglas. Probably the same guy killed her."

"She was in some dirt and weeds," Donny said. "She was naked and bloody and stomped to death."

I felt stomped. Beth turned so pale I thought she'd throw up. Beth liked Jeannie more than she liked Mama. My sister loved Jeannie. The boys rode off to see if the police were at the French's house. We didn't care about the police. I wanted to be home. I wanted to run, but I was afraid Beth would start wheezing. We walked slowly.

If Jeannie had been the Pied Piper, although we knew that the kids in that story disappeared, we would have followed her. It wouldn't have been any place bad. Jeannie could make glum Diane Taylor and nasty Harold laugh like normal kids, and she could get the Morgan boys to calm down.

Beth moved so close to me that we were bumping each other as we passed the Claussen house. Beverly was sitting on the porch. Harold Schiller was sitting on a step near her. I recognized his green sweater. I didn't think his own parents liked Harold. He always had to be first at everything and he bullied little kids. Beth said Harold was crying.

Beverly wailed at us, "Jeannie got murdered!"

Beth stopped and stood frozen. She was staring across the yard at Beverly and Harold. She wouldn't move. I pulled at her and said, "C'mon."

"But Beverly's crying too."

"It doesn't matter." I pulled at her arm and made her keep walking.

Elsa had gone home. Stevie was on the carpet with his cars. His eyes looked scared. Everything was different in the house. The colors of the carpet and the walls seemed to have changed. We waited for Mama to tell us what happened, but she just shook her head and told us to stay in the house. She stared out the window, and we knew to keep quiet.

My radio was gone again. We knew what happened to it. Beth curled up on her bed like she was sleeping. I tried to read *A Little Princess*. I'd read the book about ten times since I was seven. I skipped up to the part where Ram Dass comes to help Sara.

"How old was Jeannie?" Beth whispered. I knew she wasn't asleep.

"I don't know," I said. "It would have been rude to ask her."

"But she would have told us."

That evening after dinner, when the dishes were done and the money from the stores was counted, our parents

explained that Jeannie had been killed by a bad person.

I piped up with, "We know that already."

Mama looked hard at me, and said, "Don't be flippant."

Daddy looked sad. Beth went and put her arms around him. Stories and songs could make him cry. Mama said it was because he was European. Stevie stayed with me on the sofa. Daddy gently nudged Beth back between us. He nodded at Mama.

"Your father and I want you to know that the police are investigating this crime," she said. "They are talking to everyone in Breeze Terrace. Now, pay attention to me. *You* don't have permission to talk to them. If you see a policeman, you are to run home."

Beth spoke up. "Do you think the man who killed Jeannie will kill us?"

Daddy looked incredulous, as though the idea that Jeannie's murderer might kill us was too ridiculous to believe. He shook his head. "*Nem,*" he said. "No."

With such surety from our father, Beth slid her hand under mine. I squeezed it.

Mama kept talking. "If anyone talks to you about Jeannie or Frank, you are not to answer. You are *forbidden* to talk to anyone about this."

"Well, I can talk to Adrian, can't I?" I asked.

"No! You may not. Her mother is telling her exactly what I've told you. All of us want you children to put this terrible event out of your minds." Mother was solemn and serious. "Your father and I don't want you to read about Jeannie, talk about Jeannie, or to listen to the news. Starting from right now, no talk," Mama said. Daddy nodded.

Mother pulled my chin up. "Lynn, this isn't something to talk about with Diane, Joan, Patsy, Cheryl or Kathy, not to that little Barbara on the next block, and especially not to Adrian or Beverly." She looked at my sister and brother. "Do you all three understand?"

I put my hands in front of my face. Beth's low voice

grunted, "Uh huh." Mama had never spoken as severely to us as she was now.

Our father spoke first in Hungarian, then in English. "*Kérem szepen*, Makedt a promise."

There was that irresistible sound in his voice, something we usually only heard when he talked to our mother or was flirting with women at parties. It made me feel funny in my stomach, as though I had to obey him or I'd turn into a pillar of salt like Lot's wife. I kept my hands up over my face. Mother reached and pulled them down.

"The police may try to talk to you, but you run home or say, 'I don't know.'"

Daddy put his arm around her and kissed her cheek.

"Now, promise. All three of you, promise," Mama demanded.

Beth spoke up. "I promise," she said, clearing her throat and then drawing out the two words as though she'd never, ever, even under Chinese water torture, break her word. Stevie whispered his promise looking down at his hands. At last, I gave mine. I didn't need to promise. Mama should have known I'd never talk to a policeman about anything. She taught me that when I was little.

Daddy got up from his chair to turn on a music station. There would be no news broadcasts in our house that evening, no comedy programs, or quiz shows. Mother took us into the kitchen for cocoa and cookies. We kept adding whipped cream to our cups until everything brown in the cups had changed to frothy white. Stevie stuck his face down into his cup and made a mustache on his upper lip. Then he made big eyes like Charlie Chaplin in the our father rented last Christmas night. Our brother made us giggle, even on this terrible night.

Mother told us to calm down. We did. We tried to make everything normal because we knew that's what Mama wanted. Beth got up for a minute to show Stevie something she had learned at ballet. I chattered on with all the fifth grade gossip.

Stevie interrupted me to ask, "Will Jeannie have a funeral?"

Mama narrowed her eyes and held her mouth in a tight line so she didn't look like herself. But she didn't answer.

"No," I answered for her.

Beth scowled at our brother. "We aren't supposed to talk about it," she said.

I thought about Jeannie for a long, long time that night when I was in bed. She arranged for Beth and Stevie to see Dr. Salmon, the doctor in Beverly Hills who understood children's asthma. I never needed to go to a doctor. I never much needed anything special. And the things I wanted, nobody couldn't get by wanting.

Once when Jeannie was taking care of us after school, she was brushing Beth's hair and telling my sister how pretty she was. I complained that it wasn't fair that I wasn't pretty like Beth. Jeannie said, "Don't worry, sugar. Those freckles will disappear. When you're old enough for high heels and make-up, all the handsome princes in the world will fall in love with you. Just you wait and see."

Jeannie pantomimed a prince asking for my hand. She made us laugh. But maybe it was true. I wished I could grow up faster and find out.

~~~<<=>>~~~

Chapter 8: Boys on the Playground

Monday night's homework was tucked into our books. At St. Blaise, kids were only excused for a death in the immediate family. Jeannie wasn't in our family anywhere. I'd awakened with a dream about a cactus garden. I was playing with cats and dogs in the dream. Then I was flying over the garden with some birds. After I woke up, I remembered everything true and wished I could go back to the dream. We had breakfast and put our uniforms on.

Beth and I were both quiet on the bus. Pretty soon she nudged me. We gathered up our things and went wobbling down the aisle while the bus rattled to a stop. We jumped down the steps and began walking the remaining blocks to St. Blaise. When we reached the playground Beth waltzed off to the little girls' playground. Delores and Pat O'Hara came running to meet me. Pat had yellow ribbons in her hair. Colored ribbons were all right with our uniforms, but not colored socks, which didn't make sense.

We put our books down and went to watch the studio gate across the street from school. Sister would rather we went to St. Blaise church to make a visit with the Blessed Sacrament than watch the actors' gate if we had time before school. We liked watching the actors come in. The people we watched at the gate weren't important. They were just were extras, not movie stars, but they were actors and got paid. Some days, they wore costumes so we could tell what kind of movie the studio was making. We clustered at the fence. I squinted so I could see what the extras were wearing better. The men were wearing slinky jeans and wore cowboy hats and boots; the women wore saloon girl dresses. Some extras smiled and winked at us.

The bell rang. We ran and got in line. In Bungalow Five, Sister Mary Immaculata led our room's prayers, and the morning filled with lessons. I tried hard to put Jeannie out of my mind, but I kept thinking of how people feel when they think they are going to be killed. She must have had that feeling before she really was killed.

At recess, my friends and I ran between the rectory and Bungalow Six. We were going to act out a western. Delores wanted to be the sheriff, but Kathleen did too. Delores let her, although the game was Delores's idea. The rest of us picked our parts, except for Anna Rose. She didn't want to play if she couldn't be the saloon girl. Pat O'Hara had already dibbed that part. Anna Rose left us to huddle by the hopscotch game. Pretty soon she came back.

Three boys from our class came and stood at the yellow line that separated the girls' from the boys' sides of the asphalt. They were calling me. I ignored them. One of the boys calling me was Paul who knew more about movies than anyone in fifth grade because he was an actor. He might want to tell us something about real westerns for our game. I still ignored them until Andrew McGonigal, the smartest boy in fifth grade, yelled, "Lynn! C'mere, Lynn!"

Andrew and Paul were nice. Tommy was with them, though. He got in bad trouble at school in third grade because Sister heard him making fun of Carol Pistoresi's and my last names. He turned them into bad words. I didn't want to talk to him. I looked at Andrew and Paul.

"Did you know the woman who was murdered up where you live?" Andrew asked.

"She wasn't murdered where I live. She was murdered somewhere else."

"Okay. Maybe. But she lived up there right near you," Tommy Delaney jeered, butting in. Tommy's father was a plumber and he rode with his dad in summer and on holidays. He knew where everyone in our class lived. "So, did you know her?" Tommy yelled at me.

This was school, not home. My parents wouldn't know what I did or what I said. It wasn't exactly lying unless they asked me. I nodded my head.

Tommy ducked behind the other two boys and hit at them. "Told you!" he jeered at the boys. "Told you. Told you."

Paul and Andrew looked surprised. "Did you really?" Paul asked.

Knowing I was breaking my promise to my parents, I answered. "She was my brother's babysitter."

I was telling a kind of lie. Jeannie was Stevie's babysitter if our mother had to go to the doctor or the beauty parlor. But if Beth and I were out of school, and Elsa wasn't there, Jeannie was our babysitter too. It was fun going over to Jeannie's. Once she played monopoly with us. Stevie couldn't yet read the board or cards, and he didn't trust Beth and me not to cheat him. Jeannie helped him. He liked her better than he liked us.

Tommy came circling around in front of Andrew and Paul and his eyes were mean. He almost lunged over the yellow line dividing the playground. "She wasn't a babysitter," he taunted. "She was a whore! Just like the Black Dahlia!" He spun his basketball in the air and caught it. "My dad and mom both said so."

I didn't know the word "whore," but I'd seen it chalked on the sidewalk at the bus stop with other bad words. It was the word he'd turned Horvath into in third grade.

"No she wasn't." I said. "She was a nurse. And she was nice." My eyes stung.

"Nope. She was a rotten slut." Tommy bounced the ball up and down as hard and he could while singing, "Your babysitter was a whore, a whore, a whore. A whore, a whore, a whore." I thought he was going to sing it a million times.

Tommy bounced the ball wrong. It arced away. Paul ran and caught it and came back, but he stood away from Tommy and me. Andrew had moved farther away from Tommy too. They looked embarrassed. I just stood there, silent and stupid. I knew what a slut was. Kathleen told the rest of us girls a slut was a woman who hung around guys and got naked and let them touch her body. Jeannie never would be like that.

"I think it's true," Andrew said as kindly as he could. "My parents said her husband killed her because she was running around with men." Andrew was an altar boy. I didn't think he'd lie.

My throat felt tight. But I didn't cry. She wouldn't have done that, and Frank wouldn't have killed her. I couldn't look at Andrew.

Paul moved down toward Bungalow Five, but he was watching and listening. Tommy yelled at Paul to throw the ball back. Paul didn't. I turned and ran as far from the yellow line as I could. I ran to the fence on the other side of the bungalows. The bell was ringing. I knew I'd never speak to Tommy Delaney again in my whole life.

~~~<<=>>~~~

Chapter 9: Shoes with Little Black Bows

I wasn't sure about Jeannie anymore. She knew how to take care of sick kids. I saw her in a white uniform once, when she was helping Doc Petersen at the Breeze Terrace Drug Store after his heart attack. Maybe it was only a pharmacy coat like Doc's. Mama told us she was a nurse before she married Frank. But you could never believe what grownups said; the nicest ones would lie to you about tooth fairies and Santa Claus. Maybe she wasn't a nurse. Doc trusted her. Our parents only trusted our relatives to take care of us. Beth and I had never been allowed to go to a pajama party or spend a night with a friend. Not once. But they trusted Jeannie. She was the only one in Breeze Terrace who knew enough to take care of sick kids like my brother.

At lunch recess, my food didn't taste good. After we threw away our milk cartons and went back to the game. Delores said I was acting strange. I made myself be normal.

The afternoon was humiliating. Sister said, "Lynn Horvath. Please stand and recite the Presidents of the United States in proper order."

I got out of my desk and stood, but I couldn't remember past George Washington. The times tables, state capitals, and the American presidents liked to disappear from my brain. I could do my times tables. I knew what seven times nine was, or what six times seven was. But if I had to stand up and recite them, I went blank. Sometimes I blanked on the Pledge or the words to songs. I was a good rememberer, but not a good memorizer. I could only get A's with a pencil in my hand, not my mouth open.

"Miss Horvath, take your history book home tonight and study." Hardly pausing, she asked Andrew to recite the presidents. He said them perfectly in about two seconds.

All afternoon Jeannie's murder wouldn't go out of my mind. When the dismissal bell rang, I met Beth. As we began walking to our bus stop, I asked her to tell Mama that I would be late. "Tell her Sister Mary Immaculata wanted me to help clean the classroom today."

Sister sent home a duty schedule, but Mama didn't pay much attention to schedules. I watched Beth's blond curls bob up and down as she skipped across the tracks, and I turned walked toward the stores near the Motor Avenue intersection. I might have been committing a mortal sin. My plan was to walk home. On the way I'd spend my bus money for a newspaper. I was breaking the seventh commandment, since I was misusing my parent's money. The low winter sunshine was in front of me. The wind from the ocean whipped at my face. At the store I remembered, I went to the rack and pulled out a paper. The clerk put down his sandwich. He took my bus money and dropped it in the cash register drawer.

"So, punkin, ya gonna read the funnies?" he asked.

"No," I said, shaking my head. The bottles didn't shine in this store and there was grit on the floor. The clerk was eating right there at the counter. Daddy would have fired him. He would have said eating in front of customers was, "*Liedet Germans.*" He would have fired Elsa if she'd been a German or Russian, but she was Swiss. He didn't have anything against the Swiss. Daddy was wounded and his other brother, Zoltan, was killed on the Russian Front in 1914. He never forgave the Russians who shot them, or the Germans who forced Hungarians fight for their Kaiser.

I crossed Venice Boulevard with the signal. I stumbled on the red car tracks. It took time to get my books picked up, and the wind seemed to be trying to steal the newspaper. The Palms Theater was nearby. I headed for the theater's closest exit door. Adrian and I had gone through the exits once for fun. Each one had a little covered porch. There would have some shelter from the wind. I dumped my school things on the concrete step and prayed that Jeannie not be a bad person.

On the front page was a picture of Jeannie and Frank. The caption below it said, "French Grilled In Wife's Death." I read quickly. Her name wasn't Jeannie. It was Jeanne. I didn't know how to pronounce it. Was it Jee Ann? She was a nurse, had a pilot's license, and had been in movies. I didn't know about those other things, but she was a nurse. The paper proved the boys were wrong.

The sun moved, and I felt shivery. Whirlwinds were spinning in the dust of the theater parking lot. The newspaper claimed that Frank was under suspicion. That was dumb. Frank wouldn't have killed her. Then my heart broke into pieces. What Tommy and Andrew said was true. Witnesses said that Jeanne French was drunk that evening, and she had been seen in bars with unidentified men. Her murderer beat her over the head with a pipe wrench until she was unconscious. He dragged her into a field and stomped on her until her insides were smashed, then wrote bad words on her body with lipstick. She died naked in the mud.

I stopped reading because I couldn't breathe. When I was little I used to try and fight back when my father was hurting me. I'd kick and hit him and try to get away. Then, as I got older I got smarter. I gave up. When I crumpled down and stopped fighting, he stopped hitting me. Jeannie should have given up. She should have known to just give up.

The paper said that after the murderer stacked Jeannie's clothes on her body and threw her shoes out into the field. I wondered if those shoes were her shiny high heels with the little black bows. Beth and Stevie had clunked around in them once when we were at her house. I picked up my books and didn't care if I was littering. I let the pages of the newspaper whirl and blow away.

~~~<<=>>~~~

Chapter 10: Guardian Angels

Running most of the way except up the steepest hill, I got in the house before four o'clock. I changed and put my school sweater back on. I had to bring the clothes in from the line. It was colder now, and nearly dark. From our back porch, I could see across the bean fields toward Douglas and to the place where Jeannie was killed. I stood in the wind, yanking on the pulley, clipping off the pins and filling the basket with clean towels and shirts.

After I did my work, I practiced piano Playing *Fur Elise* over and over made me feel better. I only had trouble with one part. It made me stop thinking about Jeannie. Adrian was already learning *The Moonlight Sonata*. The Claussen girls were better than we were at talents. Beth called me when it was time to set the table. "Mama asked where you were when I got home," she whispered with a smirky smile. "I told her you'd be late and she didn't even ask why." She pursed her lips and looked like she knew what I hadn't even told her.

It was hard to smile back but I did to make everything seem normal. I still felt sick about Jeannie. I set the table in the dining room for our mother and father. Beth set the kitchen table for us. Everything was back to normal. We kids sat down to supper. Mama closed the door between the dining room and kitchen because our parents needed quiet while they ate. If we were quiet, we could hear them talking. Mama was complaining about paying the duties to send two packages to in Hungary this month. Coffee, sugar, raisins, and lard weighed heavily and cost a lot to mail. Mother never complained about the cost of buying the things she sent, but she was upset with the cost of postage and duties.

We received thank you letters from back from Hungary. In fourth grade, I took a letter to class. Sister Mary Pancratius pulled down the map and showed the class where Hungary was. I wouldn't do that this year. Sister Mary Immaculata would think that I was bragging about our family's charity. Sister Mary Immaculata made you think about why you did things, not just about what you did. "Actions only have value in the eyes of God when they are performed with humility," she said. She made us write it for Palmer Method writing practice. It meant we shouldn't do things for the praise of other people, but do them to please God.

I did the dishes while Beth and Stevie went in to the dining room table. My sister and brother made stacks of the paper money and little towers of the change while Daddy wrote everything down in the green ledger book. Stevie could already add up coins. He couldn't read yet, but he knew his numerals and could count by fives and tens. He and Beth loved helping Daddy count money. They set up the stores' change for the next day in two cigar boxes, and Daddy let them play with the rest of the money. Mama stayed in the kitchen. She pulled down the ironing board from its cabinet. She wanted to press our play clothes while they were still soft from the line. The starch smelled good. I put my hands in the hot soapy dishwater, cleaned, rinsed, put the dishes in the rack.

Mama was quiet while she ironed. She looked troubled. I knew she was grieving for Jeannie. Anna Rose told us something at recess. My work wasn't quite done, but Mama might find it interesting. I wiped my hands and sat down at the table. "Anna Rose says our whole school will get to see *Going My Way*. She heard her father tell her mother. He said all of the school could walk to the Meralta Theater."

"Your whole school couldn't fit in the Meralta Theater," Mama said. She almost smiled.

"We'd go in three shifts. It'll take three afternoons to fit all of us in."

"How does Anna Rose know so much?"

I started to answer that Anna Rose's father was in the Knights of Columbus, and knew as much gossip about school as Mrs. McCauley did, but my father came into the kitchen. When he saw me sitting at the table instead of working, he glanced at the dishes and clean sink board, but then he saw *paprikás* splatters on the stove. There weren't very many, only a few marks that were hardly big enough to see.

"Do right!" he hissed.

"Elsa gets paid to do it," I said silently, with my face turned away, wanting to scream it at him, but afraid to even whisper the words out loud.

He hit me on the side of my head. My chair skidded out from under me, and I crashed into the table and landed on the linoleum. I hurt my ribs on the metal edge of the table when the chair fell over. I was on the floor, and my skirt was rumpled up to my panties. I tried to pull it down, but before I could, Daddy bent over and yanked me up by my arm and my hair. He hit me over and over. All I could do was try to keep my hands over my face. I thought he was going to kill me this time, but Beth came running in from the dining room.

"Stop it! Stop it!" she screamed. She grabbed at his arm. "Don't you hit my sister!" she yelled as she pulled his arm away. Beth wasn't a very big seven-year-old but she wouldn't let go. Father tried to shake free of her, but she held on. Through my fingers I saw him almost lift her into the air. Suddenly he dropped his arm and she let go. He stepped back away from us. He stepped behind the chair where Mama sat.

Beth puffed her stomach out. "Don't you hit my sister! Don't you dare hit my sister!"

She looked straight at Daddy in a way I'd never had the courage to do. Her feet were apart, and her fists were clenched.

"*Es az úr is tanit! Ostoba lány! Lokott. Lokott,*" my father yelled. He wasn't yelling at Beth. He was looking and yelling at me but he moved farther back next to my mother's chair. He threw his arms up, as if in surrender, and shouted, "Leen! She is vat life you gif me. *Lány lokott. Ostaba lány!*"

Mama didn't say anything. She put the iron down, clicked it off, and turned to look at him. Beth helped me up. We backed quietly out of the kitchen. We could hear our father saying, "*Kedvesem, kinzol engem. Kérem, kérem. Kedvesem. Rendetlenség van itt.*" Daddy was praying for God to save him from me.

Stevie was curled up under the dining room table. Beth went to play with him and tell him everything was okay. I went to lie down on my bed. At school, the sisters had been telling us about guardian angels since we were in first grade. I guessed I believed in them. But like our souls, angels were invisible. They flew around us and kept us from harm.

There was a picture in the vestibule at St. Blaise across from Mother Mary Ursula's office showing a guardian angel protecting two little children as they crossed a rickety bridge over a stream. I loved that picture. But it wasn't true. In my whole life no invisible angel had ever come to stop Daddy from hurting me. It was my little sister, Beth Horvath, who protected me.

I thought about things for a long time. That night I did what my parents wanted. I decided to put Jeannie French, who had been nice to me and to all of us kids, out of my mind. I was tired and didn't want to cause any more trouble.

~~~<<=>>~~~

Chapter 11: Rozsika

The next day was Lincoln's Birthday. Jeannie had been dead for two days. I tried not to think about her or the way she died. It was a holiday, but Mama made us stay in the house. We cleaned our closets and packed up our old things to take to the Salvation Army for poor children. Adrian and Beverly didn't come over. No kids on bikes went by. Whenever the phone rang, Mama closed the door and spoke so softly that Beth and I couldn't eavesdrop. I practiced reciting the presidents so often that my sister could say them better than I could. When I put the book down I would get somewhere and stop, not knowing where I was.

Thursday morning when we got to school, I shook my head at Delores and Pat O'Hara when they called me from over by the palm trees. I ran and knocked on the door of Bungalow Five. I'd never gone to talk to a teacher before and was scared.

Sister Mary Immaculata looked surprised, but she let me in.

I stammered out that I couldn't say the presidents.

"You have studied?"

I nodded. "Yes, s-s-Sister."

She looked thoughtfully at me and asked me if could write them out. I told her I could, but it would take me a long time. She asked what I meant. I explained that if I had enough time, and a pencil and paper, I'd be able to write all the names but they wouldn't be in order. When I had thirty-two names, then I'd figure out the order. Sister looked confused. She asked me to guess where William Henry Harrison might be in order, and I said twenty-nine. She asked me who number twenty was, and my brain stopped. I didn't know. I couldn't have said who it was if I were being tortured.

Sister Mary Immaculata didn't smile. She said, "It was James A. Garfield."

"Yes," I said. "That was s-s-sad. He only was president for a little while and got shot in a train station. It took him all s-s-summer to die."

"Who succeeded President Garfield?"

"Chester Arthur."

Sister looked perturbed. "You obviously know them. I don't understand why you can't recite them properly."

I mumbled, and Sister said, "Speak up."

"I-I don't understand either, but I can't do that kind of thing."

Sister gave me a few more presidents' names. I could tell her about their lives. I told her that Theodore Roosevelt overcame asthma when he was a boy. Sister said she'd give me full credit and exempt me from having to recite.

In the afternoon, while the class was taking turns reciting, I slid away in thoughts about the cactus garden and the ranch. I liked to curl up with Grandpa on the swing under the eucalyptus trees. He never minded me being there. It was a ragged old swing and there was no garden at the ranch, only dirt and weeds, the trees, chickens, animals, and his house. Mama inherited the ranch and sold it. I could never go back there.

Delores began to recite the presidents. Sister only had to prompt her once. Delores didn't usually get A's, but she was smarter than me about most other things.

I was jealous of Delores, sad about Jeannie, and tired of my troubles at home. Patty Lacy couldn't say the presidents either and started crying. I felt bad for her. At least I didn't cry so no one knew how I felt.

Sister Mary Immaculata excused Patty to the restroom and clean up.

While Patty was gone Sister cautioned the class against self-pity. She said, "Self-pity is nothing but *backward pride.* Pride is the deadliest of all sins. Through pride, people value themselves ahead of God."

Andrew McGonigal raised his hand. "Excuse me, Sister, but if self-pity is backward pride, wouldn't that make it humility? And then, it would be a virtue."

He'd also figured out that Sister liked humility best of the seven cardinal virtues. I nodded my head in agreement. Sister glared at Andrew and flashed me a look. She told the class that Andrew was wrongheaded, and anyone who agreed with him was also wrongheaded. "Self-pity mocks humility. It allows us to put too much importance on our own insignificant feelings. Therefore it is a sin against the First Commandment given to Moses by God himself on Mount Sinai," she lectured.

After that, I tried to concentrate how insignificant my feelings were and not be jealous, sad or tired.

At music time, Sister Mary Pancratius came from fourth grade. The nuns traded around for some subjects. Sister Mary Pancratius had a beautiful voice, and she looked a little like Rozsika. She was teaching us to read the old square note Gregorian. "On the note!" Sister shouted as she came from the back of the room. She grabbed Jimmy Baxter's hand, yanked his index finger and twisted it down so hard his liturgical music book that it skidded to the floor.

He winced and bent to pick up the book. Sister was nice to the girls, but not to the boys. I'd go to purgatory for all the trouble in I caused, but Sister Pancratius would go there for unfairness. She turned to go back up to the lectern. Dennis, who sat next to me, put his thumbs in his ears and stuck out his tongue at Sister's back. I looked across the rows at Delores. We wanted to laugh, but if anyone did, Sister would figure out what had happened. She'd keep all the boys in after school to make sure she got the right one.

Rozsika used to visit us and help out, but she left our house when I was in third grade and never came back. Stevie was sick and she had come to help. I was supposed to clean the living room before the doctor came. I broke Mama's porcelain lamp when I bumped the vacuum into the leg of its table. Rozsika tried to pull Daddy away from me. He swatted her across the room as though she weighed nothing. He was yelling at her then, not me. When he turned and left the room, Rozsika got up, helped me up, and gave me a long hug. Her face was red and she was shaking.

She got her sweater and purse from the entry closet and left. She must have walked all the way home. Uncle Sandy still came to our house, but Rozsika never did again. We only saw her at the Magyar festivals at St. Juliana's Church. We'd find her in the parish hall kitchen. She'd pick Stevie up and carry him around. She always got tears in her eyes.

Mama and I were alone in the kitchen on Friday the week Sister Pancratius hurt Jimmy. She seemed sad, and I thought she must have been missing Jeannie more than Beth and I or Stevie did. I was washing the dishes and while I worked, I told her about Jimmy getting in trouble and Dennis making a face. "I don't like Sister Mary Pancratius very much, but she looks like Rozsika." I said.

"Yes, she does, but that brogue isn't Magyar," my mother replied, smiling.

"Don't you worry about Rozsika?"

"Oh, Lynn, no. And don't you worry either!" Mama exclaimed. "Your auntie has a wonderful job. She's a cook in Brentwood. The couple she works for invited her to live in their home after Sandor died. She has two rooms and a bath, and a small patio all her own." Mama's blue eyes twinkled, "Rozsika is a smart woman who landed on her feet."

It didn't seem so wonderful to have to cook for people. I shook my hands and soap bubbles flew around. "I didn't know you talked to her. When do you talk to her?"

"Of course I talk to her. We phone each other now and then. She always asks about you children, and about you especially," Mama answered. "She's happy. The doctor and his wife arrange for her to vacation in Hungary for two weeks every year, as long as she promises to come back to them. She passed her citizenship test and is building her vocabulary. They are very good to her."

"Why didn't you tell me?"

"You know why. After everything your father did for her, all the money he spent bringing Sandor and her out of Europe just in the nick of time, she interfered. No one should try to come between a parent and child."

I looked at my mother so long that she knew I was being insolent.

"Children need discipline," Mama said firmly, and stared at me longer than I could stare at her.

I thought about Grandpa and the ranch as I finished the dishes. It was peaceful at his ranch up in the valley. That's where my mother grew up, way north, past Bakersfield and Fresno. It was the best place I knew. In all the time I stayed there, I never heard him raise his voice. The one time that he was upset with me, he didn't do anything. The only thing he said was that if I loved him, I wouldn't scare him again by wandering too far away. I didn't think Grandpa disciplined Mama very much.

~~~<<=>>~~~

Chapter 12: Famous People

We were on a mountain! Actually we were only on a high hill in the Hollywood Hills, but we could see the whole city below us. Beth had the biggest smile I'd ever seen on her face. Even dopey, boring Diane Taylor was standing up straight and looking at the tower on the front of the movie star's house. Adrian went up to the door and opened it. "We're here," she called. Beverly pushed her aside and went barging in. Most of us girls and mothers were standing around in front by the cars, just gawking at the house. It looked like pictures of French chateaus I'd seen in books, not like anything American. But then, Adrian's cousin's husband wasn't really American. He was the only one Beth and I ever heard of who came from Tasmania. When Adrian first told me that, I expected him to be a native person. But he sounded sort of British.

Adrian's uncle Jack came to the door and met us and welcomed us all inside. It wasn't so spectacular inside, but the part of the house that looked like a tower from the lawn, was where the stairs curved up to the second floor next to the entrance hall. Movie stars traveled a lot and sometimes their wives went with them. Jack and his wife Margie stayed at the mansion and took care of the little Flynn babies. Mrs. Claussen showed us around, and took us to change into our bathing suits. We got to swim in the pool until time for Adrian's birthday party.

In June, we'd been in a wedding when Mr. and Mrs. Voros' son, Lorant was married at St. Juliana's Church. Beth was the flower girl. The bride's little sister, Marika, and I carried the bride's train. Stevie was supposed to be the ring bearer, but when it was almost time for the wedding rehearsal, my little brother refused to cooperate. Mr. Voros was a smart man. He bought Stevie a complete Roy Rogers outfit. It had a holster with two guns and bullets that were attached to the holster belt. First, Stevie had to agree to be in the wedding. Stevie agreed. The morning of the wedding he got stubborn again and said he'd only carry the ring pillow if he could carry one of the guns on it too.

"*Shurr you can,*" Mr. Voros told my brother. "Thees is Amerreeca. You can be cowboy."

Stevie was a cowboy in a white tuxedo. Beth walked in front of the bride. She was out there by herself, and she loved it. She stalled the whole procession by walking as slow as a snail to drop flower petals on both sides of the aisle and have longer to smile and flirt with people in the pews. No one noticed Marika and me because we were behind the bride. We were glad.

At the wedding reception Daddy took Beth out on the dance floor to dance the czardas. Mr. Voros pulled me to the dance floor. It was scary and also fun. The grown-ups were having such a good time they ignored us. Stevie ran wild with all the other boys. They crawled under the tablecloths and when women slipped their shoes off to rest their feet, the boys moved the shoes so the women couldn't find them. Marika, Beth and I, with some girls we didn't know, ran around exploring the clubhouse, and then we went back to the reception and snuck sips of champagne when the waiters weren't looking and pretended we were drunk.

But, not even a Magyar wedding was as good as going to a movie star's mansion. I wished Deloris were here too, but she didn't live near enough to know Adrian. Swimming in Errol Flynn's pool was fun, but I was too worried to play in the water with the other big girls. Beth wasn't very tall. Beverly thought she could swim, but she really couldn't yet. So I stayed with the little girls. None of the mothers was watching us. They were having cocktails at the bar near the house and talking about their bathing suits. Adrian's school friends were dunking each other in the deep part of the pool. I didn't mind staying with the little girls.

After we swam, we watched a movie in the projection room. It was full of romance and tragedy. It wasn't a kid movie, but it was historical so Mrs. Claussen had picked it for the party. We had cake and ice cream. Adrian opened her presents and then we ran upstairs and downstairs squealing and hollering. We were wild girls. Diane tripped and fell on the stairs and didn't cry. We found The Baron's grand bedroom. No one said we couldn't go in, so we did. It had the biggest bed any of us had ever seen. We pushed and tumbled and jumped on its red velvet spread. Beverly began to count. All of us fit, and there was room for more. Deirdre had been toddling after us through the house. Someone reached down and pulled her up onto her father's bed. She made thirteen. We jumped and fell off and climbed back up to jump again.

It was a long way home. Beth and I rode in the Claussen station wagon. Mrs. Taylor was up in front with Mrs. Claussen. Diane was squeezed between them. Adrian and Beverly were in the far back they started a clapping game with Marlene and a girl named Janet, but pretty soon I think they fell asleep. We were tired from swimming and the movie. The presents were stacked between my sister and me. Beth was snoring. Diane was slumped down in front so she'd fallen asleep too.

Mrs. was gossiping about someone who was going to have a baby. I pretended to be asleep too.

"Can you believe she's pregnant? You'd think she'd have more sense at her age."

"You'd think that *he'd* have more sense," Mrs. Claussen answered. "He isn't exactly a teenager."

"No, and he's probably crowing. Puffed up and proud of himself." Mrs. Taylor said. "I like her, but she's a fool to let that happen to her."

"A mason jar by the bed would have prevented it."

"An ounce of prevention is better than seven pounds of cure," Mrs. Taylor said. They laughed until they snorted, like they were the kids in the car. I didn't know what was so funny or what jars had to do with having babies.

I wondered if Nora Flynn was pregnant again. Then Mrs. Taylor said something I couldn't hear. Mrs. Claussen reached for the rear view mirror to check on us, and I kept my eyes closed.

Every kid knew someone famous. Delores' godmother was Kay Baker who sang on the radio. She came to Delores's birthday party when we were in second grade. Kathleen O'Donnell's father wasn't famous, but his voice was and not just because he sang at the eleven o'clock mass. When there was a movie, if the star couldn't sing Mr. O'Donnell's voice went on the sound track. Mr. O'Donnell didn't get credits because stars wanted people to think they did the singing themselves. Laura's father was almost famous himself. He got credits.

Paul, who sat behind me in class, had been in three movies this past year: *The Wistful Widow of Wagon Gap*, *High Barbaree*, and *Trail Street*. Sister Mary Immaculata made up folders of work for his studio teacher. Beth wanted me to give Paul *I love you* notes from her. I wouldn't do it. He might believe that they really came from me.

Thinking about Paul made me remember fifth grade and the day Tommy and Andrew questioned me on the playground, the day after Jeannie died. Everyone knew someone famous, but it was better to know people who were famous for better things than being murdered.

~~~<<=>>~~~

Chapter 13: A Party for Alex

Sixth grade wasn't as good as fifth. At home things were awful. Mama still cooked, but she didn't want to talk to us or go anywhere. On Sundays we stayed home. Beth and I spent our free time reading, or riding bikes with Adrian and Beverly. Stevie played with the Morgan boys, and Daddy worked in the garden. We went to Palm Springs once and came right home. Nothing was fun anymore.

Then in late September, our parents told us that there would be a new baby in the house at Christmastime. Beth and I were gleefully, crazily excited. Neither of us had noticed that Mama's stomach was getting rounder. She was always a soft shape. A few more inches weren't very noticeable. Beth begged to get to name the baby.

Daddy was elated. To celebrate, he took us out to The Castle restaurant for supper, our favorite restaurant. The food was pretty much like other restaurants but it looked like a castle and had a drawbridge and that was enough to make us like it best. Daddy was talkative and laughing in the restaurant. He told us he hoped the baby would a boy because then Stevie would have a brother to share his room and be his friend. Stevie didn't say anything, but he looked worried. Our brother liked his room the way it was, and he had the Morgan boys for friends. He knew what babies were and didn't see how one could be the same as a friend.

Elsa quit as soon as she found out. Mama was devastated without her.

For the next few weeks, Beth and I came home from school to greater chaos each day. The breakfast dishes weren't done. The beds weren't made. Our mother was on the sofa or in bed. Elsa wasn't kind, but she kept our family organized.

My sister threw a tantrum. "We need help, Mama. This place is a mess!" She was practically screaming at our mother. "I'd never bring anyone in this house." Beth got very rude.

"There has to be s-someone who needs a job." I tried to speak up when Beth stopped for breath. I'd never throw a tantrum. I'd never raise my voice to Mama, but Beth was right. We did need help.

Mama half sat up. "There isn't anyone," she whined. "And Lynn, don't stammer. I've said we'd pay extra, but no one wants to come to a house with children. The war ruined everything."

We didn't need a soldier; we needed a cleaning woman.

"You girls don't know how it was," Mama wailed. "Women used to be grateful for housework jobs before the war. But then they got factory jobs, and now they think they are too good for housework." Mother buried her face in her pillow.

"I don't care about the olden days, Mama," Beth yelled. She jabbed one fist at Mama's bed. "My socks are lost. I had to wear Lynn's. They're baggy on me. I'm not going to school looking ugly. No one's done the washing for two weeks."

"What can I do?" Mother whined. Her stomach looked like a beach ball.

"Get up and take care of things!" Beth demanded. "Do something. You're our mother."

Mama couldn't do much. She didn't know how. She could cook and iron shirts, brush her hair and wash ours, put on her make-up and take naps. She didn't know how to do anything else. She squished her face down in her pillow wouldn't answer us anymore.

I offered to stay home from school and do Elsa's work, but Mama said I couldn't because it was a state law that I had to be in school. So after school and on weekends, Beth and I tried our best. It was very hard. If Beth and I stayed home from school every day we still couldn't keep up. Beth wasn't good at housework. I got in trouble a lot and was scared all the time. Mama just slept. At last Beth threw a huge tantrum at Daddy. He took over the search for someone to help us.

We were saved. Through one of his customers, Daddy found a woman named Jessie Miller. Within a week the house was clean and orderly again. Jessie was tall and had lank grey hair and sad watery blue eyes, but she was kind and energetic, and she liked kids. She smelled like cigarettes. Daddy held that against her. Mrs. Taylor, Mrs. Bryant, and Mrs. Porter absolutely stunk of cigarettes, and he flirted with them.

One evening while my sister and I were setting the tables Beth said, "Lynn, if you'd move over a tad, I might could get them plates."

"Might could? Them?" Mama repeated. "I won't have Jessie's Okie-Arkie talk coming out of you girls' mouths!"

"She's from Louisiana, not Oklahoma," my sister snipped.

"At least she isn't mean like Elsa was," I retorted.

"You two girls listen to me." Mother said. "Elsa was never unkind to you."

"She didn't even like *you*, Mama," Beth growled. "Elsa made fun of you."

"She made faces at you behind your back," I said.

"She'd had a hard life. And, you, Lynn Horvath, are the last person in the world to call anyone else mean."

"I'm not mean, Mama. I've never once done anything cruel or evil."

Mother squinted up her eyes at me. "Yes, you have." She turned away. "You broke my rose clock."

"When? Lynn wouldn't do that." My sister spoke up for me.

Mama responded quickly. "She did. She put a curse on it. She said it was ugly, and now it doesn't work anymore."

Saying it was ugly wasn't cursing. "I didn't put a curse on it."

Mama grasped my hands and pulled me toward her. I could feel her rings and fingernails. "Lynn, don't you ever in your life put a curse on anyone or anything again." She glanced at Beth. "Your sister is a witch. Watch out for her."

"Maaama!" I wailed. "I'm just a kid."

My very intelligent, skip-a-grade sister gave a perfect imitation of Sister Mary Pancratius saying in Sister's exact voice, "Witches, ghosts, goblins, and vampires are the silly superstitions of the uneducated and unintelligent."

Beth said it, but Mama gave me the hard look. When we went to bed that night, I snuggled down and tried to sleep but I thought about Mama's clock. If I were a witch, I was the puniest one in the world. My curses should have killed my father when I was about three-years-old, and he was still very much alive.

Beth was thinking too. In the darkness, she said, "I think being pregnant makes women crazy. When I grow up, I'm never going to be some crazy pregnant woman. You can have babies. I'm not going to."

Her words rattled around in my mind for a few weeks, until I remembered the conversation between Mrs. Taylor and Mrs. Claussen as we drove up to Adrian's birthday party. I was shamed. I knew then that the woman Mrs. Claussen and Mrs. Taylor had been joking about was Marianne Horvath, my own mother. I pulled the blankets over my head and wished I could completely disappear. Mama had broken some kind of taboo I hadn't known about. Women in Breeze Terrace weren't supposed to have more than two children. The Horvaths were working on four. I was glad I hadn't told Beth what Mama's friends said.

Baby Sandor Janos Horvath was born at St. John's Hospital in Santa Monica four days before Christmas. Mama had been strange when she was pregnant, but she loved the baby and seemed normal again almost immediately. Our new brother was named after Uncle Sandor. That made us all happy, but Beth wanted to call him Sandy, and Mama wouldn't let her. We had to call him Alex, which was Sandor in English.

On New Year's Eve, Daddy had hired four clerks to work in

the stores so he could stay home and give a tremendous party to celebrate our new brother. Daddy hired waiters to serve drinks and clean up. A La Brea restaurant catered the food. There wouldn't be movies at this combination New Year's Eve and christening party, but there would be lots of music and good food. We got to stay up through the adults' late supper, then we were sent to our rooms.

Jessie stayed the night to take care of Alex and watch us. Beth and I had a place in the back hall where we could lie on our bellies in our nightgowns to watch the party through the bronze heater grid near the baseboard.

We could only see feet, legs and laps, but we heard everything. I picked out Mrs. Taylor's voice saying something funny. I was shamed again hearing her voice and remembering what she'd said last summer. Soon Mr. Novotny was singing songs with Mr. Voros. Mrs. Harris got really drunk and tried to kiss our father. Mrs. Harris was vulgar, but we thought it was funny. After a while, Mr. Novotny stopped singing Hungarian, and we heard Mr. Claussen start playing American. Mrs. Porter was singing. She had a rough voice but it sounded good. Mrs. Claussen's didn't sing, but in the background I could hear her piccolo laughter and my mother's clarinet laughter adding to the music. I liked the sounds of grown-up parties.

Beth went to bed but I stayed there until after Jessie had put her nightgown and robe on and looked out the boys' room door to tell me not to stay up too late.

Mr. Claussen drank a lot, but he never acted dumb. Everyone in Breeze Terrace drank a lot except my parents and the Herricks. Adrian said her parents were Jack Mormons. That meant they drank. She wished they were real Mormons. Our stores sold liquor, but our parents only sold it. They hardly ever drank it, only on big celebrations although Catholics didn't have rules against it. We could trade religions with the Claussens. If our families switched religions we'd have to go to public school. Adrian and Beverly might not like the uniforms and long school day at St. Blaise. I knew I wouldn't like public.

I finally went to bed. When I woke up later, the party was still going on. A Fourth of July smell filtered into our room this New Year's Eve night. Daddy saved some fireworks just for tonight. I got up to go to the bathroom. Mr. Foster was sitting on the floor of the hall near our room's door. I had to step over his feet. Mrs. Harris was sitting on his lap. She wasn't sitting in the normal way people sat on other people's laps; she was facing Mr. Foster. They were wiggling around and kissing sloppy. Her dress was all pushed up. They didn't notice me.

I came out of the bathroom, and I could hear guns and fireworks going off again. There were whistles and poppers too. I wished my bedroom had a window out to the front yard so I could watch the party go on.

It was 1948. I stepped carefully going back to bed so I wouldn't step on Mr. Foster and Mrs. Harris. They'd stopped wiggling around, but they still didn't notice me.

I got back into bed. The fireworks smell was still there and I could hear guns going off and people laughing outdoors in the street. The only ones missing from my parents' party were Jeannie and Frank. I'd put Jeannie out of my mind, but she crept back in. It didn't seem right that people could disappear, and parties go on without them.

<p style="text-align:center">~~~<<=>>~~~</p>

Chapter 14: Going Places, Not Going Places

On Valentine's Day, 1948, Jeannie had been dead one year and four days. As I took Alex's things from the pulley clothesline on our high back porch and stacked them in the basket, I could look across the bean fields and see the place where she was killed. It scared me to look that way. I was still frightened of men, and worried that one of them would get my sister because she wasn't frightened of anything. She walked right up to them and talked to them. Even strangers. She actually liked it when they paid attention to her. I worried that she was like Jeannie.

I lugged the laundry inside. A pork roast and cinnamon apples were in the oven. They smelled good. As I toted the basket through the hallway toward the boy's room, my father came through a doorway and spun me around. The basket and baby things flew all over. He pulled me farther down the corridor and pointed to some pieces from Stevie's Lincoln Log set scattered on the carpet. "Vy not vatching broter?" father shouted. "Mama veel falling!"

He hit me hard. The back of my head smashed into the wall behind me. The wall hurt more than his hand had. Daddy stepped over me, and the heel of one of his shoes smashed down on the edge of my hand. I couldn't help crying out. He stopped and kicked at me. "*Nem,*" he said, "You nadt hurdt."

I was hurt. How could I not be hurt? I was sitting crumpled there when I realized that I was sitting in the same place Mr. Foster and Mrs. Harris had been when the New Year came in. A silly feeling caught me. Something about sitting there like drunk, dopey Mr. Foster was funny. I wanted to laugh, but my head hurt too much.

As soon as I could see better, I got up and began to gather the laundry. Each time I bent down I was dizzy and felt like throwing up, but if I squatted down very slowly without moving my head right, left, or up and down, the spinning feeling gradually went away. I wouldn't throw up. Stevie looked around from the door of his room. I heard the front door close. It was safe. I took a deep breath. Stevie's big eyes were very serious. He didn't say anything but he began to help pick up the Lincoln Logs. This was the first time my father had hit me in weeks. I was doing better at being invisible. I pretended I was a girl version of the elusive *Shadow* on the radio. My grades had gone down and I was dumber at school, but smarter at home and there wasn't trouble so often.

I stopped doing homework this year. No one noticed. Sister was probably glad there was one less paper to check. When Jessie was sick or took days off, there was too much work. I couldn't get all of it done. Beth tried to help, but she was good at counting money and figuring things out; she wasn't very good at ordinary work. Mama wasn't either, and she was busy with the baby.

Business was very good in both the stores. Our parents bought a corner lot on a section of Sepulveda Boulevard. An architect drew plans for a three-store building. Daddy could open Lazlo's Liquors in one, and lease the other two. Daddy sold the Washington Boulevard business. Auggie came to help clerk in the Breeze Terrace store.

We were planning a trip to Hungary. *Nagymama* was in poor health and Daddy wanted to see her once again before she died. News reports from Hungary were all dark and ominous. Almost every day there was mention of Eastern Block oppression in Hungary. Sister Mary Catherine said the Hungarian Cardinal Mindszenty was a saint for standing up to the communists now. By the end of February, we all had passports and visas. Beth and I lay in bed at night and talked of meeting our grandmother for the first time. We'd dance to gypsy music and see Margaret Island, wheat fields with poppies blooming around their borders, and we were going fly across the Atlantic Ocean. We didn't think of communists.

One evening, as I took the garbage out after doing the dishes, I heard music. Mrs. Lowery played cello in a string quartet. It was practicing in their music room. It was like having the Hollywood Bowl across the fence. Music chased the stars around the sky and I stayed to listen. Soon I'd soon see Magyarország, the land where Haydn wrote melodies for Count Esterhazy and the place where Franz Liszt was born.

Everything was ready for our trip to Europe. Then, ten days before we were to leave, Daddy changed his mind. He'd been pacing and acting crazy. He raged that the right kind of baby formula wouldn't be available in Hungary, and that Alex might get sick. Mama said we'd be treated like royalty just because we were Americans, and people all over the world had babies and they grew up just fine. But Daddy went alone to Hungary. We'd never meet *Nagymama*.

While Daddy was gone, Alex's first tooth came in and he learned to sit up by himself. Our father looked handsome and distinguished coming down the steps from the plane. Mama and Beth were sparkling with happiness. I was nervous, and my brother Stevie looked gloomy. He stared at the planes taking off and landing at the airport. Daddy saw him, and understood. He promised he'd take Stevie on a plane ride. A week later, Stevie flew over Breeze Terrace in a little yellow plane. We watched from the front yard. The pilot dipped the wings so we knew our father and brother flying over.

When Daddy came home from Hungary, he didn't have one photo of his mother or his cousins. All the pictures he'd taken were confiscated at the airport in Budapest. His new, expensive camera was confiscated also. Americans were not treated like royalty behind the Iron Curtain.

~~~<<=>>~~~

Chapter 15: Camp Saint Mary of the Woods

When school was out, Beth and I each brought home a flyer for Camp Saint Mary of the Woods, a Catholic summer camp for girls up in the San Gabriel Mountains. We didn't think we'd be able to go since we couldn't even go to sleep overs, but I asked and Beth demanded. Adrian and Beverly had gone to Girl Scout camp. Beth wanted to get to go to camp too.

"Mother, you and Daddy owe us something special," she said. "Stevie got to go flying. Lynn and I didn't get anything."

Three days later, Mama gave in. Daddy looked reluctant but agreed, secure that since nuns ran the camp we'd be safe. The last two weeks of June we were in the mountains. Separated by age, Beth was assigned to one of the log cabins, and I was assigned to one of the tents. It was the first time we'd slept in different rooms since she was born. We hadn't expected that we'd be apart, or that camp would be so primitive.

We had counselors who took care of us, and they were fun. Beth liked her counselor. That part was all right. I loved Shirley, the counselor assigned to my tent. She was kind and funny.

My mother told me about periods last January when I turned eleven, but Mama made it sound like a horrible secret. Bridget Moran, one of the girls in our tent, started her period during our session in camp. Shirley told us all. That night after campfire songs, when we crawled into our sleeping bags, she lit a tiny lamp in the middle of the floor. She handed out a candy bar to each of us to celebrate that Bridget was a true woman now. That night in the tent, we told stories until late. We told each other what we planned to do when we grew up. I said I was going to be a nurse. We laughed and tossed our pillows at each other until another counselor came over to tell Shirley our tent was keeping the whole camp awake.

"I hate it here. I'm not going in those showers," my sister whispered on the morning of our second day as we met on the path before chapel. "They're dirty. There aren't any screens and bugs fly in. There was a big lizard on the window sill."

"Well, I'm not going in them either. They don't have shower curtains, and I don't want people to see me naked. I'll get clean during swimming."

"I'm not going in that lake. It's pukey. There's green stuff in it."

"Shirley said it's only algae and won't hurt us. How'll you get clean?"

"I'll get clean when I get home."

For two weeks I bathed by swimming in a small, slimy mountain lake. For two weeks, Beth didn't bathe at all. I didn't think she stunk, but Mama shooed her right to the bathtub as soon as we were home.

Although she'd been a model camper for Session 2, 1948, Camp Saint Mary of the Woods, and won three badges, my sister threw a big tantrum. She screamed and ranted that mother was mean for making her go to camp. She cried that her feet were filthy the whole time. Daddy held her on his lap, kissing her now clean feet and petting her. He promised that he would never let her feet be *feelty* again.

Mama had paid for horseback riding, but Beth hadn't gotten near the horses. I liked the way they smelled, their big eyes. I liked the way that they followed directions so easily, even when they weighed about a million times more than we kids did. I liked the lake with cattails, dragonflies and frogs. I liked the girls who came from all over the city.

We gave each other our phone numbers, but we knew we would never be able to call. Parents never let kids use the phone just to chat, only for serious emergencies. We shared addresses, but when I wrote to two of the girls who had been in my tent they didn't answer. One lived in Lomita and one lived in Monrovia. Mama said that they were too far away to become real friends.

If there had been shower curtains, everything about camp would have been perfect. There were no men, except for the men down at the stables. And they were cowboys like in the movies, not regular men. One looked like Gabby Hayes.

After summer, my sister and brother, and all the kids I knew moved up another grade. Stevie was in second. He wanted us to call him Steve, not Stevie. In the fall, St. Blaise's parish held a huge festival to collect money for a new two-story school building. Beth was chosen to pull the raffle tickets out of the wire basket on stage. My sister smiled, bowed and blew kisses from the stage. She stayed up there much longer than she needed to. She embarrassed me by showing off, but Mother and Daddy were proud because people clapped and whistled for her. Beth became the most popular girl in the whole school after that. Kids, who hadn't talked to me before, suddenly liked me. I became popular just because I was Beth's sister.

While Beth was now the star of St. Blaise School, Beverly Claussen was becoming a star in all of West L.A. Beverly at eight, was better than any of De Grasse's teenage dance students. She was invited to perform in the productions of other dance schools with older kids. Mrs. Claussen and Mama took us to see her dance at the Shrine Auditorium. Beverly's hair was pulled back and had oil on it to make it look dark and make-up hid her freckles. She'd won a scholarship to special classes at U.C.L.A. for the exceptionally talented.

Beth did fine in dance although I knew she didn't like doing it very much. She took lessons because Daddy wanted her to, not because she actually wanted to. She knew she could never be as good as Beverly was, and Beth liked being the best. By the end of fifth grade, Beth dropped out of dance class.

My sister said she was going to marry someone rich so she wouldn't have to bend and stretch all day practicing. Mama got a funny look on her face and said that getting a rich husband wasn't so easy; bending and stretching might be easier.

~~~<<=>>~~~

Chapter 16: In the Living Room

Auggie was getting older and only wanted part time clerking, and the Sepulveda store was making more than three stores had, so Daddy sold the Breeze Terrace business. Our father should have been happier with just one business to worry about, but he wasn't. Daddy was nervous all the time, the way he'd been before he went to Hungary. Only this time there wasn't anything different to cause him to be so upset.

He punched one of the drivers from Blackmore Distributing when the man came to re-stock the new store, saying that the driver was stealing from him. The distributor put another driver on our route. But after Daddy shoved the other driver into the fender of his truck, saying that driver was cheating him, Blackmore refused to deliver unless Mama was there to keep Daddy in control. Daddy accused all the clerks who worked for us, except Auggie, of either stealing from him or of looking at Mama wrong. One by one, he fired them. Mama worried and we weren't able to keep our secrets about Daddy's temper private anymore.

Finally, when Mama was as desperate as she'd been when Elsa quit, Father Király came to rescue us. He asked Daddy to sponsor a Magyar who'd escaped to Canada but wanted to come to America. The man had to have a guaranteed job. Daddy agreed. Erno came and saved our lives. Daddy calmed down. Erno was as reliable as Auggie, but younger and Hungarian. Alex had his first birthday, and things calmed down a little.

I turned twelve in late January of 1949. I was in seventh grade, and everything turned terrible again. At the St.Valentine's Bazaar at St. Juliana's two weeks later, Daddy hit Mr. Varga for trying to kiss our mother. We didn't see him do it. Mr. Varga drank too much, and drunken people got stupid, but Daddy was blamed for the fight.

Father Király helped Mama take our father out to the car. Beth held Alex while I loaded the stroller into the trunk. Mother had to drive because Daddy was still raging and cursing. Beth sat in front to calm him down. Stevie played with Alex in the back seat so the baby wouldn't get scared and cry. Everyone at the distributing houses, and now everyone among the Hungarians could see what he was like when he was upset.

Mama liked the jolly Magyar women. They treated her as if she were special because she was American. After the trouble with Mr. Varga, we didn't go to their parties, and we never went back to St. Juliana's or Palm Springs. Daddy felt that his community had betrayed him. It had been lively for all of us with the Hungarians, good food, good music, and lots of picnics. Mama seemed sad. I was sad. Baby Alex would never know the fun we'd had with the Magyars. That part of our life was over.

Mama had to go to the bookkeeper. Her instructions were few. "Don't give Alex his bottle until four o'clock. Don't let Steve stay in the house or watch TV. He can play outside."

"What about the Morgan boys?" I asked, knowing that they were waiting by the curb.

"They can play in the yard, but don't let them in the house." She picked up her purse and left. Beth and I wished we could watch TV. We were the second family on the street to have a television set, and we thought it marvelous. Beth got her dolls; I got my book. We stayed in the living room with Alex watching him bang toys on his playpen's floor. We could hear Steve and the boys through the open windows.

My sister grew bored and wanted to look at her last class picture. She wanted to list everyone in her class and thought she'd forgotten some of the boys' names. Mother's secretary was off limits, but I thought it would be okay. We knew which drawer held photos. We weren't interested in Mama's old letters. But Beth couldn't find the picture she wanted. She was frustrated and opened another drawer. The drawer held pictures, folders and receipts. Among some photo envelopes was an old leather folder with the name Andrew Cameron Frazier in the lower right corner. As Beth shoved the folder aside to sift through the envelopes, I reached for it. I didn't recognize the name on it. It wasn't Hungarian. Under its worn cover were some papers. Alex's birth certificate was on top. "Look, how cute!" I said, showing Beth Alex's tiny footprint.

"Let me see." She grabbed the folder away from me. We knelt down on the green carpet and sat back on our heels. Beth scanned the certificate and handed it to me, as she began looking through the rest of the folder. Alex was twenty inches long at birth. He weighed eight pounds and one ounce.

Beth grew very still, almost not breathing. She stared at a certificate in the folder. She shifted her weight until she was sitting flat with her knees up in front of her, the folder propped on her thighs. "Mama and Daddy were married in July of 1940," she said in an odd voice, strained and droll at the same time. "Everyone at school says that it takes nine months to have a baby, but it only took them four months to have me."

I sniped at her. "That doesn't make sense. You read the date wrong." I pulled the folder back from her and read. Beth was right. She only took four months. And that meant I didn't exist. If our parents weren't married until 1940, where was I? Something was odd about Mama's name too. Beth hadn't noticed. The groom's name was Lazlo Horvath, but the bride's name was Marianne Joyce Frazier. It should have said Marianne Joyce Bradley. Grandpa was Lawrence Bradley.

Underneath were more certificates, Steve's, and Beth's. We read through them and they were correct. Only the marriage certificate was wrong. My birth certificate wasn't there so we kept looking. Below some other property papers was our grandfather's death certificate. He died of heart failure, but I already knew that. Under that there was a birth certificate for a person named Andrea Lynn Frazier. The last name was the same as on the leather cover of the folder. I pulled out the document. I began to read, and I began to shake. The page was black with white printing. The white letters were jumping around so I could hardly read what they said.

The girl named Andrea Lynn Frazier was born at Santa Monica Receiving Hospital the same day I was. Her father was Andrew Cameron Frazier. Her mother's maiden name was Marianne Joyce Bradley. I kept on shaking, and my heart was beating too fast.

Beth took the folder and read it. She frowned, looked at me, and read it again. Then she stretched out her legs and leaned up against me.

"It's okay. You are still my sister." She said it gruffly, and she meant it forever.

My eyes were stinging but I didn't cry. I was still Beth's sister. I was Mama's child. But I wasn't Hungarian, and I wasn't Lynn Horvath. The boys were playing outside. We could hear them through the open windows. Alex was singing to us from his playpen.

"We won't tell anyone," Beth said.

I just nodded. I was still shaking. We put everything back in the drawer and closed it. My hands were trembling and it showed, but Beth acted like she didn't notice. She got up and said, "We won't ever tell her what we found out." Beth had never cared about Mama before. I didn't know why she cared now.

"I want to know why she lied to me," I said.

Beth reached down and lifted Alex out of the playpen and looked at me. "You can't ask her something we aren't supposed to know." She handed Alex to me. "Here, he needs changing."

After I changed him, we sprinkled Johnson's Baby Powder all over our baby so he'd smell good. We sprayed some of Mother's Chanel on us so we'd smell good too. She wouldn't mind that. We played with Alex all afternoon. Steve got tired of the Morgan boys and came in and turned on the TV. It was getting dark. I didn't stop him. We pulled down the sofa cushions and all cuddled up together on the carpet to watch an old cowboy movie on channel eleven.

Mama came home. She rested, washed her hands, and began to fix supper. My sister and brothers' father came in and took a shower the same way he did every evening after work. Beth and I were very quiet that evening. I wasn't angry. I was just sad because everyone had lied to me.

After we'd gone to bed, the door closed and lights out, Beth whispered, "We should never say anything to anyone."

"I know." Turning to the wall, I puffed up my pillow. Beth went to sleep, but I didn't.

I'd never been Hungarian. Uncle Sandor wasn't my uncle. It was as though Mr. Hasekura's big pruning shears had chopped me away from everything I knew. Nagymama hadn't been mine at all.

Yet, I was giddy with relief that Lazlo Horvath had been chopped away with all those other things. My sins weren't as bad as I thought. Murderous thoughts were still sinful, but he was just a man. I didn't have to honor him.

The next day had been marked on our calendar for six weeks. Beth and I were scheduled to go on an adventure. Pat O'Hara's father would pick us up in a truck at seven A.M. I couldn't brood about what I'd found out and wanted to go to sleep. I wasn't Lynn Horvath and the worst thing was that other people had known it all along, Grandpa, Aunt CeCe and Verna, Uncle Sandy and Roszika. Grown-ups lied and lied. Beth said not to tell anyone, but I was going to tell Adrian and Delores. I'd be with Delores all day tomorrow. I couldn't wait to tell her.

St. Blaise School didn't have Girl Scouts; instead sixth graders could join Sodality, a Christian virtue, prayer, and good deeds club. My friends and I joined. We met once a week after school for 20 minutes and said prayers to save people from communism. We licked envelopes, or boxed holy cards. Pat O'Hara and Delores McCauley's mothers decided to start a different club for us.

Mrs. O'Hara and Mrs. McCauley said girls our ages needed to have fun. Delores thought up the club's name, Blaise's Blazes. Mama said I could join as long as Beth was included for special events. Pat O'Hara was the baby in her family. She liked watching out for any little sisters who came with us. It gave her a chance not to have to be the one taking orders. I was relieved not to have to be the one who had all the responsibility for little kids safety.

Our club was a great success. By the time sixth grade ended, we had been to Griffith Park Observatory, to the Los Angeles County Museum, ice-skating at Polar Palace and we'd learned to knit. Our mothers decided to continue through the summer.

The morning after I found out that I was really someone else, Blaise's Blazes were scheduled to go to Catalina Island on a day trip. It was an event with my friends from school, so I wouldn't see Adrian, but I'd be with Delores all day. Beth was coming along with a couple of other little sisters. I hoped she liked Catalina Island better than she liked Camp Saint Mary of the Woods. Otherwise I'd probably never get to go there again until I was grown. Mama didn't approve of us going places without each other.

~~~<<=>>~~~

Chapter 17: Catalina Island

By the next morning, Mr. O'Hara had found a truck big enough to hold all of us and get us to the steamship *Avalon*'s dock in Wilmington. Squeezed together in the truck, there was no privacy for me to tell Delores about something that happened only in Nancy Drew books. I'd found undeniable proof that I was really a girl named Andrea.

Blaise's Blazes began to run around the *Avalon*'s decks and check out the snack bar and bathrooms. The three mothers with us found a bench in the sun on the open top deck. Beth was walking around with two other little sisters. I found a private spot on the railing where no one would hear Delores and me. Delores crossed her heart and made the sign of the cross. She promised on her mother's life not to tell anyone. I looked out over the railing at the sea and wondered how I could begin telling it. Finally, I said, "I never need to go to confession about my father again. I can hate him without breaking the fourth commandment."

"I think you still have to," Delores whispered. "The commandment means we have to honor our parents all our lives, not just until seventh grade." She was pompous about being Catholic and thought she knew everything about sins.

"Yes, we have to honor our parents," I replied. "But," I jumped around in front of her and paused to make what I said more dramatic, "... Lazlo Horvath is *not* my parent!"

As she began to understand what I had said, she screamed as loud as a seagull, "How do you know? When did you find out? Are you sure? Did your mother tell you?"

"Shush. Everyone will hear you. My mother never tells me anything. I found my birth certificate. My real name isn't Lynn Horvath."

"What is your real name? What about Beth?" Delores said, with her voice brought back down. She twisted around to look for Beth. My sister was walking with Carol Donnelly and Maria's little sisters. We could see them down the deck.

"My real name is Andrea Frazier. Beth and my brothers are Horvaths. I'm the only one my mother had from before."

"Does Beth know?" she asked me.

"Yes. But don't dare tell anyone," I said. "Remember, you promised." We stood there and looked down into the water. I had worrisome thoughts. Delores would understand and never tease me about them, so I could tell her.

"What if my real father was a criminal? Maybe he's in jail. Maybe that's why mother didn't tell me about him."

"Maybe he was killed in the war like Georgine's father."

"No. The war didn't start until 1941. My mother married Laz in 1940 before the war even started, so my *real* father had to be dead by then."

"What if he's not dead? What if your mom got a divorce?" Delores cried out. "Divorce is a mortal sin." From the horror on her face, she expected my mother to burn in Hell for all eternity.

"It's okay. It's only a sin for Catholics. She's not one."

"But your father is. It's a mortal sin for him to marry a divorced person."

"He's not my father, remember? Besides, I hope he does go to Hell forever."

Delores pulled away. "I could never want anyone to suffer for all eternity. It's a sin to wish bad things on people."

My friend was kinder than I was. All the McCauley's were. They made the sign of the cross every time an ambulance went by, stopping whatever they were doing, to pray for the person who was sick or injured.

We heard our friends calling. The Blazes were clustered in down the deck pointing into the water. We looked down to see skinny flying fish in the greeny-blue Pacific water coming up out of the water in parallel lines as though they were jumping over hurdles in a race.

Beth hadn't liked camp, but she liked Catalina. That day we rode in a glass-bottomed boat and had iced tea and a late lunch at the big hotel that overlooked the bay. She loved the grand hotel restaurant. We all sat up straight and ate politely. Most of us knew which of the tableware service we should use, and the rest figured it out. We rode a jitney up to the bird farm, and before we got back on the steamer to go back to continental America, we went down to the little curved beach. We took off our shoes and waded on an eastern shore of the Pacific Ocean. We might have been in China or Japan.

When we got home Mama was cooking supper. She had been alone with the boys all day, and the house was a mess. Toys were all over the living room. The kitchen table hadn't been wiped since breakfast. Beneath it, food was stuck to the floor. From the hallway we could tell that Alex's diaper pail needed to be dumped, the diapers rinsed out. Beth and I both raced to get things in order before her father came home. Beth did the toys while I took care of the diaper pail. Then we cleaned the kitchen and set the tables.

The next day was Sunday. Alex was a baby and too little to go to mass, but Steve didn't have to go to church at all. Horvath boys could choose. Horvath girls went on the bus every Sunday morning to St. Blaise Church. When Beth and I were riding the bus home from mass, I confessed to her that I'd told Delores about my birth certificate.

"I'm going to tell Adrian too," I added.

Beth gave me one of her mean scowls. As the bus bumped along, she was wheezing a little, and leaned her head against the bus window. "Don't you dare tell Mama," she mumbled, and then went to sleep.

Sunday afternoon was quiet. After doing the lunch dishes, I was free. I needed to talk to Adrian. I couldn't stop thinking about the leather folder in my mother's secretary. It didn't seem it right to tell Delores and not tell Adrian. I knew

Adrian wasn't going anywhere this weekend. I went to knock at the back door. Adrian opened it before I knocked. Her face looked pale and her eyes were wider than ever. She seemed anxious.

"Pop's fixing lunch. C'mon in," she said, leaning around the door. Something was wrong. I started to say no and turn away, but she pulled me into the house. We went into the kitchen where Mr. Claussen was ladling up some hamburger, rice and tomato sauce mixture from an aluminum pot into red bowls. He had an edge of a dishtowel tucked into the vee of his collar for an apron.

"Hello there, Lynnie," Mr. Claussen said quietly and cleared his throat. He nodded at me, but he didn't exactly look at me.

"Beverly's dancing," Adrian said. "We don't have to pick her up until three." We sat at the kitchen table. Before Mr. Claussen gave Adrian her bowl, he fixed one for me. I told him I'd already had lunch, but he ignored me. I tasted a little. He winked at me but it wasn't his usual wink for kids.

"It's good, Mr. Claussen. It's like chili."

Adrian piped up with, "This is Pop's favorite. He always makes it when he cooks."

"My mother's the only one who can cook at our house."

Mr. Claussen froze for a minute and didn't smile. I thought from the way I'd said it, I thought he'd have at least smiled. He knew all of us kids so well that he had to know I wasn't making fun of him for cooking. I was kind of complimenting him that he knew how. Mr. Claussen gave us each a glass of chocolate milk. While we ate, he fixed a tray for Adrian's grandmother. He put a spoon, a glass of lemonade and a napkin on the tray beside the red bowl. He picked up his drink and made the ice cubes rattle as he put it on Grammy's tray. If he took his drink along, we knew he wasn't coming back for a while. We ate slowly. I told Adrian about the Blazes' trip to Catalina. But I knew she wasn't paying much attention.

"Mrs. McCauley would have let you come too."

"No. I had to go to YW," she said, shaking shook her head. It was Adrian's first year in YW. YW stood for Young Women. It was for the girls over twelve, and she had to learn lots of prayers and rules. LDS kids didn't have their own schools. Their religion teachers had to fit kids' religion in on Saturdays.

"Hurry up. I want to tell you something," she said. "It's a secret. You can't tell anyone." She didn't need to whisper. Her father was in the living room playing the piano, and Grammy couldn't hear anything. Mr. Claussen was playing *"Bye, Bye Blackbird*, but I wouldn't dawdle to listen to him. We rinsed the bowls, spoons and glasses in the sink, left them to air dry, and went outdoors.

"We can't leave the yard. Pop wants me to go with him when he picks up Beverly." Mr. Claussen drove okay when he was drinking, but he'd want Adrian to go in the auditorium to get her sister. He didn't always walk okay when he was drinking.

"Where's your mom?" I asked her.

"That's what I want to tell you about," she said as she ran over to the Chinese elm tree and climbed up ahead of me.

I wondered where Mrs. Claussen had gone.

~~~<<=>>~~~

Chapter 18: With Mr. Claussen

As soon as we were wedged our favorite places in the tree, Adrian told what she wanted to tell me. "My mom got mad at my dad and left us." She looked tragic. I thought she'd cry. I'd never known anyone whose mother had left her family.

"Left? Like ran away?" I asked. "Just because she got mad at your dad?"

"Pop's never mean to her. She's mean to him. She says she gets tired of us." Adrian leaned back on the thick branch behind her. "She took the car to go to the store after Pop got home from work Friday, and she didn't come back. After it got dark, he got worried. The next morning the car was parked in front of the Morgans' house. The keys were in it, and Mom left him a note on the driver's seat."

My mother had never left us overnight for any reason except going to the hospital when she had the accident or had Alex. Laz had only left to see his mother.

"What did it say?"

Adrian twitched her nose and then arched her neck so her head was higher. "Pop wouldn't tell us. He told us she needed to take a little break from home."

I would have been going crazy if my mother left us. Adrian's worries made the story of my birth certificate seem unimportant. "Maybe she'll come back."

Adrian nodded and said, "She'll come back. She's done it before. But this time I don't forgive her."

"You never told me she ran away before."

"I never told anyone. She did it last year, and she did it again before Easter. It was too embarrassing. I didn't want anyone to know. Pop didn't want anyone to know."

"You should have told me. Maybe your mom told my mother."

"She probably told *everybody*. Probably the whole neighborhood knows and thinks it's funny." Adrian stopped talking. I couldn't think of anything to say to break the silence. It wasn't funny. We picked leaves and let them flutter down. I stripped a handful of little elm leaves from a branch that hung just above me, and threw them in her hair. She did the same to me. The leaves stuck, and we didn't shake them out.

"She didn't tell my mother. If she told my mother, Beth and I would have known." I said. "We'd have heard her telling Daddy or talking on the phone to Verna about it. Or she'd tell us, so we wouldn't say anything to you or Beverly on accident that would make you feel bad."

Adrian quickly understood. "If my mom didn't tell your mother, she didn't tell anyone else. She'd have told your mother first." She looked relieved. "She makes Pop feel terrible when she does this. And she makes me mad. She ought to love us more than that." Adrian stripped more of the little serrated leaves from a branch. When her hands were full, she threw them down. The wind caught them and made them flutter around. "Beverly doesn't even miss her. My sister only cares about dancing and going to Brownies."

After a little while, Adrian admitted, "Maybe Beverly cares."

Pretty soon Adrian said, "She has to care. Maybe she's trying to act brave." Adrian pulled a skinny branch down and let it snap back into place. "She's twisting her hair like she did when she was a baby."

Beverly had to be miserable. Adrian was miserable and upset. Mr. Claussen was miserable and sad. Louise Claussen was the cruelest woman I knew. "When do you think she'll come back?"

"I don't know. Last time she was gone three days and two nights. My Aunt Bev came by that time to tell Grammy that mom was down in the desert at the mud baths, and for her not to worry. But Pop was too worried to go to work."

"Mud baths?" I asked. The idea that a mother liked mud baths better than she liked her family was unbelievable. And, Mrs. Claussen was a tidy sort of person. She kept herself looking very nice even at home. I couldn't imagine Mrs. Claussen in a mud bath any more than I could imagine Beth in one.

Adrian knew what I was thinking. "Do you know what a mud bath is?" she asked.

"Nope. How would it go down the drain? How would you get it off of you?"

Adrian began to smile. "I don't know," she said.

We sat in the tree dangling our legs down and watching the street until Mr. Claussen came out of the house gripping his car keys. He almost stumbled coming down the front steps. It was time to pick up Beverly from dancing. We both scrambled down. The bark from the tree branches had left red marks on our thighs where our skirts had bunched up. Adrian ran to get in the Claussen's car. I went home.

We'd talked a lot, but I hadn't told Adrian about the folder or what Beth and I had found out. I just told her that on Catalina there was a bird farm. I still liked Mrs. Claussen. I didn't know how I could like a cruel person, but I did.

Louise Claussen came home. She came home so soon that no one else in the neighborhood seemed to realize she had been gone. Of course the girls' grandmother and aunt were there. It wasn't like the Claussens couldn't manage. But kids still needed a mother.

A day came when it was the right time to tell Adrian about who I really was, and I did. Delores had urged me to ask my mother about it and get the whole story. Adrian urged me not to. I trusted Adrian's advice. Beth said the same thing. Beth was usually right.

In the summer weeks that followed, Beth and Beverly went down to our store and wheedled Tootsie Rolls or soda pop from Laz like always, but Adrian and I grew too lazy to go along. We just sat on the lawn reading our library books or counting ants. Sometimes we would rummage through the contents of the piano bench in her house. We'd try sight-reading and singing the sheet music we found. That was about as ambitious as we were. Adrian's thirteenth birthday came. She was a teenager now. I would be one in five months.

The Saturday before school started, the Claussen house was almost empty. We were messing around near the piano. Adrian was trying *"Begin the Beguine."* Beth began weaving around acting sexy to the music. Beverly joined her, doing it a lot better and forcing Beth into a rumba.

Mr. Claussen put down the deck of cards in his left hand and clapped. "Too much talent in this room," he said.

He was kidding. Adrian knew she didn't play perfectly. My voice sounded okay on *Panis Angelicus,* but awful on a hit parade song. We actually were ridiculous, so we looked at her father and grimaced at his applause.

Mr. Claussen said, looking over his glasses at Adrian, "Honey, you're doing fine. No one gets Beguine first time through."

Beverly giggled as she began a Carmen Miranda imitation, singing, "DA da da DA da, DA da da Da da..." dancing with her butt more than any other part of her. Beth followed. Beth had more butt. Mr. Claussen chuckled. "Too bad Jeannie French isn't around to coach you kids. Little ol' Jeannie would have all of you signed up for screen tests. She'd polish you 'til you shone brighter than Margaret O'Brien or Natalie Wood."

Adrian froze, and I stopped fiddling with the fringe on the piano scarf. Our sisters stopped dancing to stare at Mr. Claussen. He was looking at Adrian, and he softly said, "Do you remember Jeannie, hon?"

Adrian nodded but she didn't say anything.

I watched Beth and Beverly. I could tell from their faces that they remembered Jeannie too. They looked serious and a little scared.

I said, "I thought we weren't s-s-supposed to talk about her."

Mr. Claussen put down the cards in his hand and looked at me, "I think it's okay now, Lynn. It's been a long time. She was a nice gal, and she loved all you kids."

"Did the police find out who killed her?" I asked him.

"Nope. Not yet," Mr. Claussen said. "I wish they would. I surely do wish they would." He picked up his drink and came over to the piano. He scooted Adrian over and slid on the piano bench beside her. We girls were as quiet as if we were in church. Mr. Claussen put his drink on the piano near the music rack and grinned at us. "Jeannie would want you girls to be happy."

When we were little girls, Mr. Claussen was building something in the Claussen back yard. He wouldn't tell us what it was. When it had walls up, and he was finishing the roof, we pestered him. Beverly danced all around it doing *tour jetes,* and Adrian sat down on his toolbox. She told her pop that she wouldn't move until he told us what it was going to be. Adrian was quiet and had good manners, but she was stubborn too.

"A chicken house," he said.

He wouldn't say any more. He had answered so Adrian got up and let him have his toolbox back. We all knew no one kept chickens in Breeze Terrace backyards. A week later, when he put shutters on the little house's windows, we knew it was a playhouse for the girls. Mr. Claussen was just teasing us.

Now we were much older. Adrian and I were too old for playhouses. Mr. Claussen began playing *"I Want to be Happy"* with his right hand, telling Adrian to find the bass clef chords. She did. We kids began to sing out the lyrics. It felt like Jeannie's good ghost was in the room singing with us. Everybody knew the words to that song. Then Mr. Claussen played *"You Are My Sunshine"* and *"When the Red, Red, Robin Goes Bob, Bob, Bobbing Along."* We didn't sing very long. Mr. Claussen had to go answer the phone and we grew tired of singing in the living room.

We went down the hall into the girl's room to play Monopoly. We didn't finish the game by the time Beth and I had to go home. Beth, as usual, ended up with the most money but Adrian had two hotels. Beverly and I weren't as competitive and didn't pay so much attention to board games so we didn't usually win them. We went home happy. It had been a nice afternoon.

~~~<<=>>~~~

Chapter 19: Witches in the Kitchen

I spent as much time as I could with Mama during seventh and eighth grades. If Laz wasn't home, I loitered around the house even when there was no work to keep me there hoping she would decide to tell me the truth. She didn't and I was so afraid that I'd upset her again that I never came near the subject of relatives much less birth certificates.

Things changed during that time. We began to lose more people, people from the neighborhood, just like we had lost the Hungarians.

Sometimes Mama's friends still came to visit, and there would be the old smell of cigarettes in the house. It didn't happen very often anymore. And if Laz was home, no one from Breeze Terrace came to visit our house.

First, Laz shook his fist threateningly at Mr. Lawler over the Lawler dog's mess on our lawn. Hardly a week later, my stepfather threatened to kill Dr. Hughes for leaving his trash can out in the street too long after the truck had picked up. Laz was yelling and waving his hands around. Dr. Hughes was scared. Donny saw him from his side of the street and told Beth and Dr. Hughes looked terrified and backed into his house. Laz did other rude things too and they began to add up. Still, at the store, he was charming with customers. But everyone around us knew about his temper.

We had no more parties after Alex's christening, but I didn't think it was because we had too many children. It was because the father of our family was too unpredictable. If there were parties in the neighborhood, my mother and Laz weren't invited. Mr. Morgan and Mr. Claussen still took Steve to the Culver Speedway with the other boys on the street, but they didn't honk the horn in front of our house. Steve went over to their house early to get in the car. Harold told my brother that Laz threatened Mr. Jenson with a knife when he came to our house complaining that Steve and his friends were cutting across the Jenson lawn. Mama told us Mr. Jenson misunderstood. Laz just had a knife in his hand because he'd been slicing an apple when the doorbell rang.

Mama seemed tired all the time. It wasn't the right time to bother her. Instead, I brought her stories to entertain her. I told her Tommy Delanty was expelled from St. Blaise and wouldn't graduate with us, and that Anna Marie's mother let her wear a bra and she didn't even need one. Mama brightened up when I told her Mrs. Morgan caught one of her boys with firecrackers and took them away from him. Mr. Morgan gave them back to the boys and let them light them off in the middle of the street. It was neat-o for the kids, but Adrian and I thought Mr. Morgan was disrespectful to Mrs. Morgan when he encouraged the boys to show off doing what she didn't want them to do.

"Adrian and I don't think Mr. Morgan has any sense."

Mother laughed a little. "I like it when a child's viewpoint matches my own."

I didn't feel like a child. A mysterious twelve-year-old creature named Andrea Frazier had taken over my body. It made spending time with my mother seem to be a kind of lie. I wanted so much to know the truth of who I was. I felt like a changeling, a different girl who looked and sounded like me, but wasn't.

One Saturday afternoon, Adrian and I were sitting on our front porch. We couldn't go to her house because her grandmother had company. Beverly and Beth had gone to the library. We could hear Laz raging in the house. He wasn't raging at someone this time; he was raging about someone. He was raging about President Truman being a socialist. Not that we knew exactly what a socialist was.

"Your father is kind of crazy," Adrian whispered.

"He's not my father," I whispered although no one in the house could hear us.

She blew a huge pink bubble and had to scrape it off her nose. "Aren't you glad he's not? He's never been that nice to you."

Adrian and I stood up and shook out our skirts. We walked down the driveway to the street. "Well, he gives me everything the same as he does his real children," I answered. "He's fair that way." Then I couldn't stop my voice from saying, "But he hits me too much. He's hit me practically every day of my life." Saying it out loud scared me, and I got a funny feeling in my stomach. I never told anyone what happened inside our house. I didn't even tell Delores how often I was hurt.

"I'd hate my mom and dad if they spanked me, and I don't forgive Mom for running away," she said. "I will never do that to my children. Not as long as I live. I'll never forgive her."

It was all right. Adrian was so innocent she didn't even understand that spanking and being hit were different things. We went to her yard and climbed into our nests in the Chinese elm tree. Holding our grudges and secrets in our hearts, we waited for our little sisters to come home.

Sister Mary Augustine taught the eighth grade. My grades weren't A's anymore, but when scores from the diocesan high school entrance exams were posted in the spring, my name was still high on the list. Andrew McGonigal's name was first; I was still third. I'd never gotten any smarter. Sister Mary Augustine seemed to resent that Kathleen, Anna Marie, Maria and I were among the top ten, because her favorites weren't there. Knowing the differences between the Pelagian and Nestorian heresies, polygons and polyhedrons, or prefixes and suffixes weren't as important to Sister as her favorites' clean desks and perfect handwriting. Kathleen was left-handed. Her handwriting couldn't slant right. My handwriting was fidgety, just like I was. Anna Marie kept odd things in her desk: acorns, pretty seed pods from camphor trees, magnolia pods that looked like hand grenades. Maria didn't do anything wrong that I could tell. In spite of good test scores, the four of us weren't having an easy year. Maria never raised her hand to answer questions anymore. Twice, Sister made Anna Marie cry. I was yelled at too, but I didn't care. The worst nun could never be as bad as what I was afraid of at home.

We Blazes found a place under the stumpy Washingtonia palms at the farthest end of the playground for recesses. We didn't do much there but toss dry, dusty date pits at each other, and laugh over what we'd seen on TV the night before. The good handwriting girls ogled the eighth grade boys. Our heroes were Charlie Chan's Number Three Son on channel eleven, and the wrestlers televised from Olympic Stadium: Baron Leone, Mr. Moto, Sandor Szabo and Gorgeous George, not skinny, pimply boys in our own class.

Our household disintegrated. Jessie had a stroke and moved back to Louisiana to live with her daughter. No other cleaning woman would stay more than two days. Laz would lock the store and come home to take the house by surprise. He'd fire whomever Mama hired if the woman were smoking, sitting down, using our phone, or not working fast enough. Alex, a friendly baby, liked all of the women and was confused and sad when they disappeared. Father Király didn't miraculously appear in the living room bringing us a female Erno to run the house. Laz got crazier, and I spent all my time doing housework, not homework. Beth spent all her time at the store making sure Laz was calm. If Erno wasn't there, Beth was.

Laz raged and threw things. The noise scared Alex. I did my best to keep the house in good order. But, for me, there was a good side to this. Once Laz had started fighting other people, he wasn't noticing me so much. In some ways, my life improved. But I missed my sister. We only talked on the bus and at night in our room. Steve was only eight. He didn't talk a lot but he'd found a job. He talked his way into a pass into the studio to sell papers afternoons after school. He got more tips because he was the youngest paperboy inside the gates. Adrian was busy all the time too. She practiced piano hours a day, and her church ward kept girls in activities after they turned twelve. The times when we sat in her tree, surveying the neighborhood and talking, had become rare.

On an afternoon, Mama and I were in the kitchen. She was sitting at the table making out her grocery list. The light was filtering in through the blinds, giving her a halo. It reminded me how she looked when I was very small, before I started school. I must have remembered back to a time when I was brave. I turned from scrubbing the kitchen counter's tile grout. It was a pleasant, still afternoon. For over a year, I'd wondered about who I was. "Mama," I asked tentatively. "Will you tell me about my real father?"

My mother stared at me. As she fully realized what I was asking, her eyebrows came together. Her lips pulled back. Words came rushing from them louder than I had heard her voice speak. "I won't hear what's coming out of your mouth! I won't!" She put her hands up over her ears and keened, "Ooo, ooo, ooo." Then, with eyes big and glittery, she cried, "I've been so good to you. Why do you want to hurt me so much?"

So softly I almost couldn't hear my own words, I mumbled, "I only want to know who I am."

She shrieked, "You know who you are. You are Lynn Horvath. You witchlet. You were born to torment me." She was weeping and angrier than I'd ever seen her. "You are a witch. That's who you are." My mother wiped her face with her apron. "See how you have hurt me." She turned her head toward the light from the window above the sink. Sunlight glanced across her face. "I've always known the day was coming when you would hurt me again. I banish you, witch." She waved her hand at me. "Go away, get out of my sight."

If I'd spoken, tears would hemorrhage from my eyes. I ran to my room and stayed there the rest of the day.

When Beth came home from the store, she asked, "What's wrong? Mama won't talk to anyone."

"I did something stupid."

She looked directly at me and pushed our bedroom door shut. "What did you do?"

"I asked her who my real father was."

Beth scowled. "Now we're in trouble. I told you not to tell her. I don't want to get in trouble because you talk too much. You didn't tell her I helped you, did you?"

"No. I just asked her who my father was. I didn't get a chance to say anything else. She was too mad."

"I'm *not* sorry for you. It was my idea to look for pictures, but it wasn't my idea to tell her. You know she's crazy."

"She called me a witch again. I think she really means it."

"Too bad you're not. You could mumbo-jumbo around and cast a spell that could transform us into a normal family."

~~~<<=>>~~~

Chapter 20: On Ocean Park Pier

When Mama took instruction to become a Catholic, Beth and I hoped she'd give up believing in witches. I never spoke of about my paternity again. Mama acted as though I'd never mentioned it at all. Except for being very religious and going to mass, she seemed her self again. Almost.

Beth thought our mother found religion because she was trying to blackmail God into helping us. I thought it was just a thank you to Father Király for finding Erno for us. Beth and I overheard Laz telling Erno and Auggie about Mama's baptism and laughing that the reason a man had to support religion was because it helped keep *veemen* and children in line.

Beth loved her father and we never said anything critical about him, but that day she made a very sour face and said, "There ought to be something that keeps men in line."

I agreed.

Although I hadn't fallen in love with Mr. Torrelli, St. Blaise's new P.E. teacher and part time actor, like most of the rest of the eighth grade girls, I had fallen in love. I was shocked to find myself experiencing such a catch-your-breath and unexpected phenomenon. After school and on Saturdays, Mr. Hasekura's son worked with him. They groomed our yard late Thursday afternoon every week. Okio was a senior at Venice High. He was handsome and lithe. Just seeing him reach up with the shears to trim the Belle of Portugal rose that overhung the porch made me tremble. I would have died before speaking to him or even looking directly at him. Beth saw me watching him through the curtains too many times. She began to tease me. Mama heard her.

"Okio is *not* Lynn's boyfriend. I don't want to hear you saying such a thing, Beth Horvath. He's Japanese."

"He's not my boyfriend, Mama. But I thought you liked Japanese people."

"Not as boyfriends," she answered curtly.

Beth didn't tease anymore, but I still loved Okio.

Pat O'Hara loved Tim Flores although we knew he was going to be a priest. She blushed red if he walked down past her desk to go to the chalkboard. Delores liked Hugh Montgomery. Adrian told me she liked Michael Herrick. Michael was a junior at Hamilton High. He and his brother had had been nice to me when I was five. I had to learn how to get to the bus stop, to school, and home again without getting lost. They were the only other children who went to St. Blaise School in Breeze Terrace, and they watched out for me.

On Beverly's Birthday Mrs. Claussen planned a perfect day as a special treat for Adrian, Beverly, Beth and me. She took us to the Deauville Beach Club. We swam in the big indoor pool. Afterward, we pestered to walk out on Ocean Park pier. Beth and I treated the Claussens to cotton candy. The sticky pink wisps of candy didn't blow all over our faces the way it usually did at the beach. It was a calm day. Calliope music drew us to the merry-go-round shed. Beth and Beverly nagged to ride.

"Well, girls, I give in," Mrs. Claussen said. She patted her tan slacks. "Look at me. I'm dressed for a ride." She looked at me. "Lynn, you won't mind will you?" Mrs. Claussen knew that I got sick on rides.

Carsickness wasn't as bad as having asthma or being crazy, and I didn't mind waiting. The carousel slowly began to move. Beverly got to pick the prettiest horse because it was her birthday. Mrs. Claussen picked a horse that matched the color of her slacks. The speed picked up and the horses began to blend together. Just watching them made me kind of sick, so I walked out of the shed onto the open pier. At the railing, I looked down. The ocean swirled around the posts with each wave. Seagulls were wheeling around, and every now and then one would swoop down into the water near the pilings to grab a little fish.

There was no warning, but suddenly a man was too close to me. He leaned on the rail and was almost touching my arm.

"Hi there, Honey. Come down here a lot? I never saw you before." He smelled like the abominable hair oil the eighth grade boys used. I jerked my head to look away from him, and there was a man on the other side of me too. I couldn't look that way either. I could only keep looking down into the water. They seemed to loom over me. My heartbeats began to thump and race each other until I couldn't breathe. There were other men behind me. They didn't bump into me, or touch me, but I was so scared my stomach felt like it was turning to liquid.

"Go to Venice?" the shape on my left asked.

I didn't answer. They were high school boys but too big.

"Santa Monica?" he asked.

I heard him strike a match and could smell cigarette smoke.

"We go to Uni," he said. "But I don't know you. I'd remember you for sure, if I'd seen you at school."

The boy on my left snorted, and the boy on my right moved in closer to me. "You go to Saint Monica's, Honey?" he asked, leaned down even closer. I couldn't get away from them.

I wanted to say something to make them go away. Nothing came out of my mouth. I couldn't stand them being close to me. I felt sick and scared. I thought I'd throw up. They were only high school boys, not men. I realized that now. But they crowded me and smelled like men. I was trapped.

"Ignore my buddy." The boy on my left said. "Come with me. Just me. Not them. Buy you a soda?"

He nudged my arm with his elbow. I couldn't stand that he'd touched me. My arm was burning where he touched me. There was a roar in my head louder than their voices, louder than the seagulls. I spun around, shoved my fists into their bellies and hit at them. Pushing my way through, I ran. I could hear them laughing and calling me. "Come back, pretty baby. We won't hurt ya'. Come back."

When I was in the merry-go-round shed, I could breathe again. The music stopped. Adrian came toward me, walking wobbly from circling around too many times. "I saw boys talking to you!" she said.

The girls and Mrs. Claussen glanced in the boys' direction. Mrs. Claussen had a funny little smirky smile. "Lynnie, boys are after you already. You're growing up," she said.

I glared at all of them. I didn't want boys after me. Adrian was more grown up than me. I was just taller.

"Lynn's got boyfriends," Beverly sang over and over. Beth hit her and made her stop.

Mrs. Claussen kept talking. "They're lettermen, Lynnie. Look at their jackets! Bet they're basketball players. What good looking boys!"

I knew where Tierra del Fuego was and what *pi* was, but I didn't have a clue as to what a letterman might be. I wasn't going to ask her. Delores would know.

Adrian noticed how uncomfortable I was, and said, "Let's get Sno-cones before we go home. C'mon."

That evening Beth and I told Steve about lunch at the Deauville Club and the indoor pool. He wasn't jealous. He'd been working at the store all day in Beth's place, and his pockets were full of the money he'd earned.

~~~<<=>>~~~

Chapter 21: Remembering Jeannie

That night, I was ready to go to sleep. My sister wasn't. She was flipping the pages of a magazine she'd swiped from the living room. I lay quietly, waiting for her to turn her light off. I had been crazy, out-of-my-mind afraid of the boys. Thinking about them standing so close to me, made me frightened all over again.

"Are you awake?" Beth asked softly enough that she wouldn't have awakened me if I were sleeping.

"Yes," I murmured. "How can I sleep when you have your light on?"

"I think about Jeannie sometimes," she whispered. "I wish that man hadn't killed her," she said.

I was snuggled in my blankets and didn't answer. I wondered if she'd sensed how desperately frightened I'd been at the railing of the pier, and it reminded her of Jeannie and the murder no one talked about.

"Daddy thinks Frank killed her," my sister said. "I heard him talking to Erno and Doc Petersen." In a low, sexy whisper, she imitated her father's voice. "Corrz husbandt do eedt. Who elz?" She was quiet for a minute as though she were waiting for me to say something, but I didn't. "When I'm at the store I hear people. Doc Petersen doesn't think Frank did it, I could tell. He said Frank had a very solid alibi."

I kept my eyes closed, but I heard Beth toss the magazine to the floor. She said, "I don't think Frank killed her either. But I don't think a stranger killed her. I think Mr. Morgan did."

I couldn't believe Beth said that. I wasn't sleepy anymore.

I'd never think of Mr. Morgan as a murderer as long as I lived. "That's ridiculous. Why would you think that?"

"It's not ridiculous," she answered. "Mr. Morgan tried to rape the boys' babysitter this past week. If Mr. Morgan would rape somebody, he'd kill somebody."

"Mr. Morgan?" I couldn't believe what she'd said. I sat up in bed staring at her. "How can you think Mr. Morgan tried to rape someone? You're ridiculous."

"No, I'm not."

"Yes, you are. It's just something stupid thing you and Beverly made up."

"It isn't. We didn't make it up. I haven't even told Beverly. I haven't told anyone but you. Yesterday practically all the customers were talking about Mr. Morgan."

"When did he do it?" I asked my sister. "Who was the babysitter?"

"Thursday night. The Morgans went out somewhere. Their babysitter was that high school girl with the long fingernails who rides our bus. Mr. Morgan tried to rape her when he took her home, but he was too drunk and she got away."

I knew the girl she meant. Besides two inch long red nails, her hair was peroxide yellow. She put her books on a seat even when the bus was crowded and people needed to sit down.

"Mr. Taylor came in for his beer, and Daddy sent me into the back room, but I listened. He told Daddy the whole story. Mr. Morgan was arrested."

"How could you not tell me?" I had trouble keeping my voice low so our parents wouldn't hear. "All day today you never said one thing about it!"

"I was going to tell you, but I was waiting for you to tell me."

"Nobody told me anything. I couldn't tell you what nobody told me."

Beth was wrong about Mr. Morgan killing Jeannie. Real murderers were smart or they got caught right away.

Jeannie's murder was still unsolved. The Black Dahlia's too. Mr. Morgan wasn't smart enough to kill anyone and get away with it for a minute. He wasn't mean enough either. He couldn't even get mean enough to make his sons behave.

Beth reached and turned off her light. "Do you exactly know what rape is?" she asked.

"No, it's bad and men do it to women. That's all I know. It goes with pillage."

"I want to know what it is. I looked in the classroom dictionary, but it wasn't there."

It was connected with brutal stuff, sex stuff, but it was like assault and battery. I didn't know exactly what they were either.

"If I find out, I'll tell you," I promised.

I asked Adrian later if she had heard anything about Mr. Morgan. Adrian said that her mother, Charlene and her grandmother laughed about it. Adrian's mother said Mr. Morgan didn't have a mean streak anywhere and wasn't a skirt chaser. Adrian's aunt said he had enough on his hands. Adrian didn't know what rape actually was either, but whatever it was, she didn't think Mr. Morgan would do it. He didn't. Later that week, it turned out that the girl had a history of making false reports. The police knew all about her. She had a psychiatric history. She never rode our bus again, but she didn't live in Breeze Terrace so we never knew what happened to her.

The next time I was with Mama in the kitchen, I asked her if she had heard about Mr. Morgan and the babysitter.

"Of course. That girl was notorious. I don't know what Vivian was thinking to hire her. And if you or your sister ever lie about anyone, and I find out, I'll take a belt to you, no matter how old you are."

I was insulted. Beth and I weren't like that. She should have known.

~~~<<=>>~~~

Chapter 22: Puberty Rites

My period started the summer after eighth grade graduation. My friends had gotten theirs, but I was the youngest of the Blazes so I didn't think there was anything wrong. Mama showed me how to manage and gave me a blue box of Kotex to keep in the cedar chest in my room. She warned me that she wasn't going to have a daughter who cried or moaned about what every other woman in the world had to put up with. Then, she told me I was never to let a man or a boy touch me *down there*. I thought that was a dumb thing for her to mention, because I'd never act like a slut. I was insulted my own mother didn't know that.

A week later, Blaise's Blazes went to the Fox Theater in Westwood to see Paul Britton acting in *The Egg and I*. We were proud that a kid we knew was in a first run movie. When I was getting ready, I joked that the movie's title was appropriate for me, biologically speaking. Mama and Beth didn't laugh. Mama didn't think periods should be mentioned, even obliquely. Beth didn't like being reminded I was older and more advanced in life than she was.

We Blazes were going to an evening showing and Mrs. McCauley and Mrs. O'Hara needed to borrow station wagons to carry all of us. The mothers wouldn't sit with us. They said we were too noisy. It was a celebration of my period starting, even if no one knew about it but me. I wished Shirley from camp or Jeannie French were here. They would understand.

Before intermission, Delores and I went out to get popcorn for everyone. If we waited for intermission it would be crowded and we'd have to line up. In the lobby, I told Delores that my period had finally begun. She asked if I had cramps. I told her I did, but my mother said I shouldn't whine about it.

She smirked, as though Mrs. McCauley told her the same thing. Then I told her the silly thing my mother said, about men and boys touching me. I sneered, "What's that have do with men and boys anyway?"

Instead of laughing, she shrieked, "You mean you don't know?" Her voice was so loud I pulled her over in a corner by the candy counter so no one would hear her.

"Know what?"

"Sex. The connection between men and periods, dummy!"

I leaned against the wall as Delores gleefully, graphically explained the facts of life to me, and she said that rape was the same as doing sex when you *didn't* want a guy to do it. She said that I could get pregnant if I *did* want him to. Sex was a mortal sin. It was men putting their penises into women.

I wouldn't believe her. "You made this up! You're teasing me. That's sickening."

"I swear," she said. "Cross my heart and hope to die. I truly swear."

When we got back to our seats and handed out the red and white popcorn boxes, she knew I still didn't believe her. As intermission began and people filed out and the seats emptied around us, Delores made the two Pats, Maria, Anna Marie and all the other girls all stand in a cluster by our seats and swear, by the miraculous medals we wore around our necks, that what she'd told me was the truth. Then, Delores whispered to them that I'd gotten my period at last, and now everyone in Blaise's Blazes was a woman. We sat down because the movie was starting again. None of us felt the least bit like women. Women were people like our mothers, not like us. We didn't want to be like our mothers. We wanted to be like Elizabeth Taylor, June Allyson or Janet Leigh.

Pat Lacey whispered to Maria to pass it down the line to tell me our mothers had to have done sex or we wouldn't have been born. It was a terrible thought, worse than terrible. Delores, Monica, and Kathleen got the giggles and we caught them too. Soon, we were shaking in our seats. We made so much noise and rumpus people in front of us had to tell us three times to be quiet or they'd call the usherette.

The giggles made Anna Marie pee her pants. Pat O'Hara and Carol Donnelly had to take her to the ladies room before she leaked through her clothes. The girls got her a pad from the sanitary machine. The pads would work as well for pee as they did for periods. When Pat and Carol told us what they'd

done, it made us laugh more.

Anna Marie swore we were embarrassing her, but she was laughing too. We threw jujubes back and forth until the people in front of us moved to the other side of the theater. But they didn't call the usherette on us.

We were laughing so much we almost missed seeing Paul Britton's big moment on the screen when he was running around with Ma and Pa Kettle's other kids and got to say his line.

I kept my promise to Beth. That night, when we were alone in our room, I gave my little sister every graphic detail I had learned at the Fox Theater about rape, sex, and the facts of life.

"That is very disgusting," Beth said.

"Yes," I answered.

~~~<<=>>~~~

Chapter 23: Queen of Heaven High School

Students at St. Blaise had been dropping out to go to public school since we were in Sister Mary Immaculata's fifth grade. Each year the sisters cranked the standards a little tighter. By eighth grade our class had shrunk to only 30 students. None of us was below the fiftieth percentile on state tests. All of us were eligible for entry to a Catholic high school, and all of the Blazes were going to the same one.

The boys were going to Hamilton or Venice, public high schools. A few boys were going to St. Philip Neri or Santa Vibiana Catholic high schools, and Andrew McGonigal, Tim Flores and Matthew Ferguson were going to the junior seminary. Sister Mary Augustine was proud of them. Queen of Heaven High School in Los Angeles was the school Sister recommended. She didn't recommend St. Monica's because it was co-ed. Blaise's Blazes unanimously chose Queen of Heaven High School vowing we would stay together forever.

Queen of Heaven had excellent, up-to-date facilities, and charged only a modest tuition. Kathleen, Anna Marie, Maria, and I had been invited to apply to Marymount or Immaculate Heart, schools our scores qualified us to attend, but we wanted to stay with our friends and ditched the application forms in the trash can near the stairway before going home.

The Red Car tracks had been pulled up from the Venice Boulevard median. Metro buses replaced the streetcars that had taken Blaise's Blazes on many adventure. The busses belched exhaust adding to the smoky grayness of the city. The city's air was only healthy at our far western edge where daily ocean winds pushed the smog back. When September arrived, we disappeared into the dinge of Los Angeles each school day morning via the Metro Bus Line.

Once we learned the bus schedule, we could plan timing to catch the same bus. We shared homework and gossip, and gave each other hilarious critiques of the television shows we'd watched the evening before with our families. Timing wasn't for the Blazes who had to transfer from other buses in their neighborhoods and depend on their connections. Rarely was Delores on the same bus I was on, and Queen of Heaven's rigid tracking system separated us during the day. I tested into college prep; Delores tested into a commercial track.

Anna Marie Urrutia, Kathleen O'Donnell, Carol Pistoresi, Laura Baronovich, Maria Gutierrez, Carol Kennedy were the only Blazes who went into the small college prep block with me. Sister Augustine would have been embarrassed if this fact had been posted anywhere. St. Blaise girls all comfortably scored above the 50th percentile, but only a few of us were above the 85th. Delores McCauley, Carol Donnelly, Pat O'Hara, and five other girls didn't. I especially hated being separated from Delores.

It seemed very odd to be broken up after most of us had been together every school day for eight years. I was upset and wished I'd deliberately answered most of the questions on the entry tests wrong. One thing good did happen soon. Pat O'Hara spent three weeks in one of the commercial blocks learning to type and file before Queen of Heaven's office noticed that, although her verbal scores weren't within the college bound placement band, she had extremely high math scores. She was moved up to college prep and we were happy to welcome her. Now there were seven of us. The tracking system eroded old friendships. The school was so big the best many of us could do was wave to each other now and then. The Blazes were broken up. We were eating lunch with girls who were in the same extracurricular clubs and had the same classes, not with all our old friends from Blaise's Blazes.

The first year passed quickly. Queen of Heaven's American-born nuns weren't nearly as strict as our Irish nuns at St. Blaise, but strict enough. The school was exotic to us. We were exposed to girls from parishes all over the city. They came different kinds of backgrounds. At Queen of Heaven, I discovered what a good life I'd lived. I carefully never got near even nice men, not even to men who were kind, but I'd watched my friends' fathers like Mr. McCauley, Mr. Claussen and Mr. O'Hara and I'd generalized from too small a sample. As fathers went, if there had been a bell curve of fathers that put my friends' fathers at one end, Laz wasn't nearly bad enough to be at the other end.

I realized how ordinary and undamaged I was. I'd only been bruised; my bones hadn't been broken. In Queen of Heaven, there were over a thousand girls. Many had endured, and were still enduring, far worse treatment than I'd ever experienced. One day in the cafeteria line, a sophomore in front of me had a black eye. I listened to her conversation with her friends as we slid our trays along, picking out our lunch items. When one friend asked her about it, she just shrugged and said, "My dad. But don't say anything. I told Sister Mary Jerome I was in a car accident. This isn't bad. He broke my mom's arm and my brother had to take her to emergency."

She was so casual about it. There were girls in our school who were bishop's placements or had their tuition paid by their parishes. Some were daughters of alcoholics. Some had run from home and now lived with relatives, or foster parents.

As my awareness grew, in some inverse parallel way, so did my doubts. When I was a child I didn't believe that there could be angels when there weren't ghosts, or that people were made in the image of God, but dogs and cats weren't. Dogs and cats ate, excreted, breathed and made decisions just like we did. We weren't very different. My questions in the confessional ended with the same response. "Pray for the gift of faith, my dear," was what Father said, no matter which priest was on the other side of the grill that Saturday. I tried. I'd been praying all my life. But nothing had happened. All my friends were devout people who believed in the supernatural. I would have been shunned if my friends thought I was some kind of atheist, so I pretended belief. I justified the pretense by telling myself that I wanted to believe, my mind just wouldn't. It wasn't quite a lie. And, I faithfully went to mass and Sodality meetings, participated in good works and said the rosary. I got A's in religion class because I understood the theory. I prayed for the gift of faith. I sang songs about Jesus in Music class, wrote poems about Jesus in English class and essays on the faith in Religion class, drew pictures of the Holy Family in Art class, and before every extracurricular activity said prayers as respectful as anyone else's. But as time went on, I knew that belief, *faith*, easy and comforting for my mother and all my friends, was something impossible for me. If there was a God, he hadn't chosen to give me that particular gift.

~~~<<=>>~~~

Chapter 24: Proven Imperfect

High school was high school even if you went to a parochial girls' school. By spring of our freshman year, nearly half of my friends had dates. We were asked out for weeknight sock hops or Saturday night movie date with a chocolate sundae at the drive-in afterwards. Every high school boy, college man, soldier, sailor or air force guy in 1951 was determined to claim his own girl. Even we modestly dressed and soft voiced parochial school girls found we were in demand.

Without any desire, and in spite of discouraging my friends with older brothers who were eager to arrange dates for me, I found myself going steady by the end of my freshman year. My boyfriend was a neighborhood boy. I'd known him since I was four, so I didn't have to be afraid of him or think of gross things like penises, rapes or murders. He was just a boy. Michael and his brother had been nice to me when I was in first grade and they were in grades a little higher. Ronnie and Michael were the only other Catholic kids on our street. Michael was a senior at St. Philip Neri High. Ronnie was in Korea now.

Dating began one cold afternoon I was walking up the hill from the Venice bus after school. Michael drove by and offered me a ride. I didn't mind the climb to Breeze Terrace, but this particular day was rainy and I was weighed down with books.

"Lynn, I want to ask you something," he said, as he slowed before driving through the intersection midway up the first long grade of climb.

I wondered if Laz might have done some horrid thing that upset the Herricks.

Michael varoomed us through the intersection, then he stopped at the curb of the next block. He looked over at me and blurted out, "Will you come to the Winter Ball at Neri with me?"

I was shocked by his question, but not so shocked I didn't know the right response. I never stammered when I talked to kids, and I didn't stammer now. "Michael, have you thought about asking Adrian?"

"Adrian Claussen?" he asked, his voice rising in an odd way.

"Yes, You could ask Adrian. She's a good dancer."

"But, Adrian isn't a Catholic!" he shrilled at me.

"You wouldn't invite a non-Catholic?"

"Never! My parents would croak. Anyway, I'd never want to." He started the car again.

That didn't seem fair. After all, Adrian was as nice as any Catholic girl I ever knew.

He didn't say anything more until we reached my driveway. "So? How about it? You didn't give me an answer."

I started to open the car door and didn't respond.

"Lynn, I have to buy my bid by Friday. I haven't been to one dance in four years of high school. I'll be graduating in June. I really want you to come as my date. Please. I'm begging you."

He sounded pathetic, and I remembered how nice he and his brother had been when I was five. "Okay," I said. After what he'd said, I didn't think Adrian would mind. Maybe she only wanted to date Mormons, now that she was old enough. My mother wouldn't mind. I'd be fourteen before the dance. But it bothered me that Michael would reject a beautiful and well-mannered girl like Adrian, while he'd found a girl coming from a house with a crazy father perfectly acceptable – just because she went to his church.

Mama was far more excited than I was. She found a pink formal at Bullock's for me. It wasn't the one I liked best, but my mother reminded me who was the one paying for the dress, saying, "she who pays the piper calls the tune."

I felt pretty but a little frightened. Michael had never danced before with a girl, and he was probably a little frightened too. We did okay. We watched what everyone else was doing. It wasn't hard. I saw Anna Marie there and met her date. That was fun, and we dated on into my sophomore year.

Catholic schools had to follow state curriculum guidelines. We'd taken first aid our first year and gotten it out of the way. Now it was Driver's Ed. Most of us had little desire to drive a car. Some of our mothers didn't know how to drive. But we took the class. Anna Marie, Laura, Maria, and I, with three of the new friends we'd made, Elena Thibodeaux, Shirley Dubois, and Mercy Jamison, were all in the same Driver's Ed class. Our new friends came from elementary schools in different parts of the city but were on our academic track. We practiced steering and braking in a cardboard car that had a real steering wheel but a movie screen was where the windshield should have been.

One of the tests we took resulted in my mother getting a call from school. The problem, the school office explained, was that I couldn't see. Mother disagreed and argued that there was nothing wrong with my eyes. She said that Queen of Heaven was challenging her competence at motherhood and was very mistaken. My vision was perfect. Since I was her child, she would have noticed if it weren't. Mama didn't raise her voice to the nun who called. But when she hung up the phone, she did raise it to me and accused me of having said that I couldn't see just to embarrass her. I didn't try to explain. There was no point when she was in that mood.

But by the third phone call, Sister Mary Antonia, the lower division dean, explained to Mama that the issue must be seen to promptly or her daughter wouldn't get credit for driver education, The Horvath family would be considered uncooperative, and Lynn Horvath's place in the school would be given to someone else. A certified optometrist or ophthalmologist had to call school confirming the examination, and his office must send a written findings report to Queen of Heaven by mail. This edict resulted in two trips to Beverly Hills. The first trip was to an examination with Dr. Roth, the optometrist on Canon Way who had fitted my mother with reading glasses.

A second trip came three weeks later when we picked up my new glasses at his office. Both times, after visiting Dr. Roth, Mama and I would stop for lunch afterward. Lunch out made me feel as though I were one of her grown up friends.

After the optometric examination on my first visit, Dr. Roth had gently told my mother that I was seriously myopic and explained that I badly needed glasses. Mama was very disturbed, but she smiled up at Dr. Roth coyly and insisted that he was mistaken. He leaned toward her, acted all flirty, and slowly explained his findings again.

He didn't change his diagnosis, but he did give her a discount on the bill. It was small consolation for his verdict that her child was indeed imperfect.

So, Mother needed the solace of a *good* restaurant. She drove the two of us to Piggy's on Sunset for lunch. "You aren't cross-eyed! I'd certainly have noticed. I don't want you wearing glasses," she complained after the pink-skirted waitress took the order on her pink tablet. Everything was pink, grey and black at Piggy's.

"You wear glasses," I said, carefully and softly, so she wouldn't notice I was arguing with her.

"Only for reading. I'm certainly not myopic. I don't wear glasses because I can't see." She placed heavy emphasis on the word see. "You can see just fine. What's the matter with that school? They shouldn't have put me through all this."

Dr. Roth hadn't said I was cross-eyed. He said that one of my eyes had a five-degree cast. I knew I didn't look very cross-eyed. If I had, the boys on the playground would have let me know by second grade. When Michael took me to the show on Saturday, I told him I was getting glasses. He asked if I'd have to wear them when we went out. It annoyed me that he acted as if it would embarrass him. Mama was bad enough.

After the exam, it was just the two of us, Mama and I, here amid a lot of strangers at other tables at the Piggly Wiggly. While we waited for our meal, I had an idea. This was a safe place. Mama wouldn't let herself look angry in a Beverly Hills restaurant. I gambled that even as imperfect as I was, nervous, stammering, shy, backward and in need of discipline, my mother would never call me a witch or shriek at me in a place as crowded or as popular as Piggy's.

I tried to keep my voice from quavering as I asked, "Mama, will you please tell me who my real father was? Maybe I inherited poor vision from him."

Mother looked at me, and around at the other patrons. Then she sighed. But she didn't shriek or even scold. My gamble paid off. Mama gave me a sideways appraisal, and she said, "Yes. Maybe you did. He seemed to see everything, but he did have a squint. You do the same thing. It's a long story, but you're old enough now."

I took a deep breath. She would talk to me at last. I wasn't prepared for the sadness of what she would tell me.

~~~<<=>>~~~

Chapter 25: A Long Story

Mama took a sip of her water. "Your father was Andrew Frazier. Everyone called him Drew. He was an engineer at Douglas Aircraft when I met him, but he'd worked for North American   also.

He called himself "a mechanic who made good," because he didn't have a college degree. Henry Ford didn't have one either. Your father designed housings for engines and improvements for the engines themselves. He'd been drawing plans for a fuselage for a new Douglas plane when he got sick.

I loved him very much. I mean, I love Daddy, but not the way I loved your father." She looked at me and drew a deep breath. "Drew was older. He was so handsome and established. He had a nice home on Bagley Avenue. His wife had been dead for three years and he was lonely." She sounded pensive and wistful. "Your father looked just like Gregory Peck," Mother continued. "You have his features and that pale Scotch-Irish skin. But his hair was coal black and his eyes darker than yours. Your hair started out black but faded."

I knew my father didn't look like Gregory Peck. Mother tended to exaggerate. She thought Laz looked like Laurence Olivier. *That Hamilton Woman* had been on TV the night before. A resemblance was there, but only if you knew to look for it. However, I did have angled eyebrows and squinty eyes, different from her big round ones. My father might have looked somewhat like Gregory Peck, in Mama's eyes at least.

"How did he die?" came out of my mouth.

Mother put her fork down and pushed her plate away. "It was the greatest tragedy of my life. We had only been married for two months when I found I was pregnant.

"Your father was astonished. His first wife wanted children but she never became pregnant. Doctors said nothing was wrong with her, so your father assumed it was his fault. He told me he didn't think he could give me children. Well, I didn't want them, so I didn't mind." She looked up at me, and realized what she had said.

"Oh, baby, don't think I don't love you. I love all of you. But you have to understand. I'd never been around children. I'd never thought about them." She looked away from me and around the room. "Drew was so delighted. And, I thought since his first wife hadn't given him a child, it was something I could do. He'd love me more than his first wife.

"Our life was so happy. He rented a plane, and we flew to Mexico for a celebration. I bought some loose dresses to wear. But then, in hardly any time at all, he didn't feel well. He was tired, and began to look ill. Doctors didn't know what was wrong. While you grew bigger inside me, he grew thinner and thinner. By Thanksgiving, people wouldn't have recognized him. I was ravenous with pregnancy, and he'd nearly stopped eating entirely. I'd go to Daddy's store and buy sweet wine for him to sip, hoping it would stop the pain spasms."

Mama stared at me and frown lines deepened in her forehead. "Lynn, you weren't even born yet, but the more you grew, the more it seemed as though you were sucking away his life and taking it into yours. I knew that wasn't true, but I couldn't help thinking it."

This was why my mother thought I was a witch. Everything seemed very clear. I felt hollowed out. It wasn't what I expected.

The pink-skirted waitress was back with our order. As she served us, Mama looked at me with the saddest look. "I prayed," she said. "Andrew gave up on doctors. I was so desperate I asked the Christian Scientists to come and read. Your father had no use for that kind of thing, but by then he was too sick to send them away."

Mama reached out for her ice water. "He was desperately sick, but he got me to the hospital and stayed alive long enough to see you. The nurses brought him in to my room. He touched your little hands. Your baby hair was black. You didn't look a bit like me. You looked just like him. It was the only time he saw or touched you, and when he said goodbye that night, it was the last time he ever spoke to me."

It seemed like an hour had passed. Noisy customers were clinking their silverware and conversing around us. Someone laughed a deep, rough laugh at someone else's joke.

"Your father didn't visit the next day. There were no phones in patient's rooms in the thirties. New mothers weren't allowed out of bed for ten days. I begged one of the nurses to call him for me. She did many times, but there was no answer. By the next day, I was frantic and nearly hysterical. I gave her the phone number of one of your father's friends, and begged her to call him.

"Bill Marat found your father in the living room of our house, in a coma. Bill carried him to the car and drove him straight to Veteran's Hospital. Your father was over six feet tall, and Bill told me later that Drew weighed no more than a child.

If I had been older and more sensitive, I'd have stopped questioning her. But I wasn't. "What was it that killed him?" I asked.

"They did an exploratory at the hospital. He had cancer of the pancreas. Nothing could have helped him. He's buried at in the military cemetery at Sawtelle."

I'd been past the military cemetery a thousand times, smears of white markers alternating with shimmery green lawn. I knew the smudged colors I'd seen were rows and rows, hundreds of rows, of white posts on a green lawn. We went by that vast, quiet park with its wide, shady trees and lines and lines of soldiers' graves whenever we went to the beach.

Mama pointed at the food in front of me. "Eat your lunch. We can't stay here all day." She pulled her plate back toward her and we quietly finished lunch. I could barely pick at my food. The bright pink, white and charcoal colors and the cartoon motif of the room seemed to jar and clash too acutely with the story I'd been told. It should have been told in a dark, somber room.

Mama sat up straight and called the waitress. Then, she looked at me and had her usual cheery smile back, just as if we'd been talking about dresses in a store window or where Laz might take us on Sunday for a family outing.

"I can't get you back to school for the afternoon. We've wasted too much time talking."

I wasn't surprised. She never thought school was all that important. Mama ordered Pink Piglet sundaes for us. She smiled the same smile she used on Dr. Roth as she asked for extra whipped cream. When our sundaes were put on the pink table, they were heaped perilously high with mounds of snowy cream. The story of my beginning was depressing, but I couldn't cry. I'd learned early on that it only gave people a sore throat and blotchy face and it didn't help. Mama had just told me the whole most terrible part of her life, and she wasn't crying.

For the next three weeks I waited impatiently for my glasses to be ready, but I didn't particularly want to have lunch at Piggy's again. Then call came that the new glasses were ready, and I skipped school again to go back again to Beverly Hills with my mother. Dr. Roth's nurse offered to show Mama a new inventory of fashion frames that mother might like to think about for her own next appointment. After the nurse led my mother down the hall, Dr. Roth explained my eye defects very carefully to me. He said that the glasses would correct my vision well, but I might always have a little trouble judging distance.

"I've always been clumsy," I said, letting him know I didn't expect miracles.

"Clumsiness is often the result of visual deficiencies. But I think you'll like the clean windows to the world this prescription gives you."

My English teacher would have called that a cliché, but just minutes later I saw a whole new world through the clean windows optometry had given me.

Beverly Hills was the first place I ever saw as other people could see. It was brilliant with color. I'd been there to get my hair done, and to go along when my sister and brothers went to the doctor, but I'd never noticed the grace of the tall palms, or seen that the sidewalk trees, flowering tropical trees with trunks like elephant legs, had individual, bright green, heart shaped leaves. I couldn't stop looking. Signs weren't smears. They held writing that I could read.

Mama decided we'd go to Farmer's Market for lunch this time. Although she wasn't happy at the blue plastic frames sitting on my nose, she seemed to like having an excuse to leave Alex in nursery school and go out to lunch - even if it was with me. She and Laz went out seldom these days.

First she had to get the car out of Beverly Hills. It was nearly eleven and there was traffic on Canon Drive so Mama crossed over to Rodeo Drive. That was a mistake. It was backed up. We were stalled in a line of cars. Mama sighed and leaned her elbows on the steering wheel. On our side of the street, out my window, one of the shops was a pet store.

A big rococo cage stood on the sidewalk in front of the store. Wearing a little red hat, a monkey was darting around inside the cage. A little ways away from the cage, a toucan perched on a red stand was bobbing his great bill. A woman, passing by wearing a black and white polka dot dress and a black hat ringed with yellow daisies, stopped to coax the monkey to give her a kiss through the bars of his cage. I felt like I'd come through a gloomy, darkly enchanted tunnel into an explosion of color. I didn't mind sitting in the traffic for a little while.

~~~<<=>>~~~

Chapter 26: The Unwritten Law

Farmer's Market was the best possible place to be on the day one could really *see* for the first time. I was so excited I chattered like the monkey we had just seen. I darted about while my mother strolled around the produce stands. Then found a place to sit and get something to eat. I had other things I wanted to ask Mother now that she would finally talk to me. But she said she didn't want to talk about my father. I could avoid that subject. After our sandwiches, Mother sent me to purchase éclairs and tea for us. When we were settled, I began to question her about another mystery that bothered me for a long time.

"Mama, why didn't you let us talk about Jeannie?"

"Jeannie?" My mother looked at me with a surprised expression as though she didn't know whom I meant.

I nodded. "Jeannie French. Jeannie. Your friend."

She looked away, and I didn't think she was going to ignore me or be annoyed with me, or both.

But she turned back to me. "Lynn, that was five years ago. Too long ago for me to want to think about."

"Please. Why didn't you want us to talk about her murder?"

She waited before answering. "Well, we parents didn't want you children to frighten yourselves. It was bad enough that we knew about all that awful business without having you children pestering us."

"But why did you scare us about the police? You made us run if we saw a police car."

"Oh, Lynn. Why must you annoy me with all this today?"

"Because I still think about it."

Mother put both hands on the little round table and looked at her nails. "Look at my manicure. My nails are already chipped. I don't think this new brand of polish is as good as my old one. I'm going to tell Margo I want to go back to Revlon."

I looked at her hands. The miniscule chips in the polish on her nails weren't relevant to what I wanted to know.

"Mother," I pleaded. "You took the radio out of our room. It bothered Beth and me. We didn't know what was going on."

"Well, there was nothing you needed to hear that week. And, we weren't concerned with you children at all; we were trying to protect Frank. You children clustered around Jeannie, and we were afraid you'd seen them having some little argument. The police were trying to blame him." She stared at me very earnestly. "Nobody wanted him arrested. We couldn't let any innocent thing you children might pop out with help convict that poor man."

"I never saw them argue. They were always nice to each other. But I can understand that you all were trying to protect someone you knew was innocent."

A busboy was winding toward us through the tables. Mother let him know with a sharp look that we weren't through, and then she turned to me with an amused smile. "Oh, Lynn, you are so young. Daddy and I never thought he was innocent," Mama said in her cheerful, light voice. "All of Breeze Terrace was positive *was* Frank killed her. Until the details came out, we thought he might have killed her. Later, we knew he hadn't. He never would have killed her the way it was done. It was horrible."

Mother noted the look of on my face and clarified her statement. "We were wrong, baby. We should have realized Frank's innocence. But, that first day or two, we didn't know what was true and what was in the paper but not true. All of us, the Morgans, Porters, Claussens, Bryants honestly thought Jeannie had driven him to it."

I was devastated. "But you liked her, Mother. She was your friend," I said. "How could you think she'd have driven

Frank to kill her? She was so nice to everyone. She was nice to him. If you thought he killed her, why would you have tried to save him? That doesn't make sense."

"I depend on you so much, I forget how young you are.

Everything is too black and white for you, Lynn. That isn't the way life is. Jeannie was my friend, but she wasn't perfect." She shrugged and looked at me sympathetically. "Jeannie was the way she was. She flirted. She liked to provoke Frank a bit. Lots of women tease their men to keep them interested."

I was only fifteen that year and didn't understand adults. She was right, though. The neighborhood women used to flirt with Laz right in front of their own husbands.

"The papers said she was a drunk."

"You children didn't see the papers. We were very careful to protect you." Mama declared. "But the news reports were all wrong. She didn't drink any more than Louise or Ann or any of our friends did. "Not nearly as much as Vivian or Helen, and nothing like Betty Harris. I don't know why the paper said nasty things like that about her.

"Beth says Mrs. Harris drives over and buys a fifth at the store every afternoon."

"That's my point, baby. Jeannie didn't look like Betty does. Jeannie's skin was clear and her eyes weren't glassy looking. You remember how pretty she was. But, Lynnie, she liked to have fun." She drew her eyebrows tightly together. "The police always try to blame the poor husband."

"If you all thought he was guilty at first, why were you trying to protect him?"

"Lynn, if Frank killed Jeannie, it would have been a *crime of passion*. It wouldn't have been a true murder, a premeditated murder. That's the old unwritten law."

"What old unwritten law?" I demanded.

"Oh, down through the ages, people have known that murder is justified if a wife is unfaithful," my mother said. "A husband had to know his wife was true to him. How else could he know their children were his?" This seemed reasonable to her, and Mama assumed it was reasonable to me. She took the last bite of her éclair and wiped her mouth.

"You mean you think a man should be allowed to kill his wife? That's preposterous!"

"Don't get so upset. You're old enough now to understand the world. Men can't help their anger. Daddy is insanely jealous because he loves me so much. And you've never once seen me provoke him. I'm too sensible to do that kind of thing. I liked Jeannie, and she was a great friend to everyone in the neighborhood, but she wasn't always sensible. She wasn't promiscuous, but she flirted."

"So you lied to the police? You all lied?"

"We didn't exactly lie. We agreed that no one would say anything. The Morgans and Taylors, Doc Peterson, everyone agreed. Helen Porter got us together. She knew Frank and Jeannie the longest. Louise was the one who was afraid that one of you children might blurt something out."

"You still shouldn't have scared us so much."

She looked up at me, annoyed at my criticism, and stood up. "Better hurry. I won't bother taking you back to school, but Tiny Tots will charge extra if we don't pick Alex up before one."

It was past noon by the time we got to the parking lot. Some businessmen coming through the Market's gate glanced at us. Mother dimpled up as though apologizing that we'd blocked a bit of the path. One of the men winked at her. She smiled at him. After they passed, she frowned at me and said, "Take off those glasses. They don't make you look a bit pretty. You've always gone out of your way to look plain."

I obeyed my mother and took the new glasses off. I'd told myself that I'd wear them everywhere Michael took me whether he liked it or not. I didn't have to be respectful with Michael. He was neither my parent nor teacher.

When Laz came home that evening and saw my new glasses he gave me a look that made Steve and Beth laugh and called me "*Ourr Meez Brrooks.*" His favorite TV show that year was about an old maid schoolteacher who wore glasses. Maybe, at last, he found a good category for me. It made me like my glasses even better. Mother gave him a sharp a look. Schoolteacher wasn't a category she admired.

Later that evening Beth came into the kitchen. "I have three boyfriends. They meet me at the bus stop and want me to be their girlfriend. It's fun."

"Beth, have you ever heard of the unwritten law?" I asked her.

"No. What's that?" She looked like she thought I was making something up.

"It is a custom, not really a law. The unwritten law says that if a woman makes her husband jealous because she is fooling around with men, like flirting and doing sex, he has the right to murder her."

Beth reached out and put the sugar bowl and salt and peppershakers back in place as I wiped the kitchen table. She thoughtfully asked, "Can wives murder husbands if they do sex with other women?"

"No, I think only husbands get to do the killing."

"It is stupid then," she said, and flounced out of the kitchen. "I'll only have boyfriends, not husbands."

My twelve-year-old sister made wiser judgments than my forty-two year old mother. But to stay out of harm, a girl was better off with neither.

At some point, boys were going to turn into men.

~~~<<=>>~~~

Chapter 27: The Power of Decision

"You have to agree with me. It's cruel and unforgiveable of the dean to kick Duane Larson out of school. I'm going to write a protest letter. I want you to write one to the dean also."

"Michael, I don't even go to your school. It's not my business."

"Dean Richards would never know that you aren't a student. A lot of letters may make him change his mind."

"It's Duane's own fault he was kicked out of school. I'd congratulate your dean for enforcing the rules he makes."

"How can you say that? I can't believe you said that."

"I said it because Duane knew cheating could get him kicked out of school. He cheated."

"Duane didn't cheat! You don't get it. One of the jerks in Calc gave him the answer sheet. Duane only passed it on. The team members did the cheating, he didn't."

"It's cheating if he helped them. He's an accessory. He knew it might get him expelled."

"Lynn, I can't stand you when you talk like that. If he can't transfer to some other college mid-semester, he'll lose his student deferment."

"He deserves to lose it. He's dishonest and what he did was immoral and stupid."

"Honeybunch, this isn't you. Have a heart. Duane may end up in Korea over this. This isn't really you. My girl wouldn't be so cruel."

But I was.

Every time we went out he wanted me to be somebody I wasn't. A week before we'd seen a girl I knew from Queen of Heaven when we were at Spinner's Drive-in. Michael made a nasty remark about her. He didn't know her. She wasn't pretty but was actually the kind of girl he wanted, compliant, and nicer than I. He got mad when I said so. Sister Mary Immaculata must have had trouble with Michael when he was in her class. I wished I'd realized that about him earlier. We got in the car after the argument. Instead of turning the key to start the engine, Michael sat posing as a brooding Hamlet. He was waiting for me to apologize.

I wasn't going to. Hamlet was too corny. Finally he turned to me. "Lynn, get this straight. I'm not happy when a girl of mine is deliberately disagreeable."

I was not a girl of his; I was a girl of my own. When I was fourteen, I hadn't minded holding hands and a giving him a dry little kiss at the end of a date. But after he started college everything changed. He wanted more than dry kisses and I didn't like wet ones. As he talked on, he made me claustrophobic.

Michael Herrick hadn't asked me take my glasses off, but I was finished with him. I told him never to call me again. When I was a freshman and he was a senior, I went everywhere he asked me. However, I was ready for our dating to come to an end. I'd told him I loved him and had promised to marry him someday when I was fourteen, but now I was fifteen. He was bossy and stubborn.

Mama thought I was being mean to "that poor boy." She said it was a phase I was going through. Adrian wouldn't want my left over boyfriend. He'd have to find some other girl. Adrian met plenty of nicer, cuter boys at Mutual, her church's club for teens.

Alex was potty trained. We didn't have to deal with the diaper pail anymore. Mama seemed better organized. She did the shopping and cooking as well as ironing Laz's shirts. I did the housework, Beth and Steve helped at the store. It wasn't good at home and we were isolated from other people, but the household picked up a rhythm that seemed to work. Mama still visited with Louise Claussen, Mrs. Morgan and Mrs. Porter. They went out to lunch every week. That gave her company and all the Breeze Terrace gossip, even if the neighbors avoided coming to our house.

Although he didn't trust clerks, other than Erno and Auggie, Laz still behaved with the customers. And except for once, before Christmas, Laz hadn't hurt me since I started high school. That one time he didn't really hurt me. It seemed that once he got worse with everyone else, he got better with me. That last trouble happened on a Saturday. I'd been working since I'd gotten up. I'd finished the windows and was scrubbing down the kitchen cabinet doors. I thought I'd earned a short recess where I could breathe air that didn't smell like Clorox. Then I start washing the windows.

I hadn't taken piano lessons since I was eleven and Mr. Calhoun retired, but Adrian brought music for the Grieg Piano Concerto and was letting me try it while she was away babysitting. The open windows brought in the morning fragrance of the roses that hung from the porch eaves. The piano was in the living room now. It was a new spinet, and its mahogany finish matched Mama's furniture. A round gilt framed mirror hung above the piano. The mirror reflected light on the keys from the windows. It did make the room elegant. My mother was proud of the room.

My brothers were outdoors. Mama and Laz were in the den going over some business before he went to open the store for Erno. Beth was running our uniforms through the washer. It was a perfect time for me to take a music break. Adrian and I liked the thunder of the concerto's opening when we were little and would listen to her parents' record player. I struggled through a page and a half of Grieg's notation, stretching my fingers, stiff from lack of practice, so I could reach the octave chords. I repeated the section, trying to get the notation down before I went back to work. Laz must have shouted at me, but I was concentrating and didn't hear him.

I glimpsed a flash in the mirror on the wall above the piano and instinctively ducked my head. One of his shoes rocketed through the air and straight through where my head would have been. It left a lightning jag crack in the mirror and a dent in the frame where it hit. His other shoe tried its best to put a dent in my right shoulder.

Mother sulked for days afterward and was cold to Laz and me. I was sorry about the mirror, but I would have been cracked and chipped if its reflection hadn't given me warning. The classical and baroque composers were more to my taste than the romantics like Edvard Grieg anyway. There had been enough thunder and bombast in my life. It certainly wasn't the first time I'd been hit by a projectile when I wasn't paying attention. But it wasn't happening so often anymore. Laz had hardly hurt me at all since I started high school. He fought with men, but was always nice to women. I guess I'd passed from being a hittable child to a non-hittable woman. The glasses would help protect me now. No one was supposed to hit people wearing glasses.

I loved my new glasses and I loved the power of decision. I couldn't get rid of Laz, but I had gotten rid of Michael. If I ever wanted a boyfriend again, one of my friends with an older brother could easily arrange it. But I didn't think I wanted one. I couldn't trust men and except for Okio, I didn't even like them. Probably, I only liked Okio because he was outside when I was in.

I wished Blaise's Blazes were still going on adventures. The club was more fun than boyfriends were. Girlfriends either liked you or didn't like you. They didn't expect that you should pretend to be someone totally different, just for them.

~~~<<=>>~~~

Chapter 28: Brahms' Marian Lieder

My family was coming to hear Queen of Heaven's chorus sing at the May Concert. Beth was in eighth grade. She wanted to see the high school where she would be going in September. Laz promised Mother that we would go to Wan Q after the concert for an early supper. It was on our way home and was Alex's favorite restaurant. My family had never been to an event at my school before. I'd duly brought home notices, but didn't expect anyone would want to come. Queen of Heaven was in Los Angeles, a long drive from Breeze Terrace. I took the bus or went with Pat O'Hara and her family if I had to be at school for some event. The O'Haras went to all school events. A few days before the concert, Mama suggested I call Michael and invite him. I wasn't going to. I invited Adrian instead. My mother wasn't happy.

Queen of Heaven High School was in a beautiful building, brick with long windows and shiny hardwood hallways. It had been built in 1925 with great attention to detail. I knew Beth would like it. Laz and Mama went to find good seats in the auditorium. Beth and Adrian kept Alex with them and went exploring. I went backstage to get ready.

For the program the chorus prepared six of Brahms' *"Marian Lieder,"* but we only performed one. Sister Theresa, the upper division dean, made a point of telling our director, that just a little Brahms was more than enough. Sister Jean Vianney took the hint. She chose Fred Waring arrangements for most of the performance. We ended with a medley the audience loved: *"I feel A Song Coming On," "It's Only A Paper Moon," "I Found A Million Dollar Baby"* and *"Fit As A Fiddle."*

Elena's paintings were hanging in the main hall with the ribbons she'd won in competitions around the city. She competed against college kids and students from Chouinard Art School. I walked my family to the display to see her work. Laz was frowning and looking suspiciously around. I didn't know what was wrong. When Mama led us into the reception room so Alex could have a cookie or two, Laz wouldn't even accept a cup of punch. I was grateful when Beth went to stand with him, calmed him. I worried that it was the Brahms that upset him. Every year he seemed to hate Russians and Germans more, ranting about articles in the paper that mentioned Germany and the Soviet Union. I hadn't had sense enough to think about how a song in German might affect him.

At Wan Q, Laz ordered for us, but stayed sullen. Adrian kept her eyes down. In a soft and dangerous way, Laz finally spoke.

"Vy school *fekete*?" he said. "Vy family go to *fekete* school?"

I knew what *fekete* meant. Beth and Mama did too. It meant black. It wasn't the language of one song that bothered him. It was the color of some of my classmates.

My mother tried to sooth him. "Laz dear, calm down. Remember where we are."

He looked around, but his eyes stayed angry.

"I didn't know, Laz. How could I know?" she pleaded.

Looking up at the ceiling, he said, "Vy sistairs send church girls to *fekete* school?" Then he looked across the table at Mother. "Vy you allow Leen go to *fekete* school? Vy the mama nadt know vadt happening to girls?"

"It's a good school," I whispered.

The waiter returned with a rolling cart carrying our food. Laz nodded to the man as though the sun were beaming down on both of them and then directed the waiter to serve. If the man serving us recognized the Hungarian accent, he'd think of Paul Lukas not Béla Lugosi. Wan Q's hostess came by our table, slinky in her mandarin dress, seating another family. She caught Laz's eye and gave him a coy little smile.

After the hostess and waiter left us, Laz commanded Mama, "In morning find differendt school."

We finished our meal. Alex was quiet. No one said anything. I knew Adrian was anxious to be home with sane people.

That evening, Beth and I could hear Laz insisting that I was not to be allowed to go to school the next morning. Mother argued that I was happy at Queen of Heaven and should continue to go there. It was the first time she'd stood up to him for me. We heard her ask, "Would you want her to go to Hamilton? Would you like it if she were running around with those tee-shirt boys or the hot rod teens?"

I knew he wouldn't change his mind.

Mother came into the kitchen. "You, Delores, Pat, and Anna Marie don't go around with any of the colored girls at school, do you? You've never mentioned any," she asked.

"We do. Pat, Anna Marie, Kathleen and I do. But, Mama, I mention them all the time." I answered. "Elena did the paintings in the foyer. Remember? She's a colored girl."

My mother's eyes grew huge. "Elena Thibodeaux is colored?"

I nodded.

"What's wrong with that?" Beth demanded, but Mama stared at me.

"You didn't tell me that. You said her father was a doctor."

"Mother, he is a doctor." I was indignant and pedantic, offended by her lack of logic. Mama's reasoning wouldn't have passed Sister Mary Immaculata when I was in fifth grade. She looked at me as though I was the one who didn't make sense.

I kept my argument going, though I knew it wouldn't do any good. "In third grade when Maria came to our school I didn't tell you she was Mexican. I never told you Carol Pistoresi was Italian. You never cared what color or nationality my friends were, Mama."

At breakfast, I found that my mother had not only taken my side in the *fekete* issue but she had won. A compromise had been made. Beth wouldn't be coming to Queen of Heaven in September. She'd go to the new Catholic girls' school, Mother of The Redeemer. All its students would be pale enough to suit my sister's father. Beth liked throwing tantrums, and would have, but her two best school friends were also going to the new Academy. She was all right with the decision. I was the only one disappointed.

Members of Queen of Heaven's Chorus were eligible to try out for the Mixed Chorus at Loyola University. Maria, Kathleen and I auditioned and were accepted. Kathleen's father, proud of his daughter's fine contralto, offered transportation.

The night of our first choral practice we were given a second audition. Kathleen and I weren't great beauties, but we were all right. Maria was a great beauty. But it wouldn't have mattered. The men of the chorus rushed us. Each man seemed to want a prize, and we were it.

What Jeannie French had told me long ago was correct. If *all* the boys didn't love me, as she'd predicted, more than enough of them acted as though they did during the fifteen-minute break during chorus practice.

We three girls began dating the chorus men, but we were failures. We didn't fail because Maria had brown skin, because Kathleen was fleshy, or because I was too shy to look a boy in the eyes. Mrs. Gutierrez insisted that Maria take her older sister along on all her dates. Mr. Gutierrez's size and glower intimidated any young man who came to the door. Kathleen and I failed on our own. Kathleen was as bossy with her dates as she was with us. The guys didn't ask her out a second time, and never learned her good qualities.

I was the worst failure of all. When a date came to pick me up, the moment we were alone, I felt a surge of panic. I'd walk on people's lawns to keep away from him as we walked to the car. I backed up against the passenger side door, my hand on the door handle as we drove. All the fears I'd ever felt as a child came rushing back. If a date tried to kiss me at the end of an evening, I hissed like a feral cat. The more he tried, the more I fought. I was untouchable and therefore, undateable.

Word got around, and the rush was over. If the glorious Okio Hasekura magically returned, it would make no difference. I could only love dream men. In my fifteenth year, I'd had over a year of experience with dating, and decided I was doomed to spinsterhood. The actual reality of men, and their expectations of either controlling a woman's mind or her body or both, was awful. It was best to just avoid the whole thing.

~~~<<=>>~~~

Chapter 29: Paint Lines

A yellow paint line on the playground separated the girls' from the boys' playgrounds at St. Blaise School. Paint lines also marked a division at Queen of Heaven. But the paint wasn't yellow. It was bright lipstick red. Girls in my track were expected to glorify the mind, not the body. Kept busy with Sodality, League for Christian Charity, Queen's Journal, the Science Club, and the Math Club, we were induced to feel superior. We were snobbish about the books we read, disdaining popular magazines as common and our family's choice of newspapers as pleblian. By the end of our freshman year, the girls from the old Blaise's Blazes who were tracked commercial or home making at Queen of Heaven were reading fashion magazines and had begun wearing Revlon Red lipstick - and using Maybelline pencil to match Marilyn Monroe's eyebrow arch.

Lured into a snobbish mind-set, the girls on my track wore scant make-up. We'd been introduced to women in the essays of Anne Morrow Lindberg and Iris Murdoch and were reading the New Yorker and Atlantic. I'd begun to see my own mother's careful manicure and mascaraed lashes as evidence of intellectual inferiority.

The paint line snobbery worked both ways. I clung to Delores as long as I could. If we were on the same bus, I'd look for a seat near her and her new friends. But her droll digs about the 'stuck-up drips' in my track hurt. Mid-way through our sophomore year I stayed with girls on my own track. The brightly groomed girls on Delores's side of the invisible paint line and we drab girls on mine separated.

Early one morning just a few weeks into our junior year, I missed the seven-fifteen bus. I'd missed my friends' bus and thought I'd be the only one from Queen of Heaven among downtown commuters. But as the bus stopped near her neighborhood east of Culver City, Delores got on. I couldn't help being happy to see her. I waved. She came down the aisle and sat next to me.

"You aren't usually on this bus," she commented as she settled down in the seat.

"Nope. I was late today. My mom's sick."

"Why do you, Pat and Kathleen go so early anyway?"

"The League meets mornings before class."

"Pray and lick envelopes for the missions? How can you stand all that?"

I shrugged. We rode almost to the next stop before I said anything. Then I decided to ask about some of our friends who weren't on my track but were on hers. "I haven't seen Patty Lacey since last year. Has she dropped out of Queen of Heaven to go to Hamilton?"

"Don't you know?"

"Know what?"

"Know that she got married."

Delores could see the shocked look on my face and looked scornful and smug at the same time. "You didn't know?"

"No one knows. Kathleen or Laura would have told me."

"My mom doesn't want me to talk about it. She's disappointed that one of her precious Blazes got pregnant. And she's crazy mad at Patty's parents. The Laceys took Patty and her boyfriend to Las Vegas to get married. "Out of the church!" as my mother reminds me at least once a day. They helped Patty commit a mortal sin. At least she got married.

I was wide-eyed, and didn't interrupt, so Delores continued. "Mom doesn't want me to talk to her anymore. She thinks Patty's a bad influence because she had to get married."

At the next stop three other Blazes that I hadn't talked to in a long time got on the bus. When they found seats around us, I became an outsider again. But that morning in history class, I whispered the news to Maria that Patty had gotten married. It went around before lunchtime.

Carol Pistoresi said she knew all along that it was going to happen because Patty's parents let her date a boy who wasn't a Catholic. Of course he wouldn't respect her. Carol was smug because her boyfriend was not only Catholic but also Italian. She thought he was perfect. But before Christmas, Carol was acting quiet and often absent. After Easter vacation, Kathleen, who was her best friend, told us that Carol and Rob Marino had been quietly married in the rectory at St. Blaise. Carol and her husband were squeezed in to Rob's old bedroom. His brother was moved to the sofa. Carol's family consented to the marriage, but they weren't speaking to her anymore and hadn't even gone to the rectory to witness her marriage.

It was an epidemic. Adrian told me that in public high schools girls dropped out to get married or else mysteriously disappeared just like they did from Queen of Heaven. It was no different anywhere. Adrian said she didn't worry about the girls who got married. She worried about the girls who just disappeared. Disappearing meant those girls were going to have to give their babies away.

By the time our senior year began, Pat O'Hara, Anna Marie, Elena, Maria, Kathleen, Carol Kennedy and I became more aware of the world. We didn't talk about sex. It was rude to ask 'how far someone went' with her boyfriend. Reticence maintained our illusion that we were all *pure*. If any girl felt passion, or acted on it, she didn't mention it.

Adrian had an almost boyfriend at Mutual. They didn't date, but talked on the phone. He was planning to go on a mission and they thought it was better that they didn't date until he came home. Beverly was too busy dancing to think of boys. A boy from Saint Monica's she met at a debate club meet was calling Beth at least twice a day. Mama liked that she was so popular. It worried me.

Pat O'Hara began dating a college man named Rich Whitfield she'd met through her family. Rich had a friend named Vince McMullen. Vince and Rich had gone to St. Thomas Aquinas High together. In our senior year, Pat arranged a double date for me with Vince, Rich and her to a Newman Club dance. I was scared, but Pat persisted.

Vince was comfortable to be around. He was tall, slim and had a very nice car. It didn't seem like he'd need someone like me. He could have a girl who was prettier and more polished than I, someone who didn't get scared, stammer, and run away.

At the end of our first double date to a UCLA basketball game, Vince said, "I'd like to see you again. You're not silly, and you never say the obvious."

"You are silly," I snipped. He was, so it proved that I did say the obvious. Vince was impulsive, funny, and he liked to dart around and talk to people.

"Would you go out with me again?"

I looked at the floor of the porch, too shy to look at him. "I would, but I'll only be friends. I can't stand men grabbing me."

He was so tall that when I glanced up to see if he got annoyed because I said what was true, the porch light lit his teeth more than his eyes. I thought he was going to laugh at me. But he didn't.

"To be honest, I don't like girls grabbing me either. Promise you won't?"

He wasn't making fun of me; he was making me smile. I recognized that it was an act of kindness, and I'd be safe with him. Vince was pre-law, and hoped to go to Hastings after he earned his BA. He had an allowance, but he was conscientious about not wasting his parent's money. He studied hard and was frugal. I'd gone out on a number of other dates that year, and they were all terrible. Vincent Patrick McMullen wasn't terrible. He didn't get physical or expect me to agree with him.

We usually went out with Rich and Pat, and the four of us had fun. We went to games at U.C.L.A, dances, and movies at the fifty-cent theaters. Vince could date other girls, and I was free to date other guys. I told him which guys I thought were cute, and he told me which girls he thought were knockouts.

Pat didn't like that Vince cursed when he was driving. When Pat cleared her throat loudly, as if to tell him: *Don't forget there are women present,* after Vince had said some four-letter word; it made me want to laugh. Pat was Irish and scrupulous, but using an occasional bad word was such a small sin in such a nice man.

<div align="center">~~~<<=>>~~~</div>

Chapter 30: Scholarship Girls

I had no plans for life after graduation. I supposed I'd get a job. Laz and Mother were firmly opposed to girls going to college. They felt it served no purpose unless the girls planned to be schoolteachers. Both of them looked down on that occupation. I stammered and was too shy to give a book report in front of the class or to sing a solo in chorus, I certainly wouldn't make a good teacher. But I had no skills that would enable me to get a job if I didn't go to college.

The girls in Queen of Heaven's commercial track learned to manage an array of office machines including the Dictaphone. They could file, type, and do basic bookkeeping. Most of them had at least two years of Gregg shorthand. Those of us who tracked college prep had a more than adequate knowledge of chemistry, physics, algebra, geometry and Latin, we could counter argue all the schisms and heretical groups from the second century in early Christianity to the Council of Trent. Our English classes had given us a proper scan of literature from Beowulf to Pre-Raphaelite poets. But there were few places in the work world for a girl who had taken college prep courses but hadn't gone to college. In 1954, three years of Latin wasn't exactly the practical equivalent of two years of Gregg shorthand.

After Christmas, the girls on my track and I began to receive invitations to Saturday teas at three Catholic women's colleges. Anna Marie, Kathleen, Maria, Elena, Shirley and Mercy weren't going to miss any. Pat and I weren't going to any. Pat's parents were struggling to pay her brothers' tuition at Loyola University, and they had medical expenses. Her dad had been sick. Her mom found a part time job to help keep the bills paid. Pat pretended college didn't matter so her parents wouldn't feel humiliated. I couldn't leave my work at home for the family on a Saturday to go off to a tea party. Pat and I assumed we would get a job somewhere. The Bank of America and Pacific Bell always needed new girls to replace the ones who quit to get married. We weren't worried.

By Valentine's Day, Elena was offered a prestigious scholarship to Trinity College in Washington D.C., her mother's alma mater. Shirley was going to apply there too. The two girls wanted to stay together. None of the rest of us wanted to leave California. Soon afterward, the nuns told Maria she was eligible for a working scholarship to Mount St. Mary's. Maria's father was very much like Laz in his resistance to educating women, but Mrs. Gutierrez brazenly defied her husband by announcing that Maria could live at home without paying room and board while she went to college. Besides Maria, Anna Marie, Laura and Kathleen were going to Mount St. Mary's College. They planned to become teachers. Mercy's family was moving again and she said we'd probably never see her again. She had a big collection of past friends.

Carol Kennedy was going to Santa Monica City College. The tuition there was low, and she could always finish up at U.C.L.A. She didn't mention her plans to any of the nuns. Those schools weren't on Queen of Heaven's recommended list. Sister Mary Francis told Anna Marie's religion class that U.C.L.A. was full of communists. Pat didn't usually contradict any of our nuns, but she said that was ridiculous. Rich and Vince went there, and they were as far from communists as anyone could be. They didn't even miss mass. And who ever heard of communists infiltrating devout Catholic college men?

Adrian would be graduating too. I hadn't seen very much of her during high school, but we talked on the phone. At the beginning of our junior year, Adrian's family moved to Westwood so Beverly to go to University High. Uni's fine arts department was excellent. The Claussens moved to Westwood for Beverly, and sweet natured Adrian defiantly refused to change high schools. Mr. Claussen taught her to drive and purchased an old car for her so she could finish at Hamilton, and she'd graduate the same time I did. Adrian drove over on a Saturday morning to tell me she'd be going to Brigham Young in Utah in September. Her pop said he'd work two jobs if he had to, so she could go to BYU. Mormons seemed to approve of educated women more than Catholics did. She was the only one I knew whose whole family was helping her go to college.

I didn't want to think about what I would do after graduation. I thought that the telephone company might good. Only women were operators. The bank would be terrible. There were too many men in banks. They wouldn't all be like Vince or Mr. Claussen. I could clean houses and take care of kids. I could work in a fabric or dress store. I might be able to do alterations. I took stock of my attributes. I was good with paper work. I was punctual and never got sick.

Before I fell victim to hubris over my good qualities, reality set in. I was still too skittery to be a saleswoman. Laz never wanted me to work in the store. If anyone spoke sharply to me, I stuttered, dropped what I was holding, or forgot how to make change. My little sister could do what I couldn't. She was a whiz behind the counter. I could barely type and didn't know shorthand. No one was ever going to pay me to sing soprano, especially when I had trouble memorizing the words to songs and was impossibly shy. The fact was that my attributes for gaining employment were limited.

All my life I had worked harder than anyone I knew. I'd taught myself ways to have a better memory. My mother hated to hear me whisper to myself or see me tapping, but the little tricks worked to help me remember. I'd managed to get through the periodic table in chemistry class. I proudly decided that the telephone company would be lucky to get me, and dismissed worry from my mind.

~~~<<=>>~~~

Chapter 31: A Thorough Interrogation

Under her black veil, with pale, unblemished white skin and black arched eyebrows, Sister Theresa looked exactly like the wicked queen in Walt Disney's Snow White. I was scared to death of her. Shaking and dry mouthed, I followed the senior aide out of my English class and upstairs to the dean's office.

Sister Theresa opened her door and, with her finger crooked wickedly, beckoned. The image of a poisoned apple flashed before my eyes. Sister pointed to a chair in front of her desk. I sat down, unable to think what I could have possibly done to be called in to the office.

Sister Theresa stood behind her desk and looked down at me. "Miss Horvath, what are your plans for next year?"

I had to give some kind of an answer. "Excuse me, S-s-sister," I said as politely as I could, "I guess I'll find a job."

"You guess? Aren't you being a little vague? Have any jobs been offered you? Have you visited any agencies to make a survey or the jobs available to a high school graduate? You'll be one at the end of this semester and it will be here soon."

"No, S-s-sister."

"You've not applied to college. Some of your teachers are concerned about this." She sat down, waiting for me to answer what wasn't really a question.

"My family doesn't approve of college. They think it is a waste of time for women." Laz not only didn't approve, he thought it ruined women. Mama was the one who said it was a waste of time.

Sister raised an eyebrow. "Then how do you plan to lead a useful life or support yourself?"

It would seem that finding a job implied I'd be supporting myself, but I knew that wasn't the right response, so I didn't say anything.

Registering my silence, Sister Theresa continued in a softer tone. She had a soft look as well. "Remember the speakers on Vocation Day? Think about what they offered as good careers for young Catholic women. Take your time, Lynn. Tell me what you would most want to see yourself doing during your adult life." Whatever I'd expected, it wasn't kindness. Sister had surprised me.

I didn't need to think. At that moment I came out of dreamland and answered quickly and honestly. "I'd like to be a nurse."

Sister Theresa leaned back in her chair and took a deep breath. "Nursing is a good choice. The convent would be better, but caring for the sick is a worthy vocation."

For girls who were essentially faithless, the convent wasn't really an option. I sat very still and waited for Sister Theresa to continue, and she did.

"Now, Lynn," she asked. "Why didn't you apply to the nursing program at St. Lucy's Hospital? Its program, in conjunction with St. John of God College, would allow you to live at the hospital, work there, and attend class all year around. You'd have a Bachelor of Science degree in nursing in only three years."

"I spoke to my mother about it last year during career week. She didn't like the idea, and my st-st-stepfather wouldn't pay for training. He doesn't think nursing is an appropriate job for a girl my age."

Sister Theresa nodded, looking thoughtful.

"And, S-s-sister, my advisor told me that I had to have a B plus average to get into nursing school. I haven't the money or the grades."

"What is wrong with your grades?"

"I only earned C's in history last year, and one semester I flunked P.E. When I was a sophomore, I received a D first semester in Geometry."

Sister Theresa pulled a file close to her and put her glasses on. She slowly read down the top paper. "Lynn, your comprehensive test scores indicate that you would do very well at either St. Lucy's or Mercy Hospital. But, will you please explain how you were able to get A's in algebra and in every science class but earned only a D in geometry?"

"I had S-s-sister Imelda. It took me a while to figure out how to please her."

"Oh, yes. Sister Imelda," the dean sighed. "I take it that your handwriting improved, and you learned to include the whole theorem with any finished problem?" Her question was rhetorical because Sister Theresa's eyes were merry. A moment later she was back to business. "Now, please explain the C's in history."

"I don't have much time for research, but if I earned enough points on the tests, I could skip doing most of the papers and still pass. So I got A's on all the tests, but skipped the papers."

"And the P.E. failure?

"We are excused during our periods. Girls were always sitting on the bench. I'd just stay with them after roll was called and use P.E. like a study hall. There were so many girls in the class, and so many s-sitting out, that I didn't think anyone would notice."

"You look fit. Don't you enjoy exercise?"

"I do enjoy exercise. I just don't enjoy games very much. But, I learned my lesson, S-s--sister. For the whole next quarter I had to take P.E. twice a week."

"There is a notation here that we sent you to get your eyes examined. I see that you're wearing glasses. Did they help you?"

My smile climbed all the way to my ears. It wasn't only Dr. Roth who gave me the glasses. Queen of Heaven did too. "My whole life changed."

Sister Theresa grinned. Her smile was so wide her teeth were showing and that was very unusual for nuns. Sister closed the folder, reached for the memo pad on the desk and made some notes. I sat quietly, trying not to fidget.

"If I arrange that you be admitted to the nursing program at St. Lucy's, will you promise you will be a credit to Queen of Heaven High School?"

I nodded my head, too stunned to say anything.

"Lynn, you've had champions working for you for many years. There are letters in your file from many nuns from St. Blaise School. They all asked that we take special interest in you." She paused, and lifting the corner of a paper in the file, she glanced at it. "Do you remember a nun named Sister Mary Immaculata?" she asked me.

"Yes," my voice came back to me. "Sister Mary Immaculata was my fifth grade teacher."

"She was most eloquent on your behalf."

I was shaking. "Thank you, S-sister," was all I could say.

"All right, Lynn. Let me see what I can do." Sister Theresa rose. "*Benedicamus Domino*," she said, bowing her head.

"*Deo gracias*," I replied, bowing mine.

In my mind I danced along the corridors and down the staircase as brilliantly and gracefully as Beverly had danced Odette's role in Swan Lake, but the hall monitors only saw an ordinary senior walking quietly back to class. Slipping silently into English IV, I took my place and opened my book like all the other students. Three weeks later I was one of the scholarship girls.

~~~<<=>>~~~

Chapter 32: St. Lucy's Hospital

The letter accepting me to St. Lucy's Hospital Nursing Program came the same week as the Class of 1954's senior prom. My mother was as excited as I was, but she was excited about the prom. Vince brought me a wrist bouquet of chartreuse cymbidium orchids and blue ribbons that matched my dress. Mama took my glasses from my nose before we left the house. I was too happy about the scholarship to argue about my glasses.

Pat and I were wearing ball gowns, lipstick, and mascara. One of Pat's married sisters did her hair, and I'd gone to the Breeze Terrace Beauty Salon. No one could tell we read good books and had taken three years of Latin. After the prom, Rich and Vince took us to the Aragon Ballroom. We danced until long past midnight. There may have been frightening men in the world. Lions and rhinoceroses might have been circling around the dance floor beside me, but they weren't going to pounce on me. I was with my very safe friends, Pat O'Hara, Rich Whitfield and Vince McMullen.

The summer went quickly. With Sister Theresa's support, I applied for a social security card under my birth name. I was now Andrea Frazier. Although I was in Queen of Heaven's 1954 yearbook as Lynn Horvath, I began St. Lucy's with my own name. In mid-August I carried one small suitcase and joined twenty-four other girls moving into St. Lucy's nurses' residence, full of hope and confidence. Following signing in, we said a prayer in the small chapel and were taken downstairs to a collation of cookies and coffee. Introductions were made and we toured the residence. The west wing would be our home. The refectory, kitchen, and storage rooms filled the daylight basement.

Public rooms, offices, and the central chapel were on the first floor. A lounge and classrooms on were on the second, and dormitories were on the upper floors. One of the girls, whose older sister worked at the hospital, told us graduate nurses could board in the east wing but had no contact with us. The boarding nurses even had a separate refectory, though the food came from the same kitchen.

My class was assigned to the third floor. Our suitcases were in the dorms ahead of us. Sister Joseph informed us that we weren't to have personal electrical appliances in the dorm. Silence was the rule at all time on the upper floors, since any of us might be sleeping when not on duty. We were never to have anyone else in our cubicles. There was a small closet at the end of the dorm for each student. Each of the five cubicles held a bed, chair, chest of drawers, hook for our robe and rack for our towel and washcloth. The only decoration was a crucifix. It was as stark as a nun's cell.

A huge, lavish, white tiled lavatory was at each end of the third floor hallway. The spotless airy rooms had everything we needed: sinks to wash our hair, two hair dryers, showers, and two tub closets where we could take an actual bath. Across from the central stairway and maintenance elevator, was a large laundry room with a chute for soiled uniforms and tagged personal clothing going to the hospital laundry, sinks for washing small items, drying racks, irons and ironing boards. There was even an alcove with sewing machines for our use. Our personal space was bare, while our common space was lavish in its function and features.

The second floor lounge had a TV, radio and phonograph, a grouping of comfy sofas and chairs, and tables for games. Bookshelves with an up to date nursing library lined the lower third of the walls. With permission from Sister Joseph or Sister Ruth, our warders, we would be allowed to bring family members and friends, even boyfriends, into the lounge. The lounge, study rooms and refectory were open twenty-four hours a day.

We were given a schedule of hours girls from each dorm could receive and make local phone calls. If we wanted to make long distance or toll calls, we were expected to use the pay phones in the hospital.

Sister Florian Catherine, in a white nursing sister's habit, delivered our formal welcome. Sister gave us a schedule for our first week, and went over the ethical practice guide for nurses. We were expected to be exemplary from the first day of our training. We pledged never to do anything to bring shame to our profession or the hospital. Afterward, Sister Joseph, in a black habit, gave us uniforms, keys to our closets, and tabs to stitch into personal clothing items. My number was 334AF, third floor, third dorm, fourth cubicle, and my initials.

During our first two full days we visited St. Lucy's wards, surgical rooms, morgue, laundry, cafeteria and laboratory annexes. The panty-girdles the hospital demanded were part of our uniform grew tighter with each hour of the tour. New white oxfords with two-inch heels gave us blisters. The nuns obviously overheard someone complaining, because in class that evening Sister Florian Catherine stressed, "A good nurse is uncomplaining in her service to those in her care."

From behind me, I heard someone's very soft grumble, "They aren't in our care yet."

The grumble might have come from one of the girls assigned to my dorm, Audrey Chester. She was bold, and although she was tall and a freckly redhead, she reminded me of my sister. The others in my dorm were Mary Eunice Cantwell, Peggy Foley, and Amparo Mendoza. Peggy and Audrey had already graduated from two-year colleges. Peggy was twenty and Audrey was twenty-one. Mary Eunice, Amparo and I were just out of high school. Amparo and I were still seventeen and were the youngest in our class.

Our third day at St. Lucy's we endured a hospital medical exam although we'd had one from our family doctors when we applied. I was dreading this ordeal. When my name was called, the medical sister in charge recorded my blood pressure and temperature. Then she asked me if I were a virgin.

"Yes." I indignantly answered.

"Then dear, let's hope you stay that way." Sister made a notation on her clipboard and smiled reassuringly. "In the case of good girls like you, St. Lucy's waives the pelvic exam. Today won't be too terrible for you."

We were subjected to scrutiny in each department of the hospital. Our body waste tested in gastroenterology and urology, blood tested in hematology, rate of breathing recorded in endocrinology. We played like silly games in psychiatry and coughed on cue, and moved on to have x-rays done in pulmonary. In the cardiology unit, we took a stress test by stepping on and off a platform while a doctor clicked his stopwatch. That evening, we compared notes and scrounged a late snack in the refectory. Long windows bounced our reflections back at us. Mostly we talked about the doctors who had examined us, laughing about the young doctors' ineptitudes and trying to agree on which was the cutest. We confided any odd or comical happenings too. I had experienced something odd. I didn't share it.

During my stop in neurology, an elderly doctor, Dr. Feynman, seemed to be taking his time. He talked on about the healing profession asked if I'd be willing to take a few more tests. His manner was grandfatherly. I wasn't nervous. Doctor Feynman insisted that I look at through a machine. He gave me other tests with colored lights and a number of exercises. I began to worry that I'd been detained too long. Dr. Feynman seemed to know what I was thinking. He glanced at the clock, and sat down beside me.

"Miss Frazier," he said. "Have you ever had a serious accident or suffered any trauma to your head?"

"No. Nothing serious, just normal kid stuff." I said.

"Never? You have never become unconscious or dizzy through an accident? Never gone to an emergency room?"

"No."

"Have you had any other serious injuries or illnesses?

"No, I've been very healthy," I said. I remembered something. "Doctor, I had convulsions as a baby, when I was two years old. My mother told me she had to put me in a tub of cold water to stop me from shaking and to bring my fever down."

"Fever convulsions? Did she take you to a doctor? What happened afterward? Did you ever have convulsions again?" Dr. Feynman asked too many questions too quickly.

"No. Never. I don't know if she took me to a doctor. I could ask her," I offered.

He thought for a while. Then he reached out and took my hand. "Miss Frazier, I'm going to tell you something in confidence. I want you to promise you won't let this disturb you."

He paused a moment. "You have some evidence of old brain injury. I know this hasn't incapacitated you or you wouldn't be here. You seem to be doing very well.

"However," he went on, "if I were to enter all the minute data from this examination on your chart, you would be sent home."

"But I'm fine," I protested.

"I see that you are fine and know the standards you met to qualify for this program. I helped write them. But any hearing loss, heart insufficiency, chronic infection, anything that might hinder a body's stamina or efficiency, is cause for student dismissal. That includes the slightest trace of brain dysfunction."

All I could do was nod my head and blink.

"I've noticed some reflex dysfunction. You don't show the type of soft signs we are finding associated with schizophrenia, and I tried to induce seizure activity in you which might indicate a mild epilepsy, and didn't. Obviously you've compensated very well for whatever may have happened to you." Dr. Feynman put down the clipboard and took my hand in both of his and I wasn't frightened. "I've made a decision not to enter these findings on your chart," he said. "Promise me you will take care of that pretty head of yours. Don't go banging it around. No riding on the back of motorcycles. No skidding on banana peels."

Peering straight into my eyes, he said, "And now, young lady, can you keep this completely confidential? I don't want to get into trouble with the hospital for what I didn't write down. All right?"

Not only did I have to do well to repay the sisters from Queen of Heaven and St. Blaise who brought me so far, but I also had to do well to repay Dr. Feynman.

~~~<<=>>~~~

Chapter 33: Olvera Street

A day and a half later, Susan Marinelli disappeared so fast that none of us could say goodbye. She was at supper in the refectory laughing and joking, and the next morning she was gone. Before our oatmeal was served, the rumor was passed that cardiology had found that Susan had a defective mitral valve.

The early sun was shining through the windows and the tall glass doors that led outside. The sloping courtyard adjacent to the refectory had high walls that muted the sounds of city traffic. I finished my breakfast and slipped through the glass door. The grass was brown and patchy. There were no shrubs or flowers, only one scaggy acacia tree. A tall statue of the Blessed Virgin stood at one end of the courtyard's rectangle. Grit and dead leaves were clinging to its base and bird droppings spotted the stone figure's veil. Cobweb filaments laced between the fingers of her outstretched hands. A cigarette butt was jammed into a crevice beneath one of her feet. St. Lucy's was dedicated to human health, but its yardmen neglected the plants growing in this small garden.

I was thinking of Susan and what had happened to her. In ten minutes the first duty bell would ring. Spreading a handkerchief to keep dirt from my uniform, I sat down on one of the benches. On the ground between the back of the bench and the wall, a tiny agave was trying its best to grow. I got up and dragged the bench a little farther away to give the spiky cactus-like rosette more space. It had been months since the last rain. I went back into the refectory and fetched some water in a paper cup. I had a cactus garden of my own.

I had my own real name now, but no one would call me Andrea. By our second week of training Sister Joseph, Sister Ruth, and all the students in the residence were calling me Andy. I enlisted the aid of my dorm mates. They spread the word. Our class tried hard, but it wasn't long until my name was pared down again, this time to Drea.

I gave up. It was only fair. Mary Eunice, Audrey, Peggy and I had nicked Amparo's name down too, and she might not have liked it either. Paro and Drea weren't the worst nicknames in the world. We students were calling Sister Florian Catherine by a nickname also, and The Florid Cat never missed catching her mice's mistakes.

During my first two semesters at St. Lucy's, I only saw Adrian once. She flew home from Provo for spring break. She'd been home at Christmas, but I was on duty when she was free. Adrian drove over to pick me up. Instead of driving back to our familiar Westside territory for the afternoon, she drove us deeper into the city. We passed Union Station, and she turned her car into the parking lot for Olvera Street.

"I like this place," Adrian said, grinding the gears as she backed to park.

"I've never been here." I answered, as gawky as a tourist.

"You have. Everyone's been to Olvera Street. Didn't you ever come here with that club when we were kids?"

"No. Never. When did you come here? When you were in Mutual at your ward? I don't remember you telling me about Olvera Street."

"I came on a field trip in fourth grade. When I was in Mrs. Walsh's class. Don't you remember? The year we studied California."

"How could I? I didn't go to your school."

"Some friend. I told you about it. You should remember."

Nothing had changed between Adrian and me in eight or nine months. Adrian scolded and I bickered. She had told me about all her public school field trips. She and Beverly went to the La Brea Tar Pits, the Los Angeles Museum, Griffith

Observatory, and the big public library downtown. Fieldtrips were the only thing about public school I'd envied.

We followed the music to watch children dancing near a fountain before going to explore the shops. Then, though we bought nothing, we spent time examining and holding brightly embroidered clothing up in front of us to admire each other's discoveries from the racks and shelves.

"Have you thought about quitting?" she asked as we walked between flowered blouses and colorful *rebosos*.

"Quitting St. Lucy's?"

"Yes. Quitting that old hospital. You could get a job or something."

"I'd never quit! And my name is Andrea now." I replied. "I never want to leave St. Lucy's. Nursing is a wonderful profession."

"Yeah, yeah, yeah, An-dree-a. You're saving lives. You, personally." Adrian gave me a wry look and then changed the subject.

"Have you been going out with anyone?" she said. "There are guys over at the college you go to, aren't there? It isn't like that cruddy nurses' residence, is it?"

"The hospital has interns and residents. They're all guys. And yes, there are guys at St. John of God. It's a men's college but last year they began offering a nursing and teaching course of study for women. I've gone out a couple of times. I still go out with Vince."

"He doesn't count," Adrian snapped, as we went back out onto the street. She was right. He didn't count for romance.

I was reconciled to my disinclination to normalcy. One man who recently asked me out at St. John of God had been attractive, but he wore a scapular. I could see the brown shoelace cord under the collar of his shirt when he bent over to pick up a pencil rolling across the library floor. The scapular defined him too well. Men with strong beliefs too easily turned into mind bullies. I wasn't going out with any more Michaels.

I couldn't explain all that to Adrian. She was such a good Latter Day Saint she'd expect me to want to date a good Catholic. She wouldn't understand.

"I've been going out with someone," she shyly confided. But she wasn't smiling. We were standing beside some sequined, spangley skirts at an open shop front. "I've been dating a junior who's on the J.V. Ski Team. I've learned to ski."

"What's his name? Do you have a picture of him?" I was glad she had a boyfriend. Movies, music, and boyfriends were the topic in the residence when we weren't studying.

"His name is Jeffery Wyler. I left his picture in my dorm. I'm not really serious about him." She looked away. "I may not go back to school after this year."

"Why?" I asked. She didn't seem homesick.

"I don't know. I might. I don't want to disappoint Pop, but staying there is disappointing me. Everyone in Provo is such a kid. I'll be nineteen this summer. I don't feel like a kid." She was staring down at her hands.

"Drop out then. Come to St. Lucy's and be a nurse with me. You don't have to be a Catholic. It wouldn't cost your family any more than BYU does. Really. I think you'd like it if you gave it a chance."

"I could never be a nurse in a million years. I don't know how you stand it." Adrian scowled at me. "Beth says you might as well be in the army or locked up in a woman's prison. And besides, I hate the way hospitals smell!"

St. Lucy's sterile corridors did smell like disinfectants. One of the R.N.'s, Molly Brundage, who had worked at St. Lucy's for forty years, told me she could still smell the carbolic acid that was used back in the early days. That phenol odor seeped into the walls of the older wards of the hospital. It made them smell clean, the same way fruit bins made markets smell sweet and money made banks smell metallic. "I like it," I said.

Adrian gave me one of her looks and punched my arm. "Yeah, I know," she said.

I smiled. Girlfriends didn't expect girlfriends to change or think like they did.

We stopped, bought tacos and soda, and found a bench to sit on. Mariachis were playing far down the street in the plaza. Adrian was quiet. My mind drifted to St. Lucy's.

At first I was afraid of the male patients, but our nursing supervisors stayed nearby. I soon found that hurting or ill, and in a hospital bed, men were helpless and most of them were afraid. Orderlies lifted and cleaned them. We only had to do nursing. If there ever was a problem, I only had to call an orderly or a floor nurse. Doctors could be a problem, but not patients. Everything was dependable at St. Lucy's, but it didn't all depend on me.

Each member of the hospital staff was identifiable by badge, cap or uniform. When emergencies happened, there was a code of procedure to handle them. There were rules, fairness, and there was order.

We sat quietly on the bench and listened to the trumpets and violins. The evening before in the student lounge, Elise, a third-year student, said that if her grandmother hadn't had a stroke, she wouldn't have begun training. She'd liked taking care of her grandmother.

Audrey Chester volunteered that she'd broken her leg in sixth grade when she lived in Phoenix. It was hard to think of her ever being a kid. She never stumbled or did anything wrong. But she told us she was in the hospital for two weeks. The nurses were so kind to her she wanted to be like them. Amparo said she liked seeing heroic nurses in old war movies on TV. She said she dreamed of being a modern day Florence Nightingale. We were all romantic idealists, but Paro was honest enough to admit it.

I'd said I'd known a nurse when I was a kid. I didn't have to say anything more. Everyone had someone they admired as a kid.

While we sat on the bench and listened to the music, I thought of mentioning Jeannie to Adrian, but I didn't want to hear her say, "Oh, sure. That's why you are doing this icky nursie stuff. You want to be like her. That is just so weird of you." I didn't think it was so weird.

Before we left Olvera Street, Adrian bought a blouse to take back to Provo with her, and a brightly colored, fired Talavera tile of a Spanish dancer for her sister. Beverly would like it. The vendor, wearing a wide black sombrero, had a table of cacti and succulents growing in ragged half-sized Edgemar Farms milk containers. Adrian saw me examining the tiny plants while she made her purchases. She bought a baby ocotillo for me. It was about four inches high.

~~~<<=>>~~~

Chapter 34: Amparo Mendoza

The next morning, before breakfast, I planted the wee spikey ocotillo along the wall of the courtyard. It was a pretty morning, and spring rains made the ground soft. The agave was doing fine. I'd transplanted it to a more favorable location, and it had doubled in size since August. The agave was a rounded, rose-like symmetrical plant. Adrian's gift would grow angular. They might squabble a bit, as we did.

Ocotillo, the ingrate, stabbed me three times before it was finally upright and tamped securely in the soil. I wouldn't get infected. I never did. And I was in a place where antiseptics were always available.

Amparo Mendoza and I had become close friends. I liked Audrey and Mary Eunice from my dorm also, but Paro and I took advantage of an option to sign up for extra classes at St. John of God College so we were together much of our time. As long as our nursing degree units were accruing on schedule, we could take other courses if we could pay the tuition. My scholarship covered any classes I wanted to take at St. John of God College. Her parents gave money for what she wanted.

Paro and I added Western Civilization and The Post Romantic Poets to our first year's courses, and we picked up a fine arts class during summer session along with Pharmacology II. We liked doing research and studying. Our nursing instructors and our college professors at St. John of God were well prepared. Paro and I plotted we could graduate in three years with double majors if we worked hard.

Adrian decided to drop out of BYU at the end of spring semester. By mid-June she found a job at Walt Disney Productions in Burbank. By August she was engaged. She called to ask me to help out at her wedding in December. I was pleased that I was included and happy that she picked her date early enough that I could make sure I'd be free that day.

I'd be one of Pat's bridesmaids in the summer of 1956. I'd already promised. It was a long time away. Vince had promised to be Rich's best man. I wondered why Rich's brother wasn't going to be best man, but Pat was vague about it when I asked her. I dropped the subject. I'd only met Rich's brother once. He was a strange sort of guy, prone to saying very odd things. Maybe he didn't want to be best man. I was glad Pat had never tried to fix me up with Tommy Whitfield. It would have been awkward explaining why I didn't want to date him.

Living at St. Lucy's we were expected to clear our dishes from the refectory tables, and carry our dirty laundry to the clothes chute from the dorms. In the hospital our status on the medical ladder was higher than nurse's aides or orderlies. We learned how to bathe and feed patients, and change linens and continence pads during our first six weeks, however those weren't things we actually would be doing when we graduated. Nurse's aides and orderlies did that kind of work. Orderlies did all heavy patient care. Nurses' aides did all non-medical patient care. Pharmacy aides checked and replenished the medicine closets under our supervision.

We learned early on that we were expected to oversee the work of others and do a practical sort of arithmetic: counting and recording patient pulse and breath, reading blood pressure and temperature, measuring and recording liquid intake and urinary output. We estimated the amount of blood loss in ob-gyn and surgical floor patients by examining their dressings, and we recorded our estimates.

While supervisory nurses checked our work, it was seldom necessary for any of us to make a correction. We learned to dispense medications and could pierce a vein and take a blood sample. We could give an intravenous injection as well as a subcutaneous one and were cautious and careful in our work.

The best part of this new life was that living and working here was easier than my life had been at home. I was only responsible for my own behavior. I was never expected to do more than one task at a time, and enough time was allotted to do that task well. I could slow down and enjoy the simple act of taking pride in what I did. By the time my second year began, if I merely respected procedures and did what was expected, I succeeded. St. Lucy's was predictable, and that was heaven.

Student nurses rotated through assignments so we could learn the procedures in all departments of the hospital, and except for one incident, my first year ended successfully.

We students had more social life than I thought we would, and that wasn't particularly good. The young residents and interns chased us around the corridors whenever Sister Florian Catherine or the charge nurses weren't watchful. It was flattering, but too much like my experience in the Loyola U. Mixed Chorus. A red-haired intern, who almost all the nurses and students thought was cute, walked me the few blocks to a movie theater and snuggled up in the dark theater to tell me he loved nurses because they were 'easy'. I was not easy. I wasn't even friendly.

Another well-mannered resident asked me out for an evening when we were both off duty. We went out to the theater nearest the hospital. But it wasn't going to work and I shouldn't have gone. At intermission, he asked me where I'd gone to high school. When I told him, he said, "That's cool. All you Catholic school girls go wild when you get away from the nuns." He had a disgusting leer. I was only wild to get away from him.

By the end of the first semester of my training, I would have turned down James Dean if he worked at St. Lucy's Hospital. The men took my frigidity in stride. Their hearts weren't broken. There were lots of nurses and student nurses, many of them were better looking than I, and probably all of them were more compliant. I understood human biology, but didn't have any inclination to practice it myself.

My sister was worrying me. I hoped she understood human biology. Mama wouldn't let her date until she was fourteen, but she had been meeting boys at the Palms Theater long before that. I tried to talk to her about reproduction and how dangerous sex was, how many girls I knew of who had to drop out of high school. She laughed at me. "I'm never getting pregnant. I told you that," and gave me one of those looks that said that in her universal view, I was the younger sister and she the older.

My friend Amparo also found it easy to resist the pestering of oversexed interns from St. Lucy's and the entreaties of the overly earnest men from St. John of God College. The interns wanted scrambly sex on the run, and the college men wanted to go from one date to marriage.

Those weren't options we accepted. Girls like Joan and Marlene said we were prudes. Maybe we were. But we went out. We weren't cloistered, and we had fun.

I could always depend on Vince if I needed a date, and Paro had an old boyfriend from high school who took her out. I told Paro I'd see if Rich and Vince had a friend she might like better, but she shook her head. She said she'd only agree if I took the friend and gave Vince to her.

~~~<<=>>~~~

Chapter 35: On the Orthopedic Floor

I didn't get through my first year unscathed. The report that was filed against me that year didn't come from a young intern or a resident who found me socially uncooperative. It came from a hateful, middle-aged orthopedist, Dr. Murray.

Many of the doctors were terse with us. They acted as though they shouldn't be forced to work with a student nurse and preferred that only a registered nurse attend them. We'd learned to tolerate that behavior. They were often terse with older, competent nurses on staff, and for no reason. I almost forgot how kind Dr. Feynman and Dr. Roth had been to me. One doctor, Dr. Roston Murray, was particularly odious. Students never wanted to work with him. He had a habit of coming up behind any of us who were standing at the nurses' counter entering records or leaning over a patient's bed tending him or her. Dr. Murray would move in on us from behind and rub up against us.

I was frightened the first time he did that to me. I jumped, dropping my clipboard and pen to the floor where they clattered away. As I bent to pick them up, he watched, grinning, his eyes on my behind. I hated the lewd insolence in that grin. The next time he came down the hall, I was ready. I lifted my clipboard, and twisted directly into his advance. It jammed hard into his belly. "Oh, I'm so sorry, Doctor," I apologized, working to turn the anger on my face into naïve and insipid sweetness. It didn't discourage him.

The third time he tried it, I didn't see or hear him coming. I smelled his after-shave. When I felt him press against me, I put my weight on my left foot and brought all the strength, force, and velocity my body could gather into my right foot's motion. I stepped back hard as he pressed up against me. The thick two-inch heel of a sturdy white nurse's oxford came down onto his instep. I was tall and climbing the hill to Breeze Terrace all those years strengthened me. I knew I hurt him.

"Excuse me, Doctor. I didn't realize you were there," I said, as sarcastically as I could. I glanced at him, sidestepping away, acting a more proper and confident woman than I was. My hands were shaking. The form I was filling out wouldn't be perfectly legible, but few things I'd ever done in life satisfied me more. I hoped the doctor would get a good bruise and find a shoe hard to put on for a few days.

I'm sure he would have left me alone after that, and it would have ended there. Except, the charge nurse and two orderlies were nearby watching. He would feel compelled to report me. I didn't think I'd be dismissed. The witnesses would work to my favor as well as his. But I was nervous and hoped I wouldn't be called in to the office.

That evening, one of the registered nurses came into the students' refectory. I was eating with five other girls. I heard her ask a girl sitting near the door if Andrea Frazier was in the room. I knew I was in trouble and tried not to show how frightened I felt. She came over to the table where I sat, and I waited for her to tell me that Sister Florian Catherine had sent for me. Instead, she grinned, pulled me up out of my chair and lifted my arm above my head.

Calling everyone's attention by reaching down and clinking a glass with my abandoned fork, the middle-aged and cheery-looking blond nurse shouted out, "In the Hospital championship fight of 1955, the winner is first year student nurse, Andrea Frazier. Standing at just five foot seven, this lightweight took on heavyweight Dr. Roston Murray standing at six foot one, though all the bets stood against her.

"She KO'd him in the fifth round with a heel to the foot and took down the Son of a Bitch!" It was a wonderful moment. Everyone in the room clapped and cheered.

I found out later that the woman was Marsha Greening, one of the nurses who had filed a grievance protesting the behavior of many of the doctors on staff. It was the first time we students knew about the grievance. One of the third year students told us it was filed on behalf of the registered nurses. No one expected, or wanted, students to get involved.

When I told Vince, Pat and Rich about it, the men stood

and clapped for me and made me blush.

"Don't be embarrassed," Vince said. "It's about time a woman stood up for herself by stomping down." Rich and I laughed, and my face cooled down.

Pat was less enthusiastic over my triumph. She said she thought there might have been a better way to handle Dr. Murray than by inflicting physical pain. I didn't get upset with her. A man had never bullied or hurt her. She'd always been respected by the men in her life *all* of her life. She wouldn't understand.

Within a week, I was called to an interview with the hospital administrator, Sister Gratian, Doctor of Nursing Science, Society of Hospital Sisters of St. Clare. Dr. Murray's report cited me for displaying a disrespectful attitude toward a senior staff member and demanded my dismissal. It was a very formal affair, and I was terrified. Sister Florian Catherine accompanied me. That terrified me more.

Sister Gratian lectured me on the difference between nurses and doctors in education and status in the hospital. Her speech ended with, "I'm sure Dr. Murray didn't do anything intentionally to annoy you."

I couldn't sit speechless. I took a breath and tried to be very calm and keep any snippiness out of my voice. "Excuse me, Sister, but I'm sure he did," I said.

Sister Gratian probably knew about the nurses' protest meetings too. She could easily think I was some radical malcontent. I hadn't been political with Dr. Murray. I'd just been angry. I hadn't even known about the meeting, but explaining seemed worse than saying nothing. The three of usat silently in the office long enough for two sets of angels to fly over. I fretted about being dismissed, but if I were asked to apologize to him, I'd quit and go to work for the telephone company. I'd never apologize to someone like him.

"Please investigate further," Sister Gratian instructed Sister Florian Catherine. A look passed between them, but I didn't know what it meant, or how this would work out. I didn't want to be dismissed and no longer felt so proudly heroic.

Sister Florian Catherine must have investigated, because it was never mentioned again. I got over feeling scared. Dr. Murray kept a satisfactory amount of space between the two of us. I got over being scared, but stayed wary. Whenever I was assigned to orthopedics, he and most of the other doctors on that floor were curt and sneering. I was very careful that I did nothing to give any doctor in the hospital reason to complain about my work. I knew that after the incident, Dr. Murray's friends would be watching for the tiniest and most minor of my faults. I didn't tell Beth. Like Pat, she would have thought I should have handled it better.

~~~<<=>>~~~

Chapter 36: The Gypsy Wagon

Beth began her senior year in high school the September I began my second year of training. She was nearly sixteen. We talked as often as possible, but it wasn't enough.

Over Labor Day I went home for two days. The boys seemed happy to see me for about five minutes, and then they were out the door. Steve had a job and was working. Alex was running the neighborhood. My sister put all her new 45's on the turntable in our bedroom for me and made sure I heard Nat "King" Cole's "*A Blossom Fell*," at least fifteen times. She played a silly song that made us dance, "*I'm Left, You're Right, She's Gone*" by a new singer called Elvis Presley. Beth wasn't giving up Nat for Elvis, but she liked him.

The household was disordered. Mama was very happy I was there because she had lists of work for me to do. The oven hadn't been cleaned since I was home at Easter. The house was dingy, cluttered, and there were cobwebs in the ceiling corners. Dirty laundry stacked up in the service area. Laz had paid for a washer and dryer, but the Breeze Terrace Laundry had closed. No vans brought clean towels and linen to our house every week anymore.

The Horvath family had to get by without pickup and delivery laundry service. Modern appliances, touted to be laborsaving, weren't nearly as good as the old laundry service. Innovation, like wartime, wasn't working in my mother's favor. It had stolen some familiar services from her and she wasn't coping well. It wasn't a good visit. Mother had never been able to keep things organized and her solution to problems was to concentrate more trying new recipes and making more elaborate meals which only dirtied more pots and made more dishes to wash.

With Beth working at the store and going to school, Mama had to do kitchen cleanup by herself. She wasn't a good scullery maid. I spent most of the visit cleaning the kitchen: walls, tile, and floors were scrubbed sterile, the pantry and refrigerator scoured with baking soda. Even the ceiling and glass domes of the lights shone from my efforts. I worked hard to atone for feeling such relief that I didn't live here anymore.

Laz didn't get better, but he'd consistently refused to go to any kind of doctor. He didn't trust doctors. His attitude was that if they hadn't helped his brother, they wouldn't help him. He thought people were better off staying away from them, and used his mother's long life in a village with no medical services available as an example. But Mama was taking some medication now. Against my advice, she had tried to give him some meprobamate that her doctor had prescribed for her earlier that year. She'd confessed to me that she had tried to persuade him, telling him he would feel more tranquil. That was what the pills were for.

Laz refused to take the medication, saying Mama was trying to poison him with Miltown. It was the first time I knew of that his paranoia extended to her.

But this visit, Laz seemed different, quieter on his own. During the two days I was there, he brooded, but didn't rage. Although he went out in the garden both mornings, he just sat in the sun. In the afternoon, he went to the store, worked for a few hours and came home. He seemed content now just to sit in his chair with the newspaper or TV, more sad than angry. He didn't seem to notice finger marks on the walls that would have made him livid just two years earlier. I knew the statistics on life expectancy, but I was young. I could know facts and not apply them to my own life or the lives around me.

Before I went back to St. Lucy's, Mama gave me an envelope with spending money. When I looked inside, I knew it was from Laz. My mother would never have given me so much. I went and thanked him.

He nodded at me, and said, *"You be goodt nurz girl."*

"I will," I promised.

Laz smiled at me and he looked at me longer than he ever had. There were circles under his eyes. His hair was completely grey. His eyes were old and weary.

I was part of the package Laz had to accept when he married my mother, not a child he could see himself in and love. I was visually impaired, hyperactive and resistant to authority, neither compliant nor loveable. When his children were struggling to breathe, I was darting here and there in perfect health. I wanted so much to apologize to him for the sullen difficult child I'd been, but I didn't know how. All I could do was imitate my sister who always knew how to do the right thing. And so as I left, I blew him a kiss the way Beth did, and I hurried out the door.

As Mama drove me back to St. Lucy's, she told me that a good daughter would be more help to the family. "You know that I need you to leave that hospital and come home."

Mama drove into the city, talking on and on about the hardships of her life. I remembered that I'd learned to sew before I knew my times tables because sewing made her nervous. Beth worked in the store before she was tall enough to reach the cash register because working in the store made Mama tired. Her nails were manicured, and she kept a standing appointment at the beauty parlor. I felt a complicated guilt. I looked down at my own hands, rough from scrubbing her floors, and resolved that I wouldn't leave St. Lucy's. I'd go and live in a hobo jungle before I'd go back home.

"You have Betty, Mama," I said. Betty Colby was new to the neighborhood. She needed money since her husband died, and she came in three afternoons a week to help with the housework. I didn't give in.

Mother didn't hold my attitude against me. She and Beth and Mother visited me sometimes at the hospital, but it was a long drive from the west side of the city to St. Lucy's. We'd have lunch in the hospital cafeteria and Beth would tell us about her adventures at Mother of the Redeemer. Mama would share gossip from Breeze Terrace.

"I saw the Herricks at mass Sunday morning," she said as she finished her dessert during a visit in the fall. "Lily Herrick told me she misses seeing you, Lynn. You ought to give her a

call. I know the Herricks miss you. They haven't seen you in so long."

"Mother!" my sister exclaimed. It was apparent that Beth had warned Mama about away from this topic.

"The Herricks miss some girl they imagined, Mother. Not me."

"You broke that poor boy's heart. Everyone would be happy if you two would get together again."

"No, you'd be happy, Mama." Beth rolled her eyes dramatically.

Mother took a long breath. "Lily told me that Michael's not dating anyone else. He's waiting for you."

"That's worse than melodramatic," Beth cut in. "If Michael isn't dating it's his choice. Dree broke up with him three years ago."

"Oh, don't call Lynn *Dreee*! Why must you call your sister by that ugly nickname? It is trashy nursing school slang. You could at least call your sister Andrea."

"Beth is a nickname, Mama. You gave me a nickname, and named me for the character in *Little Women* I liked the least. Goody, goody little Beth. Pukey Beth."

"I didn't name you for some book character. Beth isn't a nickname. It's an Americanization of Erzebet, for your grandmother. And don't use dreadful slang words around me."

Beth changed the subject. "I can drive, Drea. I'm getting my license on my birthday. Daddy taught me. I can even parallel park."

It shouldn't have surprised me. No one knew Beth was going out for debate until she made captain of Mother of the Redeemer's debate team and was going to a competition against St. Mary's Academy. No one knew she was interested in drama until last spring when the name Beth Horvath was italicized on the flyer as second lead in Mother of the Redeemer's annual theatrical production.

My sister pulled the learner's permit out of her purse and showed it to me. "I'll have my license before you will," she teased. With a grin, she jumped up.

"C'mon," she said. I followed her. We got in the cafeteria line and Beth chose another dessert for our mother while I went to the serving table and fixed Mama a mug of coffee, liberally creamed. Back at the table, Beth moved the empty

rice pudding dish away and put a piece of blueberry pie in its place. I placed the coffee near it. Mama gave us a big smile. She reached into her purse for a small tin and picked out saccharine from a jumble of Anacin and her diet pills.

"What are you girls up to now? Why aren't you sitting down?"

Beth reached for Mama's purse and pulled out her car keys. "I'm going to teach my sister to drive."

"You can't. You don't even have a license yet yourself!"

"Oh, yes I can," my sister said. "We won't keep you waiting. We'll watch the hospital doors and when you come out, I'll come pick you up. Don't worry, I won't let *Andrea* crash."

In the busy parking lot, between patients in wheelchairs and on crutches, hurrying doctors, nurses late for shifts, and distracted visitors backing in and out, my sister taught me how to start the new Studebaker and explained how a car worked. I started the engine, and stopped it. On the next visit she let me drive around the parking lot and I did well.

On her sixteenth birthday, Beth passed her California Driver's test. Laz surprised her with a car. It was only two years old and was a sleek, yellow Lincoln Capri coupe with a black hardtop and white walled tires. Beth threw a couple of yellow, red, black, and green flowery cushions in on the backseat and a red-fringed shawl over the back of the front seat. She named her car The Gypsy Wagon. By Christmas, my sister had me driving her shiny car out of the hospital parking lot and onto city streets.

Pat O'Hara was good at math, and it took a math brain to follow my complicated schedule of shifts and classes. If there were a wedding or shower for one of the Blaise's Blazes, we pooled our money to purchase one gift from the two of us. If I could get away from the hospital, she'd pick me up for the event. Best of all, she kept me up with what everyone was doing.

Kathleen left Mount St. Mary's College after her first year to enter the novitiate of our nuns at St. Blaise in their Santa Monica motherhouse. It was a good choice for her. She'd make a great teacher and would love bossing kids around.

We'd tried to keep up with the girls who went back to east to Trinity College, but no one had gotten a letter back. The closest thing was a postcard inviting Anna Marie to an art exhibit featuring the work of Elena Thibodeaux. We never heard from Mercy at all. It was disappointing. But friends did break apart when they graduated or got married.

There was some good news from two of our old friends. Pat told me that Delores McCauley had begun her freshman year at UCLA. She quit her job at the insurance company and planned to major in sociology. It had to be hard for Pat to know another girl was getting the college opportunity that she wanted so badly for herself. But she seemed genuinely happy for Delores. I was too.

Anna Marie was getting married in January. Pat and I were saving to pay for our bridesmaids' dresses. Now, in my second year, I was able to earn a little money by covering graduate nurse's shifts when I was off duty. Maria was getting married to the son of a family friend. Fortunate for us, she had sisters and cousins for bridesmaids. We could just go as guests. We didn't have to save money for dresses for that wedding. I was happy for my marrying friends, but more and more resolute that I'd never marry anyone.

~~~<<=>>~~~

Chapter 37: Adrian Gets Married

After she dropped out of college, the Claussen connections helped Adrian find a clerical job at Walt Disney Productions in Burbank. Jack Ryder was an animator in the corridor where she typed, filed and sometimes answered phones. She hadn't known him been very long, but they were getting married. Jack was at least thirty and was raising his three-year-old daughter alone. His wife died of cancer a year before Adrian took the job at the studio. He was handsome and lonely. Adrian was beautiful and single. One thing led to another. Mrs. Claussen thought he was too old for Adrian, but Mama didn't. But then, Mama thought Laz at sixty-five was right for her forty-five. Jack was only ten years older than Adrian. Adrian wouldn't have liked anyone callow or silly.

I'd asked Vince to be my escort to the Christmas wedding. He'd already asked me to be his date to his sister's wedding late in the summer, months and months away. Adrian's wedding was small and lovely. I'd never been to a non-Catholic wedding. It was a refreshingly short ceremony. Beverly was her sister's maid of honor. I took care of the guest book. Adrian's best friend from school, Marlene, would serve the tiered cake with Beth.

It was hard to find the right thing to wear. Audrey Chester came to my rescue and found a velvet dress for me. She was about my height and had worn the burgundy dress to a CYO Christmas Ball the year before. Vince took care to find out what I'd be wearing so his tie matched my borrowed dress and wore his grey pinstriped suit. At the reception after the ceremony, he bounced around talking to everyone. People always seemed to like him.

I eavesdropped on Louise Claussen's criticism of the groom. She said Jack was good looking but dull. Mama's response was to criticize Vince for not being dull enough, which gave Louise a little laugh.

Vince didn't seem frivolous to me anymore. He worked at being charming like his politician father and much of his gregariousness was just being political. And, Jack Ryder wasn't dull. He was a quiet, thoughtful man. Adrian would have hated the kind of man her mother would have chosen for her. Adrian and I both admired men who were quiet and thoughtful. We liked men like Mr. Claussen, but maybe like a Mr. Claussen who didn't drink quite so much.

Beth left her task of serving the cake to Marlene as she flirted outrageously with all the men, including Vince. Watching, I considered my little sister as a possibility for Vince when she was older. She was like him in some ways. Tonight she was wearing a simple black sheath she'd found at I. Magnin and a tiny, veiled pillbox hat. Black wasn't appropriate for a sixteen-year-old. My sister shocked some of the people there, but black looked stunning on blond Beth. Everyone glittered in the candlelight, not just the bride.

Adrian was probably the most beautiful bride I would ever see. Fashion magazine brides weren't as beautiful as Adrian. I said so to Mrs. Taylor, who came by the guestbook table to get directions to the ladies' room. She sniped, "All brides are beautiful," and tripped away.

Diane was trudging along behind her mother, scowling. For her sake, I hoped her mother was right. If so, being a bride would be the only time Diane was beautiful. She'd been a sulky child who only reluctantly left the house when she was expected to attend a party and go to school. She was going to Santa Monica City College, but growing up hadn't changed her much.

Naturally, since Adrian and Beverly were Mormons there was only a fruit punch, no champagne, yet this wedding was perfect. With Christmas greenery and candles, the white paneled reception room was elegant and classic. Mrs. Claussen, still vivacious, did the work of going around making every guest feel welcome. Beverly was a teenager now and grown to be charming, much like her mother. She helped. It was my first wedding where the punch wasn't spiked, but weddings didn't seem to need more joy than came naturally.

Laz looked young again. He wasn't as tired as he had been in September. He wore a new grey suit and silvery tie. He neither glowered nor glared at anyone. He almost looked like he had when we were young and all the women fought for his attention. Mother wore the mink stole he'd given her for her last birthday over a new green wool dress. She had a jaunty veiled evening hat the same color as her dress. Beth helped her pick out the outfit. There was no grey in Mama's hair yet, but its red-gold color was fading to a soft brown. She was heavier now, not as pretty as she had been, but she was talking and laughing happily. In spite of Laz's temper and bizarre behavior over the last few years, the Claussens had never forsaken our family. They seemed to hold onto the memory of all the good times when we girls were children and the Breeze Terrace parties seemed never to stop.

Rich, Pat and Vince came to the nurses' residence on New Year's Eve so we could ring in 1956 together watching Guy Lombardo and The Royal Canadians on TV. I had to stay in that evening because I had to be on duty at seven the first day of the New Year. Vince could have gone out with someone else, but he didn't. I wished he had. I didn't want him *really* liking me. I liked being his friend, not his girlfriend.

Pat had started counting down the days until June 9th. She and Rich would be married the week after Rich and Vince would be graduating from U.C.L.A. Vince would be Rich's best man. I'd be a bridesmaid. Rich had been R.O.T.C. all through high school and university, and he would begin his military service as a second lieutenant. Pat would become an army wife and the two of them would go wherever the army sent them. They didn't think they'd be in the city when time came for Anna Lee McMullen's grand wedding in August.

In January, my nineteenth birthday came. Beth ditched school and drove me to the exam for my driver's license. I made one mistake, but the examiner must have liked The Gypsy Wagon. He didn't mark me down. I left with my license granted.

While Beth let me drive her car back to St. Lucy's, she told me she was going to get a job on Wilshire Boulevard. She planned to work at either I. Magnin or Bullocks. "I'm going to

be an actress. I'm not spending my life running the cash register in a liquor store and putting up with Mama," she said. "I already have a job working at Orbach's after school and on weekends starting the first of February. Daddy says I can work there and he gave me permission and he'll pay my tuition if O'Roark admits me. One of the Claussen cousins is going to give him a call. I have another connection too. Gary's father is a production associate at Fox."

Damien O'Roark Studio was a well-known actor's lab on Wilshire, the Claussen cousins did have connections, and Gary was Beth's current boyfriend. I didn't doubt that my sister would do what she planned to do. But I worried about her. She was driving alone at night across town. I couldn't believe the family let her. If I'd been too cautious and skittery, she wasn't cautious enough. No one was paying attention to Beth.

~~~<<=>>~~~

Chapter 38: A Surgical Patient

No student nurse at St. Lucy's made light of death. We understood black humor, battlefield humor. We knew that wisecracks and jokes were something that eased tension in difficult times, however they weren't something we ever did. We found different ways to cope with our inability to save every patient.

One of my dorm mates, Peggy Foley, showed an odd fondness for death. She was always a little flushed when she returned to the nurses' residence if someone died on her shift. For the rest of us, the often-long process of attending the dying, preparing a body, and calling for an orderly to transport it to the hospital morgue, wasn't the best part of the job. We'd return from deathbed duty, stripped of any desire for company. Some of the girls would even drop by chapel for a few minutes before coming back to the residence.

Not Peggy. She'd come back to the residence with her eyes shining, wanting an audience. She bragged about her own ministrations to the dying and seemed never to realize that the rest of us performed the same procedures she did. One evening, Peggy told us that when she was on duty in a dying patient's room, she could anticipate when angels of the Lord would be coming to welcome her patient home to heaven. Peggy said she'd ignore other patients' call lights to keep vigil and wait for God's angels. She could feel their breath on the hairs of her arms and received a special grace from God the moment a soul was carried away.

None of us ever ignored a patient's call light. Sister Florian Catherine wouldn't be pleased to know Peggy let angels interfere with hospital protocol.

I wasn't cruel enough to ask Peg if she could also tell when demons came into the wards to carry dying patients down to hell. I controlled my tongue. Peg was tedious and superstitiously mawkish, but she meant well. And after all, I should be more tolerant.; I'd been raised by a woman who believed in witches. The nuns loved Peggy. She did have a wonderful touch with patients. But Amparo Mendoza and Mary Eunice Cantwell had a wonderful touch with patients also, and they were completely normal. Peggy was kind, but she was also creepy.

By February, I was taking four classes and struggling in Pharmacology III. I got the systems and processes, but terms didn't want to stay in my brain in their proper order and I worked hard on the rote memory work. I'd asked for night duty because it suited my study schedule, and my request was approved. For the rest of the month, I would spend my nights in OB-GYN. The department took up a whole floor. Although I might be assigned to the surgical wing and not the obstetric wing, I could still peek in the nursery window as I went down the hallway. I wished all the babies were mine. Golden tan, bronze, coffee colored, pink, in colors to match their mothers in St. Lucy's obstetric wards, I loved them all. This wasn't something I could talk about. Mother and Adrian might understand, my sister would think I'd gone sappy and brainless. In St. Lucy's residence I'd be mercilessly mocked for being a sentimental cornball. I didn't have Peggy's commanding presence. No one mocked her for being grossly ghoulish.

My first night duty in OB-GYN began at 11 P.M. I crossed the street, went through the staff entrance on Vega Street, and walked up the four flights of stairs, glad for the exercise.

I made a plan to do the stairs instead of the elevator coming to and from the cafeteria on my break as well. I felt cheery being on the baby floor. I'd been sitting in classrooms or in the study rooms too much.

I was on time to report with the others coming on shift. I got a nod from the charge nurse. Nurse Mason was a pleasant woman, and I was glad she remembered me from the last time I'd worked this duty. She looked like a Hallmark grandmother, but a very tough Hallmark grandmother who didn't stand for nonsense. She managed her floor efficiently and stayed on her feet as much as any of the younger nurses working under her.

Sister Margaret Mary was terse. "Miss Frazier, We need you in the surgical section tonight. You'll work with Laney Frederick. Laney has done a double shift and has only one aide tonight. She'll be glad you're here to help."

I gave a little head bow to signify my compliance.

"Drea?" she asked. "That's what the staff calls you, isn't it?"

"It's what everyone here calls me." I gave a little grimace but was glad she remembered me. "Is there something else?"

"Well, dear, there is. I'm glad they sent me one of the more serious students." She peered at me over her glasses. I wondered which of us she thought wasn't serious. Margie? Audrey? Surely not Paro or Peggy. They were more serious than I was.

Sister broke into my mental drift to pat my arm. "You may have to attend a death tonight, my dear. A post-op patient was sent down from the seventh floor an hour ago, very critical. She isn't much older than you." Sister stopped talking to make the sign of the cross. "The patient is getting all the treatment we can give her, but the prognosis isn't good. ER had to make out a police report. Illegal operation is what the police call it. Murder is what the church and I call it." Sister Margaret Mary couldn't hide her outrage and spoke with emotion.

"We don't even have a name for the young woman yet. Laney will fill you in on the details. She may want you to sit with the girl. If she does, that is what you will do." She looked at me over the top of her glasses. "Tend her, and pray for her soul."

I went through the wide doors into the surgical section of the OB-GYN. The lights in the hallway were dimmer, but then babies weren't being taken between the nursery and their mothers all night in surgical as they were in maternity. There was just enough light for the night staff to see to do our work. Nurse Frederick was coming out of a dark ward. She was happy I was there and explained that we only had eight patients. Three were private room women: a miscarriage, a post stillbirth delivery, and a recuperating hysterectomy. The ward Laney had just come from held four pre-op women scheduled for surgery the next day.

"I'm going to ask you to stay with the remaining patient. A botched abortion in 417," Laney said. "She's alone in that ward. It isn't likely she'll come through the night. Sally Pauley working in ER went out for a smoke this evening and found the woman, a girl really, in the ambulance entrance. She'd been dumped near the doorway, unconscious and bleeding out on the concrete. She didn't drive herself here,

that's for sure. Emergency typed her and started transfusing. Dr. Reumar did the surgery. He's about the best in the city, but he thinks it was probably already far too late to save her. She's badly infected. All you have to do is keep her IV going, check her chart for timing on her medications."

Laney listed my duties, and watched to make sure I was paying attention. "The patient is getting a high infusion of streptomycin every three hours. Keep her as comfortable as possible, and check the incision and her padding. The bleeding seems to have waned, at least temporarily.

"Call me if she gushes. Sedation is Demerol, but I don't think it is enough. She's very restless and cries out frequently. I don't think she is going to make it."

"Okay," I answered. "Don't you need any help with the other patients? Sister said you've been working a double shift."

"No, I'm fine. Everyone is settled down. You'll be saving me the strain of having to keep a close watch on this one. I'll be in to check. Call me if anything changes. She may surprise me and live until morning." Laney stopped me as I turned to get ready for the duty. "Oh, now this is important, Drea. If you can get her to talk, try to get her name, address, and the name of someone we can call. I'd rather have you with her tonight than the aide. She's a useless klutz. If the patient wakes up, she may talk to you. Without her name, the coroner's office will have additional work." She lowered her voice nearly to a mumble. "I don't know why these girls don't get themselves over to County to do their dying. Our hospital doesn't want this kind of publicity."

In the tiny staff lounge, I tucked any loose hair back under my cap, cleaned my glasses again, wiped my face with a damp paper towel, and scrubbed my hands carefully with Phisoderm. I started down the corridor to 417. Tonight I wouldn't be making rounds of patient's rooms. I wouldn't see any babies born, and I wouldn't be bringing a middle of the night breast pump or heat lamp to a sore but happy mother.

The three empty beds in the ward were dimly lit. Only a small light in the low outlet beside each bed was glowing, and it scarcely illuminated the floor tiles around it. The fourth bed, the patient's bed, seemed stage lit.

Before I stepped into the framework of curtains, I quickly checked off the five things I was trained to notice: the patient, IV flow, catheter bag, chart in its place in the slot at the bottom of the bed, nothing on the floor to impede quick access to the patient. I could see my patient, her blond head turned away, chest faintly moving up and down. Everything was in order; all was as it should be.

The patient's left arm was lying across her body, as pale as the coverlet. The IV line taped in place at the inner elbow; on my patient's slim left wrist curved a hospital bracelet. I stepped to the bed and looked down at the woman's gaunt and grey face. Her eyes were shadowed in dark rings, not by Maybelline eye make-up. Her lips were dry and scaly, no longer moistened by Revlon's "Fire and Ice". Laney was right. She was a girl like me. I'd known her since first grade and didn't need to ask her name. Her name was Delores Sinead McCauley.

~~~<<=>>~~~

Chapter 39: Sacramental Oil

St. Lucy's good training led me through the work. I checked the chart at the bottom of the bed. The IV bottle was still nearly full. My patient's vitals were checked and last medication had been administered less than an hour ago. The catheter wouldn't need replacing until shift change in the morning. I checked the surgical incision and the pad she was wearing. There had been little bleeding. I went into the ward lavatory and scrubbed my hands again and took a fresh, soft cloth and went back to the bedside. Wetting the cloth with a little of the water in the carafe on her tray, I gently wiped my Delores's face and hands, and used some hospital salve on her lips.

My mind was rushing and had no organization, and yet I was easily doing what my mind couldn't master. I felt split in two parts, one part calmly giving care and comfort, the other part was careening crazily through St. Blaise's playground as Delores and I played on the swings, and clung to the fence watching the morning studio parade. I was tortured, remembering also the pain of splitting apart as high school changed us both.

I took her hand and found only a very faint irregular pulse. Delores groaned and tried to move. Perhaps she wanted to turn over. She moaned and slumped back whimpering. A long time later, I heard her mumble something and thought she was waking up.

"Delores?" My voice sounded strange. "Delores? Can you hear me?"

She groaned again and I lifted her head and puffed the pillow beneath it, smoothing out her hair so it wouldn't bunch up and bind when she moved. She opened her eyes, glanced around, and closed them again.

"Delores?" I said, speaking clearer this time.

Her face contorted. She was so sedated she probably couldn't hear me. But then she opened her eyes again.

"Lynn. Lynn?" she mumbled. "Why are you here?"

I bent over her and slipped back into our playground talk so easily. "Dummy. Who would you expect, Kilroy?" I asked. She'd closed her eyes and grown still. "Do you know where you are? You are in St. Lucy's hospital," I told her, hoping she was still listening.

A few minutes passed. I thought I ought get Laney because Delores had been lucid for a few moments, and because I knew who she was. Before I moved to the door, Delores spoke again. "He was scared. I told him to bring me to St. Lucy's. I forgot you'd be here." Her words trailed away. A minute later she spoke again. "Promise you won't tell my mother. Mom can't see me here."

"The hospital needs to call your parents, Delores. You are very, very sick."

Her eyes barely opened and her dry lips pulled against her teeth in an imitation of her childhood smile so pathetic I couldn't leave her.

"No lie," she said. She'd slipped back into our playground talk too.

The smile disappeared and her eyes fully opened. She knew how sick she was. "Lynn," she said. "Lynn, I need a priest. I don't need my mother. Get a priest in here."

She sank back. I worried that she'd lose consciousness again and sat down beside her. She turned her head toward me and said, "I don't want my mother to know. Please don't tell my mother."

"The chaplain can be here in a few minutes. But I have to tell the hospital who you are. You know I have to. Wait for me. I'll be right back." I started to pull away but she gripped my hand tightly.

Her eyes flicked open again and she smiled. "Wait for you? Where do you think I'm going?" She let go of my hand, her head drooped and her eyes closed.

Delores made no response when I stood up. I leaned over and stroked her face, whispering that I'd be right back. As quickly as I could, I found Laney. I told her I could identify the patient in 417. I needed to see our charge nurse and call the chaplain.

Good Nurse Laney Frederick's reply was, "Go, go, go!"

I ran down the long hallway to the Nurse's Station. Mason moved to the phone quicker than I thought anyone could while I scribbled Delores's full name, address and phone number on the note pad. My writing was shaky, but I felt oddly calm. Charge nurse put the receiver down and pulled me into a chair near the elevator, She told me to sit there and put my head down and take a deep breath. She went back to the telephone.

It seemed that before I could take the first deep breath, she was back. "Drea, I'm going to call for another student nurse to finish your shift. You're pale. You look like you might pass out. We don't need you to fill another bed on the floor. I'll get an orderly to walk you back to the residence."

"I'm okay. I can stay."

She looked at me. "I don't think that is a good idea," she said.

"I'm all right. I want to finish my shift. I'll call Chaplain."

"That's done. I called Father Rodriguez before I called Admitting; he'll be here in a few minutes. It never takes him long to get here, no matter what time we call." She glanced at her watch. "By now, Admitting will have called your friend's family."

I didn't want to see Delores's parents. Confusing thoughts whirled through me. The McCauleys wouldn't want to see me either. What was happening was too sad and intimate to share with strangers, and its shame would make it too hard to share with friends. Mason didn't understand that I'd make them feel worse, not better.

"I don't really want to see her parents," I said. "May I slip away and cover the other surgical patients for Laney while they're here?"

"We can arrange it, if you'd prefer," she answered.

"Thank you," I said. I stood and started to go back to the ward, but Mason stopped me.

"It might help the McCauleys to know that a friend was with their daughter. It would comfort me, if I were your friend's mother."

"No." I said, too abruptly. When I heard that word come out of my mouth, I was embarrassed. "I'm sorry. I didn't mean to sound rude. But, seeing me here would shame Mrs. McCauley. She won't want to see anyone she knows tonight. She won't want anyone to know what's happened."

Another thought alarmed me, and I added, "Laney said that Emergency made out a police report. Delores's name won't be in the newspapers, will it?"

"The report can't be undone. There are some very bad people involved with this whole racket, Drea. The police need to apprehend them. We don't know who butchered this patient and left her here at the hospital, but someone did."

A line deepened between her eyebrows and she shook her head. "I'll talk to Father Rodriguez. I think he may be able to exert some influence and keep her name out of the papers. I'm sure the Chancery Office would back him on that. She is still a minor, isn't she? "

"She won't be twenty-one until next summer."

I was relieved to see Mason relax. She didn't think Delores's name would be published. Mason looked up at the clock. "Drea," she said. "Don't you realize that there is a good reason that you *should* talk to her parents?"

"I don't think I can do that."

In my mind I saw Mrs. McCauley skating backwards at Polar Palace showing off to a bunch of giddy teenagers and laughing on the deck of the Avalon as a gull strafed her head. I was a coward, and wanted to keep those happy images.

"Think of this," Mason insisted. "Does her family know you are training here at St. Lucy's?"

"Well, yes, they must," I slowly answered. All our families knew what we were doing. My mother knew about my friends and where they were now we were out of high school.

Blaise's Blazes had scattered when we graduated, but our mothers kept track of all of us. Mason angled her head and raised an eyebrow. "Sooner or later the McCauley family will realize that you'd know what happened here tonight. News gets around." She sighed and her shoulders slumped. "And, if your friend should surprise us and recover, she'll tell her mother she saw you. However much her family wants it kept quiet, they will worry that because you worked here, the story will get out."

"But I'd never say anything!" I was horrified at what she implied. I shared my own secrets, no one else's.

"It isn't what you'd do, Drea. It is what they'll think you may do. I'm a mother. I know the grief and guilt they'll feel will be terrible. You aren't only their daughter's friend. You are a nurse. You need to reassure them that, as a nurse as well as a friend, you won't breach the family's confidentiality."

Mason was right. I nodded and thanked her for her wisdom.

Delores didn't live long. She died nine minutes later, just as Father Rodriguez came into the ward with his sacramental case. I watched her body relax, her chest stop its faint movements. Father looked over at Sister Mary Margaret who was still standing vigil. He said, *"Dominus vobiscum."*

Sister gave the traditional response, *"Et cum spiritu tuo."*

I slipped the glass bottle from its cradle, placed it on the bed beside Delores's body, and moved the IV pole away from the bed as Laney instructed. Father methodically set up the candle, cruet of oil, box of small cotton pieces on it, and prepared to administer the last rites. He put the purple stole around his neck and gave Delores absolution. And, with ritual Latin prayers, he anointed her eyes, ears, nose, mouth, hands and feet.

I stood in the shadows while he performed the sacrament. Laney Frederick came in and stood beside me. I didn't think she was a Catholic, and I wasn't one anymore. Still, the ritual gave great significance to the passage of life.

When he finished, Father Rodriguez put all the accessories back into their case. I remembered arguments in high school about whether or not absolution administered after death could save a soul from the fires of Hell. All those questions seemed irrelevant.

Father turned to me as he was leaving the room. "Don't worry," he said. "This young woman had good intent. She wanted to make her confession. I believe God has heard her."

I was grateful for his words. My spiritual deficiencies didn't lessen my appreciation of his kindness.

~~~<<=>>~~~

Chapter 40: "Black and Blue"

It was my first criminal death. Laney explained that we didn't wash Delores's body or compose it in the usual way. The procedure was to call for an orderly and have the body transported to the hospital morgue, but we waited. I asked about the sacramental oil shining on her face, but Laney said, "Leave it there. The coroner has seen dead Catholics before. The police won't arrest Father for his interference with the body of the deceased."

About twenty minutes later, Father interfered again. He brought the McCauleys into ward 417. Sister Mary Margaret came to get me. Mr. McCauley had lifted Delores in his arms. She looked like a little girl asleep. Mrs. McCauley was holding both her daughter's hands. Laney and I stayed back, away from the bed. Not long later, Father gently led the couple out of the room. I followed. I only said a few words to Mr. and Mrs. McCauley after the priest left. Delores's parents put their arms around me. I put mine around them. We stood for a moment or two in a huddled triangle in the dark hospital corridor and created an indivisible unity. I raised my head and looked from one to the other.

"No one ever needs to know what happened here tonight." I whispered, putting my promise into words. Mr. McCauley bent down and kissed my cheek. Mrs. McCauley's tears didn't stop. But her arm squeezed me tightly, and her swollen face relaxed into ease.

When Laney came out of the ward and began to explain the coroner's procedures, Sister Mary Margaret pulled me aside. She told me another nurse had come over from maternity and would cover the rest of my duty. I protested that I had six hours left to go on my shift, but she led me toward the staff room, told me to get my coat. Sister walked me all the way back to the residence.

The crime wasn't in the paper the next morning. Delores McCauley's sin stayed a secret. My mother called me late in the afternoon to tell me that Delores had been killed in a tragic traffic accident. I acted appropriately surprised. I didn't go to the funeral. The McCauleys and I had shared Delores's death; they would understand my absence.

In March, Paro and I were free of duty and free of class on the same afternoon. I invited her to come on an adventure with me. We took the bus out Sunset Boulevard to Wallach's Music City in Hollywood. Paro was amazed at the thousands of records that were available there. She went busily through bins of 45's, 78's, and 33 1/3's, browsing for Johnny Mathis, Julie London and Elvis. I didn't need to browse. I had a very specific record I was looking for.

I'd taken American Lit and worked hard on a paper on the literature of social upheaval and racial tension. Ralph Ellison's hero in the book *Invisible Man* stayed with me. On a squalid Harlem street, the Invisible Man runs into a character he knew from an earlier time. The character's tragic circumstances lead to his death. Blues was Invisible Man's music. He played a particular recording of *Black and Blue* over and over in his Harlem basement. The Frankie Laine version of the song had been popular but it wasn't the version in the book. I wanted to hear the exact recording Invisible Man heard. I knew if it were anywhere, it would be at Wallach's.

I went through the stacks until I found it, and took it to one of the windowed sound booths, put it on the turntable, and turned the knob. Louis Armstrong's trumpet wailed; his gritty voice ground out the song's lyrics. When I graduated and had a record player of my own, and a room of my own, I would come back here and buy this record. I wasn't the Invisible Man. My face wasn't black. But, music came in sound not color. Delores's death didn't register as a social injustice, but the music helped me.

Over a hamburger and fries, Paro declared with envy, "Your boyfriend is so good looking. You're really lucky."

"Vince? He's nice, that's what's important." I was mildly annoyed. I'd told her about a million times that he wasn't my boyfriend.

"I'd want to have his pin if he were my boyfriend."

"He's not my boy friend. He's just a friend."

"So, you wouldn't be upset if someone else wanted to meet him?

"Like you?"

"I wouldn't mind."

"What about Paul? You've gone out with him ever since I've known you."

"Since I was a sophomore in high school. You know I don't love him. He wants me to marry him when he finishes college, but I never will. I could never marry someone I didn't love. I guess I'm taking advantage of him. Vince is dreamy. Paul is an old stick-in-the-mud. Want to trade?"

I didn't. I never wanted to have to deal with a new man who might not be so trustworthy. I guess I took advantage of Vince, too. But it was mutual. I was his date when he needed someone presentable for a dance or party. Taking advantage of each other is what friends did.

~~~<<=>>~~~

Chapter 41: Going Cruising

Hard work and time helped me get through the six weeks that followed Delores' death. Paro didn't like studying alone and insisted I study with her. Beth buzzed in whenever she could, even if for only fifteen minutes. Adrian called and I got letters from Pat.

Mama came for lunch every other week. In the cafeteria with Mama, I finally understood why so many people liked her so well. She had a soft, pretty voice and was always cheerful. I discovered that most of the outrageously candid comments she made were part of a deliberate comic persona she'd created. She wasn't good at organization or work, but she made a very enjoyable friend. She gave up making me feel guilty for leaving home, and I could look forward to her visits.

By the end of March, I was normal enough to be envious of Beth's Gypsy Wagon. I wanted to visit Adrian in her new home. Beth did too, but time was a problem. Depending on traffic, it could take an hour and a half to get to Encino from West L.A. by way of St. Lucy's. Freeways were being expanded, but construction couldn't keep up with the explosion in the city's population. We'd end up spending nearly three hours just in driving time. Neither of us had three hours to spare.

Adrian had been buying new curtains and drapes and choosing paint colors for the house Jack built five years earlier in Encino on the San Fernando Valley side of the Hollywood Hills. She called to tell me she was pregnant. Her voice was jubilant. She adored Jack's little girl, and was eager to give Debbie a sister or brother. Jack came to the phone to tell me how excited he was. They suited each other well.

I was jealous of Beth's Gypsy Wagon. But no one ever

deserved a car more than she did. One day that spring, she ditched school and came to the hospital when I had two hours free. Even if we couldn't go all the way to Encino, we could take a ride. We zipped out of the congested city, away from St. Lucy's and toward the beach. The bright yellow car followed Sunset Boulevard through Westwood, on past the Polo Grounds to the beach. We stopped to buy lunch, and Beth parked along Pacific Coast Highway. We stayed in the car, out of the wind, and watched the ocean change color. Eating hot dogs and soda pop in the Capri, we giggled like we had when we were little.

Cruising back from the beach to the hospital, Beth blasted Elvis and Jerry Lee Lewis from the car radio until my ears buzzed. Any time she saw a car with cute guys in it, she pounded the horn and waved, while I slouched down in the passenger seat as low as I could, afraid that some of them come after us. She laughed at me and said not to worry because she didn't honk at cheap cars, and cute guys with good cars were fun, not rude. My own dating experience denied that assertion, but it was too good driving with her to argue. A couple of times guys rushed up beside us and whistled and hollered at us. Beth waved at them and turned her head away. I got over being nervous. It was just a game she played. We had a great day, a *"Great Balls of Fire – Whole Lot of Shaking Going On"* day, a splendid afternoon. We were gypsy girls in a gypsy wagon.

Beth had never asked for a car. She'd asked for classes at Damien O'Roark's Actor's Studio. Laz gave her the car as a surprise. His years working for a director made him see acting as a legitimate profession. He knew she'd need a car to get to the classes, or she'd be spending hours on buses. Now with her part-time job at Orbach's, Beth's schedule was loaded, but before Easter, she came and picked me up again. We headed to the department store where, with her employee's discount, Beth bought me a new sweater set and pencil slim skirt, both in a soft grey blue. Beth introduced me to Mamie Silver, her boss. She told Mamie I was at St. Lucy's Hospital and Beth sounded proud of me.

My sister had the lead in Mother of the Redeemer Academy's senior class play. It was scheduled for a Friday evening in mid-May and was to be a joint production with St.

Thomas Aquinas High School. She made me promise to do whatever I had to do to get off duty, or she'd never forgive me. She coolly reminded me that I'd missed Delores's funeral. "That hospital isn't your whole life," she said. "She was your best friend."

"Beth, I only had three days warning before the funeral. I couldn't get time off."

"Well, if you don't see me at the Wilshire Ebell, I'll never speak to you again."

"How'd your school get the Ebell? Vince and I heard Murray Korda play there last winter. It is awfully exclusive for a high school play."

"I can act where Korda played. He's a Hungarian violinist. I'm a Hungarian actress. I'm as good as Dietrich." Beth cocked her head, fluttered her eyelashes and sang, *"Fallink in luf vit luf ees fallink for make beleef."* Her singing was a little off pitch, but she sounded every bit as sexy as Dietrich.

"Dietrich isn't Hungarian, dummy. So, tell me. How did Redeemer get the Ebell?"

"She sounds Hungarian. Her voice isn't thick and German sounding. We didn't get the auditorium. Aquinas got it for us. Lots of rich boys go to Aquinas."

She made her point but kept on talking. "Frank Trefoil goes to Aquinas," she bragged. "Trefoil, as in all those oil wells? As in that huge Francis M. Trefoil building down near Pershing Square? Catch up, dense Dree. Get a clue. His father practically owns the city. St. Thomas Aquinas High can get whatever it wants, as long as Frank goes there. And, as long as Mother of the Redeemer is partnered with Aquinas, we can get what we want."

My sister was good at getting what she wanted too. Sister Florian Catherine said the time could be arranged l, and I could skip classes at St. John of God on the eighteenth. Neither Paro nor I had missed a class in two years. Neither of us were the kind of people who asked for things. Maybe that was Beth's secret. She didn't care if people thought she was greedy and wasn't afraid to ask.

~~~<<=>>~~~

Chapter 42: A Grand Conspiracy

Activity in the residence also helped me out of sadness in early spring. Since January I'd been involved in a grand conspiracy. One of the most popular girls in our class was Mary Eunice Cantwell. She was sure to get recognition next year at graduation. She was already a flawless nurse. After Christmas, Mary Eunice began growing pensive and as quiet as a nun. She'd long before told us that when she was in high school she wanted to be a nun. She was that devout. Her parents wouldn't give permission, and instead she'd applied to St. Lucy's. It was a good thing she hadn't gone into the convent. Last summer, she'd begun dating a friend of her older brother and she was madly in love.

We could keep few secrets from each other. Sometime before Thanksgiving, Mary Eunice caught the most common disease of women between the ages of fifteen and forty. She was pregnant, and while Adrian was elated with pregnancy; Mary Eunice wasn't. She faced dismissal. Getting married wouldn't help. Married or single, she'd be dismissed from St. Lucy's program.

If Mary Eunice could just stay until mid-June and complete the program's second year, although she wouldn't get her degree, she'd be able to challenge the state boards for her R.N. She would qualify and could test for her certification.

Some of us were sure she and Jeff had been secretly married. She came back from two days off at Thanksgiving looking flushed. Her hair was all puffed up and she had traces of more make-up than we had ever seen her wear. Sharp-eyed Audrey noticed that Mary Eunice was wearing a long chain around her neck. We never could see what was on the chain because it was always tucked into her bra. When anyone ran into her in the showers it was under her towel.

She never told any of us, but we knew. Las Vegas wasn't so far that a couple couldn't get there, get married, and be back in two days.

As Mary Eunice's face got rounder and her figure began to fill out, Audrey came up with a subtle plan. We'd slip our candy wrappings in Mary Eunice's pockets as we passed in the hallways, and we'd sneak in to drop snack wrappers in her dorm cubicle's trash basket. Mary Eunice wasn't dumb. She knew what we were doing. She might get scolded for gluttony, but it would give Sister Joseph, our day warder, and Sister Ruth, our night warder, reason for Mary Eunice's weight gain. It wasn't enough. Before March, we knew more action was needed. All nineteen girls in our class couldn't produce enough candy wrappers to equal Mary Eunice's expansion. She'd twice been called in to the office and cautioned about the dangers of over-eating. Sister had given her a pamphlet on sound nutritional habits, and was beginning to give her stern looks in the refectory if she had more than a boiled egg and black coffee for breakfast. Paro, always thoughtful, began to take extra muffins and pocket them to smuggle to Mary Eunice later in the day.

Peggy, Joan and Minerva, were a little heavier than most of us. They came up with a brilliant idea. When Mary Eunice's uniforms began pulling much across her chest and middle, the three girls took turns lending their extra uniforms to Mary Eunice alternating so no one girl seemed to be putting too much in the laundry at once. The switch made it possible for Mary Eunice to get by for two and a half more months. I helped with the uniforms. I could let out darts and take hems up and down as needed. I didn't mind taking a sewing kit to my dorm to do the work in privacy. If Sister should barge in, it would seem I was mending my own uniform.

Mary Eunice barely made it to the first of May. Her middle had grown so prominent we thought she was going to have twins. Peggy and Audrey were at the coffee caddy one evening, and they saw Sister Florian Catherine staring at Mary Eunice. We wondered what would happen. We worried.

Nothing happened. A day went by. Another day went by. On the third of May, Sister Florian Catherine changed the duty roster. Another duty station had been added: Nurses'

Residence Records. Mary Eunice's name was listed there. For the last month of our second year, Sister Florian Catherine kept Mary Eunice busy in Sister's office, doing clerical work. The nuns had joined our conspiracy.

As soon as the semester was over and her second year safely completed, Mary Eunice let us see what was on the chain she had been wearing. As we suspected, it was a gold band. The day she left St. Lucy's, we had a party for her. Audrey and Minerva got a huge bakery cake and Paro's dad brought six bottles of champagne over to the residence. We invited the three nuns who governed our lives to join us. Mary Eunice could resign from the program, two years of nurses' training completed, certification assured, and her reputation intact. Sister Joseph, Sister Ruth, and Sister Florian Catherine were responsible for a not insignificant grace to our friend.

During the time of the conspiracy, word had come around that each of us was to contact Martha Jamison, a third year student. I didn't trouble myself to look for her. In a day or two, she came looking for me. She accosted me on the staircase, and swore me to confidence. The important thing, that she had to tell each of us personally, was the name of a doctor in the hospital who would discretely outfit any student nurse with a diaphragm.

I certainly didn't need one and started to turn away. Martha grabbed my arm, whispering, "It's important, Drea. Don't be stupid. If the Pope's damn Rhythm Method worked, we wouldn't be busting our butts covering for Mary Eunice."

We couldn't mention Dr. Howard's name to anyone, because he'd be booted out of St. Lucy's. I was surprised that he'd risk his job to help us. In a small way, I knew he was a hero, although I didn't bother to go and see him. None of us would snitch, not even the girls like Mary Eunice and Paro who followed church rules scrupulously and didn't approve of birth control. In our first two years, we had come to understand confidentiality's value in medicine, and we'd come to respect each other's decisions of conscience. We were practical women working in a practical profession.

We'd saved Mary Eunice, but Paula Stewart was dismissed from St. Lucy's before semester's end. No one knew why.

There was a dour mood in the lounge and refectory. I didn't say anything, even to Paro, but I wondered if the charge nurse's comment on the night Delores died, implying that there was a not-serious student nurse, might have been reference to Paula. She wasn't popular among us, or very friendly, though she was always invited to join our activities.

Delores's death had been a scathing, devastating attrition from my life. She'd been scraped away, just like her miniscule fetus had been scraped away. I hadn't worked hard enough to keep our friendship. Through my own vanity and weak-willed compliance, I'd accepted Queen of Heaven's snobbish high school caste system. I recognized that Delores had been lost to me long before that dismal night on the fourth floor. I'd thrown her away and was scarcely better than the person who'd abandoned her at the emergency entrance.

There were other losses also during the first half of 1956. Attrition from our class at the hospital began with Susan, whose slight heart problem sent her away during the first week of our training. Paula's absence proved it hadn't stopped. Only seventeen of the original twenty-five in our class remained for our last year.   Some compulsive record-keeper had pinned a piece of notepaper above the ironing board in the laundry room listing each student no longer with us, and the date of her disappearance. We had to confront the peril to our common goal, a bachelor's degree in Nursing Science, whenever we pressed a handkerchief or crumpled uniform collar. By the time Paula's name appeared at the bottom of the list, the paper edges were ragged and the earliest names were fading, but no one took that sorry list down.

~~~<<=>>~~~

Chapter 43: One True Mourner

In May, just when Mary Eunice found herself assigned to Sister's office, another loss occurred, this time in my family. Laz had survived a serious head wound on the Russian Front in 1918, emigrated from his own country to a place with an impossible language and different customs. He'd succeeded in business, married a young widow with a difficult infant, brought his brother and sister-in-law to America, supported his mother in Hungary, and fathered three children. He was sixty-four, nearing the average life expectancy for a man born in 1892. Mama, Beth and I thought he was getting better, his rages less frequent, and we didn't recognize that he was calmer only because his body no longer had the energy to rage. He had attended my sister's school play and seen her as the star of the show, but then was felled by a heart attack. He didn't live to see Beth graduate from Mother of the Redeemer as the school's Valedictorian three weeks later.

Cousin Verna came to stay with the family the week of the funeral. Her plan was to stay long enough to see the family through the funeral arrangements. She could help with the paperwork getting the business and properties in our mother's name.

Pat, Rich, and Vince came to the rosary the evening before the funeral. I'd told them not to come to the funeral itself. The guys had school. Pat had her job at Bank of America. It wasn't that important they be there. But it was kind that they did come to the rosary. After it, I couldn't go out with them even for a soda. I had work to do.

No store's alteration department could get the suit Mother bought for fast-growing little Alex sized in time for the funeral. I sat up late doing the work, and after a steam pressing, the alterations didn't look too amateurish. My brother's suit would be fine. Steve polished Alex's Sunday shoes along with his own, and helped him with his tie.

Father Király assisted St. Blaise's pastor with the funeral mass. Mother hired a Culver City caterer to serve a luncheon after the burial service. Verna stayed home from the funeral to supervise. The catering was set up in our dining room and also on the patio, so people could wander in and out, visiting, eating, and drinking. Except that Laz wasn't at the barbeque pit, it could have been any of our parties from times gone. I'd hoped Rozsika would be there, perhaps only to dance on Laz' grave, but Mrs. Sarkozy told me that Nagynéném Roszika had gone to Hungary for her niece's wedding. The house was full, but I didn't feel comfortable. I went outside.

Typical for May, the sky was overcast, but the garden was in an also typical California floral brilliance. Okio Hasekura had long since gone to a university, graduated, married and started his own life, but his father continued to keep the yard looking lovely. Unfortunately indoors, nothing was lovely. The walls were smeared with fingerprints, windows streaked, and carpets stained. Beth, Verna, and I had cleaned as well as we could, but the tasks needed more time than we had. We were able to get the kitchen and bathrooms shining, but couldn't do everything needed. Beth suggested holding the after-service reception at a restaurant, but Mama reasoned that the funeral party would cost less if the liquor we served were our own.

People, who should not have come to Lazlo Horvath's house, did. Mama's composure was disturbed when Laz's old enemy, Mr. Varga came to offer his condolences. He put his arms around her in a move designed to look like condolence. Beth and I glared at him and moved protectively toward our mother. He backed away. But in honesty, I couldn't criticize the man's insensitivity. I didn't see many true mourners that day. Not even in the bathroom mirror.

Reliably, the Claussens, Erno and Auggie, friends during our family's difficult years, were there. They might not have been true mourners, but they were sympathetic. Other neighbors, the Porters, Marshalls, Fosters, Taylors, and the Morgans were there, though they hadn't been in our house for years. The Bryants had long since divorced and moved away. Mrs. O'Hara came with Mrs. Herrick. They were in the altar society together. Mrs. Herrick wanted to talk to me about Michael and I tactfully found an escape by turning toward Mrs. Toth. Mrs. Herrick couldn't stay to converse with someone whose voice carried a thick Hungarian accent. She sidled back to Mrs. O'Hara.

Mrs. Harris was practically throwing herself at the suave, accented Magyar men who had been Laz's friends in better years. Wrinkles were making grooves for her mascara, but her lipstick was still bright. She hadn't forgotten where the liquor cabinet was. Mr. Claussen milled around trying to make small talk. It wasn't really appropriate for him to go to his usual spot at the piano, and he never was as comfortable anywhere else. He glanced at Beverly as she and Beth walked past him. In his face I could see deep lines. As the Horvath kids had lost their father, his daughters would lose him. Beth noticed too, and went to talk to him. Whatever she said to him cheered him and made him smile.

Beverly's pixie face had changed since I'd seen her last. She had grown to be whimsical looking, with her up-tilted eyes. Her freckles had disappeared, just as mine had.

She looked as lovely as any Claussen cousin ever had. Stunning, actually, and I remembered what Mama had once said about the Claussen girls.

Beverly had been interviewed by BYU, although she was still only a high school junior. She'd been promised a place in a dance troupe the university sponsored. Adrian and Jack weren't there. I didn't expect them. An important animation film was in progress at the studio. Jack was working night and day on *Sleeping Beauty*. Adrian wouldn't come without him.

Beth looked stricken as Mama recited the drama of Laz's death over for different people. It was a simple death. Laz had gone to read the paper after supper and died quietly in his chair. But it was hard for his children to hear the story told and retold. They had known a different father than I did and his unexpected death disturbed them. Steve edged away to help the catering crew stack plates and set out dishes. Alex seemed baffled and uncomfortable. He kept digging at the necktie he was wearing, until I told him the funeral was over; he didn't have to wear it anymore. Soon the Magyar women found him, and he was saved by a kindly coterie of extravagantly dressed women. Speaking Hungarian and kissing him on both his chubby cheeks, they made him giggle and walked him out into the garden and away from gloom.

Father Király sat on the sofa with Mother for a long time, patting her hand and nodding his head sympathetically as she talked. An hour later, Father Király followed me into the kitchen. I'd long since thanked him for helping me get the scholarship to St. Lucy's, and had never been comfortable with him. I stepped back, immune to his kind of charisma, and not needing comfort, I didn't want conversation.

Father cornered me and unctuously told me that I should give thanks to God for having sent me such a good father. I bristled at his pious lecture. Father Király knew us, knew Laz, but the priest had only seen what he wanted to see. I wasn't rude to him, but it was time for me to go back to St. Lucy's. I went looking for my sister.

Beth was ready. Mama had been telling Mrs. Taylor how St. Theresa, The Little Flower, reached down and led Laz by the hand up into God's heavenly rose garden. Mrs. Taylor must have been suppressing laughter as Mama talked. The rose garden metaphor might have eased our mother, but it was far more than Beth could handle. She'd lost her zombie look, and was working up to take on the affect of some incendiary creature from a horror film and burn the house down.

I whispered, "Let's get out of here." Beth raced to grab her purse. Alex was outdoors. Mr. Voros and Mr. Toth were teaching him to move a ball with his feet like a Hungarian soccer player. The Morgan boys and some other teenagers were slouching against the porch railing, waiting. Steve had already planned his escape. Mother had Verna. We were free.

The Gypsy Wagon sped us straight to St. Lucy's. We stayed in the lounge until late that night. Paro and Peggy came to join us. With the two of them to keep Beth occupied, I walked across the street to the hospital and went up to Sister Florian Catherine's office. She wasn't in this late, but I left her a note telling her I didn't need any more bereavement leave. I paused to use one of the payphones in the corridor near the lobby, to let Mother know where Beth was. There were still people at the house. I could hear Cousin Verna in the background saying some ribald thing, and voices were laughing over something blaring from the TV. I hung up the phone. A man passed me too closely in the corridor as I went down the hospital corridor. I swung widely away from him and began walking faster.

Almost every day, in the newspapers, a woman's brutal murder was reported. No one had killed me. I was nineteen, strong, healthy and doing well. Yet, just a moment ago, I'd flinched because a man moved too near me. My mind filled with how violent I'd become when Dr. Murray wouldn't leave me alone last year. His hulking shape pushed against me, and I'd transformed into viciousness. I'd wanted to hurt him.

I'd wished Laz dead from one of my earliest memories, but I wasn't dancing today. Chemistry classes weren't necessary to teach me that anger and fear in combination create a compound that has no antidote. I understood my own role in the dynamics between my stepfather and the grudging child I had been. It hadn't been his fault alone. But, if my friends were right and there was a god, he could have passed on giving me Laz for a father.

Stopping in the night office at the residence, I checked out bedding for my sister. Sister Ruth was glad to give permission for Beth to sleep in one of the empty dorm rooms under the circumstances.

In the lounge, my sister was telling Paro and Peggy about how Laz had given her the Gypsy Wagon when she hadn't even asked for a car. Beth began to cry, whimpering that her Daddy wouldn't get to see her graduate from high school. She would probably cry all night, grieving for the father she loved.

~~~<<=>>~~~

Chapter 44: Legacies

"Horvath men, beeg beezniz men!" Laz shouted so loud I got scared. He hoisted Stevie up as high as he could, until my brother's scalp touched the ceiling. "Son Steve vill hev leecor beeznez," Laz proclaimed. "Steve veel be hod-shod Amereecan beezniz man." He put Stevie down and our brother made his way through the crowd in the living and dining room back to the hall archway where Beth and I were waiting with Jessie. Next, Mama brought our new baby brother past us and into the party. The Magyars, who had been at the house since late afternoon, applauded and raised their glasses to our mother.

Laz pounded on the table to get every guest's attention and in Hungarian he proclaimed a grand legacy for both his sons as Mama held up the baby in his lacy white dress. Then, because our American friends were beginning to come arrive, he announced that "Bebi Alex vill hev party in dez houz in venty, tirdy yearz, help beeg broter in beezniz and take care of ol deddy and Mama."

That New Year's Eve, eight years earlier, Beth and I had felt a cruel betrayal. Laz didn't mention his daughters. Only his sons existed that night. We had new matching party dresses, blue for Beth, pink for me. We'd been to Staber's to have permanent waves. Jessie had polished our shoes. Alex's christening party was going to be the biggest evening of the year, better than Christmas. But listening to her father's prideful boasting, the corners of Beth's wide mouth turned down, and a frown darkened her face. She didn't tantrum. As Mama handed the baby back to Jessie, and Stevie went to his room to play with his toys, Beth coaxed me to a small revenge.

Liquor flowed steadily into glasses, a caterer exchanged empty platters for full ones, and the guests at the party began to clap their hands to the music that was filling the house.

Beth found a still burning lipstick stained cigarette in an ashtray and mimed a sultry Lana Turner. "Come on," she said, and we snuck into the kitchen. When no one was paying attention to us, we conspiratorially drained the cocktail glasses that weren't completely emptied. It was an act of smug childish defiance. We didn't get sick, just played our small angry rebellion until Jessie ordered us into our nightclothes and away from the festivities.

For the next few days, Beth sulked and complained. She pestered her father for as big an inheritance as Steve and baby Alex were going to get. In the only time I ever saw him annoyed with my sister, Laz ordered Mother to explain the way things were to Beth. Mama's explanation was brief and included me.

"Don't be silly," she said. "You girls know you'll never need anything. You'll have husbands to take care of you."

Now it was eight years after that gala party. Our brother Steve came to share in the same sense of betrayal Beth and I had felt as little girls. His father's promise ignored, his legacy was lost. Laz had made sure Mama and Steve knew everything that they needed to know to operate the business. He'd planned for his estate to pass to his sons in Hungarian cultural tradition, and the store produced an excellent income. But, the dead don't get to execute decisions. In spite of all his counsel and instruction, Mama couldn't face running Lazlo's Liquors. It didn't matter how it filled her bank account or how proprietary her older son felt about the business. She ridded herself of the responsibility for the liquor business promised her son, not thinking of him or his future.

At the end of probate, she sold the liquor license, all the store's inventory, interior display kiosks, counters, shelves, safe, cash register, typewriter, adding machine, back kitchen equipment, roll shades for the plate glass windows and Laz' old oak desk. And, although he was honest, understood the business, and would have stayed to help her and Steve manage it until Steve was through high school, she let Erno go.

Our brother's childhood ended with that decision. Mother didn't want the ownership of a business. Steve threw no tantrums, showed none of his father's temper or rage. Instead he became quiet and morose. He no longer spoke to Mother other than in monosyllables. Losing his birthright, he turned away to do more work for the newspaper, filling all his free afterschool time with ways to earn money.

My brilliant, seductive, charming little sister was sixteen and didn't need anyone to take care of her. A week after high school graduation, she'd appraised the situation and Beth was working full time. She was promoted to an assistant manager's job at Orbach's. I was proud of her independence, and proud that I didn't need anyone to take care of me either.

While she settled Laz's estate, Mama decided that Beth should pay room and board. The decision backfired. My sister had no father to appeal to, but paying to live at home out of her weekly check liberated her. With her father dead and Mother transformed to landlady, my sister felt that she need answer to no one. She rolled the windows of her yellow car down and let her yellow hair fan in the wind. She was free. Haughty, and full of filial vindictiveness from that time on, Beth refused to tell our mother where she went or with whom. She did as she pleased. She no longer had a father or needed a mother.

~~~<<=>>~~~

Chapter 45: The Man in the Night Cafeteria

Within a few days of Beth's graduation, Rich and Vince earned their degrees at UCLA, and a week later Rich and Pat were married at St. Blaise Church. One of Pat's sisters was matron of honor and the four of us who were bridesmaids had been Blaise's Blazes. Anna Marie found a place that dyed our shoes to match the pink organdy dresses we wore. We looked like we were cocooned in cotton candy, but it seemed as appropriate a cocoon as any for an early summer wedding. Rich, Vince, and Pat's brothers were fine in their vested tuxedos.

Pat and Rich's friends filled the church. Mama and Beth were among them. Father Duggins thoughtfully ran through the nuptial mass faster than usual because Pat's father was so ill. Gray and trembling, Mr. O'Hara gave his toast at the backyard reception then went into the house to lie down. A depression fell over everyone for a short while, but weddings are joyful events. Soon people were laughing and talking again. As the afternoon went on, the beer and wine in washtubs of ice were replenished many times. It was Vince's job as best man to make liquor store runs. We Blazes were all drinking, but Carol Kennedy was drinking too much. She lurched around hugging people. When she fell crashing into me her cigarette burned a hole in the skirt of my dress. Anna Marie sensibly took her home before she passed out.

The cigarette burn made me feel very somber, but not because I liked the dress and had to work shifts for two registered nurses to pay for it, but because of Doll and Hill's report statistically confirming the link between smoking and lung cancer. Mr. O'Hara was dying and still smoking Lucky Strikes. Nine out of the twelve of us in the wedding party smoked. Pat, Maria, and I were the only ones who didn't. Well, Pat's niece, the flower girl didn't either.

"C'mon Drea. Make Vince a happy man!" Rich called as the girls began circling for the bouquet toss. He dragged me out among them.

I didn't want to embarrass Pat, so I complied, but I was angry. I wouldn't have caught the flowers if they landed in my hands. Blaise's Blazes circled around crowing and cawing. Joan grabbed at the bouquet. It must have been the champagne that made Rich so stupid. Neither Vince nor I had ever once encouraged him to think we had a serious relationship.

The bride and groom took off, tin cans and pink ribbons trailing from the car. Pat was giddy and looking as pretty as a bride could. Rich was grinning so widely it looked like his face had split. As we gathered to wave them away, someone spilled a drink down my dress and onto my shoe. The cotton candy pink would dry screwdriver orange. The dress and shoes were ruined, and I was more than ready to flee to St. Lucy's.

We pulled into the hospital parking lot just as Paro was coming off duty. I took Vince to come across the parking lot to meet her. They'd seen each other in the lounge a number of times during the past two years, but tonight I introduced them formally. I watched as Paro nearly swooned. Vince, still in his tuxedo, could have been Rhett Butler. But, being Vince, he went for a laugh. Pointing to my stained shoe and the burn on my dress barely showing in the streetlight, he said, "Irish drunks traditionally ruin girls' clothing at weddings.'Tis a foine auld custom." He made a swooping bow to the petite girl in the white uniform beside me. And added in American English, "But, my dear, this Irishman didn't do it."

There was an extra sparkle in Paro's eyes as she tilted her head and looked up at him.

In the dorm that night, one of the girls was snoring softly. The windows opposite our cubicles were open. I'd left my partition curtain open. It had been a sultry day, and a fresh breeze came swirling through the long dorm. The soft sound of late-night traffic came up from the new freeway. I lay there and gradually the traffic noises died down.

Pat and Adrian were married. Beth was out of high school. We were all grown up. I wanted to stay at St. Lucy's. I'd worked hard so I would be hired by the hospital when I graduated. I'd move into the registered nurses' wing and if I saved money and bought a car, I could see Mama, Beth and the boys on my days off. I could visit Adrian too.

Before I went to sleep, the breeze brought a green fragrance from the patio's acacia tree into the dorm. Lingering traces of exhaust from the streets down below were replaced by sweet air drifting in to cool the room, and I began to think about someone.

I didn't want to think about him, but on this night my mind was rambling and kept returning to him and to one night in the early spring. I'd taken my break a little earlier than usual that night, and rode the elevator down to the cafeteria at two in the morning. I put a bowl of rice pudding and cup of coffee on my tray. I was just about to reach for a napkin when a plump woman, turning from the cash register, stumbled. Although she didn't fall, her tray did. A slim, blond man, wearing a coat and tie and standing immediately behind me, pulled me back toward him to safety. While the cafeteria workers rushed to clean up the spilled food and shards of white crockery, he nodded at me in a kind way, but he didn't say anything. I mumbled a hasty, embarrassed *"thank you,"* picked up my tray and moved away, sidestepping the disaster on the cafeteria floor.

From that time, I couldn't help noticing him. He had light, sun-streaked hair, and his eyes were blue. He had sharp features. He was probably a little older than Vince and Rich. He was taller than I but only by a few inches. The man had a solemn, solitary gravity I liked. If anyone were ever to touch me, really touch me, close in on me the way men seemed compelled to close in on women, it would have to be someone like him.

Now and then on night duty, I'd see him either at the long serving counter or quietly reading at one of the cafeteria tables. He looked wiry and strong. I thought he might have been in Korea, and wondered what job he held at the hospital. He must have worked in admitting or accounting. They were open all night to process patients. The staff in pharmacy and pathology worked nights too, and the men wore ties, but they wore lab coats, not sport coats. I liked the way he looked and the calm way his hands put his choice on his tray. He had a precision about him, something predictable and measured.

On my last shift before Pat's wedding, the quiet man and I were both at the counter again at the same time. I was in line behind him. He moved fluidly ahead in the line, neither rushing nor jerking as he made his choices and lifted them to his tray. I watched his hands. They were patient. He didn't seem like a person at all. He was like something different, as space and air were different from earth, and clear days were different from fog. He seemed like the bright sunlight patches I'd come upon when I was a child. This calm, silent man made me want to be a bird flying through quiet space. He put the sounds of birds into my mind. I could sing in his space. I wanted to hear his voice and know what he would say if he ever spoke to me. I knew he never would; and I would never speak to him. I was just a white uniform to him, and I never spoke to men I didn't know and seldom to ones I did. I filled a cup of coffee, signed for my food, and went to sit down.

Audrey, Joan, and Marlene were in the corner of the cafeteria where we students clustered on breaks. They waved to me as I wound through the tables and chairs and crossed the dimly lit cafeteria toward them.

When I passed the blond man's table, I was careful not to look his way, but it felt like the space surrounding him was expanding to surround me. I walked faster away from his table, but bird songs were filling my mind. As I put my tray down and squeezed a chair in between Marlene and Audrey, I wanted to hold on to the music. But, everyone was laughing and talking. It faded away. Soon, we went back to work. I glanced toward his table as I left, but the quiet blond man was gone.

While I'd been working that night, Sister Ruth posted our new schedule. Mine was changed. From that afternoon, I was assigned to the psychiatric annex from 3 to 11 P.M. I'd be taking a summer session class from 8 to 10 A.M, Monday through Friday.

I didn't mind the duty change, but I was sorry I wouldn't see the quiet man again. Not that it mattered. From the days when I was in elementary school and a gardener's son took my fancy, any crushes I'd ever had were on men who weren't in the least interested in me.

~~~<<=>>~~~

Chapter 46: Lifting Burdens

Summer classes at St. John of God were condensed, and took more study time. I scarcely had any time at all. I was off duty on the Fourth of July and spent the evening with Adrian, Jack and Debbie. We went to the Coliseum to watch the fireworks. By July, Rich Whitfield was a second lieutenant, and he and Pat moved to an army base in Florida. Working in the psychiatric annex made me think of Rich's odd brother and realize that it was possible that Tommy Whitfield was more than just odd. But Pat's last note said that Rich's family was fine, though she wished she could get home. Her father wouldn't live more than a few weeks.

In mid-summer my assignment changed again. For six weeks I'd been clinically exposed to almost every neurological or psychological disorder I'd read about. I'd charted hundreds of behaviors and learned treatments. I also discovered that people with mental ills were often eased just by a touch, no different from people with physical ills. I thought often of my sister and how Beth patted Laz's back or gave him a kiss. Perhaps I hadn't been as much the cause of his anger as his old war injury had been. Mama wasn't given to touching people, but Beth was. I had to learn what Beth knew naturally. New medications were being developed that might have helped him. The future promised so much. Electro-shock might even have helped Laz although he would have refused any treatment because of the recognition that was implicit in accepting it.

The worst of our profession was that sometimes we had to cause pain to end pain. The next on my rotation was surgery. The patients I'd see would sleep calmly through their treatment and feel nothing. In that way, it would be easier work.

In August, I was Vince's date to Anna Lee McMullen's wedding. The solemn high nuptial mass was followed by an elaborate dinner in the hillside garden of the McMullen home in Bel Air. A shade pavilion and dance floor had been erected and the garden around it was lovely. Vince's dad was again serving on the city council and knew a lot of important people. But I wasn't nervous until I found that Vince and I were expected to sit at the head table with the family and bridal party. Vince's parents, who had always been kind, were taking too much interest in me and being far too solicitous.

After all the traditional speeches, Mr. McMullen gave his wife a wink and sideways grin, and proceeded to joke to everyone at the table that he felt soon there would be another wedding in the family. Everyone began to smile and wink at me. I shook my head an emphatic *NO*, but no one paid attention. I could have been a department store mannequin. I'd never felt claustrophobic with Vince, until now. When it was time for the bouquet throw at this wedding, I hid in the garden house bathroom. Then, when the garter was thrown, and Vince didn't reach for it, I felt great relief.

Anna Lee's was an extravagant wedding. During the meal and the speeches, a band had been playing softly, and as the rituals were finished, toasts all given, the band instruments changed. A fiddler came forward, and the bandsmen who had played through the dinner moved from drum to bodhran, from piano to concertina. The sax and the brass instruments disappeared and fiddles took their place. Jigs and reels began to sound. Vince and his dad coaxed the ushers, the best man, groom, and McMullen male friends out onto the dance floor. The men's feet moved as fast as the fiddler's bow. Irish dancing was something I'd never seen. It made even watchers' hearts beat faster.

One of the waiters was watching from the kitchen doorway, tray in hand, tapping his foot to the rapid music. Vince danced toward the waiter, took the man's tray and put it down on a table never missing a step. He danced back to the waiter and pulled him out to the middle of the dance floor.

The waiter was game. He tried a few steps, and in just a few moments kept up with the men, improvising a style for Donegal reels that was more Bojangles Robinson than Donald O'Connor. Everyone at the reception went wild. Racial integration wasn't a crime on the dance floor at an Irish Catholic wedding. In spite of my earlier pique, I loved the McMullen family for that. Eventually the waiter went back to his work. The men paused to catch their breaths, the band found its original instruments.

The bride and groom danced to romantic old tunes from the thirties and forties. The guests were invited out to dance too. Whatever we might have been born, we were Irish that afternoon. The party went on into the night, and as the old folks drifted away and the music changed again to rock the sky with rhythm and blues.

My next evening off, more than a week later, Vince called. He wanted to go dancing, but the clubs were dead on a Sunday night. Without Pat and Rich, we were pretty dead. It was a dull evening for both of us. As he drove me home, I suggested that he ought to ask Paro out. He didn't say anything for a long time. "*Ebb Tide*," "*Deep Purple,*" old Sunday night standards were coming from the car radio. For once, Vince was serious. He may not have understood exactly what I was telling him, but he had to feel the tightening of the expectations of others around us. His age, his future, his religion, his parents, all were making demands that he settle down with the right girl.

He was looking straight ahead, concentrating on his driving and didn't glance toward me. "Amparo is a cute girl, Andrea. I wouldn't mind going out with her. But please take this idea seriously. Do you think you could consider marrying me?"

"I'm not interested in that. You've always known."

"Things wouldn't have to change between us, Andrea. I'm not some masher. I promise I'd never bother you that way. Here's the thing: we could just be engaged. We wouldn't need to get married until I passed the bar. That's two years away. It would be good. Someday we'd have cute kids. Your mom likes me."

I knew he was kind and respectful. An engagement would please his parents. For four years Vince had put up with my scanty conversation and snippy remarks and never expected anything from me but good humor. But time had run out. 'There's no point," I answered. "You need to find someone to love. It can't be me."

He didn't say anything for a few minutes. "Okay, Drea. I get what you're telling me." He took his right hand off the steering wheel to reach for my hand and squeeze it. "We still friends?"

"Friends always," I said and meant. "But you have to promise to ask my friend Paro out."

"I will." His carefree, cocky smirk came back. "She is really cute, you know."

"Your parents will love her," I replied. They would. The McMullens liked me. I could speak to them and to other adults without stammering now. I was modest and quiet. But Paro had those qualities and added the social poise and beautiful manners I was lacking.

That night I sat up late in the lounge. TV was showing some old movie. Sweet, gracious Paro would never come to harm with Vince. But my life had changed. He was the only man I'd met that I could tolerate, and I'd just given him away.

By mid-August, Beth was in a summer stock performance at a theater in Hollywood. Mama drove out to pick me up. Beth wanted Alex to come, and he was excited to be going to a grown-up event.

After the play, Beth had a date, but Mother took Alex and me out for a dessert. She cooed on and on about how absolutely gorgeous Beth was. And then, Mama proudly told

us that she had come to Southern California in hopes of a movie career. Her aunts convinced her that she was as beautiful as Janet Gaynor. "I was, you know," she said. I just didn't have any luck."

"If you were a movie star, Mom!" Alex squealed from the back seat. "We'd have a three-story house."

"You never told us that before," I said, amazed by this revelation.

"I was beautiful," she murmured.

I looked at her and saw many similarities to my beautiful sister. She probably had been. But then Mama had more to say.

"Lynnie, baby, have you heard of the new corneal lenses? You could give up those ugly, ugly glasses." And then, a few minutes later she said, "You haven't mentioned Vince all summer. I hope you haven't let that opportunity slip through your fingers. You haven't, have you?"

It was a good time to keep quiet. I had willingly opened my fingers and let that opportunity drop away, proud of my decisiveness. Still, I wasn't so dense that I couldn't see buried in the decisiveness the cowardice it really was. Mama couldn't face running a business, and I couldn't face being Vincent McMullen's wife. I was more like her than I wanted to be. Neither of us could face the burdens of opportunity.

~~~<<=>>~~~

Chapter 47: Beth's Tribulations

When I asked Beth if she knew that Mother once aspired to be a movie actress, my sister was astonished. Her eyes widened – then narrowed.

"She told me she and Verna moved here to get better jobs!" Beth gave an analysis of our mother's star potential next. "That was a completely dumb, stupid, impossible idea. Acting takes work, and Mama would never have had the tenacity."

Beth was tenacious. By Labor Day, she'd found an agent. She wasn't old enough to sign a contract yet, but Mama was more than willing to sign for her. In the meantime Beth had already warned Mamie Silver, her boss at the department store, that if a big role came up, or a chance at a movie or TV part, she would have to leave Orbach's. Mamie assured her that the store could work around her schedule. In about a second, Beth could turn herself into any shopper's best friend, daughter, sister, or granddaughter. She could make sales, solve problems and dissolve complaints. She said selling was all acting, so she saw work as improvisational rehearsal.

For a high school graduate who hadn't turned seventeen yet, Beth decided if she couldn't make it as an actress, she was either going to find a rich man to marry or become the manager of the best, most exclusive department in the best, most exclusive department store in the city. There was a scarcity of roles waiting as either a movie star or rich man's wife, but working at I. Magnin might be in her future. It was reputed to be the most elegant store of its kind in the whole United States, maybe the world. I. Magnin was down Wilshire west of Orbach's but it was as shiny as stage lights.

On a brilliantly sunny day in September, when each of us had free time at the same time, Beth and I drove out to Pacific Coast Highway in The Gypsy Wagon. Beth parked and we climbed down the rickety stairs to the beach, leaving our shoes in the jumble beside the bottom step like everyone else did. Children were running around, playing ball and digging sand castles. People were lying in the sun on towels.

As we walked, she told me how things were at home. "Alex can fix his own breakfast now. Steve doesn't have to help him anymore. But, Drea, our mother needs to hire someone professional to keep the house clean. She tries to get by with that dopey Betty coming in to help out. Betty does some ironing and keeps Mama company, but neither of them knows how to do anything. It is getting worse and worse. I hate that Betty. She's small-minded and a bad influence on Mama."

I didn't know Betty at all, so I couldn't comment. Beth stopped walking. "There's something else too. Do you remember how our mother wouldn't let us bring Beverly or Adrian in the house?"

"Children made her too nervous," I replied.

Beth made a face as agreement with the accuracy of my memory. "Well, now her own child makes her too nervous. She locks Alex out, literally. I had a copy of my house key made for him so he can get in to use to the bathroom. She never locked us out. It is miserable there for the boys. She doesn't even want to act like a mother. She won't clean and she cooks so much that she has to throw most of what she prepares away. The refrigerator is a mess and I'm not going to clean it."

We walked along farther along the sand. Beth wasn't quiet, but she was still fumingly angry. I should have kept quiet too. Instead, I opened my mouth. "You ought to try to help her more. She needs you."

Beth exploded. I'd never seen her anger focused on me before. "I'm not going to help her," she shouted at me. "She doesn't have a job to worry about. I do. Steve takes care of himself. All she has to do is keep things in order and pay a little attention to Alex. It's nothing! But she won't. Mamie Silver works all day, goes home, and cooks and cleans for her family. Her blood pressure is sky high. She only takes

Mondays off, and that's the store's easiest day. Mamie is fifty. She's older than Mama." Beth stood at the edge of the water with her hands on her hips.

"Mama's in mourning, Beth, You could be a little sympathetic. She lost her husband."

"Husbands die all the time," my sister said angrily. "She lost her husband? Well, I lost my father. Daddy's not here anymore, so she doesn't think she has to behave." Beth twisted up her face and stared at me. "Besides, you have no right to say anything to me. You didn't move back home to help out when Daddy died." Beth gave me a long, hard look, and tilted her chin up. "You barely stayed home long enough to come to the funeral. You didn't even help pick out the casket or his clothes."

Beth's anger was bristling, charging the air around us with hostility, and I'd become its target. The worst of it was that she was right. I forfeited any right to tell her what she ought to do when I hadn't helped more. I stood there on the beach, not moving, and afraid to look at her. There was nothing I could say. My sister was still sleeping in our old room, but we were both runaways.

"She's cheap too," my sister continued, but the intensity in her voice had lessened, "Daddy paid for my classes for a year. Tuition comes up again the first of January. I have to find the money to pay O'Roark myself." Beth looked ruefully at me.

"Mama isn't giving the boys money for lunch in the school cafeteria anymore. She told them to make sack lunches. She'll probably cut off Alex's tuition and send him to public school. Daddy would never forgive her for what she's doing to us. She has plenty of money."

Beth turned away to watch some seagulls land on a pile of seaweed, squawking. Then turned back to me and put her hands on her hips. "She isn't poor. Verna told me Mama was given a ton of money for the business when she sold it. And you know she has a good rental income from the buildings. Our house is paid for. The mortgage on the business property is a small part of what the tenants give her each month."

Beth paused and took a deep breath, "I hate her for making me pay room and board. My father would never have let her get away with that."

My sister had calmed down a few weeks later when Mama hired a professional cleaning woman. My sister told me that Mama was ultimately exhausted by Betty's ranting complaints about her ungrateful children, her neighbors, President Eisenhower, the *Nigras, Jee-yous* and *Cat-licks*. The crucifixes, holy water dispensers, and plaster saints around the house should have reminded Betty that Mother was one of the *Cat-licks*.

Mama wasn't taking a political stand by firing Betty. Mama just liked things kept cheerful. Her stand was against ranting. She'd listened to enough as a wife; she didn't need to hear it as a widow. According to Beth, the new cleaning woman was a member of St. Blaise parish. She would probably be quiet; and, in the unlikely condition that she was talkative, well, Mama didn't understand Spanish. Whatever she said would just sound like music to Mama.

~~~<<=>>~~~

Chapter 48: St. Lucy's Fund Raising Festival

A huge, first time ever, fundraising Festival was scheduled for the second Sunday in October. I needed my sister. In third, fourth, and fifth grades, the idea of knocking on doors in Breeze Terrace and asking our neighbors for money for the missions terrified me. Mama, knowing I'd stammer with strangers, gave me the mission money. When Beth was in the same grades, she won five tickets to the Meralta Theater's Saturday double feature for her outstanding donation gathering. Beth, Steve, the Claussen girls and I laughed all afternoon at *Francis, The Talking Mule* paired with *Abbott and Costello Meet Frankenstein*. My sister would shine at the Pediatric Research Festival. She would handle smiles, small talk, and sales, areas where I would be totally dismal.

Since I needed her, Beth rearranged her work schedule. Paro complained, with exaggerated pathos and great drama, that it wasn't fair. She didn't have a sister to help her. I dared her to call Vince and assured her that he loved this kind of thing. Paro called him. He responded enthusiastically.

Paro had black hair, tan skin and green eyes. Mrs. Mendoza bought her a teal green Dior copy dress with a crinoline petticoat. Minerva gave Paro a package of the new seamless nylons. Marlene contributed some clip-on earrings that just matched the teal dress. Audrey used her magical talents with make-up. When it was time for us to go out and work the crowd for St. Lucy's Pediatric Research, Paro was truly gorgeous. We were sure Vince would fall madly in love with her.

Beth arrived and was breathless. "You didn't tell me the streets were blocked off! I had to park over on Figueroa and walk miles to get here. Gimme the tickets I'm supposed to sell for you." She took the ticket books and envelope for the receipts. "I can't be late getting back to the store."

She gave me a nod that the dress I was wearing was all right and a frown because my ponytail wasn't, and we were out the door. The streets around the hospital were blocked to vehicular traffic other than ambulances and emergency vehicles. They were jammed with human traffic: people of all ages, strolling musicians, clowns, jugglers, and balloon sellers. We were told that all the big Catholic stars were here and within minutes, we glimpsed Ricardo Montalban, Loretta Young and Gary Cooper. Beth and I turned the corner at the psych annex building and a fluttery woman told us Bing Crosby was on a stage a half block beyond us. In a moment, *Wrap Your Troubles in Dreams* sung live crooned from the p.a. system's speakers up in the palm trees. I cracked wise that the song seemed fitting. Beth didn't get the joke, but then, only nurses who swaddled patients for shock therapy would find it funny; nurses often indulged in bitter humor.

Paro was working in a teddy bear booth. Vince was in his element, wearing a top hat and striped coat he'd dug up from somewhere, pretending to be a carnival barker and coaxing the crowd to Paro's booth. He saw us and waved, calling, "Step right up, folks. Step right this way..."

I would have visited Paro's booth, but Beth was in too much of a hurry to sell all the tickets. Eventually we worked our way close to a beverage and snack pavilion. Beth went on selling. I wanted to get something for her to drink. She'd been working hard for the hospital, and it was nearly time for her to leave. I found the concession line and took a place at the end. It was a warm day and the queue ran just inside the laundry building's shadow. It felt good in the shade though the crowd was still jostling. I wasn't blinded by all the stars I'd seen, radiant though they were. It was the afternoon glare of smog and sun that made me wish my glasses were tinted.

Live fiddle and banjo music sounded pleasantly brittle and not far away. People in the crowd were looking around for its source. I turned too, and found myself stunned breathless. Just beside me, standing on my right, was the slim, solemn, blond man from the night cafeteria. He was with a group of people laughing and talking. I could have reached my hand out of the line of shade into the sun and touch his jacket. I forgot my sister, the crowd, and the music.

I hadn't said a word or moved an eyelash, but the man turned toward me as if I had touched or called him. When he saw me, his face softened. His mouth began to curl upward. Little smile lines around his eyes deepened.

"I've missed you," he said.

It was the first time I heard his voice. I don't know how much time went by. The earth could have moved around its sun for all I knew. Seasons could have passed. I think I smiled at him, but don't remember if I said anything. I was too shy to say, "I've missed you too." But I had missed him. We just stood smiling at each other until the refreshment line pushed me away from him. He stepped forward too, staying parallel and close to me. I think he asked me what shift I was working now. I may have answered.

A tall, black haired man said, "C'mon Dev, we're going over to the stage on Taylor Street. Prez Prado'll be there in ten minutes. Don't want to miss it."

A stocky guy started singing *Cherry Pink and Apple Blossom White.* He was trying to mambo but he was wide and the street crowded. People were laughing at him. My night cafeteria man, Dev, looked at them, at me, and back at the men.

"Go on," he told them. "I'll find you later."

Mambo man draped one arm around the shoulder of his tall buddy and gestured toward me with the other. "Oh, oh. Watch out for jail-bait, Dev. Our buddy's in big trouble now," slurred out of his mouth.

The Prez Prado fan gave me a sympathetic look at the bad manners of his companion and tapped the mambo king on the head. They both grinned knowingly and slid away into the crowd.

"Brian's usually a great guy," the night cafeteria man said, "but he's already had at least five beers, and we've only been here an hour. He says he's drinking for charity."

"Your friends?" I asked.

He nodded. "Paul Tergian works here at the hospital too. He's on days."

We realized I was blocking the line's progress again. He stepped back to make way for me nearer him, and I stepped out into the sun. The refreshment queue kept to the shade behind me. Someone filled my place in its line. We stayed together, the throng milling around us. I think I asked the man called Dev if he was still drinking cafeteria coffee and eating lemon pie at two in the morning. He may have said something about his job or the hospital. But we weren't talking very much. Then the sister I'd totally forgotten about appeared before us, making her dazzling presence known. She was holding a red Coke cup in one hand; the money envelope was clutched in her other. She took a sip from the cup, gave a quick glance at my companion, and thrust the manila envelope at me.

"Take care of this," she said. "I've sold all the tickets in all those books for you. Did you see that old man in the grey cap? I was out of tickets. He handed me a hundred dollar bill anyway." She looked flirtatiously at the man beside me. "I know you're not a stranger. Drea doesn't talk to strangers. She's afraid of her shadow and very afraid of strangers." Beth batted her eyelashes in mock coyness and gave him a wide smile. "My sister hardly talks to friends."

"You're sisters?" He must have thought she was teasing him.

"Well, of course. Can't you tell?" Beth took off her sunglasses and stood on tiptoes to get her face closer to mine. I bent closer to her. Our facial differences were as evident as our differences in height, build, and coloring. "We *are* sisters. Our mother is the same. My sister's father was Scotch or Irish or something. We don't know what he was, but he had that kind of name." Beth was giving him more of our family history than could possibly interest him, or please me.

"My father was *Hungaaarrrian, darlink*," she continued, imitating the TV personality Zsa Zsa Gabor's accent and style. She slowly looked him over, as if she were ticking off his plusses and minuses. When she was satisfied, she tilted her head back, raised an eyebrow and, in the tone of an inquisitor, demanded, "How do you know my sister?"

Before he could answer, I said, "He works here."

"Ahhhh. What kind of doctor are you?" Not giving him time to answer, she kept on. "Maybe you are only an intern. No, you don't look that young. Maybe you're a resident. You'd need to get into a specialty. Surgery would be good, but not general surgery, that's tonsils and appendectomies, old people's toenails. Won't make money there. What would be good? Orthopedic surgery. Good money there. No, forget that. There are all those car wrecks. You'd have to work nights and weekends. You need to find a specialty where you can choose your hours and make money." Beth could not be stopped.

"Oh, psychiatry! That's it. Sit at your desk and listen to people all day. It might be interesting..." Finally she asked him what his name was and stopped talking long enough to wait for his answer.

The crinkles around his eyes showed that he'd enjoyed Beth's expansive monologue, he answered the two sensible questions she'd asked. "I work in the accounting office, and my name is Dev Cunningham."

"Then," she pulled the corners of her mouth down to make a tragi-mask. "You aren't rich." But she was getting Dev to smile. "Rich would be a whole lot better. Oh, I know bookkeepers get to count money, but they don't get to keep it. Doctors and lawyers get to keep it." She stepped forward, reached up, and tapped his chin with her forefinger, and asked him another question. "What's Dev short for? Devil? You must be a devil to get my sister's attention."

Oblivious to the inside joke between my sister and me, he answered, "No, it's short for Devon."

"That's a County in England. How did you get a name like that?" Beth didn't wait for an answer. She handed me her empty cup, signaling that she was leaving. "He's a cute guy, Andrea. Too bad he isn't rich. Now, put your name on the envelope so when you turn it in, you'll get credit."

We watched her blond head bob away in the throng of people.

~~~<<=>>~~~

Chapter 49: Not Jailbait

Devon Cunningham said, "She's right. I'm not rich." He gave a dejected shake of his head and a regretful smile, saying, "And I'm much too old to be chasing student nurses."

We stood looking at each other. He didn't move away. I turned my head slightly to watch the crowd. He did too. Our shoulders were almost touching. I glanced at him and turned shy. Looking down, I said, "You're not chasing me. We're just standing here."

The quiet, sober look I'd loved during hospital nights last winter and spring came back to his face. He seemed a little sad and didn't smile. He reached into his shirt pocket and pulled out his fountain pen. "Here," he said. "Your sister is right. Put your name on the envelope and get credit for the money."

I refused the offered pen. "No. I won't take credit when I didn't do the work." He didn't argue with me, although there was a logical argument he could have made. After all, I did get my sister to donate her fundraising skills. Instead, he looked at me with a half-smile lightly creasing his face. He put his pen away, but he didn't move away.

After a few minutes, I asked, "How old are you?"

"Twenty-six," he replied.

He stayed with me until I needed to get ready for my shift, and then he walked me back to the residence. Before I opened the door, I spun around to face him. "Twenty-six isn't old," I said.

"How old are you?" he asked.

"Not jail-bait."

"How old?" he insisted.

"I'll be twenty in less than four months."

A line deepened between his eyebrows, and his mouth tightened. He didn't say anything. He just looked at me. People in the street were getting noisy as the crowds grew. I didn't want to leave him but couldn't loiter. My time was up. I went inside to turn in the money envelope, shower and change. I didn't know if I'd see him again, but I made a wish that I would. Nineteen wasn't so young. One of my two oldest friends was married, and the other had already died. I felt far from childhood.

In a clean, starched uniform with a cap on my head and a knot twisted up and pinned where my ponytail had been, I stepped out of the building. The mass of people was thick and active, but I looked to the left and Dev Cunningham was there, waiting by an iron fence at the sidewalk not far from the residence porch. The crowd disappeared. He was all I saw. Dev looked up. He didn't smile. His handsome face was reflective, ruminative, as serious as he had seemed in the night cafeteria.

As it closed behind me, the heavy residence door made a thud and its latch clacked. Dev straightened, and came to me. Together, without either of us speaking, we made our way through the mob in the street. He watched out for me through the swirl of bodies, using his arm to hold back anyone who might accidentally step into me or muss my uniform.

When we reached the hospital staff entrance, I looked back. The crowd was still surging here near the hospital, and Mariachi trumpets were blasting from somewhere not far away. An accordion was playing too. The festival would keep going until the end of night visiting hours. Pediatric research would benefit well from this day.

The musicians were still playing and clowns and jugglers dotted the crowds in the street. No one seemed tired, and the throngs, which should have been diminishing, were still dense. I could smell barbeque and chili and remembered that long plank tables had been set up between the laundry and the psychiatric building. Celebrities had volunteered to cook and serve.

As Dev reached to open the hospital's heavy glass door for me, I said, "You'll never find your friends in this crowd."

"I found you in this crowd," he replied. His voice wasn't jocular, presumptuous, or cocky. It wasn't ingratiating or condescending. It was simply making a statement.

What I had known, this calm, quiet man also knew, sometimes the obvious needs to be said. Slipping into the hospital, to the elevator and to my work, I felt that all the quiet, calm space that surrounded him was surrounding me and would go on surrounding me. He hadn't touched me, and I hadn't touched him, but things were settled between us.

~~~<<=>>~~~

Chapter 50: The Importance of a Name

The weekend following St. Lucy's Fundraising Festival, Beth called. "I've changed my name. You changed yours when you were my age, so I thought I better do it too."

It turned out that Mr. Raudell of the famed Wallace Raudell Talent Agency New York & Los Angeles had insisted that she drop Beth Horvath for a more marketable professional name.

"Don'cha geddit?" he explained. "Beth Horveth rhymes."

My sister pointed out that he was mispronouncing his vowels. Beth and Horvath didn't rhyme, and she didn't want to change her name. Mr. Raudell didn't listen.

"Horveth? What kind a hunkie-polack name is that?" he growled at her. "The first part says whore! Geddit? Then it ends in a goddam t h. Come on. You're a kid just starting in this business. Get a good name, something real American, or find yourself a different agency. No rhymes. No fuckin' rhymin' name is going to go oudda my agency! I don't handle Paula Perky bimbos, cutesy chicks who come and go. My clients godda' have long term potential."

My sister gave in. She decided on Beth Benton. It was alliterative like Paula Perky, but it didn't rhyme. That was enough compromise. She told me she made him laugh, and the great agent Wallace Raudell invited her to call him Wally.

"I like him," my sister laughed. "He's funny."

"What do you mean you like him? You're not going out with him are you?"

"No, I just like him. But I'd go out with him if he asked."

"Beth, he sounds horrible and uncouth. He has to be way too old for you."

My sister gave me the strangest look. She threw up her hands in mock disgust.

"He's not uncouth. You just think that because you've been locked up in St. Lucy's nunnery for so long. In the industry, everyone talks like that. Especially people from the east coast. Wally is kind of old. I think he is in his fifties. But I don't mind."

"Beth! You can't be serious!"

"What do you mean I can't? *You* can't be serious. You like that guy from the festival. He's good looking, but Vince was better and he'll be a lawyer, not just an accountant. I told Mama I thought you were very dumb to break up with a rich guy like Vince and make goo goo eyes at someone who was only a bookkeeper."

"What did she say?"

"She said you were her daughter, and you'd come to your senses."

It was time to change the subject. Beth never quite believed how uninvolved Vince and I had always been and always would be, and I wasn't ready to tell anyone, not even her, how involved things had become in just a few days between my bookkeeper and me.

The first night after the festival as I had come off duty at eleven o'clock, Devon Cunningham was waiting for me. He looked at me, and I knew that he loved me.

"What do you most need to know about me?" he asked.

"Everything. I want to know everything, but I don't want you to be late to work."

Dev assured me that he was clear to start his shift a few minutes late. There were things I needed to know, and I pestered him with questions. He had been born and raised in Bishop, a town on the east side of the Sierra.

His father worked for the forest service, his mother was a housewife. He had a married sister, Nancy Poteet, and she with her family lived in the high desert country too. He'd never been married, but had come close, once when he was nineteen and once when he was twenty-three. The first time, his girlfriend had initiated the break-up. The second time, he did.

We met again the next night during the shift change, and I learned more. After the navy, Dev didn't go back to Bishop. He was eligible for the G.I. Bill and wanted to get a degree. He found the night accounts job at St. Lucy's. It allowed him to take day classes. He'd have his Bachelor of Science degree in Commerce at the end of the semester in January from U.S.C.

Philosophically, he was a deist, and he was surprised I knew what that was. He told me his mother had Indian beliefs of her own. She had been born on a Paiute reservation east of the Sierra. His father was a free thinker of Scots-Irish descent. His parents met in high school and still loved each other.

He liked animals, music of all kinds, history and football. He didn't like living in the city, and was only staying in Los Angeles long enough to complete his degree. He left me to go to work. I went to the residence to shower and sleep, hoping I'd meet his family someday and see the country on the east side of the Sierra.

I did an extra half-shift on Thursday night, but I left a note for him on my break. The next morning, before breakfast, I went to meet him. He was on his way to get something to eat and to the university for his first class. I invited myself to walk him to his car, confident that he was happy I was there.

"It's your turn," I said, as we walked along the path to the staff parking area. "Ask me any questions you want. I'll answer truthfully."

"Are you always truthful?"

"Pretty much. I don't like lies so I don't tell them."

He stopped by one of the cedar trees and grinned at me. "I don't need to ask you anything. I know all about you."

"You don't know anything about me, except that I have a sister and she's Hungarian. You've never even asked my name."

"I already knew your name, foolish child. You wear a name tag." His smile grew wider and the crinkles around his eyes drawn deeper. "I noticed the name Andrea Frazier on your tag last spring. I'd heard a story about a shy but brave student nurse with that name who stood up to an infamous doctor.

She won the affection of the entire nursing staff and all the women of the clerical staff. There couldn't be two of you."

Instead of saying anything back, I made a face at him. I wished he hadn't heard that old story. It embarrassed me. We crossed the asphalt to his car. He opened the door, slid his briefcase across the seat, and twisted around to look at me.

"Then, after that, one dark cafeteria night," he said, in his perfect, steady voice, "That same student nurse suddenly fell into my arms."

"I didn't fall into your arms. You pulled me to safety."

"Am I going to have to pull you to safety every time I want you in my arms?"

"Maybe."

He held his arms out.

It was a bolder move than I'd ever made, but the morning was chilly and damp. It was reason enough for me to step into his arms. Nuzzling up, intoxicating myself with his warm smell, I was happier than I'd ever remembered being.

But he'd told me about himself, and there were some things I needed to tell him. "I'm fierce," I whispered.

"I know," he said. He kissed my forehead before he turned to get in the car.

"Things that are easy for others are hard for me. I don't learn easily and my best friend thinks I'm weird. I stammer when I get nervous. I might embarrass you."

"You won't embarrass me. My family and I might embarrass you."

"They won't."

"My dad only went as far as eighth grade."

"And you'll be a university graduate in three months." Before Christmas, Beth Benton was in a TV commercial. She still wanted the movies, but TV was good enough for the present and the pay was good. Beth played the pretty friend of a satisfied customer driving out of Beverly Chrysler and Cadillac. She was directed to wave and smile. The next commercial she appeared in gave her a line, and by mid-spring, she had made three TV commercials credits. She was still Beth Horvath working at Orbach's, and she loved it when customers told her she looked familiar. She smiled mysteriously at them, and gave no clues.

My sister Beth mentioned her many dates, but she talked about Wally more and more. She denied that they were involved. I didn't believe her. And, with a barbed and disapproving, dueña tone, I asked her if Wally were married.

"Of course. Well, I assume he is. He has children older than me. One son runs the New York branch of his agency."

I nodded, with the confidential look and pursed little smile that we both used when we meant we understood and loved each other, and would keep trust in the things each other chose.

~~~<<=>>~~~

Chapter 51: A Rose Garden Party

February came. Anniversaries triggered memories whether or not one looked at the calendar. I told Dev how Jeannie's death affected me and why it had. But I kept my promise to the McCauleys and said nothing about Delores. He seemed to understand that if I were less cheery that month, it had nothing to do with him, or us. My bookkeeper found a way to coordinate our schedules so we could get away for two and a half days mid-week after Valentine's Day. We drove northeast to Bishop so I could meet his family. I was comfortable with his mother and sister, and his father kept busy and didn't intrude. Nancy's husband and children were easy to be around.

The mountains were beautiful. One clean desert morning, Dev's parents took us for a winter picnic, stopping for a snowball toss and hot roadhouse coffee across the state line in Nevada, before heading back. It was the first time I'd been out of California.

As the days moved into spring, my class looked forward to graduation. The ceremony would be held on June thirteenth at St. John of God College. We weren't looking forward to taking our nursing boards in July. We were worried, anxious and busy studying.

In May we each had a final interview to discuss our clinical work. I spent nights waking frequently, tormented by my deficiencies. Wild imaginings magnified any flaw I might have shown. It was one thing to pass tests, but very different to do well in the hospital. I brooded on that odious black mark on my record from my first year. What Dev saw as noble, to other eyes might appear troublemaking. By the time I was called for the interview, I was shaking.

Sister Florian Catherine praised me for my ability to focus and pay attention to detail. She said that I had the judgment necessary to care for the most critically ill and severely injured patients, and she complimented me on showing initiative. I began to breathe slower and easier. Then it became time to discuss my weaknesses.

"You finally learned to take control of your patients. I almost gave up hope, but you did learn. But Andrea, it took you two years before you could bring yourself to correct an aide or even an orderly. You would repair their mistakes yourself before you'd ask a subordinate to correct his or her own errors. You have never shown one iota of what this hospital considers leadership. Don't consider work as a nursing supervisor. You aren't suited to it in spite of the degree you earned.

"My advice is that you be satisfied doing God's work as a floor nurse. Floor nurses are the solid foundation of a good hospital." Sister Florian Catherine shook my hand and said what I most wanted to hear. "I sincerely hope you will apply to our hospital here, Andrea. St. Lucy's Hospital appreciates competence and would appreciate you." Sister smiled with amused tolerance. "But, just between us, it is a shame that someone with so much competence displays so little confidence."

Sister never alluded to the incident with Dr. Murray. As I left her office, my dense mind finally figured out what everyone else knew. The nuns who ran St. Lucy's Hospital didn't like Dr. Murray any more than its nurses did. It was my great good fortune to train in a hospital run by women.

At graduation, Paro and I took academic honors, but neither of us received one of the significant hospital awards. Peggy Foley received the Student Nurse of Distinction Award, and Audrey Chester won the Class of 1957 Leadership Award that she well deserved. During our training, the other girls tagged Paro and me as grinds, reminding us that nurses weren't paid more for having earned As than for having earned Cs. Yet, I was vainly, sinfully, proud of the gold tassels that swung from our caps. I knew my friend Paro was sinfully proud too.

Adrian, Jack, Debbie and baby Johnny couldn't be there. Beverly was graduating from high school the same day. Pat and Rich were living in Stuttgart, Germany with Richard Whitfield, Jr., their new baby boy. Pat was still grieving for her dad who had died during the winter, but she sent a memento. Dev was there with my family, including Verna who brought frail eighty-year-old Aunt CeCe in a wheelchair. I counted Paro, her parents and Vince as my family too, as she did mine.

My mind drifted during the interminable prayers and speeches. I thought of Laz and my mother. Then my mind slipped away to Delores, to the nuns who had quietly helped me, to other women I'd known:, Louise Claussen, Vivian Morgan, Mrs. McCauley, Mrs. O'Hara. Most of all, I found myself remembering Jeannie. I didn't let myself think of her sad death. I chose to remember her letting Beth and Stevie clomp around in her high heels, helping Stevie read the cards he drew during Monopoly, and giving me a precious hope my life would be better someday. When the name Andrea Lynn Frazier was called, I crossed the stage to get my diploma imagining that Jeannie French's lively spirit was there walking with me.

A reception was held in the college rose garden after the ceremony. Mama took the diploma folder out of my hands, and Beth gave me a vibrant summer bouquet with long white ribbons streaming down. California sycamores dappled light shade; the roses were fragrant. Fountains were trickling, lawns deep green. Clusters of black robed graduates stood with their guests, as I stood with mine. While flash bulbs popped, bursts of laughter would come from one of the groups and cascade into the air adding to the music of the fountains. I handed Beth back the bouquet and lifted a narrow chain from around my neck.

Just as Mary Eunice Cantwell had done, I'd secreted my wedding ring down between my breasts for months. But, the beauty of the rose garden and the happiness of the people around us overwhelmed Dev and me. I unhooked the chain, slipped the ring from it, and gave the ring to Dev. Looking at my husband, the ring still warm from my body clasped in his hand, I had a fantasy that the gold band split and grew into sparkling threads that spun out and shimmered around us, separating this golden haired man and me from the rest of the universe. The image lasted for only a second or two. There was grass beneath our feet. We were at St. John of God College. It was my graduation day. And, the time had come to make our marriage known.

Dev removed my glasses and slipped them into his coat pocket. As slowly and sweetly as he had done every private thing between us, he put the ring on my finger and kissed me.

My brothers caught on first and Steve began clapping. In his charcoal jacket, grey pants and his second best tie, Dev was a gloriously handsome groom. Unfortunately, the black academic robe I was wearing was a sorry substitute for a wedding dress. My mortarboard was not exactly a veil. But, Beth thrust the bouquet back into my arms. She took off her gaudy pearl cluster earrings and put them on me. Paro, watching, broke off a rosebud from one of the bushes near us and stuck it in Dev's lapel.

Vince grabbed his camera and ordered Dev to give me another kiss. A rain of multicolored petals stripped from the college rosebushes came down on us, and I turned to see Alex tossing them. They caught like confetti in our hair and on our shoulders. My little brother was bent upon destroying the college garden, but there must have been three hundred rosebushes. Its destruction would take more than one jolly little boy. Steve, nearly fifteen, and at six foot four as tall as his Uncle Sandy had been, was smiling down on us like some benign saint. It was the first time I'd seen him happy since his father died. With rose petals still falling, it was a moment from a great romantic movie. Paro's father was both smiling and weeping big tears. He moved closer to Mrs. Mendoza and put his arm around her.

Mama hugged me for the first time since I was about two years old. She took Dev's hand, trilling out in her pretty voice, "I'd have given you the loveliest wedding."

My sister winked at me. No matter what she was saying now, Mama in her frugal widow-woman mode would never have spent money on anything so frivolous as a wedding.

Beth examined my ring. "No diamond!" she exclaimed. "No engagement ring?" She turned to face Paro's and my combined group of friends. Beth knew how to work the crowd. She spread the fingers of her left hand, fanned them out in front of her, and announced, "Before I ged marriedt, Darlinks, I veel haf a beeg, beeg diamondt."

My sister swung her hips, looked seductively at her audience, and then segued to Paro. She lifted Paro's left hand so everyone could see the full-carat square cut diamond on my friend's finger. The clapping began all over again. We paraded to the to the refreshment tables where our exuberance turned punch into champagne and cookies into wedding cake.

Dev and I had been married since our trip to Bishop in February. Sarah and Everett Cunningham stood up with us in a Nevada courthouse. And, in spite of meticulously careful use of Dr. Howard's prescribed diaphragm and anti-spermicidal vaginal ointment, I was two months pregnant.

With luck, I could work for three or four months more before St. Lucy's policy forced me to take leave. Dev would continue working at St. Lucy's until he found the job he wanted. When he did, I was willing to give up everything I'd known, and everyone I loved, to go where he wanted.

I'd discovered to my embarrassment and to my delight, that I was as sluttish as any blowsy camp follower. If Devon Cunningham chose to go off to the Sahara Desert, I would happily trudge along behind him, pack on my back, baby in my belly, and up to my knees in sand.

~~~<<=>>~~~

Chapter 52: Honeymoon Summer

After graduation, Dev and his friends helped me move out of the residence and into my husband's small studio apartment near the hospital. We hadn't had a traditional honeymoon, but that was all right. We hadn't had a traditional wedding either. I wasn't going to tell anyone I was pregnant. They'd find out when it became obvious.

As a wedding present, Beth brought little things to glamorize the apartment: a nicer shower curtain, some colorful dishtowels, throw pillows as bright as those in The Gypsy Wagon. She had a discount at Orbachs and now and then picked up a pretty blouse for me. Mama bought us sheets and towels; Sarah and Everett, my in-laws, bought us a set of dishes and pots and pans.

Dev was still working nights and I began work as a floor nurse in the hospital the day after graduation. I wouldn't receive registered nurses' pay until I'd passed certification in July and I was still spending time studying. Our schedules didn't always match, but we had time to tell each other all our secrets and make the unspoken promises that bound us to each other more than a marriage ceremony could. I learned about the women who had come before me in his life, and all that he endured growing up poor during hard years when his parents had struggled. I told him of the extravagant joys and some piteous shames in my life. Every word we spoke to each other, we never forgot.

"You need to know something important," I confessed one afternoon after my shift, as I took my uniform off and hung it up. It had been a particularly trying day. I'd been assigned to orthopedics, and work with Dr. Roston Murray. Dev was lying on the bed. We'd have supper together before he left for the hospital. But first, rankled by a rude doctor, I needed to talk to my husband.

"You need to understand how much I don't like men."

"You hide that attitude well." He grinned and lifted an eyebrow, beckoning me to the bed.

"This is serious. I'm trying to tell you something, and it's hard. I've never liked being around men. I hate being alone with them or working for them. Remember when I told you I was fierce?"

"I remember."

"Well, I am. It isn't so good to be the way I am. That fierceness made me enjoy hurting Dr. Murray. I liked it so much I wish I could stomp on his foot again. I'd do it harder and meaner. I want the men who molest or bully and hurt women to be shot dead. I might enjoy shooting them myself."

He was watching and his expression had changed. He was paying careful attention to what I was saying.

"Dev, you think I'm quiet and shy. Your mom and dad think I'm a sweet, nice girl and they are happy you picked me. But that's just how I act. I'm not a nice person at all inside. My mother knows. She says I'm a witch. I know she is superstitious and silly, but sometimes I worry she's right."

I slipped out of my shoes and stockings. He hadn't said anything, but was somberly watching me.

"The thing is, Dev, *you're* a man. I don't want to be any danger to you. I don't ever want to hurt you. I'm afraid that someday I could."

"I'll never do anything to make you want to hurt me," he said.

It was said so simply and honestly that I nodded at him, knowing that though we had said few words, he understood. Something had passed between us that I would never forget. It was something that would last forever in my memory, but it didn't last long in actual time.

Dev grinned, gave me a lecherous look, and said, "Come here witch woman. Take the rest of your clothes off. Your glasses too."

I took my things off but danced farther away, then stopped to stare back at him. "I'm fierce and I'm also selfish. There is one thing you must promise. Promise me no other witch will ever ride that broom of yours."

"That's an easy promise to give. Dev Cunningham isn't a man to take risks. Come here."

I came. I never had trouble coming to any of his invitations.

In early July, my class took the state nursing board exams. Candidates from all the hospital schools in Southern California were bussed and billeted for the two days of testing. Proctors walked up and down the rows of tables where we were tested and monitored the hallways and restrooms. Sister Florian Catherine had given us confidence as we got on the bus by telling us that if we weren't going to pass with top scores, St. Lucy's would have washed us out long ago. All of us did well.

That summer, Pat and Rich called from Stuttgart. I'd sent Pat the apartment phone number for emergencies, and this was an emergency. Rich was very worried about his brother, but the army wouldn't give him leave. He knew I barely had my R.N., but he wanted me to visit his parents to assess Tommy Whitfield's behavior and make suggestions that might help the family. So, on a warm morning in the late summer, I drove out to their family home in Baldwin Hills. At night, twisting strings of light threading out from the city into passes and canyons would look like a jeweled necklace from the hills, but by day the mountains across the city seemed one curving, jagged and impenetrable, blue wall. As I walked toward the house, a curtain in a window of the house next door moved. No one was mowing a lawn. No children were riding bikes.

Tommy was standing on the Whitfield's porch, ringing the doorbell over and over, his flat and uninflected voice repeating without stop, "The communists are coming. The communists are coming..."

"Hello, Tommy," I said, interrupting him. "It's nice to see you again. I'm Andrea Frazier, Rich's friend. I've come to see your mother."

My words halted the manic doorbell ringing. Tommy Whitfield, thin and glassy-eyed, mumbled about Jesus and devil communists and backed away from me. He went down the side steps from the porch and disappeared down the driveway. I waited a moment and knocked at the door.

Inside the house all was quiet. With a forced but still graceful politeness, Mrs. Whitfield brought me a glass of iced tea. She then sat beside me and told me Pat had written her that I'd been married. She offered her congratulations and said how much she and her husband thanked God for bringing Pat into Rich's life. Only then, released from the convention of manners, would the haggard woman tell me about the family's troubles with their son.

"He stopped going to class. A friend of ours found Tommy a job, but he couldn't keep it. He makes no sense and doesn't understand what we say. Our doctor made a referral to a psychiatrist, but Father Warren told us to pray and give God a chance to answer our prayers. Father felt that a psychiatrist would confuse Tommy and make him doubt the faith. He said God would never send us what we couldn't endure with His grace. Father persuaded us to give God time. We are good Catholics, Andrea. We've prayed for so long, but Tommy doesn't get better. We don't know what to do."

Mrs. Whitfield found her handkerchief tucked into the sleeve of her sweater. Her voice breaking, she finished her description of the family's distress, saying, "No friends stop by after church anymore. I can't leave the house even shop for groceries until my husband gets home from work. The neighbors avoid us." She huddled down in her chair. "I don't blame them. Tommy scares them. He scares me too. But Father Warren is a wise man. I don't want to go against his counsel."

Remembering the isolation we'd felt in Breeze Terrace because of Laz, I reached out for her hand. With as few words as possible, I reminded her that St. Lucy's was a Catholic hospital, and I could assure her that though not all St. Lucy's physicians were Catholics, they were all respectful of their patients' personal beliefs. I gave her a list of doctors on staff.

Pat wrote a month later to thank me. She was afraid she was pregnant again, but Rich was relaxed now that he knew his brother was in treatment. The senior Whitfields had chosen Dr. Margolin from St. Lucy's psychiatric staff. He diagnosed Tommy's disorder as classic schizophrenia, even to the age of onset for Tommy's symptoms.

The diagnosis saddened, but didn't surprise me. Pat and Rich wouldn't want fairytales. So as I was writing back, I told her that they should only expect care, not a miracle cure. Schizophrenia was a serious disorder and Tommy's prognosis not hopeful.

Dev came behind me and leaned down to put his arms around me as I finished the letter. I read the letter Pat had sent me, and my answering letter, aloud to him. He didn't know Rich or Pat yet. Someday, when they were back stateside, he would get to know them. Dev's friend Paul and his girlfriend Tricia were good friends now to both of us, though I still wasn't comfortable with Brian, the mambo man. Dev liked Adrian and Jack. And, of course, he knew Vince and Paro well by this time. Paro was working at St. Lucy's too, and Vince was always around.

"They are certainly opposites," Dev said of Vince and Paro after we'd gone to the Beverly Caverns with them and listened to Teddy Buckner and his All Stars. "Amparo is so quiet and proper. Vince is so lively.

"Beth would seem more his type. Paro said tonight that you introduced her to Vince. I'm surprised you didn't try to fix him up with your sister."

"Beth would have given Vince far more competition than he could ever handle," I replied.

~~~<<=>>~~~

Chapter 53: Cousin Verna Talks

In mid-summer our great aunt CeCe died. We hadn't seen much of her or Verna during the years Laz was disturbed. Cecelia Bradley Beauchet's ashes were scattered to the wind. Our great aunt had been raised a Baptist along with our grandfather, but while Grandpa continued to be a Baptist until his death, somewhere during her life our great aunt became a Theosophist. Consequently, she didn't think that her old body needed any special resting place or funeral since she'd be moving into a new body and just continue on. This made it easy for Verna. Verna sold the house in Pasadena, retired from her job, and purchased a cottage on a mountaintop in Maui, Hawaii.

On the first of August, she called Beth to tell her there were a few items she thought Beth and I might want from the house before she shipped her belongings. Beth was insistent we do this. She picked me up and we drove to Pasadena.

The Hawaii bound Verna threw away her usual caustic humor and replaced it with effusive hyperbole. "Oh, the balmy ocean breezes! The smell of pikake in the air! I want you both to come and stay with me on Maui. From my veranda you can see the blue ocean on opposite sides of the island. There will always be room for the two of you."

I noticed that she didn't mention Dev. It didn't surprise me. Actually, it surprised me that she invited me. My sister picked up on a more significant omission.

"You'd want us to bring Mama with us, wouldn't you?" Beth coyly asked.

The question brought the instant and expected reaction. "Don't you girls dare bring Marianne. Don't you dare! I love your mother more than anyone else in my life. You know I do. But I don't want her staying in my house."

Imitating Mama's high sweet voice was difficult after years of cigarettes, but Verna tried her best. "'Would you get me a cup of coffee, Verna? I hate to bother you, but I'd really like one of those cookies from the kitchen too. You wouldn't mind getting me one, would you? Oh, Verna, are you going to run a wash? If you are, would you run my laundry too? Verna, if you're going into the guest room, would you bring my purse with you when you come back?'" Then, in her own, very sarcastic voice: "Well, Marianne, I wasn't going in the guest room, but I'll go and fetch it for you."

Verna took a deep breath and then her eyes got a merry twinkle. "I promise you two that I'll fly back to see your mother at least twice a year. I'm not abandoning her. She's my closest relative in the world, and I love her more than anyone else I know. But if the hostess burden is on her, it won't be on me.

"Enough of this, you both understand. The sunroom is full of junk I don't want. Take whatever you like. The rest goes on the Salvation Army truck."

Beth put dibs on a jewelry box filled with cameos, beads and glittery pins. I sorted out some photos, an old patchwork quilt, things I knew my sister didn't want. Beth found shawls and fans from the early part of the century and a marble bust of Shakespeare. I took the old, worn Bradley Family Bible. I liked its shabbiness, and I'd soon be able to add a Frazier-Cunningham name to the entries of Bradley family descendants it held.

The three of us lugged the items out to the back seat of the Gypsy Wagon, and then we sat on the front porch steps in the shade to drink some iced tea. I felt a deep sorrow that I'd never be here again. But I didn't want nostalgia today and squelched any thoughts of Aunt CeCe, her kindly manner, and her home on this shady street of old homes where I'd stayed as a tiny girl before Beth was even born.

"Verna, maybe you'll get married again," my sister said.

"Not me! I'm too old for that sort of foolishness."

"You might find a handsome gray haired hula guy on Maui," I teased.

Beth rushed into the opening. "How many times have you been married?"

Verna raised her eyebrows at Beth's impudence. "Not as many as your mother."

"Mama was married twice, but we thought you'd been married more," I said.

"No, get this straight. I was the one who married twice. Marianne doubled my record. She's been married four times. She tells you girls what she wants to be the truth, not what is."

Beth and I stared in disbelief, as Verna continued. "Your mother ran off and married a college boy, Bobby something. It was annulled, of course. She was only fifteen. She married Jim Claiborne here in Los Angeles. Jimmy was a lot of fun." She rolled her eyes lasciviously and lit another cigarette. "Your mother didn't want him spending his money on that casino ship out of Long Beach Harbor. She divorced him. She got a nice alimony. Lynnie, your mother and Drew Frazier were perfect for each other when he came into her life." She paused long enough swallow a drink of the tea. "Drew loved her dimples and that sweet way of hers. He had a good career, a nice home, and his first wife was dead. He was lonely. Marianne was just what he needed.

"After his funeral, Marianne was lost. She wouldn't stay with mother and me. She wouldn't go to your grandfather. She just sat with you on her lap in that house waiting for some miracle to bring Drew back. Mother and I drove all the way there on weekends to make sure she had groceries. Mother worried so about you. You were a terrible baby. You screamed and squalled all the time."

Verna looked at Beth. "Then, Beth, your father came into the picture. He knew just what to do for her. Lazlo Horvath knew them from the neighborhood. Laz would drop in on your mother every evening to make sure she was all right. He took her flowers and candy, the newspaper, little presents for you, Lynn. And, you girls may not want to hear this, but it is true.

Marianne couldn't live without a man. She was in Laz Horvath's bed before Drew had been dead six months."

I was angry. Mother was a widow now, and she wasn't out chasing men. Just the opposite, we wished she'd find someone, and she wasn't interested. Verna had been snide. It didn't seem to bother Beth. She and Verna usually saw things the same way.

"Your mother was so helpless she wouldn't leave the house to buy baby food. Lazlo left that poor wife of his running the liquor store," Verna continued, "while he went out running errands and taking care of your mother."

"Daddy had a wife? Mama was *the other woman?*" Beth demanded an answer. I was too stunned to say anything. This wasn't right. The *other woman* was supposed to be a dark haired, sinister home wrecker, not a soft voiced, pretty woman like our mother.

"Yes," Verna slowly said. "But you girls have to understand. Your father was head over heels about Marianne, Beth. She was so young and beautiful. Men fell for her, and she looked just like a Madonna with Lynn in her arms. Ilona Horvath might have been an attractive woman once, but she'd lost her bloom. Ilona wouldn't divorce him, so Laz forced the issue by moving your mother and Lynn into the apartment right above them on Venice Boulevard. Oh, it got very ugly for a time. Ilona threatened to kill your mother."

Verna reached over and grabbed my hand in her bony one. "Lynn, Marianne took you up to the ranch to stay with your grandfather. I had a good job I couldn't afford to lose. My mother had just had surgery. We couldn't manage you. You weren't screaming so much by then, but you walked early and were darting around getting into everything. No one could keep you still. Sandor and Roszika were still in Europe. Your grandfather just turned you loose with the dirt and the chickens and the two of you got along fine."

Beth looked horrified, but now Verna couldn't stop. "Flaunting your mother in that poor woman's face finally drove Ilona back to Hungary. Once she was out of the country, Laz could claim desertion and finally get a divorce. It took a while. When it was final, Mother and I kept you right here in his house while Laz took your mother to Yuma to get married. I swear you didn't cry once the whole time they were gone. You were quiet as a mouse."

We were tired as we drove home. We were still absorbing the drama of our family history. Beth didn't even turn the car radio on. I thought about Ilona Horvath. We both lived on the outside edge of Mama's life. I wondered what happened to the woman Laz and my mother drove away. It was chaotic in Eastern Europe before the war. Did Ilona survive Hitler? Did she come back to America? The yellow Capri skimmed through the Arroyo Seco, toward Los Angeles and the apartment where Dev and I lived. My sister broke into my somber considerations to say, "If Verna would only move to Park La Brea Towers instead of stupid old Hawaii, I'd be able to move in with her. My life would be perfect."

"Your life will still be perfect. You'll be able to go to Hawaii to see her."

"That'll be fun. She invited you too. We'll drink Mai Tais and sit under palm trees."

"Nope. You're her favorite, not me. You notice she didn't invite Dev, and she knows I'd never go without him."

Beth nodded. A few quiet minutes went by. We were still absorbing the history Verna had shared with us.

"I'm going to have a baby in late December or early January," I said.

Beth didn't say anything, but she took her hand off the steering wheel long enough to give me a tap. She and Mother had already figured it out and were just waiting for me to make the announcement.

"My baby will probably be a terrible baby. It'll scream and squall all the time."

We got the giggles. Beth had to suppress hers for our safety because she was driving. So I worked at suppressing mine too. I turned around and leaned over the back of the passenger seat until I could pry the jewelry box open. Grabbing some strings of amber and onyx beads, and a Chinese-y carnelian necklace, I turned forward again to decorate the rear view mirror. Beads hung down to the dashboard. A vermeil heart glittered along the strand. The Gypsy Wagon was festooned magnificently. My sister smiled.

Beth didn't say very much as she drove me home to my husband. She looked distant, as though she were dreaming. I knew she wasn't dreaming; she was carefully organizing the details of her first trip to Hawaii.

~~~<<=>>~~~

Chapter 54: Settling In

Dev became the payroll supervisor for a consortium of three small community hospitals in the San Joaquin Valley, and we moved about two hundred miles north of Los Angeles. He would have preferred the eastern side of the Sierra, but the small population in the high desert limited opportunities in his occupation. With the baby coming, it never occurred to either of us, to our families or to our friends, that I'd become anything other than a wife and mother. We'd left the city to become country people. Dev's salary was less than he would have earned in Los Angeles, and he had been invited to apply at St. Lucy's, but he wanted to feel free again, and the cost of living was much lower in rural areas. We'd be able to save more money for our future. We rented a clean, older three-bedroom house in a small valley town for no more than our tiny studio apartment in the city had cost. Salaries were lower in rural areas too, so we lived as frugally as we had as students. It was already our habit so not hard to do.

Of the consortium's three hospital communities, we picked La Cordillera for our home. It was nearest the Sierra. The town's economy was based on citrus, grapes, walnuts, almond and stone fruits. To the west the land grew flat and became a patchwork of vineyards, grain crops, and alfalfa. Around town were peach, plum, almond and walnut orchards. To the east, in the foothills at the edge of the mountains, citrus groves gradually gave way to cattle ranches. The range, *La Cordillera* in Spanish, of the Sierra Nevada was spectacular, the highest mountains in the lower United States.

La Cordillera was truly a rustic paradise, but it wasn't perfect. The climate was the best in the world for producing sweet fruits and abundant crops. But it took a pregnant woman who had been raised near the cool Pacific Ocean by surprise. The day when we moved into a small rental house in La Cordillera, the temperature reached a hundred and five degrees.

Fortunately, Dev's parents had come to help us settle in. I tried to help unload the truck we'd rented, but after an hour of work, Sarah Cunningham noticed that my pregnancy-swollen face was red from heat and exertion. She soaked a towel under the faucet in the bathtub to wrap around my head and insisted that I go and sit under a sycamore tree.

The rental house's drains were blocked. Dev called the landlord, but he'd gone dove hunting. A neighbor told us that there was only one reputable plumber, but when Dev went to find him, he was hunting with our landlord. Dev and Everett spent the afternoon and most of the evening digging up the front yard to clear the blockage. Sarah and I did our work later, in the cool of evening, glad that the electricity was on, the sinks no longer overflowing, and proud of our men's know-how. We managed to get the cupboards washed, drawers and shelves lined, things put away, and I stretched flat on my back on the hardwood floor, luxuriating in the cool, damp air rushing in from the aluminum box in the window, grateful for both good in-laws and the person who had invented the strange apparatus my Cunningham family called a swamp cooler.

Beth visited in early October. Her yellow Capri was loaded with things Mother had purchased for the baby. The baby's room was ready with new curtains I'd made and a crib from Dev's parents. My sister surveyed the town, and had complaints to make. La Cordillera had only one theater and its offerings were all in Spanish. "My movies would have to have subtitles if they were shown here."

"What movies? Are you starring in any movies?"

"That's beside the point. This place is pathetic. No supermarkets! You only have two tiny grocery stores. There were no mushrooms in either, and they only had Spanish paprika. Who ever heard of a place where you couldn't get Hungarian paprika? How can you live here? You don't speak Spanish."

"I'll learn."

"I think you've turned into a poor person."

"We like being poor persons."

Beth found a few things she liked, but not many There were no jets roaring across our skies. The cars, pick-ups, farm trucks and school buses didn't become traffic jams. There was greenery everywhere, and it was organized, domesticated greenery that appealed to my sister. She liked the geometry of farm and ranch boundaries. "I'll come here when I need a rest," she said.

I was happy. Sunset turned the mountains brilliant with reds and purples over the darkening band of citrus groves. I had never seen so many stars in the sky before, or seen such spectacular moonrises. I only knew the season-free coastal climate, broken by short episodes of cold Pacific fog in May and the dry Santa Ana winds in October.

Now I learned how the four seasons manifest themselves in most of the temperate zone. The valley's hot dusty summer smell changed to a damp cinnamon fragrance one morning, and without other warning, it was fall. Leaves on the trees turned color and it felt good to put on a long sleeved shirt. We took walks in the evening when Dev came home from work and gleaned walnuts from an orchard already harvested. Dev showed me how to cure the nutmeat in the oven so it wouldn't get fruit worms. We had enough to store for a year.

We would make our life here in La Cordillera. Beth would come visit. So would Mama and my brothers and Dev's family. Our first child would be born here, perhaps before the New Year, 1958, began.

~~~<<=>>~~~

Chapter 55: The Beauties of Winter

In December, a damp chilling fog set in and it was winter. It wasn't the white New England winter of Christmas cards, rather the world turned grey, black and umber. Leaves on the ground skeletonized; their cellular material broke down and turned into soil. The native sycamores' bark whitened and the trunks of other leafless trees darkened as rain came filling reservoirs and snow came covering the mountains. Wind machines and smudge pots activated in the citrus groves.

Mother didn't come to visit until after the baby was born. My brothers had activities and jobs, and she didn't really trust leaving them alone. They weren't bad, but they might bring a girl into the house, or even bring in the Morgan boys. She didn't trust young people's impulsiveness. But she loved babies and was anxious to be with us for her first grandchild's early days.

Right on schedule, just after Christmas, Sarah Anne Cunningham was born in small, forty bed, La Cordillera Hospital. From her pre-natal heartbeat, my obstetrician, Dr. De Angelo, predicted she would be a girl and she was. We named her Sarah Anne Cunningham for her two grandmothers. Sallyanne was right for her. The fates were better to me than they had been to my mother when Mama bore her first child. Sallyanne was a cheerful baby, not prone to squalling or screaming. My husband was handsome and strong. My first pregnancy hadn't brought tragedy with it.

Dev came to my room with Mama when she arrived at the hospital, and then he left us alone to go down to the nursery and gaze at his daughter. I expected my mother to come in bubbling over, her smile deepening her dimples. Instead, she came in looking far too serious. I would have been frightened for my child, if I hadn't just held and fed our newborn a few minutes earlier and seen how healthy she was.

"Baby," Mama said, calling me a pet name that seemed both ironic and sweet in the circumstances. "I have something I need to say to you before I say anything else." She had rare tears in her eyes. "Listen to me. This is very important. It is what your grandfather told me the day you were born. I thought it was cruel, but it wasn't." My mother sought my eyes. Hers were filled with all the words she had never spoken, and I had never heard.

Then she gave me a message passed down from her father, the only parent she had known, and the only grandparent I had known. "Baby," she said. "You have given a hostage to fortune and you will never be carefree again." I recognized it as a quote from Sir Francis Bacon I'd heard in college, and recognized its awesome implication for the first time. Though not yet quite twenty-one, I had gone from girl to guardian.

Mama stayed for a week. None of my friends' babies were breastfed. They thought it vulgar, and that it would ruin their figures. Mama encouraged me to nurse, and I knew on my own that if my child needed cow's milk she would have been born a calf. I was confident that if my figure were ruined, Dev would love me still.

Mama, of course, did the cooking that week. Knowing I'd far rather clean than cook, she was afraid that Dev would leave me for my culinary deficiencies if not for changes in my figure. She informed me that she didn't want me sent back to her house because I couldn't cook a decent meal. She didn't know that I could serve Dev oatmeal for every single breakfast and canned corned beef hash with tomato slices for every single supper, and he wouldn't complain as long as the food was wholesome and prepared in a sanitary manner. But Dev did enjoy his suppers during Mama's visit. She saw his joy in our baby and me. My mother and my husband were beginning to see each other's strengths.

In La Cordillera I found things I'd never known, loving physical intimacy with another human being and the sweetness of having a child from our two bodies come into the world.

I would have been happy to be some old-time frontier wife with a new baby every other year. And I found that Dev was suited to the role of husband and father. He could have been some old-time frontier husband. There was never a minute when I didn't know where he was. He was either at work or with us. As time went on I was to appreciate his constancy and diligence. The surprises that came with marriage and our removal to this rural place were good ones.

I hadn't lost Paro, Pat, or Adrian by moving away from the city. We wrote long letters, and indulged in phone calls when any important event occurred. I'd promised to be a bridesmaid in Paro's wedding, and so in February we went back to the city. I had a gurgling, happy baby to show off, and it was good seeing the family and Dev's and my old friends.

In the spring, with Dev's savings and a G.I. loan, we purchased an older, run down home on one of the shady streets in town. We worked to repair and renovate it and were quickly able to sell it for twice what it had cost us. New people began to fill my life, and I acquired new skills suitable for a place with transient services. I learned to use a hammer and shovel as well as a stove. I liked the unstylish simplicity of the people I met. Country and small town people showed a lack of concern with the superficial and took the essential very seriously. That suited me.

Mama and Beth visited often, usually separately, and Dev's parents crossed the mountains to see us every season. Everett, Sarah and Dev would follow the game seasons in the Sierra and the Coast Range. The hunters skinned and gutted, and plucked feathers. I learned to package and freeze venison, and cook the meat the hunters brought home.

Dev rented a rototiller and put a garden in our backyard. I obtained booklets from the county agricultural advisor and learned to freeze food, make jams and jellies. Sarah taught me to crochet. Our second Christmas in La Cordillera, I made six different kinds of cookies. I was a legitimate housewife, in training to be a ranch wife. The ranch soon followed.

My nursing skills wouldn't go to waste. Accidents were common to people in rural life dealing with machinery, barbed wire and animals. I practiced kitchen triage, my kitchen often a first aid stop on some neighbor or neighbor child's route to an emergency room or doctor's office.

Our early years together passed quickly and our family expanded. With real estate profit and help from a Cal Vet Farm and Home Loan, we purchased forty acres on high ground east of town. The lower thirty-acre section, on sloping alluvium, was already planted in mature citrus trees. On the rocky top of the knoll, there was a view all the way across the valley to the coast range. We built our home there. I had two more pregnancies bringing tough little boy babies, and wielded a hammer wearing an aluminum-framed baby backpack as easily as my mother-in-law's grandmother worked to tend her family and build a wickiup while wearing a cradleboard. Mama couldn't resist needling that Dev was making me work my life away. She'd forgotten how hard and how long I'd worked in her house. I was working for my own home with Dev. The more we accomplished, the happier we were.

When we finished the house, we added a barn and erected fences to protect our garden from deer and livestock from California's boldest predators: coyotes, raccoons and dog packs. Bobcats were too shy to come near the ranch house. If we saw mountain lions or bears, we were to call Fish and Game. Dev tucked that number, along with the fire department's, on a card above the phone. We had a shotgun for emergencies, but I never had to use it.

We had two more children, rowdy little boys. Sallyanne had brothers named Andy and Ev. We named the boys for our fathers, Andrew Cameron Frazier and Everett Wilson Cunningham. I didn't think it was possible to be as happy as I was.

Dev bought sheep and goats. We kept chickens, ducks, and rabbits. Most of what we ate we grew and almost any problem I couldn't solve when Dev was away at work, I could find a solution with advice from a little book called *The*

Homesteader's Handbook.

A threat did come one day when Dev was at work. The little ones were napping, fortunately. I was ironing Dev's shirts. Our dog's bark warned me, and I killed a rattlesnake near the porch with a hoe. It was more difficult that I expected. It took many strikes of the hoe's blade. The snake did not want to die, and its rattle made a horrendous buzz the whole while. I was hitting at it. I was terrified the whole while too. But my fortune held small hostages who played in the yard around the house; I took no chances that before Dev got home it would disappear into the shrubbery to come out when my babies were outdoors.

I chopped it into so many pieces that the chickens came from the vegetable garden to run away with its parts. I had to shoo them away. It was a justified murder. With respect to my half-Paiute mother-in-law, I apologized to the spirit of the snake as I buried its body, as respectfully as Sarah Cunningham would have. Not that I really believed in spirits.

Dev was able to break his vacation into two parts so that in the pleasant days of fall we could go on a visit to West Los Angeles. Then, its climate was at its best. We'd stay with my mother or with Adrian and Jack, and make time to visit old friends like Paro and Vince, or Dev's friends Paul and Brian and their families. Traveling with small children wasn't always easy, but we managed. They loved going to the beach and splashing in the surf, the boys knocking each other down and wrapping seaweed around themselves to play monster and chase their sister.

We developed a yearly travel pattern. Each April, we drove to Bishop for a visit with Dev's family. The road over Tioga Pass was seldom opened that early in the year, so we usually went the long way around, down through Bakersfield then over Tehachapi Pass and up Highway 395. The east side of the Sierra would be bursting with wildflowers and the sharp mountain escarpment, so different from our view of the Sierra from La Cordillera was still snow-covered. Grandpa Everett and Grandma Sarah, Nancy and her two older children took our children fishing in snowmelt streams in the pines. I was happy to stay and keep the fireplace burning at the Cunningham homestead with any children still in diapers.

The clean desert air and glorious view was enough of a vacation. The drive itself was worthwhile even in a car crowded with occasionally squabbling children and all their paraphernalia. Poppies and lupine would be blooming on the high hillsides, and the ugly, weedy shrub that was black and spikey all winter down in the canyon gullies had burst for in pink tamarind blossoms.

~~~<<=>>~~~

Chapter 56: Vacation in Encino

The ranch satisfied Dev's need for space and physical work. He studied citrus culture and read pamphlets from both U.C. Riverside and U.C. Davis. As soon as he felt knowledgeable and had a routine for managing the grove, he built terraces and trucked in topsoil for gardens at the top of the hill around the house. We planted shade trees and shrubs: Mexican willow, olive, ironbark eucalyptus, pomegranate, fig, pistachio, almond, and oleander, plants that took little water and built a cactus garden beside our patio. I graced it with a small statue of St. Francis, for although I had trouble believing in anyone's god, I'd never had trouble believing in good people. St. Francis was welcome in our garden. Sarah Cunningham's spirits of the earth were welcome too, and real creatures, roadrunners, hawks, crows, blue jays and doves came to live with us as the trees grew and shrubs spread.

We spent nearly every weekend working on the ranch, but one beautiful, glowing day, when our oldest child was nearly four, we bundled the little ones in the car and went for a long drive. Dev wanted to see a place I'd been so fond of as a child. I knew times past did not come back, but my grandfather's ranch was an hour and a quarter's drive north and west of our place in La Cordillera. We found the property. The line of eucalyptus trees was still standing, but the old house, windmill, and pump were gone. A low modern house, new barn and horse corrals took their place. Only the trees my grandparents had planted in 1911 remained.

By the fall of 1962, we were well established and I had friends, other ranch wives, but I missed my brothers and wanted to see our old friends again. We had an invitation and accepted, we loaded the station wagon with baskets of clean diapers, a folded up play pen, snack crackers, cans of soymilk formula and drove to Los Angeles.

The confusion caused by a little baby beginning to crawl plus two toddlers was too much for Mama. So although we spent time with her, we stayed with Adrian and Jack in their large child-welcoming Encino home. It had a clothes dryer! There were disposable diapers in stores now, but they were imperfect and irritated our children's skin. Adrian and I both used soft and airy cloth in spite of the daily work our choice involved.

The Ryders had plenty of room and a yard designed for kids. Adrian had pestered me to bring the family to see them. The three days we were there, the men took over most of the care for the six young children. Adrian and I were pampered.

Our last full afternoon in Encino, Baby Everett was sound asleep in his playpen beside Adrian and me as we lounged under a shade tree. Sallyanne, almost four, was hanging onto the side of the pool and kicking as Debbie Ryder played swim coach. Our roughneck two and a half year old Andy and the little Ryder boys were having a mock battle with Styrofoam alligator floats. Dev and Jack worked as lifeguards and peacemakers.

Beverly was coming to see us. She was now a major performer with Spirit of Elation Dancers. She'd arrived in Los Angeles for a few days before the troupe began a tour of the South Pacific. Waiting, Adrian and I were sipping the Kool-Aid that Dev irreverently called *Mormon Vin Rose* and looking at Adrian's collection of women's magazines.

In a little while, the chain link gate leading from the street rattled and Beverly appeared, truly stunning. Her auburn hair was a brighter red, and she was wearing a pink blouse over a flowered skirt. She stopped at the pool fence long enough to greet the kids splashing in the water, give Jack a kiss and say hello to Dev, then came to us.

"It's about time," Adrian mock-griped as Beverly gave her a hug.

Beverly swished away from her sister, looked around, and whined, "Where's Beth? I want her here."

"I thought I told you. She's in Hawaii," Adrian said, "She has a part in a film."

"It's only a tiny part," I said. "But she's staying longer to visit Verna."

Beverly scrunched up her face until it looked like one sad wrinkle. "Phooey. I have something I wanted to tell you all together. Now it won't be the same."

Adrian stuck a toe out and nudged her sister's leg. "So what is it? Tell us."

Beverly took a deep breath, let it out, and announced, "I got married."

Adrian stared at Beverly's left hand and wailed, "How could you not tell me?"

"I'm telling you now. The only other people who know are Mom and Pop."

"Did you marry Gordon? You didn't marry someone I've never even met, did you?"

"Of course I married Gordon. We drove to Elko on Monday. You know I'd never marry anyone else."

Adrian glared. "You're pregnant! That's why you didn't have a decent wedding."

"No, Adrian. I'm not pregnant. We didn't want a big wedding. I didn't need six toasters and fourteen sets of placemats. I'm going to be touring for the next six months!"

~~~<<=>>~~~

Chapter 57: Young Mothers

Debbie, Johnny and Donnie kept shouting, "Aunt Bev! Aunt Bev!" So, Beverly got up, grabbed a skimpy bathing suit from the big bag she left on the grass, and went in the house to change. A few minutes later she was in the pool. Sleek, as graceful in the water as on a theater's stage, Beverly practiced a few smooth dives and swam down to the kids playing at the shallow end.

Adrian, dour and unsmiling, watched her sister. "I would have gone to Nevada to be with her. I'd have chartered a plane out of Burbank and gone by myself if I had to."

"When Dev and I were married in Tonopah. I didn't tell Beth."

"I know you had a reason to keep things secret, but that doesn't make it right. It wasn't fair to your family or to me. It was rotten. And now my sister does the same thing to me that you did to Beth."

"Your sister spends lots of time in costume. She might not have wanted the nuisance of a wedding. The dress, the rehearsal, it may have seemed too much for her."

"Don't make excuses for her," Adrian growled. "She's not your sister."

Eventually, Beverly climbed out of the pool and came back, shaking water out of her hair to splatter over us like some kind of backyard baptism. "I remembered how kids pee in pools. Icky!"

"It's sweet pee from our sweet babies, sister dear," Adrian chided. Soon you'll have your own babies and you'll see."

Adrian was beginning to feel better. But Beverly objected to sisterly smugness. "No, Adrian. Gordon and I aren't ready for children yet. We'll wait to have them when we're ready."

I joined in, supporting my friend's point of view. "Ready has little to do with it, Beverly. Dev and I didn't plan children for five years. In four and a half years we've had three babies, and I'm pregnant again."

Beverly's arched eyebrows came together. She looked over the two of us and took note of every slumped muscle and ounce of shifted fat on our bodies. Adrian's first pregnancy had given her broken veins and blue streaks on her thighs. I was thinner than I'd ever been, but the wasp waist I'd been so proud of had expanded by three inches. I knew I looked haggard. I'd had morning sickness with this pregnancy I hadn't had with the others.

"I'll *never* be like you two," she said. "I'll have children when I *want* them. My children won't be accidents."

"I wanted my children!" Adrian exclaimed. "How can you imply I didn't? They weren't *accidents*."

It was only fair that I be candid. "I wanted my children too," I protested.

And then, I avoided committing a sin of omission by being honest. "But we would rather have waited a while before they began arriving. It would have been better for us to have waited a year or so before they began arriving."

Dev was getting the kids out of the pool for snacks while Jack locked the pool gate. Debbie and Sallyanne helped herd their little brothers into the kitchen. The yard grew so quiet we could hear waves in the pool lapping its edge in lengthening intervals.

Beverly's certainty was presumptuous. A jump-rope rhyme sang through my mind: *First comes love, then comes marriage, then comes Beverly with a baby carriage.* "Healthy women get pregnant, Beverly," snipped out of my mouth. "You can't have sex without taking that risk. You have to be aware of that."

"Drea's right," Adrian said. "You'll get pregnant. Except for you and Beth, all the girls our age from Breeze Terrace have kids now. Adrian leaned toward her sister. "Oh, I take it back.

There is one girl who doesn't have kids, Diane Taylor She'll be living with her parents until she's seventy."

Adrian made a strong point. Pregnancy did follow marriage. All the married nurses, except Peggy, from my graduating class at St. Lucy's were mothers now. Everyone I knew from school was too. "Good luck with your plans, Bev, but no protection method other than sterilization is truly reliable."

Beverly had an odd expression, almost a smile, almost not a smile.

Expecting Mormon disapproval, but knowing I'd tell them eventually, I blurted out, "I've decided to have a tubal ligation when this last little one is born."

Beverly and Adrian were both shocked, but not speechless.

"You'd have yourself sterilized?" Adrian gasped. "You *can't* do that! What if something happened to Sallyanne and the boys? What if they were all killed in a wreck or something? Drea, you can't consider anything like that. Too much could happen."

"I have considered it. We're insurance poor now. Dev's a good father, and he adds coverage every time I have a baby. He's so afraid something might happen to him, and he wants us protected. He worries all the time."

"Men are supposed to protect us and worry. That's their job," Adrian told me. "If Dev can't cope, then he should get himself fixed. You shouldn't be the one who does it."

"He offered to have a vasectomy. I won't let him."

"You're so crazy. You've always been crazy." She threw her hands up. "Why not let him?"

"I don't know," I answered. I didn't know, except I didn't want him altered in any way.

"That's just stupid. You're a nurse! Tell her, Beverly. Tell Drea she can't go have some crazy drastic surgery when it's so easy for a man to do it."

Beverly flipped her damp towel at us. "You are so out of it, you two. She doesn't have to have surgery. Those days are done and gone."

She went across the lawn and picked up her big purse. Here," she said. She pulled out a plastic case and tossed it to me. "Haven't either of you ever heard of Enovid? There are *pills* that prevent pregnancy now. They work."

Adrian glanced disdainfully at the little pill case, but I picked it up and read the label. I was disturbed. Dr. De Angelo hadn't told me this was available. He must have known about this form of contraceptive. He should have told me. It is what I got for having a Catholic doctor. He was in the Knights of Columbus, but he had economic motivation too. The more pregnant patients he had, the more money went into his wallet.

The kids came running out with popsicles in their mouths. Adrian yelled, "Don't run with sticks in your mouth."

Beverly jammed the packet back in her purse, and tossed it the lawn, not far from the playpen. I froze, my heart racing. Adrian flew out of the chair. "Your purse! Beverly! Your purse!"

"What is wrong with you two? My purse won't hurt your precious lawn."

"I don't care about the lawn. Use your brain, Beverly. Think." Adrian said.

"We need to be very careful." I said calmly, trying to explain. "When I was at St. Lucy's, a beautiful little four-year-old died because she got into medication she found in her grandmother's purse." I picked up the purse and sat back down, holding it.

Beverly understood, and her eyes filled with tears.

Debbie came running across the yard with purple Popsicle smeared around her mouth. "Auntie Bev, come watch me do my positions. Miss Marsha says I'm her best dancer. I'm just like you."

Beverly grabbed her niece up and hugged her. They walked over and turned the patio into a stage. Adrian shook her head and said, "We can't expect a dancer to think like a mother."

I took the Beverly's big purse inside, put it high up on the top of the refrigerator and came back out. Ev was still asleep. I could get some sewing done.

"The kids love their Aunt Beverly," Adrian said. I wish she lived here and they could see her more."

"How did we miss hearing about the pills? There must have been reports in the paper. I don't remember seeing any. I knew an oral contraceptive was in research, but I had no idea it was on the market," I commented.

It seemed like a long time went by. We could hear the kids giggling with Beverly. A breeze came up and rattled the leaves in the tree above us. Baby Ev stirred in the playpen and was beginning to wake up. I thought I could feel the new baby in me move, though it was early to feel life. My mother used that expression *feel life*. In old books it was called the quickening.

"I hadn't heard of any contraceptive pill at all," Adrian said. "But I don't watch the news or read the paper anymore. The news is all about bombs, Russians, fall-out shelters and building more missile silos."

"I don't either."

"Over and over nuclear war all it is. Death and destruction. I begged Jack to have a shelter dug when we remodeled the cabana, but he wouldn't do it. He says we'd all just die anyway when we found the rest of the world gone. I know he's right. But I'm so scared. I cry for no reason. And I panic when jets fly over. We get sonic booms, not enough to hardly feel, and I think it is nuclear missiles and we're at war."

"I do too. Dev tells me I'm not being rational. He says the Russians aren't going to waste their warheads on orange trees and cattle ranches. But no place is safe. I get nightmares that my babies have radiation sickness and wake up scared. I stay scared and don't want Dev to leave us to go to work. "You've called me crazy since we were little kids, Adrian. But I'm so terrified all the time, my husband is beginning to think I really am."

"You're not crazy," Adrian said.

Sallyanne ran to join Beverly and Debbie on the patio. The three boys, not to be left out, push-pulled, slid, and stumbled their raucously noisy way across the yard, so they didn't send them away.

I found a needle and thread in a sewing kit I'd brought out to hem playsuits for Andy and Ev. They'd be able to wear them when we went to see Paro and Vince and their new baby Jason tomorrow.

Adrian was sitting quietly, watching Beverly and the children. "I think she will be a good mother someday," she said.

"I think so too."

~~~<<=>>~~~

Chapter 58: Beth Takes Wilshire Boulevard

The actress in the Horvath family was raking in money. The annual income from my sister's steady jobs in film, TV, and commercials equaled what she earned at the department store. In effect, Beth had two full time jobs. She had a small apartment off Olympic Boulevard, and dressed in clothes from Beverly Hills boutiques. The yellow Gypsy Wagon had been traded in on a bright red Chevy Corvette, Gypsy Wagon II, and she was proud of her savings account. Then, before Thanksgiving, Orbach's offered her a marketing position in their national headquarters in Newark, New Jersey. Beth well understood how rare it was for a woman to be offered a move up the corporate ladder. The promotion offer forced her to take stock of where she was, and where she was going. She came to a decision.

She was a capable actress, prompt, intelligent, and cooperative with directors, but she'd expected to be a star by the time she was twenty-two. Years had passed busily, but she was nearly twenty-five. She blamed the Wallace Raudell Talent Agency that her career wasn't where she wanted it to be. With Orbach's promotion dangling before her, she took action. She confronted Wally, the man she'd trusted with her future. Two days later, she drove up to La Cordillera to tell me what happened during their battle.

Beth stormed into Wally's inner office the morning after she had been offered the corporate promotion. "I'm not happy," she announced, frowning at him.

"What's up?" Wally asked. He beamed a patronizing, fix-it-quick smile at her.

Beth's demands soon erased the smile. "I don't want to do any more stupid commercials or voice overs or walk-ons," she told him. "People know my face and voice, but they don't know my name. I want to be someone. I want starring roles in movies and TV, roles with Beth Benton on the credits. You've known that for over five years." She paused a second to glare at him. "And, you haven't given it to me."

Wally's response was, "Whaddya talkin' about? You got a good career, making good money. I got a long list of little chickies out there beggin' for half the jobs I get you. Gimme a little gratitude."

He then made a mistake that infuriated Beth. He waved her away, negotiation ended. As he reached for his phone and spun around in his chair to look out the window dismissing her, she spun into a wild, enraged virago.

"Grateful? Grateful to you?" she shouted. "I get parts because I'm good, you jerk. Not because of anything you're doing for me."

Wally swiveled back to face her. His face was red, and he slammed the phone down.

"Get oudda here," he said. "Get oudda my sight. I never done nothin' for nobody else like I done for you."

Beth puffed up as tall as she could and attacked. "I've been with this agency for six years, and I'm still doing idiot commercials. You get me nowhere parts in shoddy little B pictures no one I know would even see. I'm sick of the junky jobs you get me. You haven't done a thing for me but squeeze your percentage out of every nickel I've earned." She did a quick, on the spot calculation. "I gave you eleven hundred and forty-seven dollars and sixty three cents this year alone."

Wally slammed his hand down on the desk and said, "Think of the money I made for you! You are gettin' goddam rich on the jobs I give ya. You got special treatment from Wallace Raudell all the way down the line from the first goddam fuckin' day you came in here."

Beth didn't whine. She yelled. "Then why am I still doing schlock? I never missed a call, always knew my lines, put up with whatever crap a director handed out. You knew what I wanted and I don't have it." She gave him her ultimatum. "Get it for me, Wally. Or I go to another agency."

"So go," Wally yelled back. "You ungrateful bitch! I give you work a hunert girls would die for."

"You have no right to call me that. I'm not a bitch, and I deserve more than you give me!"

"You got it backwards. I give you more'n you deserve. Without me, you got nuttin'." He shook his fist at her. "Screw you!" he shouted.

At that, Beth picked up a paperweight on Wally's desk and tried to hurl it through the plate glass window behind him. The heavy tempered glass shuddered and bounced the paperweight back to chip the mahogany desktop. It barely missed chipping Wally.

Wallace Raudell's face contorted. He looked like a rabid bulldog. He stood up, shouting, "Get oudda my office. I never want to see you in here again. No one could make a star oudda of you. You ain't marketable as a star." Slowing down, he sat back down. "Hollywood already got Kim Novak. You're just a copy of her. But you don't even got her shape and you're geddin' fat! Go home and check your mirror."

That stunned my sister speechless. But Wally wasn't through. He pointed his finger at her and said, "Screw you, Babe. Sit home watchin' commercials, you dumb little slut. You sure as hell won't be in 'em.'' Wally took a deep breath, and then leaned back. "I worked my butt off for you. Get your ass oudda my office. Don't come back. Screw you, Beth Horveth."

Beth turned and walked out. In her entire life, no one had ever spoken to her as Wally had. She left his office experiencing, in camera frame order, every variant of indignation or outrage she had ever faked for a lens.

But Beth was a practical and observant woman. She wasn't so distraught that she couldn't see what was going on around her. Wally's new secretary was leaning on a filing cabinet in the outer office. Wearing a slinky, shimmering, low-cut dress with perspiration rings under the arms she was showing the mail boy some cleavage, ignoring the multiple phones ringing on her desk.

Farther down the hall, past Wally's agents' offices, Trudy, the ancient crone who had long been his secretary, sat with her back to the waiting room. Trudy was coughing in a haze of Lucky Strike smoke, her bony shoulders rhythmically convulsing. Beth didn't slow her march down the hall to pick up the *Harper's Bazaar* that had fallen from the old woman's desk. Beth did slow for an instant to notice that it was ten o'clock in the morning, and the ashtrays and trashcans were full. Janitorial obviously hadn't done its nightly work.

Beth stepped through the waiting room on her path to the corridor. Plants shriveled in dusty containers on corner tables. A crumpled receipt, a gum wrapper, and fragments of torn pages from *Variety* were littering the floor. A nervous hopeful sat with a photo portfolio on his lap. The other chairs in the waiting room were empty. Beth took it all in.

Turning, she tripped herself back into Wally's inner office. My sister stretched her five feet and one inch as high as three inch heels let her and took a deep breath, hoping that filling her lungs with air would somehow make her taller. She planted her feet apart, put her hands on her hips, and stared at Wally.

"The Wallace Raudell Agency is coasting on what it used to be. You may have a great reputation, but it's dissolving. Do you know Davis Theatrical Management is on your tail? I got a nice call from Larry Bingham this week, and I bet I'm not the only one of your moneymakers who did. This agency is dead. How many clients have you lost?"

The enraged, red-faced Wally flinched ever so slightly, just enough to let Beth know she was slicing through his tough skin. She continued on. "Calls from interested directors don't reach us, Wally. I don't know how many jobs I've lost in the last two years because I got the call up too late to schedule it. Other actors tell me the same thing has happened to them. I can give you names. Do you even see what's going on around here?"

The agent screamed at her, pointing at the door. "Oudda here!"

Beth didn't leave. She held her battle position on the nubby carpet. "The bookkeeper messes up. Our checks aren't cut promptly. Taxes and union dues are deducted sometimes, but not at other times. Complaining hasn't helped, either. You go on thinking the Wallace Raudell Talent Agency is big stuff, while the whole damn place falls apart. You're on Wilshire Boulevard. It's the best location in the city, but two years from now you'll be working out of a trailer in Van Nuys. I'm only twenty-two years old, and I could manage this place better than you do."

Wally was so furious he lost his voice and hissed, "Shit. You're in my office talkin' shit. I handle the best talent on the West Coast. I'll always handle the best talent on the West Coast. You think some little gettin' too chubby chick knows how to run a business? Screw you! You couldn't run the stapler on Betty's desk."

"I could save your business, but it's not worth my time. I don't care what happens to you. I wish I'd aimed that paperweight at your stupid, ugly, fat, bald head." When she left, she slammed the door loud enough for everyone, down to the pathetic would-be Marlon Brando in the waiting room, to feel the concussion.

Before Beth's heels clicked out of the agency and all the way down the marble corridor toward the elevator, she was thinking about the money Orbach's offered her with the promotion. Newark wasn't that far from New

York City. Park Avenue was probably a lot like Wilshire Boulevard. Newark wasn't that far from Philadelphia, Boston or Washington, D.C. either. She thought she'd like it on the east coast. Wally's son Leland ran the New York Agency. Leland could probably get her a part off-Broadway, but she might just like working work at Orbach's corporate headquarters.

Before the elevator doors opened for her, Wally chased her down. "Ya think you know so much? I give ya the job," he sputtered. He took her arm, twirled her around and led her past the single waiting client, past Trudy, past the agents' offices, past Betty and the mail boy where he waved his arm in a grand, all encompassing gesture. "Here! I give ya my agency. You think somethin's wrong? Then, chickie, you fix it."

"Okay," she said.

My sister stopped the narrative at this point. She just sat there across my kitchen table, smiling at me.

"Don't stop there," I said. "What happened then?"

"We went back to the office, and Wally screwed me. Then we worked out a contract and the terms of my salary. I'm his business manager, not office manager. If I clean the agency up in three years, I become a partner."

I was still struggling to understand what she had just said. I understood the partnership and contract part. It was the other part that upset me.

"Wally screwed you? You mean like... screwed your body? Right there in the office?"

"Drea, you have always been so dumb. Naturally, my body." Her eyes twinkled. "And, the office is where we were. Sister dear, it was about time. I've always wanted him to."

"Not really."

"Yes, really. I like him. He's funny."

She told me that before, I just didn't realize all she meant.

After Beth had left for home, when Dev and I were lying in bed I told him about the change in my sister's career. I tried to put in all the details just as she told me. When I got to the part about Wally screwing her body, my husband chuckled.

"Drea, you are dumb. Of course he screwed her body. This is a semantic consideration. If it were her mind he was after, your sister would have used a different verb."

"I don't get it," I said.

"One screws bodies. One fucks minds."

"Oh."

He pulled me up on top of him. My nipples brushed the hair on his chest as I stretched up the length of his irresistible body. I could love this man's strong bones and long smooth muscles freely and without restraint, precisely because he never fucked with my mind.

~~~<<=>>~~~

Chapter 59: A Breeze Terrace Wedding

Beth never worked before a camera again. Instead she straightened out the Wilshire Boulevard agency. Within a year, my sister fired nearly everyone who worked for Wally, starting with Betty, his pseudo secretary. Beth would have kept Trudy on staff in some capacity, because she knew Wally loved the old woman and approved of his loyalty, but Trudy's cigarette cough killed her two months after Beth took over.

As the office emptied of its less than sterling employees, Beth persuaded a number of people from Orbach's, including Mamie Silver and Bill Gower, the head bookkeeper, to come to work for the agency. She tried to entice Dev to move us back to Los Angeles so he could clean up the agency's accounts, but we would never go back to the city.

In three years, the nameplate in the agency building's lobby and on the gilt letters on the glass of the agency's door changed from The Wallace Raudell Talent Agency to Raudell-Horvath Talent. The business had expanded to take over the whole ninth floor in the building. The number of agents working for Wally tripled, and the office staff expanded to fifteen.

The single negative in my sister's life was that her childhood asthma had returned. But through Steve's doctor's recommendation, she'd connected with a good allergist in Century City and was taking tests and responding well to treatment. Beth had enough free time so she was taking classes in business law at

U.C.L.A. just for fun. She moved into a swanky apartment on the eleventh floor in the southwestern most building in the Park La Brea Towers complex as soon as she signed the contract with Wally Raudell, realizing her teenaged dream.

Beth's life was as glamorous as a movie star's. She knew what was in and what was out in restaurants and entertainment venues, and would call me to fill me in on where she had been with her various dates. Always discrete, Wally and my sister never went out together in public.

Time was beginning to travel faster. Older people had told me this would happen and they were right. Dev and I hardly could blink without the kids moving up a grade, needing larger sized clothing and acting quite mature. Our children were housebroken, and even quite civilized. However, what Dev and I considered civilized wasn't sedate enough for white carpets, white drapes and German crystal. When we visited my sister in her gleaming tower during our annual visit to the city, we either left the kids with Mama or Adrian. The kids only got to know Aunt Beth through her visits to our house. She visited often, and she spoiled her nieces and nephews more than we liked. She spoiled me too. I may have been the only woman in La Cordillera who wore Chanel to go to the lumberyard or feed store. Not that there weren't other women who wore Chanel. But they lived on big properties, and sent their ranch workers to do the hauling. We didn't send anyone to do what we could do ourselves.

Now and then, when Beth came for a weekend, she brought Wally with her. No one knew him in La Cordillera. He seemed to enjoy having a weekend away from the city. He was a proper guest. He slept on the sofa in the den, while Beth used the guest room. Aunt

Beth's friend became part of our Cunningham family. Wally enjoyed being in the country and talking to Dev about property investment. However, Beth was talking to me about getting Wally to invest in Hawaiian property for his retirement.

During vacations with Verna, Beth had grown to love the islands. After she treated Mama to a week there, she promised Sallyanne, Andy, Ev, and Jennybeth that she would take each of them on a separate trip to the islands the summer after their twelfth birthday. I was pretty sure Hawaii would win. Wally would learn to surf before he became an orange grower.

Not even Hawaii could tempt me away from La Cordillera. The ranch had definitely turned out to be a good investment. Even on a bad year, the grove paid the mortgage and property taxes. Twice a day, at sunrise and sunset, the whole valley below us turned golden. We felt, without irony, that we lived in Voltaire's "best of all possible worlds." We had named the ranch *El Corrocamino* for its dominant form long-legged avian wildlife. But Dev and I were home lovers, not roadrunners.

Our son Ev was the ring bearer at my brother Steve's wedding in May of 1966. Andy and Sallybeth had a wonderful time at their first formal wedding and made their uncle and new aunt proud by their good behavior. We stayed with Adrian and Jack, and since Adrian had a babysitter for her children, we paid half her fee and left Jennybeth in her care. She was a lovely girl from the Ryder's ward, very used to small children. Debbie was there to help the sitter, and Adrian's younger children and Jennybeth were too young and impetuous to endure such a long day of propriety and politeness.

The ceremony was at St. Blaise and the reception held at the posh Rancho Californian in Westwood. Mama finally had the wedding she had dreamed of. Best of all, from her point of view she didn't have to pay for any of it. Steve hosted the rehearsal dinner on his own at a restaurant in Palms. But Mama played hostess grandly.

Janet was from a St. Blaise family, but it was a small one. I was afraid she'd find us overwhelming. But at the dinner I discovered she was almost star-struck by Beth's few years of TV and small film parts. But then that happened. Beth's smalltime fame had boosted both her brothers' popularity among young women in the parish. The halo effect lasted longer than her acting career had. But then, some of her commercials were still being shown.

Paro and Vince seemed to be having a grand time. Vince was a deputy district attorney now, and often served as a spokesman for the office. His name and photo were in the paper and on TV, and Mother treated him like a celebrity. She paraded him before the bride's family and guests, introducing him proudly. Paro and I sipped our champagne on the club balcony and talked for a long time. She wanted more children but hadn't gotten pregnant and that frustrated her. Jason wasn't a baby any longer. Vince had chattered through the dinner. He'd flirted a bit with Beverly, but Gordon didn't mind. Vince spent some time talking to Alex. When he found that my younger brother was interested in studying law, Vince encouraged Alex to apply for a summer internship with the District Attorney's Office. It was a very kind thing for him to do. An internship with Los Angeles County would look very good on a scholarship application.

The bride and groom cut the cake; the bouquet was thrown. All the toasts were made, and music started. As soon as the ritual dances were finished, Paro and Vince were on the dance floor. They danced most of the evening. Beth, Beverly, Adrian and I went table-hopping to greet people we knew. My sweet husband watched out for our children so I could visit with old friends and the kids wouldn't sneak champagne.

Steve's bride Janet was a stylishly pretty girl. We'd talked at her shower, and at the rehearsal dinner. She'd been pleasant. Beth came up to us as Steve's new bride was advising me that if I'd only get contact lenses and try a more bouffant hairstyle, I might be really, really attractive. I didn't think Janet had much understanding of a ranch wife's concerns. Beth walked toward us and the bride fled away to other people.

"Janet doesn't like me," my sister growled. "Did you notice she scurried away when I came up beside you? She's already decided I'm an evil step-sister-in-law."

"You're a little evil, but not that bad. You'd never be evil to anyone Steve liked. She's probably just intimidated because you are *somebody*."

"Yeah, I'm sooooo famous and important." Beth said sarcastically. "You're the one she should watch out for. You're the witch in the family. I hope Mama didn't tell her that."

"She doesn't have to worry about either of us as long as she's nice to our brother."

My sister looked very thoughtful. "Steve needs some attention. He's been so good for so long. He goes by to check on Mama and Alex all the time. Much more often than I do. Oh, Fudge! I just realized how hard it's going to be for Janet to cope with Mama. It isn't just her superstitions, either."

"Janet's probably realized how Mama depends on Steve. We need to be extra nice to her."

"We will be," Beth said. "We will be excellent sisters-in-law." We clinked wine glasses on the promise. Beth took my hand and we went to pour excellent sisterly blessings over the new bride. Beth would coax her into liking us. She was very good at that kind of thing.

The reception wound down. Late in the party, when he and Beverly, his favorite partner of the evening, finally left the dance floor, Vince was happy to come sit with Dev and me. Jack and Adrian were tired too and getting ready to leave. Jack said he'd leave the light burning for us. Paro, who'd abandoned Vince early to sit and talk, thought it best that she and Vince go home too. Dev went out to the parking lot with them to make sure Vince wasn't driving. He'd had too good a time to be safe behind a steering wheel.

I sent the kids to say their goodbyes to the family. The bandsmen were putting away their instruments. Mr. Claussen took over the club's piano and I didn't want to leave. Mr. Claussen was very drunk, but his fingers hit the right keys just the same.

Sallyanne and Andy fell asleep in the van on the way to Encino. Ev was singing softly to himself. His voice was sweet as he went through the repertoire of songs he knew. He was Mama's favorite of our children. Jennybeth was the most like her. Though she didn't like the bother of children, she loved all her grandchildren.

Louise and Don Claussen seldom saw Adrian's children. The Claussens couldn't stop drinking; Adrian couldn't excuse it. She wouldn't take her children to places where alcohol was served. Paro wanted another child and couldn't get pregnant. Anna Marie was pregnant with her sixth child and didn't seem to take any joy from it. Although she was the bride's cousin, she and her husband couldn't stay for the reception. They were too Catholic to use birth control and couldn't afford a babysitter for longer than the marriage ceremony itself. His schoolteacher salary didn't stretch very far. I didn't know what she'd do.

As we drove back to Adrian's, I thought about the choices women had been given in the past few years. For women like me, who felt sick when taking the pill, other safe contraception methods had become available.

Ev finally stopped singing and fell asleep. We'd have three children to carry into the guesthouse at Adrian and Jack's tonight. Jennybeth had been put to bed with Adrian's little ones. I kept my voice low as we drove through Sepulveda Pass toward Ventura Boulevard, but my thoughts on the changes in women's lives induced me to say, "I think that the IUD was the greatest discovery in the twentieth century."

For a little while Dev didn't say anything. Then he said, "Drea, that comment shows how intellectually limited you have let yourself become. You're a nurse. Forget aeronautics. Forget electronics. Think about insulin? Think about penicillin? What about the Salk vaccine? What about the advances in surgical procedures and anesthetics? I'm not saying you have your head up your ass, but it isn't far away from there."

I began to laugh visualizing where, anatomically speaking, he thought my head was, and he was laughing too. We were tired from too many days in the city and too many people today. It was all right. Tomorrow we'd be home.

Pat and Rich missed the wedding. Pat was at home nursing three small children with the chicken pox. Pat, like Paro, didn't approve of my fallen-away Catholic status, but separated it from our friendship in the same way she would separate any political differences we had.

She'd made me promise to call her when I got home and tell her all about the wedding. I kept my promise and called her Sunday evening.

We'd seen Rich, Pat and the kids a few weeks before the wedding when they'd looped up into the valley overnight on their way to visit one of Pat's brothers in Phoenix. It was out of their way, and we were happy to see them. During the evening, Rich told Dev that he knew he'd be in Vietnam within the next few months. Pat didn't mention that at all. She chattered on about her life in base housing and the kids. I listened. She was living with nightmares and sleepless nights. As the bomb scared Adrian and me, Southeast Asia scared Pat. We didn't talk about the probabilities that she was facing.

Advancements in pharmaceuticals for schizophrenia helped Tommy Whitfield, but he still needed constant monitoring. Pat told me that the hospital had received funding for an occupational program, and one of its stations was a large garden.

Tommy's behaviors were well enough controlled that he could sometimes leave the hospital grounds. The kids adapted to his visits to their home. Tommy's contorted expressions, rhythmic rocking, and incessant muttering didn't seem so odd when viewed within the context of Grandmother O'Hara's tongue clicks and Grandfather Whitfield's Parkinsonian shuffle. Pat and Rich were good parents, as Adrian and Jack were, and as Dev and I tried to be.

More than just the wedding itself, chicken pox kept Pat and Rich from getting to spend some time with Paro and Vince. The men's friendship had held up well over the years. Rich was Vince's son Jason's godfather. We saw them less than they saw each other. We had the ranch and four children who were beginning to have activities through school or scouts that sometimes cut into our vacation plans. We didn't get to L.A. very often and when we did, we had to spend time with my family, Adrian and Jack, and Dev's friend Paul and his wife and children. I was lucky if Pat could get to the city during the time we'd be there so I could see her. Our trips to Bishop too were shorter, and they had to coincide with the kids' spring break from school.

We'd made lots of friends in La Cordillera, but grand reunions with our old friends were harder to manage as the children grew older. They were becoming less and less frequent.

~~~<<=>>~~~

Chapter 60: Concerns of Conscience

By 1967, man still hadn't walked on the moon. Sallyanne was in fourth grade, Andy in second, Ev in first. Jennybeth was anxiously waiting to begin kindergarten in the following September. A December child, she already knew her address, the alphabet, and numbers to one hundred. Her sister and brothers were teaching her basic addition and subtraction to their father's delight. She hated being left behind when the school bus came each morning. I agreed to let her go to the only preschool in La Cordillera, Happy Days, run by the Baptist Church. I dropped her off there each morning, and came back home to an empty house. Now, I was the one left behind. I was thirty and felt that the best of my life was over.

I'd sequestered myself for ten years in a rustic fantasy and shut out everything frightening. I stopped singing along with the Doors' *Light My Fire*. Fires made me see burning; burning made me think of napalm. I put Mozart and Haydn LPs on the stereo turntable, and carefully avoided turning on the radio or TV in my empty house. America's involvement in Vietnam replaced my Cold War terror, but the media was full of war protests and civil conflicts. I hid from everything threatening and wanted to hear nothing ugly. And every day I counted the minutes until I could get in the car and ransom my youngest child back from the Baptists.

I sat with Dev as we watched news coverage of the deaths of Medgar Evers and John Kennedy and I still tried to deny the tragic impact of assassination and troubles in the nation. I could have been watching some old John Wayne movie for all that I let reality intrude on me. I kept my mind locked in the toy box with Andy and Ev's trucks and stuffed animals, Sallyanne's and Jennybeth's Barbie dolls.

Then, one day, Sallyanne came home from school. Our oldest child seemed perturbed, but denied anything was wrong. I didn't realize she was saving her concerns for her father. That evening, as I prepared supper, I heard her telling him about something she had seen from the school bus.

People were carrying signs and blocking the road. I listened as Dev patiently explained the need for social equity. He balanced the plight of those who worked on ranches against the interest of owners who needed labor, and people who needed food. Sallyanne was paying attention and asking intelligent questions. By the time she'd reached fourth grade, my child had outgrown me. Dev joked that he had five children, not four. There was truth behind his humor. I was cowering in denial, and I didn't like the person I'd become.

I decided to become a grown-up again and checked with the county nurses' registry. Before the mail brought a listing of job openings, Clara Buchanan called me. She was Doctor De Angelo's nurse. I'd known her from our first weeks in La Cordillera and through my pregnancies we'd become friends. I was no longer Doctor De Angelo's patient, but Clara was eager for me to apply at the office. Clara wanted longer weekends so she'd be free to attend weekend events with her husband Don, an international judge for Arabian horses. The job would suit me. I'd work Monday and Friday. Clara would work Tuesday, Wednesday and Thursday. It would be easy to coordinate our work. She had a practical and efficient manner.

I was hired. Doctor De Angelo outlined his expectations. I'd be taking the usual samples and recording the usual measurements, maintaining records, and attending at the women's physical examinations. Doctor asked if I would also do pre and post-natal counseling, advising his pregnant patients on health, nutrition, physical and emotional changes. Clara, since she was older, would more appropriately counsel his menopausal patients.

I hadn't been Doctor's patient since Jennybeth was born. I'd wanted a more progressive doctor. However, the times had changed even for Dr. De Angelo. Women were demanding pills instead of saltines for nausea and pills instead of fans for hot flashes. Before I agreed, I reminded Doctor that I was only a nurse and couldn't prescribe medications. He reassured me that before any patient left the office, he would review my assessment and write any needed prescriptions.

Mama didn't approve. "Surely Dev makes more money than that. Don't tell me you are so poor you have to go to work! Why would you do such a thing?

Adrian didn't approve either. "Oh, Drea, must you? You're a mother. How can you leave the kids for some job?" She thought I was defecting from womanhood and turning into a feminist. My mother would never understand any woman going working who didn't have to, and Adrian didn't realize how apolitical I was. I wasn't going to burn my bra or march in any demonstration. I was going to go to work two days a week.

Dev's mom, Sarah, didn't approve, but only because she was afraid I'd taken on too much. "Seems like you got enough on your plate with four kids, a husband, and the ranch. Don't you go get yourself worn out. Women get sick, if they try to do more'n they're able. That boy of mine can help. He knows how."

I assured Sarah that Dev did help, and it was thanks to her for the way she had raised him. She smiled, nodded proudly, and went on quietly crocheting a cap for me that matched the ones she'd made for the girls. And of course, my sister not only approved, but also understood. "Well, it's about time you did something. You've been turning into Susie Homemaker. You've had Cheerios rattling around in your head where brains used to be."

Dev had taken over the grocery shopping a long time ago, when I was busy with two energetic toddlers, a year-old baby, a tiny nursling and was exhausted. Now, to make it easier for me to get to work in the morning, he added the task cooking breakfast, while I made sure my now bigger children had socks that matched, lunches fixed, and no one spit toothpaste on a sister or brother. Dev also became proficient at running the washer and dryer. He picked Jennybeth up from the Baptist Nursery School at two P.M. and he arranged to be home from work when our other children's buses arrived and they came trudging up the hill. As I became a mother with a part-time job, he was my greatest support.

As nursing jobs went, working for Doctor De Angelo was easy. I liked working with the patients, and Doctor was a talented doctor in the delivery or surgical room, well respected for his technical skill and a man who was always polite and never overstepped bounds. Yolanda, our receptionist, scheduled the gynecological appointments for mid-week, the maternity patients for Monday and Friday to fit Carla's and my workdays.

Five months after I started working in the office, Melanie Taylor, a young friend of ours who was a county social worker, brought a woman to the office. The woman had multiple physical problems. Melanie felt that someplace other than the overcrowded, overworked county clinic should assess this woman's case. When I took the patient's history, I found that the woman's husband had abandoned her. She had five children, a leaky heart valve, scoliosis, and a history of tuberculosis.

It was apparent that the patient had reason to be seriously depressed, and she was terrified that she was pregnant again. Doctor confirmed the pregnancy. His words and manner destroyed the respect I'd held for him.

Ignoring her detailed patient history, Dr. De Angelo said the same thing to this sick, malnourished patient that he said to every other pregnant woman who came through the office. "Oh, my dear, you'll do fine," he said. "You just take it easy for the next few months, and take your vitamins. If you keep your weight down, this baby won't get too big and delivery will be easier." He patted her knee, washed his hands at the examining room sink. "I'll see you next month," he cheerfully said and left the room giving the woman no help and only placebo advice.

Tears formed in the woman's eyes. Dr. De Angelo belonged to the Knights of Columbus, the Rotary Club, and Kiwanis. He was a local civic patron who gave generously to charity, but his cavalier dismissal of this patient angered me.

"My kids. I got to take care of my kids," the woman was mumbling as I helped her sit up. Tears dripped on the sheet covering her lap.

I put one arm around her, and with the other, I reached for a box of tissues on the counter next to the examining table. The patient was twenty-eight, just my age. Malnutrition, overwork, and illness made her look aged. In the firmly kind diction I'd learned in training, I said, "Get dressed but wait here. I'll be right back."

When I came back, I gave my patient a piece of note pad paper. I'd printed out the name, address, and phone number of a trio of well-qualified OB/GYNs in Kings County who shared a practice. I'd heard of the medical group's liberal practices for determining which patients needed a D & C.

"Ask Miss Taylor to take you to these doctors. They can help you."

The patient started to say something to me, but I stopped her by putting my forefinger to my lips in the universal sign for secrecy and walked her to the reception desk.

Anger is mute in timid people, but felt no less. I wished I were brave enough to speak up to Dr. De Angelo. I'd tell him how his carelessness and condescension disgusted me. But I wasn't. I was only brave enough to go behind his back to recommend another doctor for his patient. He paid my wages, and I had probably committed an ethical violation. I'd call Clara when she came back on Tuesday and tell her what happened. Clara would tell Doctor if she felt he needed to know.

When I began working in the office, Clara told me about a horrible practice that was being used by poverty-stricken women in the farm labor camps. A woman needing to end a pregnancy carved a stiletto from slippery elm bark. She softened its surface by boiling it, then soaking it in water overnight or until slimy astringent mucilage from the thin bark covered the homemade dagger. Then the woman would then drive its tapered point through her cervix. Holding the stiletto in place in her vagina, if she could lie still for at least four hours, the fetus would usually abort.

After Clara shared this horrifying story of desperation and self-mutilation, she told me the bark could be purchased at any drugstore, no prescription needed. "Doctors around here see cervical scarring from that stuff, and it doesn't always work. It came in with the Okies in the thirties. It is purely *Grapes of Wrath*." Desperate women needed better and more humane alternatives to slippery elm bark.

~~~<<=>>~~~

Chapter 61: In The Patio by the Cactus Garden

I went home still thinking of the troubled woman in the office. Dev wasn't on the tractor. Instead, this afternoon he was across the yard checking the Suffolk ram's ear for foxtails, trouble for an animal. Jennybeth had doll clothes scattered all over the side porch. I had to step around the kittens, our old ranch dog, and my younger daughter's play to get into the kitchen. All was calm and orderly there. Andy and Ev were doing their homework at the dining room table, with Sallyanne supervising. A bossy big sister, she'd made a rule for the boys. They couldn't watch TV in the evening unless homework was done perfectly in the afternoon. The ranch's antenna only picked up two channels, but *Lost in Space*, the kids' most favorite show, would be on tonight. I washed my hands and put away the groceries Dev left on the countertop. I was in luck. He'd put the ice cream in the freezer. It hadn't melted in one of the grocery bags.

After supper when the kids were doing the dishes, the animals all fed and penned for the night, Dev and I went out to sit on the patio. I told him all that had happened that day.

The sun was setting on the Coast Range across the valley making the cactus garden glow with color more vivid and fierce than any city's neon. It was an exquisite evening.

"You don't have to work, honey. You can walk away from that job," Dev said.

"I know. But I like the work. And it's good for me to be there."

"If it had been Beth or Beverly in that woman's place, would you have given her the name of a doctor to end the pregnancy?" my husband asked.

"If she had to face what this patient has to face, yes. The woman is so sick, Dev. Even if the pregnancy is terminated, she may still die. I did what I could."

"You didn't talk to Melanie about it?"

"No. I gave the patient the information. I was afraid that if I talked to Melanie, it might seem like we were in collusion. Doctor De Angelo may fire me, but I wouldn't want him to lodge a complaint against her with Social Services for conspiring against him."

"But you said you were going to talk to Clara about it."

"Yes." I knew he saw an inconsistency in my reasoning, but he'd figure it out. Clara had worked for Doctor De Angelo for over twenty years. Nothing could threaten her job. Doctor's whole practice depended on Clara, but Melanie had only been with the county for three months. She could be hurt by a complaint lodged with her supervisor.

As night came and shadowed around us, Dev went in the house to check on the kids' work progress. I heard the TV come on. Our children would lose themselves in a starry future with Will Robinson and the robot.

As the evening darkened, I turned my chair around so I could look out past the new barn and watch the moon rise over the Sierra. The bright moonlight washed over our hill. It found reflective bits of mica embedded in the patio's paving stones, tiny fragments so inconsequential against the light of the sun that I'd never noticed them in the daytime.

The side door closed. Dev came back to sit with me, bringing each of us a half glass of Gallo Rosé. Stars came out all over the sky. I told my husband of something I'd never mentioned to anyone. But he was the sharer of my life's secrets, and I needed to tell him of the night a girl named Delores McCauley, the sharer of my childhood's secrets, died in St. Lucy's Hospital. I remembered every word Laney Frederick, Charge Nurse Mason, Sister Margaret Mary, Mr. and Mrs. McCauley, or Father Rodriguez spoke that night, and everything that Delores said to me, and I to her. When I finished, the story was as much a part of his memory as it was of mine.

We let the kids watch TV until late. It was almost ten when we went back inside. Jennybeth had fallen asleep on the floor. I carried her to bed, managed to get her nightgown on her sleep-limp body and tucked her in, while Dev scooted the other kids to the bathroom to brush their teeth. Their bantering sounds came echoing down the hallway, sweet, rich, laughing sounds. I let the present sweep in and reclaim me from the past.

~~~<<=>>~~~

Chapter 62: St. Lucy's 1967 Reunion

Late that summer, my nursing class held its ten-year reunion. I went to Los Angeles by myself, staying in Breeze Terrace with Mama. Husbands were invited, but Dev didn't really want to go. I didn't want to leave him or the kids, but I very much wanted to be there. Paro called to invite me to stay at her house, but I felt I needed to spend time with my mother. Pat was coming as Paro's and my guest. I picked her up at her mom's house for the reunion and we went together.

Audrey Chester was flying in from Germany for the reunion. Our old dorm was expected to be present. I couldn't remember Peggy's husband's name but he was the man she dated occasionally when we were in school. She looked the same except bigger. So did he. Peg was a supervising nurse at a big Lutheran convalescent complex in Orange County. We celebrated our tenth reunion in one of St. Lucy's conference rooms. The cafeteria catered, and our student favorites were on the menu. Few husbands or boyfriends were there. It was practically a ladies' night at St. Lucy's. Mary Eunice brought her husband. He was the only man sitting at our dorm's table. Mary Eunice had finished her Bachelor's at a secular college but said she felt she belonged to St. Lucy's.

Audrey walked into the room, forgivably a bit late. She had come farthest, from a base in Florida. She was still in the army, and I'd expected she be wearing her military uniform with lines of earned ribbons on her chest and a jaunty cap. Rather, she made her entrance in a party dress and brought a girl friend with her. Mary Eunice and I began waving. Audrey and her friend came toward our table holding hands, and acting affectionate in an intimate manner. Paro frowned. She leaned over and whispered something to Pat, and just as they reached the table, Paro flounced away.

Paro, Peggy, Audrey and I had been dorm mates for three years. Mary Eunice had been with us for two of them. We knew each other well. We saw that Paro's rapid defection from the table stabbed at Audrey. She tried to smile, but her lips pinched together for a moment too long before the smile broke through.

"She's a little uptight, isn't she?" Audrey's friend asked her, one eyebrow cocked. An 'I told you so' look was on her face.

"She always has been," Audrey answered. "Drea, did Amparo ever marry that cool friend of yours? Vince, I think his name was Vince."

"Yes. You were already overseas. They have a little boy now, Jason."

Her face relaxed back into her easy humor and she slipped her arm around her friend and looked around the table. "Pat! I remember you," Audrey said. "You visited so often, you were almost a member of our class."

Pat tossed a smile to Audrey and her friend. It was a good smile. Only someone who'd known Pat from childhood would know it was forced.

"*Pleeease*, come sit with us," Mary Eunice said, her voice full of genuine welcome.

"We will. We will." Audrey turned to me again. "What about you?" Audrey asked me. "You married the lanky blond guy down in accounting, didn't you?"

I grinned and nodded. "He's home taking care of the kids."

Before the two sat down, Audrey introduced Sherry Lambeth to each of us.

"Are you in the army also?" I asked, making her welcome.

"Yes, but tonight we are both civilians." Sherry twirled around in her party dress. During dinner, Pat told the two that she was an army wife, and the three of them found bonds of commonality. Audrey and Sherry were worried about the war in Southeast Asia. Both felt that one or both of them would be sent there in the next few months.

"Rich knows he's going too. He just doesn't know when." Pat said. "I'm going to hate it, but I knew he wanted the service when I married him."

"Someone needs to protect America," Audrey said with a thumbs-up gesture. "We go where we are needed most." The U.S. Army Nurse Corps had to appreciate having someone like Audrey in their ranks.

Joan Freeland came over with Joan Turner to tell me she was glad someone in our class snagged the cute man in the night accounting office. She said loudly that Marlene had tried her hardest to interest him. Marlene, sitting at the next table, was intended to overhear this and laughingly admitted that it was true. "He wouldn't come and sit with us in the cafeteria. He wasn't very friendly with any of the rest of us, you know."

"Stand-offish," Joan Turner laughed.

"Ah, but that's exactly what I liked about him," I quipped back.

The party began to break up by ten o'clock. Paro had spent most of the evening with Peggy and her husband at the reception table. As I went to saying goodbye to them, Paro's left hand was clenching the medal she was wearing around her neck. She seemed tense. Perhaps she and Peggy had been bemoaning my fall from the true faith. I understood and didn't take offense. People talked about people, and at that moment, I didn't think the true faith was helping Paro very much. She'd been rude to Audrey, and obviously wasn't happy.

Dev's dad retired from the Department of Fish and Game, and he and Sarah spent more time with us. I was always happy to have Sarah around, and the kids loved their grandfather. Marriage hadn't diminished my reluctance to be around men, but Everett was always careful to remain a comfortable distance from me, either through a natural reserve or perceptively sensing my wariness.

My mother finally became reconciled to the child born in her thirty-ninth year. She even seemed to appreciate having

Alex still at home. He'd always been likeable; it just took her a long time to figure out what everyone else knew. Both my brothers were safe from the threat of Vietnam. Alex had an injury during his sophomore year in high school that left him with a permanent limp and classified 4 F. Steve had a wife and child, plus his asthma history disqualified him from service. America's involvement seemed to be affecting many families. I felt guilty over my relief that the men in my family were safe.

When Laz died, Steve was only fourteen. Mama had curtly told him that she would only supply him with and food and a bed where he could sleep. Anything else he wanted, snacks, clothing, haircuts, spending money, he would have get for himself. He did. He ran a crew of paperboys every afternoon after school for the Herald Express, sold newspaper subscriptions on weekends. Beth helped him get a bank account.

Before Steve was sixteen he had a work permit and found a job in retail that paid better than the Herald Express. When Beth bought a new car, she gave him her old one.

Steve was too proud to beg our mother for any money for clothes or school supplies, and knew she wouldn't have given it. He'd been promised college and his father's business. He received neither. He had no time for sports or clubs, but his responsibility earned him one job after another, each one better than the one before.

He had done well and on his own. He was now managing a floor at Bullock's Westwood, rising quickly in responsibility and earnings. He and Janet, with their baby daughter, were shopping for a house out in the San Fernando Valley, where they could purchase a four bedroom two and a half bath house for what a dilapidated, two bedroom cottage would cost in West L.A. Gas was cheap, and Steve could commute over Sepulveda Pass to Westwood in less than a half hour.

Alex received a scholarship to Thomas Aquinas Prep at eighth grade graduation. He was witty and well organized. His size made him a good prospect for football. Like Beth, he was popular. He had the girth, height, and weight to appeal to Aquinas's football coach. After the field injury sidelined him, he became a better student. He'd applied for the internship with the county that Vince McMullen had suggested, and that helped him to a scholarship to Loyola U. He was in his second year there, working part time in the District Attorney's Office.

The best thing that happened in 1967 was that the Ryder's adopted their second baby girl. Adrian and Jack had five beautiful, energetic children now, Debbie, Johnny and Donny, Melanie and Michelle. We kept each other up to date on our families' activities. She told me of Gordon and Beverly's travels and gave me news of the people from our old Breeze Terrace days. Vivian Morgan was a widow. Michael Herrick was married and was living in Long Beach managing his uncle's factory. His brother Ronnie was working at Rocketdyne in Santa Suzanna, and according to Adrian's sources he was still single, brainy, weird, and collecting horror comic books. Bossy, bratty, obnoxious Harold was a psychologist in Portland, Oregon. Who would have believed that?

~~~<<=>>~~~

Chapter 63: A Military Action

1968 rang in without the fireworks of New Year's Eve of Alex's gala christening party twenty years earlier; Dev and I opened a mini-bottle of champagne and shared it. Our families called with phone wishes for a bright New Year. Vince called too, just before we went to bed. Paro sounded happier, but maybe it was the champagne she was drinking. The next morning, I called Adrian to wish her a happy New Year and then called Pat and we talked for a long time. She saw the New Year with her children and her mother in Culver City. When Rich was deployed to Southeast Asia, Pat and the children moved out of base officer's housing into the O'Hara home in Culver City. They didn't know how long he would be overseas, and Pat wanted the support of her family more than the support of the other wives on base. She wouldn't be lonely at her mother's house; she could enroll them at St. Blaise, and Culver City wasn't far from Rich's widowed mother in Baldwin Hills.

"God won't give me any thing I can't bear," Pat said. She bolstered herself up with the sayings she had always heard at school and home. Though trite and illogical, the axioms seemed to help her. But, that year, none of Pat's prayers and novenas could keep Rich Whitfield out of Vietnam, and they didn't bring him home safely.

Rich was killed in February of 1968 at Lang Vei. He had been serving as an intelligence officer at Khe Sanh, and was sent to Lang Vei just before Soviet tanks overran the southern sector. Eleven years earlier, Tommy Whitfield had made a bitter prediction from his schizophrenic visions when he stood chanting that the Communists coming. A shell from a Soviet built PT-76 tank killed his brother.

Living in agrarian bliss of La Cordillera hadn't insulated Dev or me from the war. Our county had the greatest percentage of casualties of any county in California in 1968.

We both knew good hardworking people who lost sons, nephews, brothers and fathers. Rural area working class boys didn't get student deferments, it seemed that way too many were going from the high school football field to military flag draped coffins. Insane politicians were bleeding away our nation's young men. Rich was Pat's husband, but he was also Dev's and my friend. I'd known him since I was sixteen. My heart was with Pat and the Whitfield family, and also with the families of Johnny Sanchez and J. C. Corter, young men who had worked in our grove and were now gone.

I understood the protesters marching in the streets. I remembered the propaganda films at the Palms Theater matinees during World War Two. Our whole neighborhood felt wild exhilaration when Hitler was routed to his underground bunker, and when the Allies won the war. But clearly to my mind came the memory of how victory's glory tarnished a few months later when as a naïve third grader, I read of the bombings of Hiroshima and Nagasaki on the newspaper racks. Glossy magazines, in the beauty parlor where Mama took Beth and I to have our hair done before our parents' parties or other important events, ran photo features for years afterward about people who were maimed and died in Hiroshima and Nagasaki. I was born at the wrong time to be able to support any nation's war crimes.

Dev was older and he had a different military viewpoint. Pearl Harbor and the Invasion of Poland happened during his childhood awareness.

My husband could champion the need for our nation's use of the A-bomb to conclude the Second World War. But he wasn't convinced that this new Southeast Asian war was excusable. La Cordillera was solidly RED, WHITE and BLUE, but our friends in the town were all quiet people like we were, people who spoke through their votes, not by carrying placards or marching in the streets. But, when the news featured kids on American college campuses chanting: Hey! Hey! L.B.J.! How many kids did you kill today? I was silently chanting along with them.

Rich Whitfield was a hero. I believed that. But a good man dying in an unwinnable war was far too great a price to pay for an ideology. I felt little patriotism that year. No attack had been made on America. I saw no reason for that war which killed my friend's husband.

Rich's funeral was held at St. Blaise, and he was interred in Holy Cross Cemetery. Pat's father died nearly ten years ago, and Rich's father died just two months before he did. They were buried there too. Dev was away at a conference for small hospitals in Houston, and I had the ranch, children, and a job to worry about. I'd already promised Dr. De Angelo that I'd cover for Carla for two weeks while she and her husband were in Brazil at an Arabian horse show. I sent flowers on behalf of the Horvath and Cunningham families, and my mother and sister went to the rosary, and Pat and I talked for a long time on the phone that week. She was finding her family difficult and not the support she had expected. She'd been the baby of the O'Hara clan, and although she'd been a wife and mother for twelve years, her family wanted to make every decision for her.

"We planned for the possibility that Rich might be killed. He was a soldier," she said. "The kids and I'll be okay. My brothers make me scream. They want to control how I budget my income, put their names on my bank account, and tell me where to live. I'm going to do what my husband and I decided together, not what they want. I'm not staying here at Mom's.

I'd like the kids to continue going to St. Blaise, but my mother clucks at me about everything. The kids think she's the boss, not me. She medicates my children after I've told her not to."

"Your mom would pour cod liver oil down the kids' throats twice a day and send them to school with a flannel round their neck smelling like Vicks Vapo-Rub."

"You remember."

"I remember you hated it."

"I'm thirty-two. But my whole family still sees me as the baby. My mother-in-law doesn't. Elaine depends on me to help her with decisions about Tommy's care. She sees me as a sensible young woman who worked for the Bank of America and had money saved before she was married. Mom thinks I need her. I don't. And Elaine needs me and the kids."

Pat didn't take time for grief. Within two months, she found an older, four-bedroom house she could afford in St. Mary Magdalen parish in Thousand Oaks, not far from the state hospital. It had a good parochial school within walking distance She invited her mother-in-law to move in with her and the children. Pat O'Hara Whitfield enrolled at San Fernando Valley State College the following September as a freshman, and easily passed all her entrance exams though it had been nearly fifteen years since she graduated from high school.

~~~<<=>>~~~

Chapter 64: Never To Be Called Sandy

By 1971, Beverly gave up dance troupe tours and the birth control pill. Soon she and Gordon had a darling wee baby named Cassie who had her mother's auburn hair. Gordon found a good job through the Claussen's Hollywood connections. He was working as a location manager for Twentieth Century Fox and he and Beverly had purchased a big ramshackle home in Topanga Canyon. Adrian told me that the yard up in Topanga was beautiful with a shady sloping terrain that led to an intermittent stream. She would happy to have her sister living near.

Steve and Janet had two children, Karin and Doug, and made a yearly trip to our ranch on their way to and from water skiing at Bass Lake. My brother Alex had a degree in philosophy and was working full-time in the District Attorney's office. He planned to attend law school, but hadn't enrolled. After two years with the county, he surprised the family by applying to Vista, the domestic Peace Corp. He was sent to Trenton, for a break-in period, and then assigned to Detroit where he worked as an ombudsman for indigents needing legal counsel. He came home full of stories of his work helping an urban under-class negotiate the complexities of the judicial system. The second time he came home for a visit, he brought a spunky Arizona-born woman with him. Her name was Sandra Kaplan. She was his supervisor in Michigan. Raised in Tucson, she'd earned her M.A. from University of Arizona. Sandra was as committed to helping the least favored segment of society as my brother was. They were passionate about their work, though neither was passionate about long eastern winters.

Mama, Steve, Janet, Beth and I, all pointed out that there were poor people who needed help in California too. Sandra laughed heartily and told us that her family said the same thing in reference to Arizona. As soon as they met, Sandra and Beth became great friends. If I hadn't been so busy, I would have been jealous. They had much in common though, areas where Beth and I had never had any commonality. Both were career minded and loved travel. Neither was interested in a domestic life or a house full of children.

During her twice-yearly visits to Verna's retreat in Maui, my sister had become enamored with Hawaii and not only for the islands' beauty. For nearly ten years Beth had watched as tourist traffic grew with the American economy. Airfare was inexpensive enough that even supermarket checkers and bank tellers were able to save enough for a vacation in Hawaii. Hawaii Five-O was the weekly favorite of people in the nation. TV shows and movies were being filmed in the islands and that indicated to Beth that there was a need for an agency like Raudell-Horvath in the islands. My sister couldn't pass up the business opportunity.

"Hawaii is exactly like Hollywood was sixty years ago. It needs us," she nagged, as she pestered Wally.

"You do it," he answered. "I'm not doin'it. Whadda ya think? I'm gedding ready to retire."

But he couldn't resist her. Wally appropriated the money for Beth's venture, and five years later, my sister's and the Raudell-Horvath Agency were providing Hawaii's best entertainment for concerts, bistros, advertising, movies and TV. Beth took a lease on a Waikiki penthouse as nice as the one she had Los Angeles and was commuting the Pacific twice monthly managing a well-staffed business office there.

Beth was the organizer for all our family events and made sure that even though Dev and I were too busy to fly to Hawaii, we didn't miss anything important. Dev and I'd first met Sandra at a party at Beth's Los Angeles apartment.

Beth introduced Alex's companion, saying, "This is Sandra, *never to be called Sandy.*"

Beth made me laugh, but Mama, Janet and Sandra didn't get it. Dev didn't either. It only took Steve a second or two, and he broke a smile as he remembered a conversation that had taken place years and years ago earlier, when we were children. Sandra didn't understand and looked perplexed.

"You can call me Sandy," she protested. "Most people do. Really, I don't mind."

Janet was quick to say, "I'm already calling her Sandy. It's a cute name and suits her."

Sandra wasn't the kind of woman who would feel flattered to be considered cute. Steve, more perceptive than his wife, noted the look that crossed Sandra's face. "But you don't know the story," Steve told his wife.

Beth took the floor slipping into a pose from musical comedy. "No, Stevie. I get to tell her. When Alex was born, I began to call him Sandy. It's the Hungarian equivalent of Alex. Sandor is Alex's birth certificate name."

Sandra nodded. She knew that much.

"Our mother wouldn't let me." Beth shook her finger at Mama.

Steve broke in. "Sandor had been our uncle's name. We'd called him Uncle Sandy, so we liked calling our new brother Sandy. Mother was so mad. She forbid us to call him that. She said Alex was *never to be called Sandy*."

"Why not, Mother Horvath? It's only a nickname," Sandra asked.

Mama evaded the question. Instead, she said, "I was upset. I wasn't *mad*."

So Alex answered for her. It was his story. He'd heard it all his life. "Mama thought that the names Stevie and Sandy sounded as though they belonged to a pair of Cocker spaniels, and weren't appropriate for her kids."

Mama spoke out indignantly. "I didn't say that! You tell the story that way but you never once heard me refer to you children as kids. That's a vulgarity." Having scolded us, Mama turned to Sandra. "What I said, my dear, was those names would make my sons sound like a pair of Cocker spaniels, not like my beautiful *children*. And they would."

"Okay, Horvath family," Alex's girlfriend put her shoulders back, raised her chin, and announced, "I truly don't want to be considered a dog. I hereby state that I am Sandra-never-to-be-called-Sandy." She turned to Alex and fluffed his hair. "Handsome boy, I think you should begin using your real first name. Sandor sounds *tres chic*. Sandor and Sandra. It suits us."

And then they told us that they were engaged. Beth, Janet and Mama had noticed the diamond ring but it was on the wrong hand, so they didn't get the implication. I'd noticed that Alex and Sandra were exceptionally talkative and affectionate, but not the ring. Sandra wasn't going to put it on the proper finger of the proper hand until they had made the announcement to both families. She was a few years older than Alex and this was her first marriage. She wanted to do it quietly, but right.

~~~<<=>>~~~

Chapter 65: Poison in Paradise

Beth invited all of us to visit her in Honolulu, and my brothers did although we didn't feel we could go so far from our small ranch, and the trip would have been expensive. But the best thing Beth did, from Dev's and my point of view was something she did for our children. She promised each of her nieces and nephews a week in Hawaii with their auntie on or around the date of the child's twelfth birthday.

Beth always kept her promises. Sallyanne visited during Christmas vacation in 1969, Andy the summer of 1971. Ev had his trip the summer of 1972. Jennybeth's turn would come this year. She was going to spend Christmas 1973 in Honolulu.

Between the kids, the ranch, and our jobs, even as Dev's salary increased, we hadn't felt we had the time for Hawaiian vacations, but my brothers, their wives, and three of our kids had already gone jetting across the Pacific with Beth. Our younger daughter was driving us crazy with anticipation. She was marking all the calendars in the house - including the one in her dad's office and had pictures of airplanes and palm trees taped to the door of her room.

In early December, as Jennybeth's long anticipated visit to Honolulu approached, Beth made a morning visit to a resort on Oahu's North Shore. She wanted to audition four dancers who worked in a small club there before she signed them. It was a break from the managerial work she did and helped keep her current.

The weather was clear and clean. There was almost no traffic as she drove across the high plateau between Oahu's two mountainous regions. She was familiar enough with the area to know that taking Kaukonahua Road would cut a few miles from her drive. Sun was glinting on the green cane fields, the mountains deep blue behind them. She had a brief thought as she passed the Schofield Barracks turn off that the strafing of the airfield there had taken place when she was just a baby. It had been thirty-three years since that historic morning.

When she reached the North Shore and her appointment, she found she liked the dance act and agreed to sign the young performers to a six night, two matinees per week gig in Kona beginning the first of February. She expected that they'd wow the tourists, and was feeling good as she started back to her office in Honolulu.

Windows open, Beth was driving her new pimento red Triumph Spitfire, Gypsy Wagon VII, back to Honolulu and singing along with Don Ho. Her route turned away from the beach to re-cross the isolated center of the island. Sand and ocean gave way to tall cane. After what seemed only a few miles, her car's engine failed. She let it coast to the right shoulder of the road, set the brake and raised the convertible top against the islands frequent showers. The landscape had been lovely earlier that morning was now rather lonely. Cane fields on either side of the road were high barricades. She felt like she was in a sky-topped green tunnel. Beth didn't frighten easily, and it was a lovely day. After trying a number of times to start the car, she locked her briefcase in the Triumph's tiny boot, took her keys and her bag, and began walking.

Beth trekked about a quarter of a mile when a nearly new Buick Riviera came from behind her. Its driver offered to give her a lift to a telephone. She was wary, but he was well dressed and well spoken, a nice looking man around thirty. It might be a long time before any other car came by and would be a horrendous walk to Wahiawa where she could get a tow. Her feet already hurt. The man introduced himself as Jeff Howard, telling her he was an insurance agent in Pearl City. He looked pleasant and legitimate.

But as they drove, the man wouldn't respond to any of her conversational openings. Beth was uncomfortable. The more she talked, the odder he seemed to be, taunting her with his lack of response. She asked him to stop the car and let her out. He continued to ignore her. The hairs on her arms stood up. She felt panic enough to risk jumping out of the moving vehicle. Reaching for the door handle, she couldn't get it to open. As she yanked at it, the driver caught her by the hair and pulled her back toward him. Steering the car with his left hand, he used his right hand to push her down onto the floor of the car. When she was down in the foot well, he began smashing at her with a heavy, metal object.

Beth squirmed enough to keep the first blows from seriously hurting her, but he hit at her again and again as he drove. She managed to get her hand on the man's shoe and put all her strength into forcing his foot off the car's accelerator. Distracted, and trying to control the car, he dropped the weapon. As he tried to kick her hands away, the car spun across the opposite lane into a shallow ditch along the left side of the road. The car's front driver's side fender hit the dirt shelf below the cane, the hood popped up and the passenger door swung open. Blood pouring from her head and almost blinding her, Beth scrambled out, climbed the ditch embankment and began running down the highway.

The driver's door was jammed against the steep side of the ditch toward the cane field. Beth had a slight head start, but she knew he was stronger than she, and she could hear him thrash his way out the passenger side of the car after her. My sister kicked off her shoes and ran barefoot down the cracked macadam road. She could hear him climb up the ditch and then heard the noise of his shoes behind her. She ran, gulping air, and not looking back.

Before her, the cane on that right side of the road ended. In the open land ahead, she could see a farmhouse. Beth swerved toward it. A thin, aged farmer wearing a conical rice hat, shirtless, with rolled pants and bare legs, was working in a garden in front of the house. Beth, screaming and bloody, ran toward him. The farmer assessed what was happening, for he yelled something loud and ran toward her. He raised his hoe as though he held a Samurai sword in his hands, and he ran toward her attacker as the door of the farmhouse opened. Two women and some children rushed out onto the porch beckoning and calling her to the safety of the house.

Beth's attacker saw the family too. He turned and ran back to the Riviera, got it started and backed it away from the embankment, then raced the car forward along the ditch until he came to a place where the Buick could get back on the highway. It gunned past the farmhouse and was gone.

"I only have a little headache. They ran me through every possible test this afternoon before they'd give me anything for it. By then I didn't need anything. I was used to it." My sister wasn't happy. She had two sets of stitches on her head, one set on her left shoulder, and she was covered with contusions and bruises. "My feet hurt worse than my head. They're scraped from the road."

"Do you want me to fly over? I can easily. Carla would cover for me."

"No. I'll be okay. I'm even breathing okay. Can you believe that? All this and I don't have to use my inhaler."

"Of course not. You're your own adrenalin factory."

"I don't need a nurse, Drea. Mama offered to fly over too. But Verna's here. She caught the afternoon flight out of Maui, and Wally got the first flight out of LAX he could. He'll be here in a few hours. I don't want him to see me looking bald and ugly, but he's coming anyway.

"My hair had to be shaved half off. They think the guy hit me with a tire iron. I kept wiggling and got my shoulder up, so he couldn't kill me. But the cuts bled so much I'm surprised I didn't need a transfusion."

"You better come home. The guy might still be a stalker."

She ignored me and changed the subject. "A cute cop was the first to get to the Ishida's farm, even before the ambulance," she said. "His name's Tom Fonseca. You'd really like him. You especially. He had a Portugese grandfather but he looks like Okio Hasekura did. You had such a crush on Okio you'd adore Tom. He's been here twice today. He told me not to worry. I was in the wrong place at the wrong time, that's all. My description matched those given by two other women who were beaten and raped this year. Tom says the police are sure the guy's killed at least two women in addition to the ones that were hurt. Their wounds were similar, and similar to mine.

"The man who saved me, Mr. Utaro Ishida, saw the guy's license number and remembered it. His wife and daughter and all the grandkids came out on the porch, and that scared the guy off." The delivery of Beth's stream of words suddenly slowed down. Her medication must have starting to take effect.

"Drea," she said. "The second time Tom came in to see me, he said the guy who attacked me is a dead man. Drea? Dree, are you there?"

"I'm here." My mind had jumped back in time. I was thinking of Jeannie French's murder when Beth and I were children. Beth could have died the same way. A pipe wrench or a tire iron, both objects were heavy pieces of metal. My sister was very alive and talking to me. I felt nauseous and frightened for her. I didn't sleep the rest of the night.

Seven hours later, feeling grungy and wishing I were in Hawaii, I was at work when Beth called from the hospital.

"Wally's here already," she said. "He's been with the police. They towed the Gypsy Wagon. My briefcase was in the trunk. But that's not why I called."

"What's going on? I know you are all right because you called me."

"Don't say anything to Mama, she'd get freaky. But, Drea, the guy who attacked me is already dead."

"Literally dead?"

"Yes. He's literally dead. I know that someone killed him.

"How can you know?"

"My cop stopped in again. He showed me the man's picture. It was definitely the man who attacked me. Tom told me I had nothing more to worry about, ever. He was very positive, Drea. Honestly, he looked right in my eyes. It was as if he were telling me the guy was dead without saying it. Tom said the identification was confirmed at the man's house, and his partner found my purse under the seat of the guy's car." She stopped talking, and I heard her take a sip of water and put the glass down. "He gave it back to me. The purse. Do you get it? They didn't keep it for evidence. You don't need to say anything, not even to Dev. Maybe the police didn't kill that guy, but someone did. He's dead and I'm glad."

Two days later she called to tell me that she heard a brief report on TV that the body of an unknown white man was found in a cane field near Wahiawa. It was estimated that he'd been dead two days.

"Remember how you killed that rattler on your property when the kids were little? Think about this. There aren't any snakes in Hawaii. There aren't any rattlers or cobras. No one wants poison in this paradise."

~~~<<=>>~~~

Chapter 66: Overlooking Waikiki Beach

Beth was soon commuting between the agencies in Los Angeles and Hawaii again. She wrapped colorful scarves around her head until her hair grew back and continued to be glib about the attack. Beneath her flip comments, her anger lingered. The attack changed her.

My sister's first action was taken to insure that the Ishida family was generously rewarded. Soon after that, she dropped all her social clubs and became an activist for abused women. She surprised people, because it was the first time she'd seemed to show much social commitment. Mama worried about her radical change of interest. Steve said it was the way she was handling what had happened to her. Alex and Sandra were proud of the way she integrated her own experience into doing good for others. I spun back to hard days in my own childhood. It wasn't the first time in her life that Beth Horvath had been a champion for the weak and helpless.

Beth began by volunteering her business expertise two days a month to help victimized women on Oahu. She rented and refurbished a dilapidated space in a shopping center and began employment-training classes, persuading other managerial women willing to volunteer time to provide training and employers to provide job opportunities. As the months passed, piggybacking on Wally's knowledge of general fund-raising methods and the organization of charitable entities, she made presentations to civic and social groups. She'd flash her smile, quote statistics and hand out flyers.

I couldn't help admiring the positive way she integrated her own terrible experience into becoming an activist.

"Few of these women were randomly attacked like I was," she told Dev and me. "This is different, and it isn't some nut case hurting them. Their husbands and boyfriends are trying to kill them, physically or spiritually or both," she insisted.

I'd worked in an emergency room. She wasn't telling me anything I didn't know. Neither of us ever referred to the house in Breeze Terrace, or our childhood. Those memories were something always present but never voiced between us.

Both in Hawaii and at home in West L.A, the focus of my sister's life changed. She spent hours, days and weeks helping women who were psychologically beaten down get job training, legal aid, apply for financial support, and work out co-op child care.

Our youngest child's birthday trip was deferred because of the attack, but Jennybeth finally had her Hawaiian week with Aunt Beth during spring break. Instead of the scuba lessons and helicopter rides her sibs chose, Jennybeth asked if Beth would invite Wally to be there so he could take Jennybeth, by herself, to lunch at the old, pink Royal Hawaiian Hotel on Waikiki. "Just the two of us," she informed

Auntie Beth. "You don't need to come along. I want to feel like I'm Wally's date." We knew she wanted to pretend she was Beth for one afternoon. Beth was flattered, and I understood.

Wally took Jennybeth to lunch; Beth took her shopping and to Maui to see Verna and drink virgin Mai Tais on her terrace. And Jennybeth came home happy. Her purchases, too numerous to carry home on the plane, were mailed from various stores and gave her a sequence of presents to open for the following weeks.

Wally's third wife, after a long illness with cancer, died early in 1975. Not long after, Beth supervised the sale of Raudell-Horvath Los Angeles to Wally's son in New York. Wally was ready to retire. He wanted to sell Raudell-Horvath Honolulu, but Beth refused. By then, she was on the Hawaiian State Council for Women, and working as part of an active legal advocacy group. She wasn't ready to retire from anything.

A discrete time after the death of Wally's wife, Mama, Alex and Sandra, Steve and Janet, and Dev and I, along with the adult members of Wally's immediate family, flew to Hawaii for Wally and Beth's small, quiet wedding. My sister had taken rooms for us at the Halekulani. Mama and Verna were set up in the most luxurious suite I could imagine. I went down the hall to visit them the morning after the wedding. Mama was in a peacock chair near a huge window that overlooked Waikiki Beach. Her lips were pursed and she was frowning.

"I don't know why your sister had to marry that coarse man," she said as I walked in. "He's too old for her. Why did your sister have to go and marry such an old man?"

Verna kept quiet, but gave me a look.

"You did, Mama. You married old men," I said for both Verna and me.

"It isn't the same. I didn't have Beth's advantages! She didn't *have* to marry an old man. She could have had anyone. Wally will just die off on her, and she'll end up a lonely old widow with no one to look out for her."

"Most of our husbands die off, Mother. No matter how young they are. Mr. Taylor died young. Don Claussen too. Mr. O'Hara did, and Mr. McCauley. Now my friend Pat's a widow and she's my age. Women outlive men. It's the real curse we have to face."

I'd made my point well, but Mama had more to say. "Well, my beautiful daughter didn't have to end up as some man's fourth wife. That's shameful. Why couldn't she have been a first wife? You were a first wife. It embarrasses me to think my gorgeous daughter is just another bead on the string of Wally's wives."

"Mama, Laz was your fourth husband. Wally was only married once before. You're the one with the string of beads."

"Don't be snippy with me. And don't be spiteful."

Verna rolled her eyes and left the room. She'd had enough of Mama this morning.

"Your sister, with all her money! Steve and Janet had a nicer wedding. Who ever heard of a wedding in someone's own apartment? That was tawdry."

"Mother, Beth's home isn't an apartment. It's a garden penthouse. It was a lovely wedding. Think about the flowers and the musicians. Everything was just beautiful."

"You always stick up for her. You do that even against your own mother."

I went into the suite's kitchenette and fixed Mama a sandwich and cup of tea. Food always put her in a better mood. I was in a very good one. Tomorrow we flew home. Dev and I planned to sneak away alone, without the family, and dance the fragrant tropical night away.

"Why did you fix tuna? I'm more in the mood for egg salad."

"Do you want me to call room service?"

"No. It will do. I just would have liked the other better."

Beth and Wally weren't going on a honeymoon. Work was what my sister liked, and that's what they were going to do. The agency had new talent to assess and process, and Beth was to address a conference on domestic violence the following weekend.

Our mother decided she wanted to stay in Hawaii a little longer and was going to change her flight to extend her visit. Verna made a personal sacrifice and invited Mama to come and stay with her on Maui. It was Verna's wedding present to Beth.

~~~<<=>>~~~

Chapter 67: Talking to an Old Friend

Alex and Sandra married quietly and left their work in Michigan to move to Las Vegas, halfway between the Horvath family headquarters in Los Angles and Sandra's family in Scottsdale. Sandra, never-to-be-called-Sandy, took a management job with the Department of Social Welfare, and Alex began working as legal liaison for the indigents of Clark County. They liked Las Vegas and being nearer both their families.

Dev and I bought forty acres of pasture adjoining the back of our property. Steve earned another promotion. Beth and Wally were thriving on the islands. All was well as we moved into mid-life.

Beth's continuing work with abused women didn't interfere with her relationship with Wally. He had a strong and generous attitude and had long been a well-known contributor to civic and social causes. He was proud of her social commitment. I hoped marriage and the experience that she had undergone with the attack would temper her often-brash desire to do exactly as she pleased. Not that I wanted her changed; But I did want her safe and able to enjoy some of the simpler, less ambitious and less frantic delights of life.

My childless sister was able to keep better contact with Adrian and Beverly than I was. Beth never let more than a month or two go by without seeing or calling each of them. But, the older my children seemed to grow, the more I seemed to be running around barely keeping up with my obligations to them, my job and my husband. The same was happening to almost every woman I knew who was around my age. We were suddenly part of a new working class, and we were struggling. Our mothers hadn't worked for wages and couldn't teach us how to manage a family and a job. We were the first generation of middle class working mothers. I wasn't successful. I'd have been swamped without Dev's help.

Andy and Ev were both running track and on the swim team at La Cordillera High School. Sallyanne, who wanted to be called Anne now, was in her first year of college and living in a dorm at Fresno State, coming home on weekends. "Sallyanne is *too cutesy*," she told us. "I'm not a little girl anymore."

"Well, change it. I did when I was your age," I answered. "Your dad and I would respect that."

She gave me a very funny look. "I thought you'd be upset."

"No, I wouldn't be upset."

She was a dear child, nearly an independent woman. I didn't worry about Sallyanne or the boys. I worried about Jennybeth. Our youngest was striving to join every single junior high school club, concentrating far more on activities than A's. She dreamed of being like her Auntie Beth, but seemed more like her maternal grandmother. Her Auntie Beth did get A's.

Two years after Beth's wedding, an invitation to another reunion of my nursing class arrived. It had been twenty years since the class of 1957 graduated from St. Lucy's Hospital and St. John of God College. The same committee was putting it together, and the invitation itself was filled with so much flagrantly pious phrasing and covered with so many roses and crosses that Dev said it looked like the handout at a mortuary viewing. Peggy must have designed it herself. I knew Paro had no part of its design choice.

I sent in my regrets, though not because of the invitation. I was crazily busy on weekends. I was on the costume committee for La Cordillera High School's drama department. This spring's offering was to be *Taming of the Shrew,* and the costumes elaborate. I felt obligated to sew, since both our boys had speaking parts, and freshman Jennybeth had a crowd scene part. She expected a costume as elegant as the gown I was making for the senior who was playing Kate. I'd had to explain to her that that wouldn't be appropriate.

Sallyanne was living in a campus dorm and had an on-campus job, but came home with her laundry every other weekend. She didn't have a car, so one of us had to pick her up and drive her back. The other kids were too busy in school to help around the ranch as much as they had earlier. I had to help more.

If Dev and I were lucky, we found time to sit in the patio at the end of the day. Sitting down anywhere wasn't happening very often. We had to sneak foreplay in between sprinkler checking and mucking out the barn, and usually fell asleep immediately after the actual activity, so there wasn't much afterplay going on either. We were too worn out to be able to stop and think about how happy we were. Though, beneath the fatigue, I think we knew.

The phone rang one evening. It was a wonderful surprise. Paro called me. I hadn't talked with her for a couple of years, though we still sent handwritten notes to each other tucked into our Christmas and birthday cards. Her voice sounded the way it had when we were students, cheerful and easy. Whatever seemed to have upset her so long ago was gone. She'd heard from Peggy who collected the RSVP insert envelopes that I wasn't coming to our class' twentieth reunion, and wanted to touch base.

"Jason is going away to college. Vince talked him into Georgetown, and we're sure he'll get in. Oh, Andrea, my son doesn't need me anymore, and I don't want to cripple him by clinging."

"You wouldn't. You aren't like that. Do you think you'd like going back to work?"

"You went back to nursing. Do you like it? Are you happy being back at work?"

"It's been nearly ten years now. Working is good for me. I did medical office work for a few years, and that was only part-time. But for the last few years I've been doing nursing work for La Cordillera Public Schools. It's a full-time job and pays well. Oh, I do volunteer work too. I volunteer as a stand-by nurse at for St. Catherine's school in Taylorville, the town south of La Cordillera. The nuns appreciate having someone that they can call on when medical problems come up. My superintendent lets me do that as long as I make up any of the time I'm there, so the taxpayers aren't providing St. Catherine's with my service.

Paro's voice cooled. "Does St. Catherine's know you're a fallen-away Catholic?"

I was a run-away Catholic, not a fallen-away one, but Paro wouldn't understand the difference. So I said, "I told the sisters that I wasn't a Catholic, which is the truth. I told them that I wanted to volunteer my nursing expertise to repay the church for the excellent training I received at a Catholic hospital, which is also the truth." Getting our conversation back on easier ground, I asked, "What does Vince think about you going back to work?"

"He'd rather I not. He likes me doing the charities because it makes him look good, but I'm tired of that."

"You might not be satisfied with school nursing, Paro. I do head lice checks and talk to the fifth and sixth grade girls about menses. I do a bit of counseling with parents when the boys run around the playground like young roosters, or the girls start nasty cliques. I teach a class for expectant minors at the high school. I sometimes have the opportunity to intervene if I find kids are in bad situations at home or in class. School nursing is more like mothering than like medical nursing. It doesn't feel like hospital work."

"I'd rather go back to hospital work." Paro said. "You are so lucky with your houseful of children, but I'm not living your life. My life is lonely. Jason doesn't need me anymore. And hospital nursing would give me a community again. The very best time of my life was at St. Lucy's. School nursing would remind me daily how much I missed by not having more children. I wanted to adopt, but Vince wouldn't consider it. Whenever I'm around children I miss the children we didn't have so much I want to cry. I wanted a big family, Drea. I couldn't work around children."

I had no idea she'd lived with such grief. Every baby announcement I'd sent her probably caused her pain. Every word in a chatty note or phone call from Pat or me about our daily lives must have turned to arrows piercing her. "Shift work would mean being away from home at night," I said.

"Vince wouldn't even notice. I see him on TV more than at home. Parties and politics are what he loves, not me. Club and charitable work is very hollow, Drea. I've made no real friends." Her voice sounded so despondent, I couldn't believe I'd been so wrong about her life. "When Jason leaves for college, I'll be alone all the time. I think I'd love doing shift work in a hospital again. Nurses don't have time to get lonely."

"Oh, Paro. You won't be lonely. Anna Lee must be a good sister-in-law. You certainly have friends. There's always Peggy." Mentioning Peggy would have gotten a laugh from the old Paro. "It's McMullen. Vince is like his father. His dad is all parties and politics too. Vince's mom was always in the shadows, but she seemed to enjoy her life. She seemed happy.

"I do love Vince, and he is awfully good to me. But our life isn't like yours. Don't think it is. You are very lucky. I better go now. It's been good talking to you. I'll call and let you know if I get a job somewhere."

I didn't want to give up the conversation. It had been too long since we really talked. "Promise. I'll be waiting to know what you decided. Give Vince and Jason my love. Jason probably doesn't remember me."

"He does. He remembers a time we came up to the ranch. If I apply for a hospital job do you think Dev will give me a character reference on his office letterhead?"

I was pleased to have heard from Paro, and I hung up the phone receiver smiling. The idea that Amparo Mendoza McMullen, the past president of a dozen charitable organizations in the city of Los Angeles and the wife of a popular county spokesman would need a character reference from the comptroller of a small town Central Valley hospital consortium was beyond ironic.

~~~<<=>>~~~

Chapter 68: Envy's Limits

A short time after Paro called, Pat called. Pat had been such a popular guest ten years ago at St. Lucy's 1967 reunion that she received her own invitation to the 1977 reunion. Without giving me a chance to tell her I wasn't going to be there, she told me she wasn't. She'd promised to chaperone a school math club trip that weekend and hoped I didn't mind.

"I can't mind," I told her. "I won't be there either. I'll miss seeing everyone, especially you and Paro."

"The three of us should meet for lunch on a Saturday. It would be fun. You haven't gotten together with us for years."

"You'll have to meet Paro without me. I honestly can't get away until summer. I'll try then."

"Yes, you can get away. Just take a Saturday. Drive down in the morning."

I wasn't Pat. Dev and I had jobs, children, and ran a ranch in our spare time. I couldn't do everything she did. Over the past six years, she'd graduated from college, spent a graduate year earning a teaching credential, and begun teaching high school math in Ventura.

Her energy would have taxed any man wanting to date her. She worked full time, had three children living home, did parish bookkeeping audits, and took care of a now very frail mother-in-law. She watched over Tommy Whitfield. Every other Sunday she checked him out of his care facility so he could enjoy a proper Irish Sunday supper with the family. Her children had grown up thinking that having a schizophrenic uncle was no different from having a developmentally disabled brother or an alcoholic grandpa like other families might have. With all she had filling her schedule, no concert came to town, no first run movie, no circus or fair that Pat didn't make sure Elaine and the kids attended with her.

My children missed out on those entertainment venues. Dev hadn't been entertained as a child, and he didn't think they were important. The opposite had happened to me. I grew up attending so many events and amusements they lost significance. Perhaps our children suffered some cultural deprivations from our miserliness and unconcern, but we thought that they'd survive. We lived a simple life. Still, as Pat rattled on about the last touring Broadway show she'd seen, I felt guilt. Tragedy hadn't forced me into the compromises she faced. Pat's husband had been dead for nearly ten years. I was with mine every day. With callous unfairness, life had given to me while it had taken from her.

"Are you dating anyone?" I asked.

"You know I don't have time for that."

"Well, you need some kind of a social life."

"You're talking about sex life, not social life. I have more social life than you do. I'm doing fine. I have my kids and I'm not one of those women who needs a man around." The nuance of Pat's comment made a pejorative implication that I *was* one of those women. I didn't take offense. Maybe it was genetic. Verna said that same thing about my mother once.

"Besides," she went on. "The single guys I meet are divorced. I'm not about to take on some man who's already a failure."

"What about widowers?"

"There aren't very many out there, Drea. You find me a Catholic widower who is rich, handsome, and would and treat my kids right, and I'll think about it. Okay?"

"Okay."

"Another thing. He has to live here in Thousand Oaks. I'm not moving. I like my house, and Elaine will be staying with us until she dies!"

Pat started giggling. She must have worked her way into my mind and seen what I conjured up for her.

Al Crespo was on the board of one of Dev's hospitals. He'd donated a hundred thousand this past year to Angel of Mercy Hospital in his wife's memory. I knew he was Catholic, because Dev and I had gone to Dora Crespo's funeral. I described him, and then she really started giggling. Al definitely wasn't handsome. He was at least thirty-five years too old for Pat, and outweighed her by around two hundred pounds.

Pat was feeling good. She finally found a solution to a worrisome problem. Tommy Whitfield had been literally thrown out on the streets. The taxpayers were protesting and the legislature was cutting many services. The farm project at the state hospital, which had helped calm Tommy and gave him occupation with supervision, was discontinued; next, any state hospital mental patient who was manageable with medication was evicted to outpatient status. That meant to his or her family or a licensed foster home and often that meant eventually to the streets.

Care of the mentally ill was being decentralized, and the consequence was a care disaster. Few families could adequately manage mentally ill patients, and private care providers often weren't any more competent than patients' families.

Tommy's behaviors, even with medication, didn't allow him to live in a home with children. Pat found adult foster homes for him, but soon he'd go missing. She'd have to search for him, usually finding him un-medicated, ranting, picking up cigarettes from the street and begging for beer outside liquor stores. Once she found him thirty miles away from the home. He couldn't tell her or the police how he got there.

My friend's life was like running a marathon in city traffic. She had Tommy's crisis to manage, the stress of motivating apathetic algebra students, her own three kids to keep healthy and out of trouble, the responsibility of her aging mother-in-law. Elaine couldn't drive herself to post-surgical physical therapy, but Pat was getting her there three times a week.

"I've found a place in Oxnard run by a woman who has an adult Down syndrome son. I visited without calling and liked what I saw. Mrs. Sanchez' boy and the other residents were clean and busy. Her family helps her. This yard has a high fence and a gate that locks. Tommy wanders, but he's never been violent as long as he gets his meds.

"Reagan and the state legislature have stripped Sacramento of any feeling for the common people." She took a deep breath. "I know it's not only the governor and the Republicans. Civil libertarians among the Democrats are petitioning for people like Tommy to have the right to decide for themselves. Tommy can't keep his pants zipped up. He isn't capable of deciding anything. The voters are allowing this to happen, but they are making a terrible mistake."

With Pat's narrative I suddenly realized that the sorry people I'd noticed cluttering the street corners here in my area were the newly ex-institutionalized. I wasn't a political person, but I knew that what was happening to the mentally ill was shameful. In our area, poor, farm labor families were struggling like Pat was, and in fieldworker families, everyone in a household worked. There was scarcely supervision for children, much less for mental patients sent back home.

"Laura Michael's father was picked up for shoplifting a month ago," Pat continued, needing to vent. "He's an alcoholic and suffers from dementia. He did so well in the State Hospital. He worked on the farm there too. In the foster home, he was gone for two days before he was caught trying to steal a bottle of Jim Beam. He couldn't even tell the arresting officer who he was. Laura's the one who told me about Mrs. Sanchez. Every time I get a call that Tommy has run away, I expect to find him dead. Two days without his meds, he begins ranting. One of these days, he'll annoy the wrong person."

I envied Pat's energy and buoyant enthusiasm. I envied her honest and unwavering goodness. But I didn't envy her life.

I'd never envied Paro's life either. She was perfect for the kind of high style urban class the McMullens moved in. She would grace Vince's arm anywhere and had the range of social abilities and skills to be an outstanding politician's wife. But although she lived the life most women dreamed of: European vacations, household help, a gorgeous Bel Air home, beautiful clothes, and elegant banquets in fancy hotels, she was very unhappy. The little ponds Pat, Adrian and I swam in weren't as wide or sparkling as Paro's were, but they pooled deeper and had warmer water.

~~~<<=>>~~~

Chapter 69: Topanga Canyon

Paro and Pat's phone calls prompted me to call Adrian that evening. Debbie Ryder was engaged. Adrian and Jack's older son, Johnny, was on his LDS mission, distributing copies of the Book of Mormon all around Puerto Rico. Donny would go in a year or two. The baby girls Jack and Adrian had adopted were already in junior high school. Adrian didn't admit it, but she was a working mother too. She was children's music director at her ward. She was teaching after-school piano lessons also. Her students went through their finger exercises while her own girls read or played board games at the dining room table. She was strict about TV time, and more censorious about content than I was. Beverly, happy with her little family, was dance coaching and working as director for her ward's theater activities. Contributing talents was part of the LDS ethic of service.

"It is about time I heard from you," she said. "I call you twice for every time you call me."

"I'm busy. You know I work full time now, Adrian."

"All right. I forgive you. When are you and Dev going to come back to civilization? I have Beverly here, and if you'd just come back, I'd be so happy. I can understand Beth spending half her time in Hawaii, but there is nothing glamorous about that old place where you live. There aren't any sidewalks. There aren't streetlights at night."

"Without streetlights, stars are brighter. We love it here."

"You're just saying that. Last time we came home from that ranch of yours, it took three visits to the carwash to get the dust off our car. Why do you have that long dirt track instead of a proper driveway?"

"Our lane isn't dirt, it's road base and it's very durable."

"You are so contrary. It's not asphalt or cement. It is just like dirt."

"Jesus walked on dirt roads, Adrian."

"That was then. This is now. There wasn't any civilization back in Bible times. You don't have to live like that."

"Adrian, We love living here. It's so peaceful here. Through the window right now, instead of traffic roar, sirens screaming and jets overhead, I'm listening to crickets and night birds."

"Owls, bats and bugs. No thanks! Call an exterminator!"

For over thirty years, our conversations began in a barbed ritual then segued to family talk. This time was no different.

"What's Beth up to?" she asked. "I talked to her two weeks ago, but she is always up to something new. What about Steve and Alex? Tell me what's going on."

I did. Talking to an old friend was simply good. We talked about our mothers. Louise was a widow like my mother. Don Claussen had been dead for over six years. Louise sold the house and she and her sister Charlene were sharing a Santa Monica apartment. Louise found a part-time job in a Venice boutique. She was selling consignment movie clothes. Louise would still be vivacious. She'd be good at the job.

A few weeks later, Adrian unexpectedly called me. "You'll get shower invitations in the mail. Beth and your mom will get them too. I'm going to call them. I really want you all to be there. I hope Beth can fly over for it."

"It's that important? You know I'm not good at that kind of social thing."

"It's very important. The party is for Beverly. She's having a baby in June. I want you to bring Sallyanne and Jennybeth too. My girls will be there. Think of it as a reunion, not a girly party."

I should have felt guilty accepting the invitation, when I couldn't make time for my class reunion. But I didn't. I wanted to see the Claussens, my mother, and Beth. If my daughters came along it would be a mini-vacation. I promised we'd be there if we possibly could. We'd pick up Mama and take her with us to Beverly's party. The girls and I could spend that night in Breeze Terrace and come home Sunday morning.

This pregnancy was Beverly's fourth. She and Gordon had a daughter, Cassie, who was seven, and little sons, Bobby and Gordie, who were four and two years old. My girls were happy to come along. It was Anne's first chance to practice driving on the interstate. Jennybeth was ecstatic to be going to a city.

Topanga Canyon wasn't far from Encino. Sycamores grew along the curving, hilly road leading to Beverly's house. The canyon could almost make living in Los Angeles endurable. Beverly's house wasn't as dilapidated as her sister had described it. It was a good place for a family. Cassie and her cousins, Adrian's Melanie and Michelle, met us at the car. Anne and I helped Mama up the hill to the house. With age and her increasing weight, Mama's limp had become a lumber. Then the girls dragged us around to show us the back yard. There was a trampoline and swing set out under the oaks, and big rocks for kids to climb on. Gordon and Beverly did a grand job of making a country home in the city. Three of the women from Beverly's ward were serving as hostesses for the children. They'd set up an outdoor table with games and refreshments on the deck off the kitchen. I went indoors but Jennybeth after greeting Adrian, Beverly, Louise and Charlene challenged Anne to a game of Ping-Pong and chose to stay out with the children.

Louise had changed little. She, Charlene and Mama had reached their sixties and were the elders at this party. The pleasant LDS women gave the three older women lots of attention. Mama understood the rules: she bragged about Beverly as though she were Mama's own child, and described,

in her own pleasing voice and grandiose style, all Beverly's childhood dance recitals and performances. Mama may not have been perfect as the mother of children, but she was excellent as the mother of adults. Beth and I were proud of her performance, and saw why the neighbor women dropped by to visit her so often when we were children and she was a shut-in. Mama was fun.

However, twice during the afternoon there passed a puzzled look between us. Beth and I sensed that something else was wrong. It was too cheerful a gathering.

Conversation wasn't allowed to lag for a moment without some Mormon lady perking it up. The churchwomen hovered over Beverly. Adrian wasn't darting her usual verbal arrows at her sister, Beth, or me. Something was very wrong.

The shower games began, and I escaped to the yard to sit on the deck steps watching the children run and play. It was a beautiful afternoon in the canyon. I could smell the rich, warm earth and feel a slight current come through the trees. It seemed like home. A few minutes later, Adrian came out of the house and sat beside me. For a while we didn't say anything. We could have been children again, sitting in the tree beside her house, holding a companionable silence. Then she told me what was wrong.

"Beverly's husband, that stupid jerk, has left her." Her tone was low enough that none of the kids hear us. Adrian's soft brown eyes were angry.

"Adrian, that can't be true."

"It is. He's been gone a month. He has an apartment somewhere in Burbank but won't even tell her where it is. She doesn't have his phone number. If she needs him, she has to contact him at work."

"He's left now? With her pregnant?"

"He didn't want this baby. When he walked out, he claimed she deliberately got pregnant to keep him trapped. That was the worst of it all. Up until that day, she didn't have a clue there was anything wrong. Jack thinks he has someone else."

"Oh, Adrian. I'm so sorry."

"Not as sorry as I am. I'm ready to kill him."

Those words, coming so harshly from my gentlest friend's mouth, were shocking, and full of passion.

"What'll she do?"

"She doesn't have a clue. She's just waiting, hoping he'll come home. Jack and I want her and the kids to move into the guesthouse or take our whole upstairs. But Beverly won't leave the canyon. She's so stubborn. She hopes Gordon will come to his senses and come home. I don't think he will. We were wrong about that guy. He's rotten. He left her without any money and closed their bank account. Even her gas card has been cancelled." Adrian twisted around and took my hand as though we were little girls.

"Drea, he took the Honda, their good car. All she has is that rattletrap Buick to haul the kids around. Jack and I have given her enough money to get a lawyer so she can get support and at least fill the refrigerator."

"What about counseling?"

"He refused. He hung up on Bishop Michaels and then on Jack." Adrian found a pebble in a groove of the decking and tossed it out to the ground. "The church is helping her right now. The elders are bringing food, and all the sisters in this area are taking turns transporting Cassie and the boys to ward and school events. We take care of each other." A smug look broke across her face as the old Adrian reached out to give me a little slap. "See, you should join the LDS Church."

"Dev isn't going to leave me."

"How do you know? He could."

"Oh, you think Jack's going to run off with some ink and paint girl at the studio?"

"Not Jack."

"That's my point. Not Dev either."

"Okay, okay." Adrian stretched out her legs. "We'd better go back inside."

"Not until the shower games are over."

"You stay if you want, but I better go in. Explain this to Beth and your mom. Beverly wants people to know what's happened, but she doesn't want to talk about it herself."

I stayed on the deck and watched my daughters and Adrian's daughters keeping the little ones running about gleeful and happy. The children were laughing as they raced over the rocks and under the trees. Topanga Canyon was an idyllic place, a retreat within the city. But if Mormon families were breaking up, then chaos was circling around everyone.

~~~<<=>>~~~

Chapter 70: Worse Things Can Happen

We kissed Mama goodbye, but before we started for home, I drove the girls around Breeze Terrace, showing them the tree where Adrian and I used to sit, the small shopping center, and the bus stop. I slowed in front of the house where Jeannie and Frank had lived but didn't stop the engine. Over the fence on the side of the house I could see the top of a swing and slide set. I was so rich with Dev, our children, our family and friends, and the family we'd made for ourselves that my timorous, fearful childhood here in Breeze Terrace had been crowded out. It held memories of people I loved, but too many painful scenes were there too. There was much that I hadn't chosen to share with my daughters.

"It's okay looking at all your old places, Mom," Jennybeth sighed with weary resignation, "but I really think we need to get something to eat before we have to go all the way home. We'd better get going."

It was uncanny how much my younger daughter's clear, fluty voice sounded like my mother's. Jennybeth, like Mama, had never been harsh or shrill in speech, but both were occasionally capable of being tactless, and each usually said exactly what she thought. I made my daughters wait for lunch until we were in Valencia. Anne drove all the rest of the way home. Dev took her back to campus in the ranch truck. He needed to pick up some things at Fresno Ag while he was in Fresno. They were open on Sundays.

Less than a week after we were at the shower in Topanga Canyon, a fire broke out in Beverly's house in the night. Beth was the one who reached me. Cassie and the boys were all right, but Beverly was dead.

The fire happened on Sunday night. The Topanga Fire Department interviewed the neighbors and children, and its investigators speculated on the chronology of the episode. Beverly woke around eleven P.M., possibly hearing the smoke alarm. The boys' room was next to hers. She was able to get them out of the house. She directed Bobby, the elder boy, to take his brother's hand and run to a neighbor's house. The child remembered noise, smoke, and his mother telling him what he had to do. He was quoted by the L.A. Times and on TV saying, "Mom yelled at me to take Gordie to Mrs. Padakis's house and call 911, and I did. Mrs. Padakis called 911 for me."

Beverly's body was found half way up the interior stairway. The investigators were certain that she'd re-entered the house to get to Cassie who slept in an upstairs room. By the time the fire department arrived, neighbors were fighting the fire with hoses pulled from their own homes. The first neighbor on the scene had been driven back by the flames. Heat and flames were pouring out the windows. He found Cassie in the back yard, crying for her mother. Except for a sprained ankle and some scratches, she was unhurt. No one could find Beverly.

Cassie had staked claim to a small attic bedroom off the loft, demanding a place where her brothers wouldn't bother her. It was an aerie, an indoor tree house. Her friends could play or stay overnight, and the little boys were forbidden to go upstairs to pester. During her interview at the hospital, Cassie said that she woke up and smelled smoke. It scared her. That month her second grade class had watched a fire safety presentation and she remembered what the fireman told the class. The door was hot, so she didn't open it. Cassie unlatched the screen of her window and climbed out onto the jutting shed roof of the kitchen. She tried to find a way down, but couldn't. When she saw flames at the window behind her, she jumped. She landed in a shrub, her ankle hurt, but she was alive.

I didn't go to Beverly's funeral. Dev was on his way to a conference in Portland to with other small hospital comptrollers, and the funeral was scheduled for the same day as the dress rehearsal of *Taming of the Shrew*. The boys were wrestling around, roughhousing to distract themselves from the tension of learning lines and studying for quarterly tests, and Jennybeth wanted her skirt shortened. But I could have gone. The kids were old enough to manage without me. I didn't want to see Beverly buried.

When the determination of the origin of the fire was published, it began in a junction box. The original owners of the house rewired it to code in the early fifties. It had been inspected when Gordon and Beverly bought the house. There was no one to blame. Adrian was determined to get custody of Beverly's children. She and Jack had been to a lawyer before the funeral to begun custody proceedings. She told me he lawyer didn't give them much hope, but he was a member of her ward and she trusted him to help.

"The kids are at your house, aren't they?" I asked her as we talked.

"Only Cassie. Gordon came and took the boys. He doesn't deserve them. Cassie refused to go with him. She is still crying herself to sleep. I want to keep her in the same school so part of her life is normal. Her teacher is great but I'm driving her all the way to Topanga every morning and picking her up in the afternoon. The good thing is that Gordon doesn't want her crying like this. I have to get her back to normal, but once she is, he'll try take her away from us."

Within five months, Jack and Adrian had spent thousands of dollars trying to gain custody of Beverly's children. The best their lawyer could get was liberal visitation rights. The children could be with the Ryders for every holiday and one weekend a month. The rest of the time, they would live with their father.

Gordon had begun to clear the fire debris in Topanga. He was planning to design and build a new home on the ruins of the old as though nothing had happened there. I'd never heard Adrian so angry as in the telling of these events. I didn't have any comfort for her. I just listened.

Losing Beverly to such a horrendous accident sent us scurrying around the ranch correcting any safety hazard we could find. My mother's words from the day of Sallyanne's birth wrapped themselves around us. Dev and I had given hostages to fortune.

Not until Dev had been over every inch of the ranch, checking the spark screens over engines, motors, belts and blades, tightening roll bars on the tractors and trucks, and going over every bit of wiring in the ranch buildings and house, and making sure the kids knew exit routes from their rooms and the smoke alarms worked could we sleep well again.

~~~<<=>>~~~

Chapter 71: A Call from North of Sunset

Citrus groves were green year-round, but in the gullies of the foothills where water had run in winter and early spring, the wild grass headed out and turned tan. Summer's bronzy tones came and etched the leaves of the native Sycamores. Dust dulled the deep green of oaks in the pastureland and beneath them, lazy cattle rested in the shade.

A Saturday morning, not long after breakfast, I'd been outdoors and came back in to hear the phone ringing. The call was from Vince. Hearing his voice both pleased and concerned me. I'd been apprehensive since Beverly died. "Is everything all right? Are Paro and Jason okay?" I asked, much too abruptly.

"Sure. *Calmate, chica.* They're both doing great." His familiar joviality reassured me. "I just wanted to call. Hadn't talked to you in a long time."

Vince's mom died not long after he and Paro were married, but his dad was still a big part of their lives. Mr. McMullen would be seventy now. "Your dad? Anna Lee?" I asked.

"Relax. Be cool. Everyone's fine. Dad's still in that big old place, but Yolie watches out for both him and the kitchen, She and her husband are living in the apartment above the garages. We aren't far away, and Jason spends a lot of time with his grandfather. He's doing fine. It's been a long time since you and I had a conversation. We haven't really talked in a long, long time. You and Paro communicate, but I'm out of the loop. We still friends?"

"Of course we're still friends. Always friends."

I assumed calling Paro was the same as calling Vince. Husbands and wives, what you told one, you told the other. But maybe they didn't share every bit of trivia. They were in a different social class from us and seemed to have a different kind of marriage.

"How's old Dev?" Vince asked.

"Old Dev isn't much older than old Vince. He's trying to figure out how to quit his job and become a full-time rancher. He wants to buy more pasture east of the barn. My whole salary goes toward my husband's belief in Manifest Destiny." Vince knew I was bragging, not complaining. "He's at a farm equipment sale, but he'll be back in an hour or so. I'll have him call you. You can talk about sports and the senate's foolishness. Guy stuff."

"Just tell him I called, okay? I'll be out all day myself. I just wanted to talk a little."

"Then talk. Tell me what you've been doing. How's the super job going?"

"The same as always. The money's good. Amparo told me you'd gone back to nursing. But, Dree, come time-traveling with me. I've been thinking about the day the two of you graduated. Remember the college rose garden? Pat and Rich weren't there, but they were the only ones was missing."

"Some of my other friends were missing too, but it was still one of the best days in my life. I know it was for Paro too. You'd given her the engagement ring. And, we ..."

"And we toasted your marriage with punch in paper cups. It's been twenty years. Know what? I still have the pictures I took that day, Alex covering everyone with flowers, Beth getting her face in practically every shot. Your sister's big-time now. She really did well, didn't she?"

"She did, but so did you. Beth's interests are expanding out into community action. She's doing all kinds of good work for women's causes, in addition to running the agency in Hawaii."

I knew better than to kill a good memory with a bad one, but couldn't help myself. "Did you know that our friend Beverly Harper died a few months ago?"

"Yes, she was your friend Adrian's sister. I wanted to call you then, but got busy. I remember dancing with her at Steve's wedding."

"I'm surprised you remember anything from that wedding. Paro had to drive you home."

"C'mon. I wasn't as drunk as you think," he chided. "Paro sent flowers for Beverly's funeral, but I should have called you. Kept meaning to." Vince cleared his throat. "How is Alex? I used to see him around the department. We were sorry to lose him at County."

"You helped him so much, but he'll never go to law school. He likes the work he does. He and his wife work for Clark County in Las Vegas. The pay is poor, but they're into good works, not money."

"Aw, there's plenty of time for law school. He's not thirty yet, is he?"

"Getting there. He's happy working as a judicial ombudsman. He likes working with the poor. Excuse me, *the disenfranchised*. My baby brother corrects my terminology."

"There is a need, and people should do whatever makes them happy. Give him my best, next time you see him. Give everyone my best, your mom too."

"Vince, why don't you and Paro drop everything and come up here next weekend? Jason could spin brodies around the rows of trees with our boys on the ATVs. You could too. You'd like it. I love to see you all again."

"I'm sorry we missed the barn-raising. I wish I'd been there."

"It was twelve years ago!"

"I know. I'm still sorry. Rich told me it was some party. He said before it was over, around midnight, you and Pat, and some other gals took lanterns down the hill to stop traffic on that road below the grove. About fifteen guys took turns racing the kids' red wagons down that crazy dirt drive of yours. Pat said only one woman would try it."

"And she broke her wrist. That was our neighbor's

seventeen-year-old, hardly a woman yet, and hardly typical. Julie's racing cars during the season at Oak Canyon track now. We don't follow racing, but if Rich were here, he'd love it. He'd have Pat and the kids here all the time watching the cars go around, and I'd get to see more of them."

"Ah, Lynnie. I miss Rich. I've missed you and Dev too. Hey, got to go. My other phone is flashing."

"Talk Paro into coming up, okay?"

"Yep. Will do. Take care of yourself. Take care of Dev."

"Of course. The kids too."

We both hung up. Vince hadn't called me Lynnie since I was in high school. I spent the rest of the day thinking of him darting about taking pictures of us in the college rose garden that one singular day. I didn't need to rush to dust the guest room or freshen the sheets and pillowcases. It wasn't likely that Vincent P. McMullen would step off Los Angeles County's political racetrack for a rustic weekend.

Paro went to banquets and cocktail parties, but her life had constraints. Jason's life was constrained too. I doubted that the boy had ever ridden horses through the hills, swum in the fast cold current of a river, driven a truck on a grove track, or scaled rock falls at twelve thousand feet in the Sierra. He certainly hadn't shot at tin cans on a fence post.

Statistically, serious accidents causing death or disability were more common in rural than urban areas. Farm equipment, roads with poor lighting and no signals at intersections took their toll. Twenty years ago, Dev and I had thoughtfully appraised the risk-to-benefit ratio. We knowingly chose to raise our family here. We worried, but our kids were tough and resilient, honest, hardworking, uncomplaining, and nonexclusively fair. They carried the six cardinal virtues of our own private creed. I was proud of them.

Before he went to Vietnam, Rich titillated Vince with that story of our barn-raising party. All the men were feeling a little too good that night. Not that we women weren't.

Two bodies jammed into each of our kids' red wagons, they

went flying down the eight percent grade of a long rough, curved dirt driveway. The man in front steering crazily, the man in back providing balance and ballast, they tried to hold to the track long enough to make the tee onto the paved road below the ranch before crashing. Moonlight was their only guide.

Vince could allow himself a vicarious pleasure with the story, but he would never have tried the real thing even if he'd been with us.

The McMullens were not going to come and visit us the next weekend. When they did come, they'd have a reason not to bring Jason. Neither Vince nor Paro would want their prep school boy running rowdy with an old friend's country kids.

~~~<<=>>~~~

Chapter 72: Ocean Swimming

At noon, the Monday after Vince's call, my mother phoned me at work. Beth called me there, but Mama wouldn't. I knew something was wrong as soon as I heard her voice.

She'd seen a TV news report that Vincent P. McMullen, Official Spokesman for the County of Los Angeles, had been found dead. His body washed up on an Orange County beach. Suicide was suspected. All I could think was, why was Vince on an Orange County beach? The McMullens lived nearer Santa Monica or Will Rogers, or even Malibu if he wanted to go ocean swimming. He and Paro didn't have a beach house at Newport. There was a gap between the words *found dead* and the words *suspected suicide*. My brain was processing too slowly. As Mama talked, I looked around my desk and the stacks of books and test papers jumbled on it, but what I saw was Vince dancing with Beverly at my brother's wedding. Twirling, centered on the dance floor as everyone watched. They were so beautiful, and now they were both gone.

I called Dev's office and left a message telling him that I'd be at home if he needed to reach me, and checked out of the district office for the rest of the day. I barely got in the house before I began to throw up. Too aware now that Vince had called to say goodbye, I found a blanket and curled up in the porch swing to wait for the kids and Dev to come up the hill and home to me. Red Cat came and climbed up next to me. But I needed more than a blanket and a tomcat. I wanted Jennybeth to come up the lane from La Cordillera school bus's early run with a smile on her face saying, "Mom, you're home early! That means we'll have something really good for supper." I wanted to see my sons get off the athlete's bus to charge up the hill toward the house, grab-assing and horsing around, shoving each other, and laughing over something that had happened at practice. Most of all, I wanted Dev.

He had been at a board luncheon meeting, but came home as soon as he received the message at his office, before the kids were out of school. "I'm sorry," he whispered as he held me. I still needed him to comfort me for Beverly's loss, and now I'd added another sad attrition. Dev didn't change into ranch clothes. He sat on the swing with me, his touch better comfort than words could ever be. We stayed beside each other, looking across the valley, and waited for the kids to come home.

I did fix something really good for supper. In a strange slowed motion, as though I were pulling the strings of a puppet that resembled me, I defrosted chicken breasts and made *papricás* and sour cream. Andy came in to help. It was his nature to stop what he was doing to give comfort in that simple way. Jennybeth helped her father and Ev take care of the ranch's afternoon chores so Andy could stay with me. It was their way. At supper, I just moved the food around my plate. It was a sorrowful evening. I had little to say to anyone. I barely brought myself to ask the kids about school.

That evening I called Paro. A woman answered, thanked me for my call, and said she'd give my name to Mrs. McMullen. An hour later, the phone rang. Jennybeth answered.

"It's for you, Mom. It's probably about Mr. McMullen."

I told my daughter I'd pick it up in the bedroom, and went there.

Paro's voice came hoarsely through the receiver. "Drea, did you know about Vince?" she demanded.

"Oh, Paro. My mother called me as soon as she heard. I'm so sorry. What I can do?"

"Did you know about it?" Her voice was icy, angry.

I was confused, and asked, "Know that he died?"

"I think you knew."

"I don't understand. I didn't know until my mother called. I couldn't have known."

"Vince left his address file open to your name Saturday. Why did he call you? What do you know?"

"I don't know anything. Vince did call me. He only said that he hadn't talked to me in a long time, and that you and Jason were both fine. He asked about Dev, and told me that Anna Lee's kids were growing up. I invited you all up to the ranch."

"That's all?" She sounded so hostile and accusing that I became defensive. I didn't know why she was angry with me.

"It's absolutely all we talked about."

There was too long a pause, and then her voice changed. She sounded aloof and dry. "What do you know about him?"

"What could I have known? I haven't seen you two in so long. You didn't tell me he was having any trouble when you called. He didn't tell me. Was it work? Was he depressed?"

"I think you know."

"Paro, please tell me what you are talking about."

"I never want to talk to you or to hear your voice again." Paro crashed the phone down. Before the noise ringing in my ear cleared, I was sick again and ran to the bathroom. Then, like any other normal, forty-two year old woman in trouble, I called my mother.

Mama's light voice soon calmed me. "Now, baby. Of course Amparo is upset. Her husband killed himself. If he talked to you last, naturally she'd blame you. She needs to blame someone. Be understanding. She'll know you couldn't have stopped him even if you'd know what he was going to do. Phil Donahue had a show on this very thing. Baby, no one can help someone who decides to do that. She couldn't have stopped him either."

"But Vince, Mama. Why would Vince do that?"

"Well don't ask me to understand. He was so handsome and had such a good job. I heard her drag a chair nearer the phone. "What will the family do about services for him? The church denies suicides a Catholic burial."

"Was it suicide for sure?"

"According to the paper."

"Was there anything more in the paper?"

"There isn't an obituary yet, but the evening paper is right here. I'll read what it says. *'McMullen was a highly respected spokesman for Los Angeles County. A family member cited depression and over-work as possible reasons for his death. He leaves his wife, Amparo Mendoza McMullen and a son, Jason Ignacio McMullen, his father, James J. McMullen, a former Beverly Hills city councilman, and a sister, Anna Lee Prather.'* That's the end of the article except for a paragraph on his education and his work with the county."

How could anyone hide depression so well? Clinically depressed patients in the psych annex were dismal, unable to eat, sleep or communicate. They showed behaviors opposite to any I'd seen in Vince. As soon as Mama and I hung up, the phone rang again. It was Pat, calling from Thousand Oaks. She was hyper in that manic way some people are when they are shocked. She had known Vince longer and closer than I had. He was her husband's closest friend.

"I talked to Paro this afternoon," Pat's voice raced. "I don't know how to say this, but she doesn't want to see you, Drea. It's totally crazy, but she thinks you knew about it. She said he called you the morning before he killed himself. Did he? Did he tell you anything?"

"Nothing." I felt guilty for something I hadn't done. Dev came by and put his hand on my shoulder. I leaned my head against his arm as I continued explaining. "He called me Saturday morning, and it was unusual, but he sounded completely normal." Talking didn't squelch my sick feeling. "My mother asked about services."

"Everything is under control there. Don't come down, Drea. The funeral will be private. Paro told me the family doesn't even want me there, and Rich was Vince's best friend." She sniffled and blew her nose. "He called me too, two weeks ago."

"But she's blaming me for his death."

"She's just blaming you because he called you last. If he'd called me last, she'd be blaming me. She's acting out, but you shouldn't take it personally. She's been through a lot. This is what she told me: Saturday night when Vince didn't come home she tried to file a missing person's report. The police wouldn't file it. They told her to come back Monday. By Monday, his body had been found.

"Vince left the Mazarati parked at Seal Beach. His shoes, coat, wallet, and the note were on the passenger seat. Oh, Dree, the media has been awful. Reporters beat the O.C. Sheriff's Department to Paro's door. Vince knew all of them. You'd think they'd show more respect."

"Vince left a note?"

"Yes, he did. There is no question but that it was suicide. Paro told me he wrote that he felt that she and Jason would be better off without him."

After Pat's call, I called my sister.

"You were smart to break up with him," Beth said. "He seemed so rich and so perfect, but look how stupid he turned out to be." It was an awful thing to say, but it made me feel better. I could count on my sister to punch me with her own kind of blunt objectivity. She'd never had my morose tendencies.

That night, it was Dev who helped me drive grief, confusion, and sadness away from the two deaths by fulfilling my searing need for him. Sex was the only thing intense enough to keep me tied to the present. That night he kept his arms around me until the worst of my sorrow for Beverly and Vince dissipated.

The next morning I was all right. We took care of the animals, the kids went off to school and we went to our jobs. The old rule still applied: One only missed work for the death of members of the immediate family.

It was hard concentrating on the things I had to do that day. I visited two schools where I was giving a first aid class. I tried to sit and have lunch in the faculty room and pay attention to the teachers' chatter of difficult or easy classes, changes in the sports program and the next school assembly.

In the afternoon, I checked out of my office and drove over to St. Catherine's. I'd been asked to sit in on a consultation with a family. One of the nuns worried that a child's unusual sleepiness after lunch was possibly symptomatic of diabetes, but the family resisted getting a medical exam for the little girl and thought my presence would help force the issue. It was difficult, and the father stubborn. But the mother agreed that the child's behavior had changed, and frequently she perspired when she hadn't been active. It was a successful consultation. The medical appointment was scheduled and Sister Rosa wasn't blamed for wanting the best for the child.

Late in the afternoon, after I'd gotten home, Pat called to let us know Vince would have a Mass of Christian Burial at some obscure parish in the San Fernando Valley. She was calmer. Vince's pastor successfully pled his case to the archdiocese: Vince was suffering from extreme mental illness, therefore incapable of the volition necessary to commit a mortal sin. I wondered if poor people were entitled to the same archdiocesan charity. Perhaps they were now, since Vatican II, and no longer banished from consecrated ground.

"The McMullen family is trying to keep the location of the funeral from the media. They aren't talking to reporters. The D.A.'s office is handling any news releases. Paro didn't want the family to post an obituary, but they had to do that.

"When Anna Lee and Mr. McMullen wanted to establish a scholarship in Vince's name, she fought them. She's not being rational."

"You can understand what she is going through better than anyone else."

"No, I can't understand. I don't have to make excuses to our children for Rich's death. He was an American hero. He didn't kill himself."

"But you were widowed and angry. Remember how upset you were?"

Pat's voice softened. "I was. I could have killed my mother the day we buried Rich, and she wasn't that bad. Lynnie, she was just being a mother doing what she thought was right. I'm planning to have Father Flores say some masses for the repose of Vince's poor soul. My prayers will be that Amparo gets through everything that has happened to her."

~~~<<=>>~~~

Chapter 73: In Bed with Dylan Thomas

On Wednesday Beth left me a message telling me that she was in Century City, and asking that I call her when I got home from work. Before I changed out of my work clothes or started supper, I returned her call.

"You need to call Alex," she said.

"Alex? Mama was going to tell him about Vince. I don't need to call him."

"Yes, you do. Hang up right now and call our brother."

I did what I was told, but waited until he and Sandra would be home from work.

"That's a bummer about Vince," Alex said as soon as he recognized my voice. "Sorry. I know he was your friend."

"Yours, too. Alex.

"I know. I owe him my degree and my career."

"Beth said to call you. What do you know that she thought was so important?"

"You may not want to hear what I know."

"Alex, Vince was the one of my friends who kept everyone else's spirits up. Suicide really bothers me. I want to know anything you can tell me. Talk."

"Okay, but don't go rumor this around. Others don't need to know."

"Know what?" My thoughts filled with pay off scandals, kickbacks and bribery. Those things were impossible to connect with Vince in any way.

"He was a good guy. Don't think he wasn't. But Drea, the thing is, Vince was gay."

"Gay? Vince? Explain that."

"You know what I'm saying. Homosexual."

"That's ridiculous. He was married. He and Paro have a child."

"You are so naïve, Drea. Lots of gay guys are married. Some of them have kids. Maybe he was bisexual. I don't know. He was careful not to bring it into the office, but a few of us knew. Not everyone."

"I can't believe that."

"Then don't. You don't have to believe me."

"But you had to tell Beth so she'd tell me to call you."

"No. I didn't tell her. She called me and asked."

"Why would she think that? Alex, I'm not naïve. Some of the people we know are in different relationships. They are good concerned professionals, and loyal friends. But it doesn't make sense for Vince. I can't accept it."

"Wally knew about it. He told Beth. She just called me for confirmation. You don't have to accept it, but it's true. Vince was a cool guy. He never hit on any of us when I interned in the office. But we knew. We didn't talk it around. It would have killed his career and we liked him. Listen to me. He had a friend who used to stop by and pick him up for lunch. They had something going on."

"I have friends I meet for lunch. We don't have *something going on.*"

"I saw them together, Dree. Lots of times. They even looked alike, only the guy was black. Dressed nice, probably another attorney. One evening after I'd graduated and was working full-time, I had to work late. I saw them together in the parking lot. Men don't touch each other like that. I never told anyone until now, but take my word on this, Vince was gay."

Everything I'd known about Vince spun around me. Paro's increasing unhappiness over the years, and her distancing herself from me now moved to a different context. There was a reasonable and sad subtext to everything she had said.

"This is so hard to deal with."

"Well, no one ever knows what's in someone else's mind. But, honestly? Honestly I think he killed himself because someone was trying to blackmail him. Something ugly was happening. People are shits. They really are. Especially in politics, even small time county level politics. I think someone was threatening to out him. People were jealous, and Vince was popular and moving toward being the next D.A."

"That's horrible."

"Yeah. It is. After Beth called, I got in touch with Scott Casserly. He's still working in the office. He told me Vince had been acting edgy for about month. No one knew exactly why. Things were going fine at work. It wasn't that, so Scott thought that there must have been some domestic issue. Scott and Alonzo talked privately about the gay angle but didn't say anything to anyone else. Now no one there is talking to anyone, not even the guy at the next desk."

"Vince called me last Saturday, Alex. He asked me to say hi to you for him. He said you were a good kid."

"I'm not a kid anymore."

"No, you're not. I'm not either."

"Is there going to be a funeral? Scott hadn't heard anything about services. I ought to be there if there is. Sandra and I could fly in to LAX and stay at Mama's. Don't say anything about this to her. You know how Mama is. Suicide is bad enough. She'd never cope with what she sees as perversion."

"I'd never bring this up with her. No need to come to the city. His services are going to be private."

Sandra came on the line to tell me she was sorry about my friend. She told me that her department had just authorized counseling sessions for families where one parent was gay. "It's difficult for the wives and kids." Sandra said. "One of the men in my office calls this the year the closet doors opened."

This is what Paro knew, and I didn't. When I'd dated Vince I was happy he was a polite and respectful date. But I wasn't sixteen anymore. I should have figured it out. Paro had grown wan and sad over the past twenty years, the classic profile of a neglected wife. Vince was gay, not bisexual. Paro gave him a cover. She made his public life go smoothly, and he knew she'd never divorce him. She was too proud and too Catholic.

As we got ready for bed, I told Dev what I'd learned from Alex. He listened, eyes wide, unable to maintain his usual coolly analytical gaze.

"You didn't suspect?" I asked.

"Never. He always seemed affectionate with Paro when we were around. Of course we didn't see them that often. You know, babe, Vince wasn't an average sort of guy. I thought it was that Catholic school business that made him different. Rich was kind of different too. Sort of prissy. I've always thought you Catholic school kids were kind of warped."

I gave him a scowl, but he just gave me back a weak smile and raised eyebrow.

"Actually, Drea, Vince didn't act as prissy as Rich did. But Vince *was* different. Running too fast. Wanting everyone to like him. That whole politician thing." Dev paused to set the alarm for morning, and he looked at me with a thoughtful expression. "I knew he wanted to be like his dad. He wasn't quite a man on his own. But, no, I never thought he got off on other guys. That's something I thought I could always pick up on. Guess I was wrong."

"He never made a pass at you?"

"No."

Dev climbed into bed. I reached up to snap the light off and squirmed down next to him. He turned toward me, his right hand coming around to cup my breast, his left hand traveling lower. "Babe, you know I would have told you if he had."

Yes. He would have told me. Our marriage had been one long running conversation. "There's more, Dev. Alex said Vince had been in a longtime relationship with a man. The interns suspected, because they saw him with the same man too often during the time Alex worked there. Alex said he saw Vince with the man once in the parking lot after he graduated when he was working for the D.A. full-time. They were being too intimate. Alex thinks someone may have been trying to use that knowledge to extort money or preference from him."

"Then his suicide makes sense."

"I hate that I contributed to all this. Paro hates me."

"C'mon. Don't make yourself too important here, babe. You tend to do that."

"I'm not. His death isn't my fault. But it is my fault Paro married him. I threw them together."

"You're still making yourself too important. She had plenty of time to evaluate his character on her own."

"His vile, cowardly, and treacherous character."

"Hey, don't be so hard on him either. You've never once faulted your friend Audrey for her similar choice. Tony Butler, in your office, is as queer as they come, and you've never once nailed him for having a bad character. You know kinks in one's wiring aren't something people would choose. It's got to be a bitch of a life."

Dev's hands began moving slowly. What Dev was doing to me, I liked. What he was saying, I didn't. "You don't need to lecture me. It's not Vince's gender preference I'm criticizing, it's his character."

My mind went to the reception after Anna Lee McMullen was married: Vince out on the dance floor leading the McMullen men in that fast Irish dance, clogging over to the tall, good looking black waiter. He led the man, a dark mirror image of himself, out onto the dance floor. Maybe it was the same man. As a friend, I felt so betrayed. I couldn't imagine how Paro felt. "You aren't a woman and you won't understand, but what Vince did to Paro was beyond cruel. It doesn't have anything to do with gender preference; it has to do with exploitation. A person of character would never have dragged someone else's life into his lie. Vince used Paro. He destroyed her."

"Then, he used you too. Don't blame yourself."

Dev kissed me so long and sweetly that I slipped into his warmth. But that night I dreamed of Beverly twirling in toe shoes out on the lawn in Breeze Terrace, something she never did out of a dream. She took good care of her toe shoes. Beverly wouldn't have risked grass stains. Then I slept again and woke in the cool darkness. I raised myself up to see the illuminated clock over the mound of Dev's body. Curling back down next to him, I slipped the tips of my fingers under his weight so gently he didn't wake up.

It was not yet three A.M. An old Dylan Thomas poem I hadn't thought of since college filled the night around our bed with unquantifiable images: pride and secrets typed like fortune cookie tabs were scuttling across a great round moon. I recognized that my fragile and insubstantial body, snuggled here this night beside the man I chose to love, was merely that of a figure from a poignant old poem wherein "...lovers lie abed with all their griefs in their arms...."

That figure was all I ever would be. My husband's quiet breathing was real; and my only authentic, definable presence was that of an anonymous lover inside a poet's too brightly illuminated lines. I felt my grief for fey and forever lost friends.

~~~<<=>>~~~

Chapter 74: Surname Ramirez

My mother's secrets made my childhood a torment, and Vince's secrets turned what should have been a time of grace and fulfillment in Amparo Mendoza's life into a torment. Mama was a simple woman who wanted a new life less painful than her old one. I still begrudged her lie that made me believe Laz was my father for so many difficult years, but it hadn't been an act of malice. My sister was wrong, though. Vince wasn't stupid. He wasn't a simple man. Vincent Patrick McMullen had been raised with moral certainty. He was a university graduate with a law degree. He knew what he was doing. He stole Paro's life, and arrogantly wasted it.

But time went by. Seasons passed and good things happened again, successes and promotions in our friends and families' lives, as well as in our own. In the next year, I discarded my guilt at my connection to Paro's unhappiness. I was so busy there was no time for prolonged examinations of conscience. Present social reality trumped past social responsibility.

Mama called tittering because Verna found a courtly old gentleman in Maui. Speaking for herself, Mama proclaimed, "I don't want any old geezers coming around me. I'd never marry again. I've been married enough." She said that men only married women who were past menopause for their money ... or to get an unpaid nursemaid. She wasn't going to share any of her assets or carry anyone's bedpan. Mama gave my sister, brothers and I great entertainment. Verna must have listened to her, because she avoided the pitfall. She kept her gentleman, but wouldn't marry him or let him move in.

As the seventies closed, I felt like I'd passed through an

ominous tunnel of losses and come out into a brighter decade. The Cunninghams, Raudells, and Horvaths were whole and sound, happily welcoming the eighties in. Life for my immediate and extended family was good.

Pat's first son graduated from college, and her daughter was engaged. Pat O'Hara Whitfield was the head of the math department at her high school in Ventura, and had a widower courting her. He was diminutive and literary, an English prof at Northridge, and nothing at all like Rich had been. It was good to hear her giggle like a teenager when she talked about him. We met them at a jazz festival in Monterey one weekend and found him witty and charming.

In the Ryder household, after much time and thousands of dollars, Jack and Adrian had permanent custody of Beverly's children. They lived in the Ryder house in Encino, but spent some school holidays with their father and his new wife. Adrian's girls were delighted to have Cassie with them and get to be big sisters to Beverly's boys. Adrian was concerned about Cassie, who blamed Gordon for her mother's death. Her logic was simple: If her father hadn't left them, her mother would still be alive. Dr. Davies, the psychologist counseling Cassie, was working on getting her to understand what the doctor called, "the irrationality of *if* thinking." Dr. Davies felt that underneath Cassie's anger was guilt: if her mother hadn't gone into the house to find her, Beverly would still be alive. Internally, she blamed herself and while projecting the blame to Gordon eased her, it was unfair. Gordon didn't set the fire. The therapist sounded like a thoughtful woman.

My niece Karin, was on a team that won the North Valley regional cheerleader's competition and was going to state level to compete. Her little brother, Doug, was pitching well on his Little League team. Dev's nephew, Allan Poteet, won a national award for skeet shooting. Our young Cunninghams were doing fine, though they hadn't won mantle trophies.

Anne was going to graduate from Fresno State University in June and had begun work on a teaching credential. Andy was right behind her keeping top grades and expecting to go on to medical school. Ev was playing in the high school marching and pep bands, and sat in with the Tulare County

Symphony during its Christmas concert. Jennybeth was doing as well as she could, considering that her major area of concentration in school was popularity.

In March of her senior year, Anne came home from campus one weekend with a sturdy, dark-haired man in tow. It had been over a year since she'd mentioned anyone special, so we were pleased to meet her beau. After a pleasant supper, Anne and Rudy Ramirez sat with us in the living room and told us that they were getting married.

"It seems soon, Mom. But Rudy and I've known each other for a while. We thought this out and we know what we are doing."

Dev hadn't liked any of Anne's dates in high school or in college. I didn't think he would now. He gave me a look that told me I was supposed to handle the parental interrogation. On the other hand, I'd always liked Anne's dates and boyfriends. Dev said I was too easy on young people. I attributed it to my supreme confidence in our daughter. This child of ours was very like her father. She didn't act on impulse.

"Well, your dad and I are surprised. When do you two plan to get married?"

"As soon as possible, Mom."

"Oh," I said.

"Yes," Anne said.

Our daughter needed give no further explanation. I looked at Dev and knew he wasn't quite ready to be either a father-in-law or a grandfather. He was probably thinking he shouldn't have ever become a father. But he loved his daughter. It would all work out.

The solemnity of the young couple before us, and the memory of our own choice in each other, mediated our concerns. I got out of the wing chair to go and sit on the floor by Dev's rocker, leaning against his legs.

"We'd better start making plans, Honey," I said, patting his knee.

"I'm not supposed to make the plans. I just pay the bills," the father of our bride grumbled, but a grin broke on his face.

Dev's mother was happy and promised that they would be there. Sarah said that they'd leave a day early in case there was late snow over Tehachapi pass. Then she handed the phone to Everett, who tactlessly asked Dev if Anne *had* to get married. Dev ignored his father's question. But at the end of the conversation, Everett said, "We'll be there, *grandpa*."

On my side of the family, Mama made a predictable response. "Anne is getting married in three weeks?" There was a pause of about three seconds and she sighed noisily. "Oh, so that's how it is. My first granddaughter hardly gave me time to get a new outfit. How many people will be at the wedding? I have to know what to wear."

"Just the families. You don't have to wear sequins, Mama."

"Just the families? Then it won't be much of a wedding."

"Rudy has about six or seven brothers and sisters and most of them are married and have kids. Then there are the *padrinos* and *madrinos*. A niece and nephew of Rudy's will be dressed as miniature bride and groom. One of his grandfathers is flying in from Guadalajara..."

"Oh! Guadalajara! Well, I will have to look my best."

Within the month, we welcomed a new son, Rudy Ramirez, into our family. His family became part of ours and accepted Dev and me in spite of our cultural reserve. Rudy's families, on both sides and across many generations, were wild about the bride's aunt Beth. My sister stole everyone's attention at the reception away from the bride, and then compensated by lending Anne and Rudy her Waikiki penthouse for two weeks and giving them the flight tickets to get there.

Six and a half months later, Francisco Devon Ramirez, named for both his grandfathers and called Paco for short, arrived in the world. Anne stopped college for neither marriage nor motherhood. She was earning a bi-lingual teaching credential. Rudy's mom, who didn't work for wages, was baby-sitting and making sure Paco had two languages right from the crib.

"Dad loves the baby, doesn't he?" Anne said one Sunday while we were fixing supper. "I was afraid he'd be upset that Rudy was a Mexican."

"Your father is one quarter Paiute Indian! How could you worry about that kind of thing?"

"I don't know. It makes a difference to many people here. Tanya and Julie, in my dorm last year, didn't want to be seen with Rudy and me."

"Well, what would you expect from those two? They are valley kids. In a lot of ways, this valley still thinks it's 1939."

"Mom! You always defend the valley to Adrian and Aunt Beth."

"No place is perfect. It's better now than it was, but there are still problems."

"Yeah. Some of my friends' attitudes."

"Some of mine too."

"You haven't dropped those friends?"

"No. People aren't perfect, either. Do you think I should drop Carla, or Michelle, or Lonnie over ideological differences?"

"Well, no. But I hate bigotry."

"Changes take place lots of different ways, sweetie. Some of them are subtle. Not all meals are cooked at high heat."

My daughter would thrive. But she'd find that landlords might not want to rent houses to people with a Spanish surname. Anne and Rudy would be seated far back by the kitchen in many restaurants. I gave her my advice, but knew she'd bristle at seeing her husband treated with discourtesy, her children discounted in school. She wouldn't be passive.

~~~<<=>>~~~

Chapter 75: Mama Takes A Survey

A year and a half later Paco's brother Joey Ramirez entered our life. Ten months later, Anne told us she would have a third grandchild for us. Dev decided to fence a play area in the kitchen garden area of the hilltop, and invest in pre-school play equipment. I was carrying baby pictures in my wallet in full grandmother mode and couldn't complain.

My sister called. She was working up a tantrum and wanted to scream her anger at someone who would love her no matter how loud she was. She and Wally were in Los Angeles for a big civic event that was very important to him. He was going to be honored during a huge banquet at the New Otami Hotel in downtown Los Angeles. The trouble began when Beth refused to accompany him. Wally had been a great fan of the Kennedys and one of the awards he was to receive was for his contributions to Bobby Kennedy's Center for Justice & Human Rights and to the national group, Common Cause. Beth was as staunchly Republican as Wally was Democrat.

"I'm not going," Beth shrieked into the phone. "He can't make me." I'd been listening to her rant for twenty minutes and it was hurting my telephone ear.

"But it is such an honor," I pleaded on Wally's behalf.

"Why doesn't he give money to B'nai Brith for scholarships or to Planned Parenthood, or something worthwhile instead of where he gives it? He could give it to me. I'd use it for women, not on some stupid bleeding heart liberal Kennedy nonsense."

I didn't point out that percentage of the population felt helping abused women was bleeding heart liberal nonsense.

Instead, I said, "It wouldn't hurt you to be nice to him."

"Yeah. Tell me what to do. You don't go anywhere you don't want to go. You didn't even come to Beverly's funeral."

Beth and Wally screamed at each other for two days before my sister gave in and went to the banquet. She had a wonderful time and met people who remembered her from the days when she was working in the entertainment business. She was photographed with Governor Brown. The photo came out in *Los Angeles About Town*. She sent me a copy. Beth was wearing a gorgeous tangerine gown, and Wally, with his eye-patch, looked like a short, wide, tuxedoed pirate. The governor did his best to look like California's governor and not like he was someone waiting in line to get a dance with my sister.

Everyone was doing well. Jennybeth was in college. She'd resisted the idea, but Beth encouraged her to get at least an Associate of Arts degree. Rudy was running a packinghouse in La Cordillera, and commuting to Los Angeles for grad work. He would get his M.B.A. mid-summer. Three packinghouses near La Cordillera had offered him jobs in advance. Agri-business was doing well in the Central Valley.

Andy had been accepted to medical school and was up in the Bay Area far from his girlfriend, La Tosha Wilson, who was doing the same thing in Southern California. They'd met at a health occupations conference when they were juniors but hadn't been able to get into the same medical school. Our house was a mid-point rendezvous for them and we'd grown fond of her.

Ev was majoring in music and math at Pacific College. He was a member of the Fresno Symphony and had a steady Mennonite girlfriend. In the world of dreams, he'd play jazz sax, but he knew there was a non-dream world. He was taking education classes too. There were always job openings for math and science teachers.

We built another, smaller house across the cactus garden from the ranch house for ourselves and persuaded Anne and Rudy to move into the big ranch house. Dev retired early to be a full time rancher. Rudy helped him on weekends when things got busy. It was good having children around the ranch again. The proximity didn't hurt any of us. There was lots of space on the ranch.

In 1983, my sister, brothers, and I nagged at Mama until she finally agreed to put her house on the market and move near one of us. We worried about her. Nearly all her friends in Breeze Terrace were gone. Though she didn't like to admit it. She had grown socially isolated. She had stopped going to church, claiming that the new pastor was only interested in her money. "One of the things I liked about Catholics was that the church didn't demand tithing like the Protestant churches. I might just as well have stayed a Methodist. Father Werner wants his hands on my checkbook, and he's not going to put them there."

With noticeable rivalry, Beth, Steve, Alex and I were determined to woo Mama to our own areas. As we moved into middle age, we'd begun to spoil her. We competed for her attention far more than we had as children, and so we spent time scouting our neighborhoods to find a house, apartment or condo that would suit her. Mother visited each of us in turn to examine what we'd found and make her relocation decision. First, she'd explored Hawaii with Beth and Wally. Then she came to see us. La Cordillera was second on her survey schedule. She was unimpressed by the best our area offered.

"Dev and I would make sure you got the best medical care. Anne lives here. She could check on you every day if I couldn't."

My mother rolled her eyes at Anne's name, as if to remind me that the baggage of Anne's children wasn't an inducement. Mama called them her *beloved little boys*, and liked buying presents for Paco, Joey and baby Lydia, but she didn't like their actual physical presence much.

I ignored her eye rolling and blithely went on, "During our fog season, you could fly to Hawaii or stay with Alex and Sandra in the desert. It is only six weeks. The Blossom Trail is beautiful in March and trees color up like New England in the fall. In summer there is an endless supply of fruits and vegetables." I was eloquent, and I remembered practical considerations. "Think how much easier it will be for you to get to fruit stands and the market. You wouldn't have to drive. I could take you. You wouldn't have to tote bags of groceries."

"I've seen the kind of markets you have. Not the kind I like." She compressed her lips, frowned and made a quarter turn away from me, her eyes never leaving mine, definitely showing aversion. "You know, baby, this valley is what I ran away from."

"Well, do you think you'd be happier near Beth?"

"I'm not going to live in Honolulu. It's a terrible Asian place."

"Mother, how can you say that?"

"Now, baby. You know I like Asian people. I just don't like so many of them all in one place."

"Sometimes I'm ashamed that you're my mother."

"Well, Andrea. Lots of times I've been ashamed that you're my daughter. You and Alex. You both turned your backs on opportunity. I think you two did it to spite me. You had good chances given you, and you walked away from them."

"Mother! By opportunity, do you mean Michael?" I lowered my voice for a sad inclusion, "Or Vince?"

"Well, I admit I was wrong about Vince, but Michael has done very well. He's running his uncle's plant in Long Beach. He lives in Palos Verdes in a huge house overlooking the ocean. He's married to some dull little thing. I know he'd leave her in a minute if you came back into his life. Lily doesn't like her at all."

The next morning, I fixed my mother a nice brunch with freshly ground Kona coffee from Beth and freshly squeezed orange juice from the grove. She seemed in a good mood, but then her expression changed. She looked broody and then she began to tell me of a conversation she had recently with Rozsika.

"When I told Rozsika I was going to sell my house, she invited me to move to Bainbridge Island near her. I'd never go there. The sun only shines about three times a year." Mama stopped eating and sat back.

"That's awfully far north, Mama."

"It is. You know, baby, Rozsika was very rude to me. She invited me to live with her and then she attacked me for letting Daddy punish you when you were a child. She's never let that drop all these years. And what could I have done? Of course, he disciplined you. Never. Verna brings up that old stuff too. Neither of those women had a child. They don't know what its like." Mama thoughtfully sipped the coffee and looked out the breakfast nook window at the Sierra.

"Daddy had to discipline you. He couldn't just let you do whatever you wanted. Rozsika had no right to talk to me like that, especially after your father and I did so much for her. You know you were never abused. I don't know how they can say such you were."

Laz wasn't my father. I got busy rinsing off the skillet and running the garbage disposal so I wouldn't have to look at her. My childishness embarrassed me. I was almost forty-six years old, a grandmother, and still carrying a childhood grudge.

"Come and sit down with me, Andrea," My mother ordered. I finished the work I was doing and obeyed.

"You know you weren't abused. Daddy loved you just like he did his own natural born children. He gave you everything in the world. No child in the neighborhood had more than you did. Everything you wanted, he got for you. He treated you just the same as he did his own children. You had everything, bicycles, beautiful clothes, parties, toys, lessons, a good education. I want you to tell me that you know how good he was to you."

I had to think carefully. This wasn't really about Laz. This was about my mother and me. I had to find the right words. They came to me. "Mama, look at it this way. If you hadn't married Laz, I wouldn't have Beth, Steve or Alex. What would my life have been like without my sister and brothers? Your marriage filled my life with people I love. I would never want to change that."

She eased comfortably on the kitchen chair. I went and picked up the coffeepot and refilled her cup. She blew her nose, and I put the pot on the table and my arm around her shoulders.

"I know you two didn't get along, Andrea," she said. "But, baby, you know there was nothing else I could do at that dreadful time in my life. We needed someone to take care of us."

"I know, Mama.

The phone rang, but it was a wrong number. My mother sat and glanced at our weekly paper. Dev had brought it in earlier. She seemed at ease. I looked out the window toward the barn and the Sierra. The mountains beyond our foothills were so high and brilliant in the morning light.

The kitchen was quiet, other than the noise of the mockingbirds out in the cactus garden outside. The refrigerator made one of its usual gurgles and the clock pinged its quarter hour sound. The air smelled of maple syrup, coffee and scouring powder, sweet, bitter, and cleansing.

I looked at my mother sitting quietly looking at the newspaper. The two most painful and difficult conversations of my entire life had been with her, and both had taken place in a kitchen.

~~~<<=>>~~~

Chapter 76: Lunch in Visalia

A few weeks later, Beth drove up and we had lunch in a restaurant on Visalia's Main Street, not far from the hospital where my students were doing their clinical work. Beth was three years past forty now, but still gorgeous. She'd let her hair grow out in its natural color to see how blond she still was under the salon color. She was so pleased she'd kept it natural ever since. Here in my valley habitat, she was a brilliant bird escaped from a tropical aviary. It was fun watching the waiters watch her.

Beth was beautiful but irate. "She didn't like anything I showed her. Wally and I aren't on the mainland enough anymore to watch out for her there. But she didn't like anything in Honolulu. I found beautiful places for her and she didn't like any of them. She made me crazy. I called Verna. She was okay with Mama moving to Maui, as long as she had her own house. So we flew to Maui. She loves flying, you know. Says she feels like Aladdin on his magic carpet."

"But would she consider Maui?" Maui was no more urban than La Cordillera.

"She hated it. She said that Verna might like Maui, but it was too close to where Father Damien had his leper colony. Mama said she wouldn't risk getting some horrible disease. I reminded her that in over twenty years on that island, Verna hasn't caught anything but a couple of boyfriends to take her out to dinner."

"She doesn't like it here either. She says she escaped from this poverty stricken valley and isn't coming back. She complained that there aren't enough high line items in our grocery stores."

"She's right. I told you that twenty years ago."

I didn't mention what Mama said about Honolulu being an Asian place, not wanting to torch any of Beth's incendiary fuel. Any slight to her two heroes, Utaka Ishida and Tom Fonseca, and Beth would throw a tantrum that would light up the sky between California and Hawaii, Aurora Borealis *al sud*.

"I don't think she'll like Las Vegas, Beth. Mama's too much of a bigot to live near Alex and Sandra. Vegas has a big African-American population. Remember when you were in eighth grade and you couldn't come to Queen of Heaven High School because black girls were enrolled with me."

"Oh, That was Daddy. Mama isn't really a bigot. Her generation just thinks it ought to be. Remember when she took us to see Nat King Cole?"

I did remember. Mother held her forty-eighth birthday dinner at Ciro's because he was doing the dinner show that week. It was very long ago. Beth was only sixteen. I had just met Dev.

Beth's smile grew wide. "I knew you had to remember. Nat was better than Neil Diamond, Stevie Wonder and the Beatles put together."

I disagreed about the Beatles. No one was better than the Beatles. "I remember Mama sent fifty dollars up to the stage so he would sing *Mona Lisa* just for her. It was a waste of money. He would have sung it anyway. He always sang it."

"But not specifically for her. She grieved more when Nat King Cole died than she did when Daddy died." Beth frowned. "Kill the nostalgia. Move up to the present. I didn't drive all the way here today to talk about Mama, as interesting as that subject has always been. I want to tell you about a girl I've been working with."

"The one with the baby and the rough ex-boyfriend?"

"No. That hulking problem is in prison for the next three years. This girl is one of our own agency clients. Her husband is a bastard. He put her in the hospital three weeks ago, and its not the first time he's bashed her around. She's got a tremendous voice and has a local following. Her husband is a civilian employee out at the naval base. He's such a jerk he tried to tell her she should only sing for him. She's great and really loves performing. Her family is all stateside and have no money, so after she got out of the hospital, I went with her when she appealed for a restraining order."

My sister went into a long narration of both the woman's talent and marital troubles, and while she talked I thought of some of our young nursing students and their difficult relationships. I was only half listening.

"Dree," she asked, startling me back to the present. "Have you ever thought about Jeannie?"

"Jeannie? Jeannie French?"

"The Jeannie who used to take care of us and was murdered. That Jeannie."

"It was Jeannie French," I said. "You were only seven. I didn't think you still remembered her."

"I do. I think about her a lot. I didn't tell you, but Mama really talked to me this last visit. She told me that Ilona Horvath, Daddy's first wife was sterile. She hadn't conceived in the twenty-five years of their marriage, and he wanted children. He promised Mama that he would take care of the two of you if she'd agree to have a child for him." Beth sat back with a cynical smirk. "I was just a business arrangement to our mother." She reached into her purse and got her makeup out. "At least my father wanted me."

"I wanted you too. That makes two of us, so cheer up. It's more than a lot of people have at birth. How does this connect to Jeannie French?"

"Just a minute and I'll answer you. Let finish." A moment later she clicked her compact shut, and put it and her lipstick away. Grooming done, she continued. "It connects because that same afternoon, Mama told me that Jeannie helped women in our old neighborhood find licensed doctors to give them abortions. Back when it was illegal. Mama said back then women had to go to back alley hacks or go to Mexico. Our mother is so strange. She told me that getting rid of a child was the one sin she never committed, as though she regularly robbed banks."

My sister made an exasperated face and went on talking. "I bet she never told you this. Mama said that she knew a woman who died from an abortion when she was young. It left her too afraid to ever have one herself. Think about that. If that hadn't happened, she might have ditched every one of us."

"Mama didn't tell me about the arrangement with your father, and she didn't exactly tell me that Jeannie helped the neighborhood women get abortions, but she implied that. I know it was Jeannie who found the pediatrician in Beverly Hills who practically saved Steve's life. Jeannie was popular and had contacts in the medical community. It could have been true. Mama never actually used the word abortion."

"She didn't use it with me either. Mama is too superstitious to say words like abortion, venereal disease, or cancer. As though saying things out loud makes them happen. She said 'women were in trouble'." She meant pregnant. A pensive and thoughtful look came into my sister's eyes. "I'm glad *Roe versus Wade* was affirmed by the court, and women aren't trapped anymore."

There was much in her face and voice that I'd never ask about, but I did ask her about something else I'd considered. "Beth, do you think Jeannie might have been killed because she helped someone?"

"You mean like giving a doctor's name to the wrong person? Maybe."

"If a doctor lost his license, he could have become vindictive. Her murderer was angry. It wasn't just a sex killing."

"I remember thinking Mr. Morgan killed her."

"It may have been an enraged husband. Remember when people used to say that a man's ideal woman was barefoot and pregnant?"

"I heard that when I was a kid and decided that barefoot woman would never be me." Beth reached for the bill. "Drea, you're not anti-abortion are you?"

"No. I never chose it for myself, but I am pro-choice. If the pill and IUD hadn't come along when they did to work for me,

I might have had an abortion. Dev loves our kids, but four stressed him to the breaking point. We would have been ragged with five."

"One woman I've counseled told me her husband put her BC pills down the toilet and threatened to kill her if she took them. It's a relief to know you aren't politically archaic. You're so conservative about everything. God, Drea. You still peel potatoes and carrots. Don't you know you can buy them pre-prepared in any market."

"I only live conservatively. I vote liberal."

"You don't *really* vote liberal?"

For once I didn't back down from confrontation. "Yes, I really do. I don't understand how you can live so liberal, be Wally's wife, and vote conservative."

I did get a smile out of her. We both understood the complexities of choices offered by a democracy, and we'd never been alike. I tried to change the subject to tell her about my new job. Five years earlier, I'd earned my Master's and had been teaching in the nursing program at College of the Sequoias. But Beth was impassioned and single-minded. She didn't want to listen to me chatter. She wanted to talk.

"The women I help have to fight. If they don't stand up for themselves, men will keep battering, beating and breaking them down. I want to get self-defense classes going in every programs where I volunteer, martial arts training courses."

"Oh, be realistic, Beth. It doesn't matter how many self-defense classes women take, men can kill us whenever they want. You're slipping into fantasy if you think Karate and Tae Kwon Do will make any difference. By the time a boy's fourteen, he is three times as strong as a woman of the same height and weight. Self-defense training is no answer."

My sister looked astounded at what I'd said. Then she said, "Sometimes you are really dumb. If I hadn't fought when I was attacked, I'd be dead and you'd be sitting at this table alone. That asshole near Wahiawa was bashing me on the head with a tire iron and I fought back!" Beth's face was radiant with pride at having made her point, and her eyes were driving her passion into me. "No kidding, Drea. I'd be dead if I hadn't fought back."

"I'm glad you're not dead."

"You'd better be. You're so lucky to have me for a sister."

We left the restaurant and walked along Visalia's Main Street in the leafy shade. Beth stopped and pulled me into a shoe store and scandalized me by buying a pair of sandals that cost a hundred and forty-five dollars. She could have gotten sandals for twenty-five dollars at J.C. Penny's that were every bit as good.

~~~<<=>>~~~

Chapter 77: Leaving Taking

After more than forty years, the last member of the Horvath family moved away from the neighborhood of Breeze Terrace. West L. A. real estate was in great demand, and Mama made a nice profit on the sale of the house. She wisely didn't sell the Sepulveda property that generated her comfortable income; she had good tenants and felt she could manage the leases in absentia. Mother surprised us all. She didn't pick Beth's, Steve's or my locations for her new home. She chose to move to Las Vegas near Alex.

Mama told Steve he had been a wonderful son; however, she concluded, he and Janet were too busy with their children and social life. She felt that they might chafe under her physical demands, as she grew older and needed more help. "Alex and Sandra don't have so many distractions," she said.

She didn't offer an explanation to Beth or me for rejecting us. The choice confounded us. Our gregarious, personable, save-the-world brother had always seemed Mother's least favorite child. During his childhood, she'd resented his energy as though vigor was something he did to annoy her, not a facet of good health. I'd expected that Mama would follow the money and either settle in Hawaii near Beth or in Northridge near Steve, and I was wrong. I asked for an explanation.

"I want to be near Alex and Sandra, because Alex interferes with me less than you other children do. I like freedom to do whatever I want. Janet and Karin snip about what I do, and you two girls do too. You're always trying to control me."

"I've never tried to control you!"

Mama didn't say a word, but she gave me one of her looks.

After my first shock at this indictment, I came to understand. My adult children were beginning to interfere with me. My daughters suggested I cut my hair and shorten my skirts. Ev didn't like me using the same colorful driving phrases that he accepted when they came from his father's mouth. Andy was the only one who didn't seem to mind the way I naturally was. Beth claimed Mama chose Las Vegas not because of Alex's tolerant nature but because of the town's glitz, glamour and glitter.

Everything settled down in the following months. Spring moved toward summer. Jennybeth was graduating from Reedley College and Ev from Fresno Pacific. Wally and Beth brought Verna to the mainland in early June for the graduations. Sarah Cunningham drove over with Dev's sister and her daughter and they stayed with us. My family decided to make a grand reunion of the weekend and took party suites in a Fresno hotel. Mama flew in to Fresno from Las Vegas with Alex and Sandra. Steve and Janet drove up and brought Janet's mother along. She'd been depressed since her husband died and Steve thought the trip would cheer her. They didn't bring Karin or Doug, both now old enough to be busy with jobs and activities.

Dev had the idea that I prepare Mama for her meeting with Andy's future wife by sending photos of La Tosha and Andy that he'd taken during spring break and I did. Mama was prepared. Within two hours, of meeting La Tosha, she seemed as fond of Andy's young woman as we were. Beth had been right about Mama. She wasn't really a bigot. Her generation's rigidity only left a thin scattering of xenophobic dust on her shoulders. Time helped Mama brush it off.

We had a barbeque the last evening of the family's visit. The ranch had two kitchens now, and that made it easy. The tomatoes were ripening, and there were early apricots in the orchard. Wally and Beth gave the graduates obscenely big checks. Our older kids weren't jealous. They had been treated with equal generosity when they'd graduated.

The children had grown independent. Jennybeth was working in the cosmetic department of Gottschalks in Visalia while she was in school and loved her job in retail. Ev would stay to get a graduate degree and teaching credential. As the festive week ended and the guests went home, Dev and I were smug and cuddly. Our children had turned out well in spite of our mistakes as parents. We hadn't raised them alone. Grandparents, aunts, uncles, teachers and many friends had helped us.

Later that summer my husband and I drove over Sherman Pass on our way to Bishop to see Sarah. Rudy and the little boys would take care of the ranch. The pass was only opened in the summer, and seldom traveled except by hunters, foresters, and loggers. It connected the mountain hamlet of Johnsondale with Highway 395, crossing into the lower Kern River canyon and climbing back up. The view from its crest was glorious. The Sierra backbone stretched northwest displaying knobby vertebrae: Olancha, Kaweah, Whitney. The peaks of mountains reached above 13,000 feet, and still had snow in clefts. We stayed there for a long time in the cool, high mountains, sitting on pine needles and slowly sharing a picnic lunch. The mountains refreshed us, reminded us that we were part of some marvelous, gigantic thing, impossible for a feeble human mind to comprehend. The task it had given us, as it did any organism to maintain our health and care for our young, was now finished.

Dev embraced our new freedom. I had moments of sadness, missing my disappeared children, not always seeing them in the adults they had become. I missed the mischief and silliness. But those mother-grief moments came less often now that Anne's Paco, Joey, and Liddy had come to fill the places of my lost babies. I could see along with Dev, that a different sort of life was opening. It would be a time of joy and satisfaction, and perhaps even greater happiness.

In the night, in mid-September, the phone rang. Dev woke up before I did. He was answering while I was still thrashing out of some dream and trying to reconcile the noise of the phone with its plot.

"Hon, wake up. It's your mother," he said.

I came awake, his words transferring my terror at an after-hours phone call from my children's welfare to concern for the Horvath family. Dev handed me the phone.

"Our Beth is gone," my mother said as soon as she heard my voice.

"Mother, what are you talking about?"

Her voice sounded weary and distant. "She's gone. She's dead, Lynn. She had an asthma attack, and Wally found her in the bathroom. She was lying on the rug not breathing."

My sister was too young. She was too much alive. I'd just talked to her. She couldn't die. I listened to my own voice and wondered whose it was, and denial left me. I knew Beth could die. Anybody could die.

"I told Wally I would call you all. I've talked to Steve and Alex. I called Verna too. Oh, she loved your sister so much." There was a space of time when I spun around somewhere thinking I love my sister so much. *Why are you talking about Verna? Why are you saying these terrible things?*

Mother's voice kept talking and talking. "Wally was still at the hospital. The paramedics couldn't do anything for her. They tried for over a half hour but they couldn't help her." Finally she paused. I could hear her breathing and I had no words to fill the space.

"Baby, I'm tired and need to rest now. Alex came over as soon as I called him. He and Sandra are with me. I'll talk to you again in the morning."

I was nodding my head and realized she couldn't see me. "Okay," I said. "Okay."

"Lynn, Lynn. Did you ever think it would come to this? Our little Beth was never as sick as Steve. He's the child I thought I'd lose, not Beth." I heard her fumble the phone, and Sandra's calm voice in the background as she took the receiver to hang it back up for Mama.

"Bye, Mama," I said, knowing she couldn't hear me, but needing to say it anyway.

Dev pulled me down on the bed. He pulled the blankets up and half leaning over me, tucked his arms up around me making a cradle. "I'm so sorry," he said. I felt dampness on the pillow beside me and on my shoulder. My sister left me, and he was softly crying for Beth while I had no tears. I just stared into the darkness of our room.

A long time later Dev turned over in his sleep, his breathing even. Slipping away from him, I went into the living room and wrapped up in an afghan Elaine Whitfield had sent me years ago. There was no moon out our windows, but the little towns and cities of the valley below our hill illuminated little pockets in the night. The afghan was soft. Its wool carried a sheep smell, even through all the processing, a comforting smell synthetics never had.

The manufacturing of yarns shouldn't have been filling my mind when my sister was dead. What kind of vacuous, uncaring person was I? Other trivial things came to me but didn't stay long enough to become thoughts. But I didn't sleep. My sister's face kept coming into my random floating thought and I tried to hold it, knowing that soon I wouldn't be able to grasp her expressions clearly. She'd be like grandpa, Uncle Sandor, Jeannie, Beverly, Vince and all my other lost people, remembered, but without detail.

In the morning when Dev got up, he came to find me. I was aware enough to ask him to call the college office and tell Marcia, the secretary, that I'd needed leave time.

"I have to tell the children," I said. But then I turned my face away from him and curled into the sofa again.

"I'll take care of everything," he said. He pulled me up into his arms and then walked me back to our bedroom. I climbed in and rolled over to sleep on his side of the bed where it was still warm.

~~~<<=>>~~~

Chapter 78: The Competent Horvath Brothers

In this time of crisis, the Horvath brothers turned out to be Mama's competent children. As insubstantial as a ghost, I was no help to anyone. By the afternoon of that first day, Alex and Sandra had Mother on a plane and had flown with her to Los Angeles. Steve was already in Hawaii to help Wally make arrangements to bringing Beth home for burial. She'd left a will and a note with her lawyer. Wally had a copy of each. Beth wanted her services held in St. Blaise Church and had specially requested that she be buried next to her father at Holy Cross Cemetery in Culver City.

Dev made reservations for the two of us at a small inn in Chatsworth, not many miles from Steve's house in Northridge. Anne and Rudy promised to take care of the ranch and our animals and make sure Andy, Ev and Jennybeth were kept informed of the arrangements being made. Clara, retired now, had been happy to pick up my lesson plans and take them to the college. She even volunteered to substitute for me.

We checked into a small inn in Chatsworth and drove to Steve and Janet's house. My sister-in-law had created a beautiful home. It had fresh flower arrangements, pretty showpieces, and decorator items. Magazine-perfect, there was none of the farrago of books, musical instruments, unfinished projects, and pets that littered our home. Karin welcomed us. Alex and Sandra had gone somewhere. Janet was out stocking up on groceries for the week ahead. Mama was in the living room.

"Can you believe this could happen to me?" Mama asked as Dev and I came toward her.

She didn't expect an answer. Mama was sitting in a wing chair, a wadded handkerchief in one of her hands and a crystal rosary in the other. "You see what life done to me," she murmured as I put my arms around her. I wasn't the daughter she wanted, but she didn't push me away.

The next morning, while Steve and Wally were escorting Beth's body home, Alex, Dev, Sandra and I sat in the dining room with Mama. No one but Mama was hungry. The only thing the rest of us savored was gloom. Coffee was getting cold, omelets congealing. Then, abruptly, Mother cut through our morose apathy. "I need to use the phone. Oh, Sandra, get me the phone."

Sandra jumped up and brought the phone to the table. Mama fumbled to pull an address book from her purse, put her glasses on, and found the number she wanted. As she began to dial, Mama felt us watching her. She looked around the table and brusquely dismissed us. "You children go about your business. I need to make a call now."

Janet slipped back into the kitchen. Sandra, Dev and I got up to leave the dining room. Alex remained in his chair across from Mama. We, the more compliant members of the family, went into the living room. Someone had left the TV on. A morning show was blaring. Dev turned the set off. Sandra picked up a decorator magazine from the coffee table, but didn't open it. We made small talk. Rather, Dev and Sandra did. I was only vaguely aware of what they were saying.

It wasn't long before Alex came in to join us. He had a strange expression, surprise and annoyance blended. He sat near us and leaned forward conspiratorially. "Do you know what our mother is doing?"

Dev shrugged and said, "Haven't a clue."

I just shook my head, but Sandra whispered in her droll way, "Who could ever predict what your mother would do?"

"She's calling her lawyer. She wants Randy Dwyer to change her will. She wants Beth's name taken out of it. Damn, you guys! Beth isn't even buried, and Mama's re-writing her will."

Sandra allowed a sly and tolerant smile to wash across her face. Dev didn't look as mother-in-law tolerant, and he wasn't smiling.

"She wants Randy to draw up a whole new will and fax it to her here," Alex said. My brother rose to go back down the hall to the dining room. I followed him.

Mama looked up at my brother and me. She knew what we were thinking and gave us a smirky look that said: *Don't meddle in my affairs*. Deliberately ignoring us, Mama looked toward the kitchen. By then Dev and Sandra were standing behind me in the archway.

"Janet, dear?" Mama called.

"What do you need, Mother Horvath?"

"Steve has a fax machine in his office, doesn't he? I need its number." Janet came through the kitchen doorway with a notepad and pencil.

"Mama, you can't do this," Alex said.

"It's my business, not yours. It needs to be done."

Janet gave her the number. Mama tucked the piece of paper into her purse, smiling up at my sister-in-law. "Thank you, dear. You'll need to keep checking the office for a fax coming in for me today." Mama turned back to her breakfast, sighed, and took a bite of toast.

"This is very wrong, Mama," Alex cautioned. "Steve would agree with us. Wally doesn't deserve this kind of a slam, especially right now. You're embarrassing me."

Mama puffed up. "I'm protecting you, that's what I'm doing. I could die tomorrow. Nobody knows what might happen." Her eyes grew squinty and her face tight. "I won't have that old man getting a full quarter of everything I own."

"He was good to Beth, Mama. He's been good to you too."

With a look that closed the topic to further discussion, Mama turned toward the kitchen again. "Janet, honey, did you already put away the orange marmalade?"

The Braden Brothers hearse was waiting at LAX when the plane arrived that afternoon. Alex and Dev had taken the 405 to greet Steve at the airport. Wally's son, Leland Raudell, was there to meet Wally.

The five men had a late lunch in one of the airport restaurants and coordinated logistics for Beth's services. Wally's son was competent and thoughtful. He would organize temporary management of the island agency. The rosary was scheduled for Thursday evening, and the funeral would be held on Friday. The pastor of St. Blaise parish was arranging a solemn high requiem mass.

Sandra took mother shopping for a mourning outfit to get her out of the house. Janet needed a rest from toting and fetching. I went back to the quiet of the inn and its shady garden until Dev called, and I had to go back to dinner in Northridge.

That evening trouble came. Beth asked to be buried next to her father in Holy Cross Cemetery. However, the plots on the hilltop where Laz was buried had long ago been filled. The only vacant plot was Mama's purchased and reserved place beside him. Mama refused to give up her plot. She stubbornly declared, "I was your father's wife. Beth was only his child."

My brothers glanced at each other, then at me. It was our sister's last request, the only thing now that we could do for her. Alex offered a suggestion only half in jest. "When you die, Mama, we'll have you interred in Daddy's grave with him."

Mama sucked in her breath and slowly let it out and said, "Don't be ridiculous."

"It's not ridiculous," Alex said, forming a plan as he spoke. "Tandem grave sites were already being offered for couples in the cities back east when Sandra and I were living there. Land is becoming scarce even in graveyards."

"This is California. We have lots of land," Mama answered, clenching her teeth.

My husband came to Alex's support. "He's right, Marianne. I read about it in *Forbes* or *Fortune*, one of the business magazines. It's not a new concept. Cemeteries have been doing this in Europe for a long time."

"I know about the catacombs," Mama dismissed Dev by answering sarcastically.

"Not the catacombs, in modern cemeteries. This is an environmentally sound concept."

Steve, sitting next to our mother, bent toward her and took her plump hand. Her rings flashed in the low sun coming in the west windows. "Just think, Mama," Steve said. "You'll be a style setter. You and Daddy could have the very first double-decker grave in Holy Cross Cemetery."

Sandra's hearty laugh tore through the room.

Mother sharply said, "What's so funny? That wasn't so funny."

Sandra calmed herself enough to choke out, "Just think, Marianne, you'll get to be on top for all eternity."

Mama poised herself. Then, she tilted her head and looked sharply at my brothers as they stifled their laughter. "What if I die this week or this month? What if Holy Cross doesn't allow it?" She looked from one of her sons to the other. "I won't be buried in some weedy corner near derelicts or in some potter's field down by Holy Cross's back fence. I don't want you putting me in some awful place."

"There aren't any awful places in Holy Cross," Alex said.

Steve added, "Mother, Holy Cross is full of Catholic movie stars. It's the Beverly Hills of cemeteries."

Alex grinned and began a litany of names. "Think who'll be there with you: Bing Crosby, Charles Boyer, Jimmy Durante, Jack Haley, Mario Lanza." His blue eyes were twinkling. "Mama, those tenants aren't going to let that nice neighborhood go down."

Mama's eyes grew huge. Instead of being appeased, her face looked truly horrorstricken. She reared back in her chair and pushed farther from the table. Her voice soared tremulously as she said, "Oh, VAMPIRES! I won't be buried with Béla Lugosi! Don't you dare put me near VAMPIRES!"

"We won't put you near any vampires," Steve promised. "I swear. Don't worry about a thing. Alex and I'll spread so much cash around the cemetery office, that if you can't be with Daddy, you'll have the best grave in the whole place."

Sandra broke into raucous laughter. Dev and my brothers couldn't hold serious faces any longer.

Though I understood the psychological benefits of funereal humor, I was remote from its relief. Mama ruthlessly wrenched the family's focus away from my sister, and Beth was a woman who earned and was due our undiverted attention.

But Beth, with our help, had captured the hill and it was a righteous win. For while Mama had counted four husbands and Laz had counted two wives, my sister was the only daughter Lazlo Horvath ever had and he had been her only father.

~~~<<=>>~~~

Chapter 79: Necessary Alterations

Death ceremonies wrested people away, and I didn't like giving up my dead. I resisted getting into the car to go to the funeral; then at the church, I wanted to wait in the car for Dev until it was over. But he nagged at me, insisting I be there with him, saying that if Wally and Mama could get through it, I could too. Beth's mass had candles, incense and quiet prayer. St. Blaise Church did death well. The service was severe, formal and liturgical. There were no impromptu eulogy vanities from a front lectern. The old church of our childhood held death in great respect. Starkness, blackness, solemnity were the ritual. We were there to grieve. Death wasn't seen as celebration. For that, I was grateful.

Beth would have gagged at the hope symbols of roses or doves. She wouldn't have wanted us tranquilized. She would have wanted absolute assurance that we could not survive without her. More than just a solemn high requiem mass, she would have wanted what our times didn't allow: wailing, the gnashing of teeth, the tearing of hair and the rending of clothes.

After the service and graveside prayers, Wally hosted the family and close friends at Leland's home in Bel Air. Steve already knew how Beth died. He'd filled out all the forms in Honolulu pertaining to her death that Wally's shaky hands couldn't manage, but he didn't think an exposition of Beth's manner of death was his story to tell. Her death certificate stated that she died of asthma, but it wasn't a simple death from a chronic disorder. Wally told the family what happened on the day that Beth died. It was his story to tell.

"Beth knew this young kid who had trouble with her husband.

She was one of the agency clients. Had a great voice, fuckin' wow audience appeal. Husband was a jerk," Wally began.

"Beth helped 'er get a restraining order and a new place to live. Son of a bitch threatened to kill 'er if she filed for divorce, so for da hearin' cops were gonna be alerted. I told Beth not to go to court with the girl. I yelled at 'er to let da cops take care of it. But she wouldn' listen." He leaned forward. His hands were on his knees. "I woulda stopped 'er. How ya make sense out of that? Her not telling me where she was goin'." He stopped to wipe his eyes. "I woulda stopped 'er. She got the security guy from the agency to go along with them, but she didn' tell me nothin' about it."

"They got to court. Everything was fine. The divorce was gran'ed, no trouble. They come out of the building, all hell breaks loose. The ass hole son of a bitch jumps out from between two cars. He shoots his wife dead. Point blank. The girl is bleeding on 'a ground. The husband turns to his gun to Beth. Security guy pushes Beth down and covers her with his body. A courthouse cop shoots the guy down. All over in about two secon's."

Wally looked around and said, "It was big news in Honolulu, but you got too much shit of your own. You wouldn'a seen it on TV over here. She didn' want me to call Marianne or any of you. Said she'd do it when she was ready."

Wally broke down and motioned to my brother to continue for him. Steve's calm, resonant voice picked up the narrative. "At the courthouse after the shooting, Beth refused to get in the van with the paramedics. She only was scraped on one arm when she hit the pavement. And she insisted she wanted to go home and change. Her clothes were streaked with the victim's blood. You know how your Beth was. One of the detectives told her she'd get home quicker from the hospital than she would from the crime scene, so she finally got into the ambulance with the paramedics."

Wally straightened up and broke in. "She called me from the hospital and tol' me to bring her clean clothes and a pair of shoes. Then hung up. I din't know what was goin' on. I thought she'd been inna accident. I got there as fast as I could. Your sister was so mad. She was chewing out the detective. I heard 'er when I got outta the elevator, alla way down the corridor. She wouldn' answer his questions. She was mad at me, too, an' I came fast as I could find her stuff. She said she was only going to talk about what happened once, so we bedder pay attention.

"Beth was so pissed. They tried to give her Valium after the interview. She wouldn' take it. She yelled at me that I got the wrong shoes and threw them at me. How'd I know what the fuck shoes she wanted?" Wally seemed to crumple down. "After it was all over, an' she made da statement, I took 'er home."

Steve finished. "Beth and Wally had an argument. Wally didn't want her to watch the news coverage, but she insisted on seeing it. The next morning she insisted on going to work, but there were reporters all around their building, so Beth worked from home all day, cancelling any appointments that couldn't be handled on the phone. Mid-afternoon she began wheezing, took her pills and used her atomizer. She seemed to feel better. Wally fixed her a cup of tea, and made her a sandwich in the evening. She coughed a little. He was worried and wanted to take her back to the hospital. She refused but said if she still felt sick in the morning she'd call her allergist. They watched TV until eleven. Beth was still wheezing and said she was going to go to bed. Wally rinsed the dishes, took out the kitchen trash, and went to join her. Beth was lying on their bathroom rug, not breathing."

Swollen eyed, Wally looked around at all of us. "I loved 'er the first time I saw 'er. What was she? Sixteen, seventeen? I swear I never made a move on 'er. Never once. Not for years. But I loved 'er."

Even Mama, tougher than all of us together, was weeping.

Beth's estate lawyer read her will in his firm's conference room on Saturday morning. Verna had flown home to Maui, but Wally, Mama, my brothers and I were asked to stay over and to be present for the reading. I didn't want to be there without Dev, but he thought it improper for in-laws to be at the reading. He, Janet, and Sandra waited out in the building's courtyard grateful that it was a pleasant day.

Our sister left an identical and significant amount in stocks and securities to Steve, Alex and me. She left twenty-five thousand in trust for each of her nieces and nephews to claim at the age of twenty-five. She had already established a generous educational trust for the grandchildren of Mr. Utaka Ishida, the hoe-wielding farmer who had come to her defense during the attack near Wahiawa. The bulk of my sister's estate went to support abused women and children in the state of Hawaii. Wallace Raudell and Stephen Horvath were to act as co-trustees for the bequest. Sister Mary Immaculata's influence was apparent, because Beth's legacy was to be distributed anonymously. Beth didn't want praise to tarnish the value of her gift.

With the exception of a few specific pieces designated for her nieces and for Wally's granddaughter Marcella, Beth left her jewelry to me. Mama was upset that she wasn't mentioned in Beth's will until Alex pointed out, "It wasn't personal. She didn't mention Verna in her will either, Mother. She didn't expect to die before you."

"My daughter was always practical," Mama sighed, temporarily mollified.

Dev and I drove Mother back to Northridge, so she could lie down. My brothers and their wives went to lunch with Wally, Leland and Beth's attorney. As we drove out Sunset and through the Santa Monica Mountains on the 405, we were very quiet. But when we cleared Sepulveda Pass, and could look down at the sprawl of the San Fernando Valley, Mama broke through the introspective silence in the car.

"You don't appreciate diamonds, Andrea. Beth should have left all that jewelry to Sandra and Janet or her nieces."

I smiled a little and looked out the window, but Dev was unable to ignore what Mama said. He fired back, "She didn't love them, Marianne. She loved Andrea."

Bereavement authorities say the death of a sibling is the hardest loss from which people recover. We are more like each other than we are like our parents or our children; we share a fusion of genetic commonality and early learning. I knew I would never survive Beth's death. Stocks and securities, rings and necklaces were scant compensation for the loss of my sister.

Yet, in the months after Beth died, Dev pulled me toward him and away from the devastation of that loss – just as on a night in the hospital cafeteria years earlier, when crockery shards flew like shrapnel, he'd protectively drawn me toward him. He held me clamped so tightly in the vise of his arms that my broken parts began to bond back together. Then, knowing that he mirrored the alterations of all those things that had broken in me, I turned, held his hands, stroked his hair, and kissed his face. He was bereft of a sister too. We honored Beth by allowing anguish to wash over us. Without the protection of armbands or black clothing to warn others away, we withdrew to each other, and allowed ourselves a time necessary for grief.

Two years later, we attended Ev and Rhoda's wedding. Mennonites don't dance, but they eat well. We came home from the reception needing exercise to burn off both too many calories and too much goodness. The house was inky dark and cold when we came in. I took off my coat and hung it in the hall closet while Dev turned on the lights, the heater and the radio. The latter was set to Radio Bilingue from Bakersfield. The wilding cadence of *ranchera musica* surrounded us. Though rockabilly was more to his taste, Dev shouted, "Viva Vicente Fernandez!" and twirled me around.

No family members would barge in on us. All our family was spending the wedding night in Fresno. Rudy, Anne and the little boys were with Rudy's parents. Jennybeth was staying over with one of the other bridesmaids. Andy and La Tosha had splurged on a hotel room at the Radisson to be near the rest of their extended Horvath and Cunningham relatives who had come to see our schoolteacher son married.

Dev reached out to turn the Mariachi music even louder. Accordions droned. Violins soared. Trumpets blasted. I broke away from him long enough to put my glasses on one of the bookshelves and come back to his arms. We danced up and down the living room, around the dining room table, down the hallway and back. I was a teenager in Olvera Street again, this time with my love. The sedate mother-of-the-groom dress I was wearing spun itself into ruffles and red petticoats; Dev's suit morphed to black satin with silver buttons and spangles.

We came through all right. My husband and I had loved each other for a long time; we would dance to whatever music we heard, and neither of us would go where the other couldn't follow.

~~~<<=>>~~~

Chapter 80: The View from a Place of Shelter

Yesterday two women were gunned down in the parking lot of a mountain resort about an hour's drive from our ranch. One had been granted her divorce decree earlier that day; the other was the attorney who represented her. The crime was eerily close to being a reenactment of my sister's death, although Beth was never tallied as an official victim of that old crime.

So much has changed since 1947. While Dev and I were in Los Angeles for Jack Ryder's eighty-fifth birthday this year, Adrian and I drove across the city to West Los Angeles. The homes in our old neighborhood in Breeze Terrace, small by today's standards, now cost close to a million dollars to purchase. A cool Pacific wind was blowing. The tree where we used to sit had grown immensely. We didn't get out of the car to climb up into it. We are old for climbing trees, and it stands in someone else's yard.

Southern California's metropolis stretches from Ventura to San Diego. The neighborhood of our childhood is hidden behind clusters of tall buildings and the vast elevated concrete river of the 405 freeway. There are no more bean fields. Newspapers have gone electronic; our grandchildren talk to their friends on Skype. Yet, every day, everywhere, women are beaten, raped and murdered by the men in their lives or by random men finding them to be available victims. Progress in human behavior hasn't kept up with progress in human technology.

Adrian didn't want to drive by Jeannie's old house, but I was the driver. I got to choose. The house is a different color now. A skateboard was on the front lawn. It has been nearly sixty-five years since she died. I don't know who killed her. I never will. I do know that she was neither an alcoholic nor a slut.

She was a lovely, out-going woman in our neighborhood. Newspapers created a person never seen by the people around her. We saw Jeannie's many acts of kindness. Anything else I might say about her is only an inference drawn, only my belief, not necessarily anyone's truth.

Here, in the patio next to the cactus garden, the afternoon shadows are stretching longer, reminding me that my own metaphoric afternoon is moving toward night. I reflect, and know I've been good to the people in my life. I've been a wife, mother, nurse, and teacher. But I'm flawed. I've accepted more from the people I've loved than I've given them. I've seldom initiated action, whether for good or bad. I rationalize my passiveness as character flaw, not sin. Timidity isn't a sin, but it's not a virtue either. It isn't the same as humility.

As to my sins, a better daughter would have sacrificed more. I could have left nursing school when my mother needed me. I didn't. I know I made mistakes when I raised my children. They were thoughtful and well intentioned, but they were mistakes nevertheless. There was time for me to atone for my sin of abandoning my mother. There was time also for my children to grow to be parents themselves and make a few well-intentioned mistakes. I can shrug off any guilts arising from these sins.

But, without atonement, any act of contrition rings hollow, and my conscience twists itself around two sins that I can't shrug off.

When I was ten years old, I betrayed Jeannie French's memory to some boys on a school playground. When I was fourteen, I let Delores McCauley slip away from me through my own vanity and pride.

There has been no gracious allowance of time for me to make atonement for either of these sins, and they linger like the shadows of black birds come hovering over me in an irregular but predictable migration.

After Beth's death, Wally's generous heart failed. He died in 1985. Although he never went back to Hawaii, his bequest tripled the fund my sister had begun. Her gift was given anonymously, but Wally wanted her name remembered. His endowment is called The Beth Horvath-Raudell Foundation for Women, and it continues Beth's work throughout the islands.

Steve and Janet divorced the same year Wally died. Steve's second wife, Bebe, is very like Rozsika and the Hungarian women of our childhood. Always ready for singing or dancing, or to cuddle some child, she shows her love easily. Bebe spoils my brother and watches out for his health. He looks ten years younger than he is. He is still straight and tall. They take long walks, play tennis, and go on cruises. They visit Alex and Sandra, Dev and I, and spend much time with Bebe's family also. Steve's wife is a stylish urban woman. Bas Mitzvah marked Bebe's coming age, while mine was marked by Confirmation. Yet we've found we have much in common. Alex and Sandra won't ever retire. They are in transition from being employees to being volunteers. A tremendous team, they have never tired of helping people who needed help, and they have shown enough social conscience to earn a grand karmic reward. I take great pride in both my brothers and love their wives as sisters.

Sarah Cunningham died sixteen years ago. Her quiet Paiute way, a strong, solitary, controlled sense of self that I admire, shows in my children as it does in my husband. They don't fidget. They don't fear. And they don't complain about what life gives them. I miss her, but see her daily in the faces of my family.

Paro flew in from Washington D.C. for St. Lucy's fiftieth reunion. Our numbers were small, as one might expect. Paro stayed near me that evening, her face relaxed. She plans to bring her grandchildren out to the ranch and have Dev and me accompany them on a tour of Yosemite and Sequoia when school is out. Her grandchildren are getting old to be traveling with granny, but maybe it will work out. Her son Jason is a legislative analyst, and she had moved to be nearer him and his family ten years ago. Jason's children are handsome and dark-haired in the photos she carries. Paro's cordiality was its own apology for our estrangement. Our conversation carefully skirted around Vince. Time has graced me with better perspective. Vince was only twenty-four when he and Paro married. In the nineteen fifties, few men had the courage to stand up against moral convention. At that time he would have felt he would lose his soul along with losing everyone he knew and loved. I've finally grown wise enough to realize that marriage was a fragile branch Vince reached toward, not an evil he committed.

Audrey Chester was able to defy convention. Maybe our gender is more accepting, or perhaps just braver. She and Sherry have been together almost as long as Dev and I have. They live in a seaside retirement village in North Carolina. We flew to visit them two summers ago. We sat on their porch, drank California wine, and watched the ocean. On a daily basis, the Atlantic is a gentler sea than the Pacific. Its waves are smaller and farther apart.

My friends, Adrian, Pat, Paro, and I have lived to an age when whatever kills us won't be premature. Women's cancers took many of our friends too early. Kathleen, Anna Marie, Mary Eunice, Joan Turner, Vince's sister Anna Lee fell to that disease. Their mothers felt the dreadful pain of survival, as Mama did when Beth died.

The mothers of women in my generation lived during a halcyon time for middle class women. Antibiotics vanquished the infectious diseases; cancers were not yet on such a rapid rise. The Great Depression was over. Our mothers enjoyed a grand leisure that my daughters, daughters-in-law, and granddaughters can only imagine: morning visits to the beauty parlor, afternoons filled with shopping, cocktails, bridge, canasta, Tupperware parties and the ladies' matinees at the Palms or Meralta theaters. Most had household help at least one day a week and the heavy laundry was sent out.

My mother's gargantuan appetite propelled her into diabetes. One of her nurses told me she came to check Mama's oxygen and IV bag one morning during the last few days Mama lived. Mother greeted the nurse with a lovely smile and asked, "If it wouldn't be too much trouble, dear, could you please ask the hospital kitchen to send up a piece of that lovely cheesecake they served at supper last night?"

It was far too late in Mama's life for her nurse to worry about carbohydrate grams. The good woman went down to the kitchen, found the treat, and spoon-fed bits of cake into my mother's mouth. It was an act of kind humanity.

About a year after our mother's death there came a point in time that seemed to put her to rest for my brothers and me. Alex and Sandra were in Los Angeles for an advocacy conference. Dev and I, Steve and Bebe met them. We three couples enjoyed a jolly meal in a high-rise restaurant, and then drove Sunset Boulevard out to Will Roger's State Beach. Alex and I immediately raced down to the water and slipped out of our shoes. We waved to the others who were spreading a blanket Dev brought from the truck. Steve came down to the water and took his shoes and socks off too. We walked as the surf rhythmically, repeatedly, sent arcs of inch-deep water across our toes and funneled the water back to its depths. Waves and distant seagulls were the only noise.

After a while, Steve stopped, looked out to sea and broke our reflective silence by saying, "You know, I never forgave Mama for selling the business my father left me.

"And I never forgave her for lying to me." Sliding out of my mouth were traces of ancient, residual bitterness.

"Hey, you guys!" Alex chuckled. "You two didn't have it so bad. I never forgave her for locking me out. The whole damn neighborhood used to take pity and give me lunch." He dug a hole in the wet sand with his toe where some little sand crab tunnels were bubbling.

"I always loved her. Even when she did that." Steve said.

"I did too," I affirmed. "I loved her all my life."

"She did it her own way, but she was a great mother," Alex said. "The proof is that we've all had good lives, and not one of us ever spent a night in jail."

We walked along at the edge of the surf, stopping now and then to let the waves swirl around and tug at our feet before they rushed back to Mother Ocean.

"I wish Beth were here," I said.

"She is here," my brothers replied in a duet of such resonant sureness that I could feel our sister was walking with us. The sun began dropping faster, and we had gone far down the beach. We turned to go back, pick up our shoes and socks, and join the others.

I hope that Dev will outlive me. I don't want to be anywhere without him. He has been my joy and delight for well over fifty years. We argue on matters such as whether Bessie Smith or Janis Joplin made the best recording of *Careless Love*. I favor Janis. But we've seldom had a serious argument. In things that matter, we've always either agreed or let the one who made the most logical argument make the choice or decision. Well, usually, perhaps not always.

My husband is vigorous at over eighty. He runs the ranch with a little help from Rudy and our grandsons. They work with U.C. Riverside on approved biological controls in our groves. I work one day a week at Nordgren's Women's Clinic in Fresno. I began volunteering after retirement from the college ten years ago. I work as a pre-termination nurse-counselor. Dev growls at the cost of the fuel for the ninety-mile round trip, but I persist. My life's one bravery is that I have walked the gauntlet of pro-life placards and taunts with my head held high and my step unhurried. I remember Jeannie. And I haven't forgotten Delores.

The women I counsel sometimes ask me if I ever terminated a pregnancy of my own. I'm honest and admit that I never did. We then discuss the many alternatives: adoption, open adoption, agencies that will give a woman support. Older women seldom ask.

Adrian has had a beautifully busy life. To this day, her house is filled with people taking sanctuary, as her mother's house was. She and I are bound by the deaths of two women whom we loved, and each strives to fill the place of the sister the other lost.

Pat is still devoutly attending mass every Sunday. She and Adrian don't approve of my volunteer work. Both deny that there is a need for abortion since birth control became reliable. The framework of their lives has never put them into contact with poverty-stricken immigrant women, teenagers with neither money for prescriptions nor supportive parents, cancer patients endangered by hormone-based medications, or menopausal women who thought that they were safely beyond concern and find themselves pregnant. My life has given me a different perspective. We maintain our fondness for each other by tolerantly avoiding conversation about the work I do.

Adrian called yesterday to give me her latest grandchild and great-grandchild count. Pat calls often and for the same reason. I think they count coup on me.

My friends aren't concerned with the problems of exponential population expansion. Their belief systems single out mankind for some special position in the universe. Mine doesn't. I worry that my own species is crowding other species out. My mother had too many children for Breeze Terrace's waspish sensibilities. I know I had too many for the good of the planet. Human habitation has covered the globe like the scabs of a deadly plague. There are too many of us for the other living things. We are crowding them out. My imagination sees a giant ecological finger pointing at me from somewhere other than the Sistine Chapel.

I have grandchildren also, they are the joy of my life and they come in more colors than pink. In spite of my guilt at contributing to the critical over-population of my own kind, I like the thought that some of my grandchildren are part of the new people who are not purely any one race or other. They are therefore able to proudly claim descent from the world itself.

Dev's and my wanton fertility led us to produce more than merely our own replacements, but I ease my guilt by claiming a residual family allotment. Neither Beth nor my brother

Alex produced a child. Ergo: species balance is maintained, not exceeded, and our impetuous productivity is absolved.

It's a silly rationale and one with a wide fissure in logic. But selfish to the core and very much my mother's daughter, I find a soft and comfortable justification for any of my actions.

The three of us, Adrian, Pat, and I, are relics of another time: Norman Rockwell grandmothers, the godmothers from Walt Disney's *Sleeping Beauty*. We are matriarchs of joyous dynasties, the meek who wondrously inherited the earth. We three come as close to perfect happiness as life allows, and it's too late for hubris to bring me down. My ride on the swing is almost over.

As though I'd called to him, Dev comes out to sit by me on the patio. He's brought an article he knows I'd like. Spring often comes early here. Fiddleneck and lupine have begun blooming on the winter green hills behind the barn and along the barbed wire pasture fences. In two months La Cordillera's citrus trees will send out a fragrance that will perfume the whole county. My husband begins to read to me. I reach out to touch him. How could I have resisted him when I was nineteen? I love him to this day.

Afterword

Novels are born when two or more persistent memories collide
in an author's imagination and make a strong, insistent
demand. This novel begins with the persistent memory I have
of a woman named Jeanne French. She was real. Her murder
is still unsolved. Some scenes in the book, such as the party at
Errol Flynn's mansion and the girls' conversation on the
Catalina steamship, are very similar to memoir. However,
Acts of Kindness, Acts of Contrition is not a memoir. It is
fiction. We carry the impressions of many events that didn't
happen to us, incidents that we saw and heard in the media,
dramatic happenings to people we knew. Often those
borrowed memories are as strong and insistent as our own.
They too have authenticity.

Acknowledgements

I wish to thank the following people for their contributions to this book: my friend, Beverly Krantz Richardson, Porterville, California, and my sister, Theresa Cord, Sedona Arizona, for their kind willingness to read and critique the manuscript in its earliest and most raw form; Sandor Havasi, Agoura Hills, California, for generous assistance with passages using the Hungarian language, Marilyn Fordney-Havasi for her commitment to young dancers through the Fordney Foundation for DanceSport; Lanore Scott, Orange, California, for prodding me to bring the manuscript to completion; Deloris Mahnke, Porterville, California Sedona, Arizona for serving as reader; Gloria Getman R.N., Exeter, California, for sharing the experience of both the training of nurses during the 1950's and the practice of nursing to the present time; Lois O'Connor, Camarillo, California, for sharing knowledge of care for the mentally ill in California during the latter half of the twentieth century; Arthur Neeson and the Exeter Writer's Guild Members for worthwhile critiques of many scenes; Margaret Dubin, Oakland, California, for her long and valuable personal friendship and professional validation; Gayle Wattawa, Berkeley, California, for her encouraging comments; Malcolm Margolin, Berkeley, California, for his long support of written work pertaining to California's arts, history, ethnic and cultural richness.

My very special thanks go to my husband, Bob Ross; and to our sons and the daughters they brought to us, Chris and Zoila Ross, Ted Ross and Winnie Clark, Nathan and Maria Ross, and Andy and Monica Ross; my brothers Joe and John Stigmon and their wives, Susan and Kathleen; my sister Theresa Cord and her husband Bill; for their gifts of love and patience during the time I've been preoccupied with this work.

Sylvia Ross
March 19, 2012
The feast of St. Joseph

Sylvia Ross is the author-illustrator of *Lion Singer* and *Blue Jay Girl*, books for children. Her stories and poems have been published in a number of anthologies, and also featured in *"News from Native California,"* an esteemed quarterly magazine. She is of Native (Chukchansi Yokuts) descent and an Oregon Trail descendant on both sides of her family. In early adulthood, she worked as a cell painter for Walt Disney Productions in Burbank, California. Later she taught for many years at Vandalia Elementary School in Porterville, California, which was, and is, the school attended by most of the children from the Tule River Indian Reservation.

Acts of Kindness, Acts of Contrition, a mid-century themed novel concerning women's and cultural issues between 1940 and 1980 was a finalist for the James D. Houston Award in 2010. Though born and raised in West Los Angeles, Mrs. Ross and her husband have made the Great Valley of California their home. They live in Eastern Tulare County.

Made in the USA
Las Vegas, NV
14 August 2021